ABIGAIL TRENCH

ALSO BY RANDY OVERBECK

Leave No Child Behind
Cruel Lessons

The Haunted Shores Mysteries

Blood on the Chesapeake
Crimson at Cape May
Scarlet at Crystal River
Red Shadows at Saugatuck

ABIGAIL TRENCH

A Novel of Washington's Spy Ring

RANDY OVERBECK

DIVERSION
BOOKS

Diversion Books
A division of Diversion Publishing Corp.
www.diversionbooks.com

For more information, email info@diversionbooks.com

First Diversion Books Edition: June 2026
Trade paperback ISBN: 9798895151648
e-ISBN: 9798895151631

Design by Westchester Publishing Services
Cover design generated with the assistance of Ideogram
and edited by Libby Kingsbury

Printed in the United States of America
1 3 5 7 9 10 8 6 4 2

First of all, I'd like to dedicate this book to my wife, Cathy, and the entire Overbeck family, who believed in me through it all. Also, with the 250th anniversary of the Declaration of Independence, I'd like to dedicate this story to the many unsung heroes—like my fictional hero, Abigail Trench—who sacrificed so much during the American Revolution to give birth to this incredible country. Their names and identities may be lost and buried in the annuls of history, but I've learned, for every Washington and Hamilton, there are hundreds of men and women who struggled in these dangerous times to secure freedom for their children and, ultimately, us. Their passion and dedication won the war and inspire me to this day.

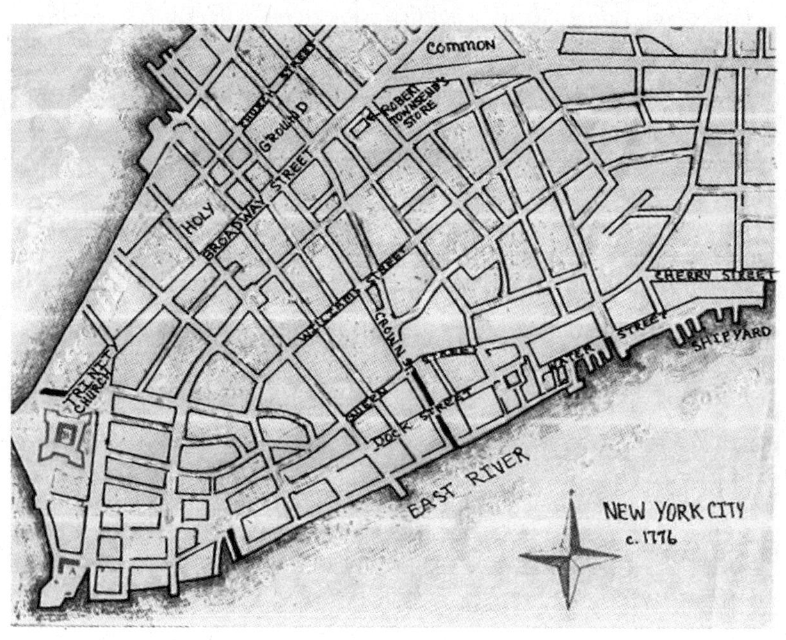
COMMON
ROBERT TOWNSEND'S STORE
GROUND
HOLY
BROADWAY STREET
CROWN ST.
CHERRY STREET
STREET
SHIPYARD
DOCK STREET
EAST RIVER
TRINITY CHURCH
NEW YORK CITY
c. 1776

AUTHOR'S NOTE

Abigail Trench: A Novel of Washington's Spy Ring is a work of fiction.

In the framing of this narrative, I have tried to portray the events and historical figures as faithfully as I could, using primary sources when possible as well as various other historical resources. In September 1776, a major fire did destroy much of Manhattan, and Nathan Hale was hanged along with a wooden effigy of George Washington, and nearly twenty thousand spectators witnessed the execution of the bodyguard-turned-traitor Thomas Hickey, the largest such crowd in American history. However, as this is fiction, I readily admit to using some literary license in the interpretation of events and in the framing of the story.

Because of the incredible secrecy surrounding the Culper Ring and of the passing of 250 years, the historical details of the ring are sparse and many have been lost in the centuries past. For example, though scholars have largely agreed there were six men involved in the spy ring, the identification of the last of these was not confirmed until 2020. The primary sources also make reference to a woman who assisted in the espionage activities, though, again, particulars are lacking. In the documents recovered, she is never named and only referred to as "355." There has been some deliberation among scholars about possible historical persons who might have been the woman spy, but there has never been any definitive or convincing evidence that points to a specific person. For this story, I have invented the character of Abigail Trench, teacher and tutor, and have her step into the role of the female spy of the Culper Ring.

I hope you enjoy this literary expedition to the world of Revolutionary War America and Abigail's journey from small-town teacher to secret spy in her new country.

I wish C——could fall upon some more direct channel by which his Letters could be conveyed, as the efficacy of his communications is lost in the circuitous rout. If he could fall upon a method of conveying his Letters to Genl Maxwell at Elizabeth town, or to Colo. Shreive at Newark, they would come to me with more dispatch, & of consequence render his corrispondance more valuable.

As all great movements, and the fountain of all intelligence must originate at, & proceed from the head Quarters of the enemy's Army, C——had better reside at New York—mix with—and put on the airs of a Tory to cover his real character, & avoid suspicion, In all his communications he should be careful in distinguishing matters of fact, from matters of report. . . . Many other things will occur upon reflection without an inumeration of them; I shall therefore only add my wishes that the whole may be placed on such a footing as to answer the end most effectually, & that I am Sir Yr Very Hble Servt

Go: Washington

—Letter from General Washington to
Robert Talmadge providing directions

I

SUMMER, 1776

New York City

ABIGAIL

1

Abigail Trench had never seen a man hanged before. Yet here she was.

Out in the country on Long Island, where she and Father had made a home for the past three years, she'd heard only rumors of men in the colonies hanged for murder or thievery. Now she was about to see for herself.

They'd arrived in New York City only two days earlier, and this morning she'd set out to knock on doors, looking for work. She was a teacher—or rather, had been a teacher at the small school in Smithtown until they'd had to leave everything and flee here.

Yesterday she spent the day visiting three charity schools and received the same response at each. No openings—and no expectation of any in the fall. The headmistress at the third school, which met in a rundown tenement near the river, had at least shown her some kindness. After Abigail shared her references from both London and Long Island and explained her story, the woman—a plump, middle-aged redhead with a rosy face—had nodded sympathetically and pursed her thick lips.

The woman had said, "I'm sorry. We'd love to have ya if we could. With the rebels and the war breaking out, everyone's in a panic around here. Unfortunately, school's not the first thing on people's minds." She'd pressed a finger to her lips and studied Abigail. "You could check some of the mansions over on Water Street. Some o' those rich folks may be lookin' for a tutor—if they're stayin'."

So this morning, Abigail followed the woman's advice. Hurrying south toward Water Street, she cut across the green—and stopped. A huge crowd had gathered in the open space, people standing shoulder to shoulder on the mud- and grass-covered ground, many of them stamping their feet. The crowd spread out in a fan, and she saw no way around it. *It must be something about the war and England*, she thought. It was all anyone talked about.

It had dawned another warm morning. A sluggish breeze carried the aromas from the crowd, opposing scents layered atop one another—heavy sweat and body odor, alcohol and vomit, foul flatulence, and, mixed in somewhere, even a trace of expensive perfume.

From where she stood, she could see no faces. Everyone was turned away from her, facing east and talking at once. A cacophony of voices rose and fell—gruff men's shouts, children's giggles, the anxious chatter of women. One older woman blabbered above the rest, her voice cutting through the din.

"I hope they go through with it this time. Las' time we come out here, the officials changed their mind and gave us nothin'. I'm losin' customers every minute we stand out here, and losin' customers means losin' coin. My family's gotta eat, ya know."

The prattle came from a chubby woman at the edge of the crowd, not too far from where Abigail stood. Like all the rest, the woman was turned away, and all Abigail could see was the back of a bobbing head of blond hair.

"Now if'n they actually give us somethin' so we can have a lit'l fun, then I figure it'd be worth any loss in earnin'." The woman's short arm shot up above the crowd and a plump finger pointed ahead, the way they were all facing.

Abigail peered in that direction. Being small—just over five feet—she could make out only a narrow glimpse of the river between the rows of heads. The morning sun slid from behind a cloud, its brilliance turning everything to silhouettes, and she raised an arm to block the glare.

She nudged the person in front of her. A woman turned and looked Abigail up and down, eyebrows lifting, her coiffed brown hair barely stirring with the motion. The woman wore a yellow dress with long sleeves and buttons down the front, pink petticoats showing beneath. She tucked delicate hands into a white pocket apron tied at her waist. Abigail had not yet had the time—or the money—to purchase "appropriate female attire," as Father had said, and still wore the simple gray frock she'd used for most tasks in the country.

"What's going on?" Abigail asked, pointing to where everyone was staring.

The woman gave her a haughty glance and huffed. "Well, we're here for the stretching, of course."

"The stretching?"

Next to the brunette, a man in a fancy waistcoat and striped breeches leaned over and, in a polished voice, said, "We don't ever miss a stretching." Adjusting the tricorn hat atop his obvious wig, he continued, "It doesn't happen often enough, I say. Teach them hellions a lesson." He slid his arm through the woman's, and both turned back around.

Puzzled, Abigail edged around the crowd, searching for a place where she could see. As the sun slid behind another cloud, she stared ahead. At the far end of the green, above the heads, she could just make out a simple wooden structure—a crossbeam with support timbers at either end.

Abigail moved down the row and came up behind a woman dressed more simply. She tapped her on the shoulder, just to the side of the blond curls that cascaded down her back. The woman turned with a scowl, but it faded when she saw Abigail. She was probably no more than sixteen, several years younger than Abigail.

Abigail offered a small smile and raised her voice over the din. "We just got to town." She pointed to the crowd. "What's going on?"

The girl—not woman—returned Abigail's smile, her lips bright red. "We've all come out to watch Ian swing."

"Swing?"

The girl chuckled. "You know, *swing*." Her small hand made a gesture of pulling on her neck.

Abigail gasped. "You mean hanging? They're going to hang a man?"

"That's what I said. Swingin', hangin', it's all the same." She lolled her head from side to side, tongue drooping.

Abigail shuddered. All these people had gathered here to watch a man hanged? She let her gaze roam over the crowd, doing some quick counting. More than a hundred people—and a lot of children, just like the ones she'd taught on Long Island. The youngsters darted between the legs of their elders, sometimes screeching with glee. Who would bring their children to watch a man's neck snap?

She wanted to run—leave, go anywhere but here. Do what she'd come out to do. Knock on a door or two and search for a position. She surveyed the heads in the crowd ahead. A sea of men's tricorn hats, women's cloth bonnets, and more than a few military hats told her all she needed to know. Those she needed to see were probably here anyway.

The girl had turned back toward the gallows. Abigail tapped her shoulder. "What's he done? What's his crime?"

The girl faced Abigail and her eyes brightened, a brilliant green, almost emerald, set in a flawless oval face. "They claim he raped Miss Geraldine. Rape and theft, accordin' to the handbill." She handed Abigail a printed sheet. "At least, that's what Jamie says. I can't read."

Rape. The mere word made Abigail flinch. Her hand shook as she tried to read the paper.

At a trial of his peers, Ian McKenzie has been found guilty of rape and theft. By the laws of New York City, he has been sentenced to be hanged by the neck until dead on this day, the fifteenth of June, in the year of our Lord, seventeen seventy-six.

Rape.

Abigail couldn't breathe. She and Father had come here to escape—though they'd had little choice but to leave. *Rape.* The word conjured up the ugly episode.

Maybe she *could* watch this man be hanged.

2

Abigail nudged her way up beside the girl, who noticed and shifted to make a little room for her to squeeze in. "I'm Molly, and this here's Jamie," she said. The girl gave the arm of a young man a little squeeze. The boy—really, he couldn't be more than sixteen—nodded. He had a wiry build with long arms and small hands, and a pleasant enough face topped with a mop of unruly brown hair.

"I'm Abigail." She let out a breath. "Abigail Trench."

Before she could say any more, a commotion rose at the front of the crowd and everyone quieted. A voice boomed across the space. "Ian McKenzie, you have been found guilty of these crimes. Do you have anything to say before the sentence is carried out?"

The answer, when it came, drifted weakly over the crowd, the words coming out in squeaks. As he spoke, Abigail realized the accused was also a mere boy, his voice not yet changed. "I'm sorry. I meant no 'arm. What I did, I did for love." Then he hollered over the crowd, "I love you, Geraldine."

An anguished gasp escaped from someone near the front, followed by loud, frantic sobbing. After that, the crowd came to life, responding with jeers and sarcastic chants of "He did it for *love*." Laughter followed, loud, boisterous, and nervous.

Abigail stretched up on her tiptoes, trying to get a glimpse of the accused, hoping her ears had deceived her. As she strained to see, the torso of a young man came into view above the heads of the crowd, his slender, clean neck caught in a noose of rough hemp. Beside him, the figure of a cleric stepped onto the platform, the black-and-white collar visible. The boy looked to the minister for some final reprieve.

His face was young—cherubic almost—bright pink skin blotched with pimples, a small nose, thin, drawn lips. And hollow, terrified eyes. Stringy black hair hung down his forehead almost to his eyes. His shoulders were narrow and the noose surrounded a skinny neck. His lips opened and closed, but no sound came out.

From the side, someone barked a sudden command, the order audible even above the babble of the crowd. As she watched, the boy's head dropped a foot and jerked up and back. He squirmed, his face going into spasms. His eyes bulged, growing impossibly large. His lips opened and closed like a carp on a riverbank.

Abigail wanted to look away but couldn't. This young man—this, this boy—had *raped* a girl. To harden her heart, she tried to imagine another face there, *his* ugly head inside the noose, the scars on both cheeks popping from the exertion. She failed, the contorted boyish face filling her view.

Abigail figured the whole thing would be over quickly. But it wasn't. As she watched, now unable to tear her eyes away, the young man's face twisted into one horrible grimace after another as his lips kept up their useless motions.

Still standing on her toes, she tore her gaze from the spectacle ahead and took a quick glance around—to Molly and Jamie and the others. All stood staring straight ahead, their gazes fixed on the gallows and the figure hanging there. From among the crowd, curses erupted, followed by jeers.

"Swing, you useless lubber!"

"Won't filch no more now, will ya?"

"Hey, look. He browned himself!"

The crowd howled with laughter.

Abigail gulped and brought her eyes back to the condemned—she reminded herself, *condemned*—as his ears, cheeks, and chin turned the color of beets. His huge eyes seemed to be staring at *her.*

This young man, this boy, was a rapist. Not hers, but still a rapist. He deserved this.

How long had he been hanging? It felt like hours, but Abigail realized it had only been minutes. Standing there on her toes hurt. She dropped back onto her heels, giving her stretched feet a break.

A gruff voice near the front yelled, "Hurry up and die, ya bugger!" More shouted taunts from other spectators followed.

"There he goes. He pumped ship. Won't be long now," called another onlooker, and a hail of laughter followed.

Abigail squinted, trying to make sense of the slang. Her gaze cut to Molly, and the girl must've recognized Abigail's confusion.

Molly rolled her eyes. "Means he pissed himself."

Abigail gave a slow nod and rose back up onto her tiptoes. Up on the scaffold, the boy's movements slowed, and his lips opened sluggishly. As she watched, the blush of color in his young face seemed to drain away, turning the flesh a sickly blue-gray. Then his tongue dropped. All activity ceased.

A moment of silence followed, the quiet so intense Abigail could hear the water flowing past in the river. Then the peace was broken. The crowd erupted in cheers, loud catcalls and clapping, the children joining in the yelping.

Abigail couldn't believe her ears, couldn't believe any of it. Bile rose in her throat and she fought it down. Mouth clamped shut, she hurried to the edge of the crowd. There, she retched, over and over again.

3

"Get it all out," a soft voice said behind her.

Abigail felt a gentle hand on her back and turned to see Molly with a sympathetic grin on her face. "Your first hangin', huh? Ya get used to it."

God, she hoped not. Straightening, she brushed at the bits of sausage and vomit spattered over the front of her frock. The little she'd eaten that morning now streaked her outfit and lay on the ground at her feet. And she stank. She couldn't knock on any doors today. This frock and bedgown was the only outfit she owned. She'd have to go back and wash the whole thing.

"Come on," Molly encouraged, taking her arm. "Let's go back to the Pelican, and we'll get ya somethin' to help."

Molly led her back across the square. The crowd headed off in different directions—some toward the waterfront, some toward the streets beyond, some toward Water Street, where Abigail had been heading. That would have to wait. Ahead, mingling with the departing crowd-goers, Jamie weaved and ducked, stopping to grin, trade a few words, even laugh with a man before moving on and repeating the same performance again and again.

Abigail nodded toward Jamie and the dispersing crowd. "What's he doing?"

"His job."

By the time they reached the eastern end of the green, the other gawkers had gone, though Abigail could still hear loud voices arguing on a side street. Now only Molly, Jamie, and Abigail stood on the trampled grass. Abigail stepped up to the front of the gallows and stopped. Molly halted beside her. Abigail stared up at the figure, listening to the wood creak as the thin body swayed in the slight summer breeze. Catching another nasty odor, she saw the boy had soiled himself, a large brown stain at his crotch. Now she understood some of the crowd's cruel taunts.

Up close, his face looked impossibly young, his thin body emaciated, his eyes bulging. She choked, ready to vomit again, but her stomach was empty. She dry-heaved twice, then regained her control.

Turning to Molly, Abigail asked, "Won't they take him down?"

The young woman shook her head. "They leave 'em up a day or two, sometimes three. S'posed to be a lesson fer others."

Abigail straightened. "Well, at least he deserved it. I mean, he raped a girl."

"Pro'bly not." Jamie came up alongside. "I learnt young Geraldine and he fell in love and had laid together. When her father found out, he was furious. He dredged up the rape charge and then crammed up the thievery." He shrugged. "Least that's what I heard."

Abigail felt her resolve, fed by her own dark experience, crumble. That poor lad. How hard-hearted was she to have entertained such ugly thoughts? She stared at Jamie. "He can do that?"

Jamie said, "If you're important enough, you can throw the hatchet like that, and everyone goes along."

"Hatchet?" Abigail asked.

Molly laid a hand on her arm. "He means lyin', don't he?" She didn't wait for an answer but tugged on Abigail's sleeve. "We best be goin'."

Casting one last glance at the corpse, Abigail trailed the two as they sauntered down the road beside the wharf, their feet making hollow echoes on the wooden planks of the raised sidewalk. The river below was dark and turgid, sluggish waves lifting garbage, butchered animals' carcasses, and fish heads that bobbed in the foul water as the stench drifted in the humid air. Four ships sat docked at the piers, sails furled, decks empty, rocking gently in the slight waves.

Molly and Jamie led, and Abigail followed as they weaved through knots of people coming the other way. Once, they stopped, leaning against the rough timbers of a building, as two Black men passed them shirtless, sweat pouring down their chests. Cursing in a tongue Abigail didn't recognize, the men dragged a wagon overloaded with barrels.

A little ways down the noisy walkway, Jamie ducked into a doorway beneath a wooden sign with a rough drawing of a large bird—a pelican, Abigail guessed. The two women followed. Inside, the space was dark, and it took a moment for Abigail's eyes to adjust. Six rough-hewn tables sat around the small room, each surrounded by squat wooden benches, all unoccupied. To the right, a wooden bar ran half the length of the room, and a man with an unkempt beard and a disheveled shock of black hair leaned on the scarred surface. He wore only a waistcoat, hairy arms poking out both sides of the vest. Jamie gestured to a table in the back, and Molly and Abigail headed that way. A minute later, he joined them, holding a dented gray tankard filled about a third of the way with brown liquid. He slid it toward Abigail.

"Take a good swaller. It'll help yer stomach."

Abigail took a tentative sip and almost choked, the liquid burning her throat. She coughed, and Molly slapped her on the back a few times.

"What was *that*?" Abigail rasped.

Jamie smiled. "Jus' a bit o' American whiskey. Good for what ails ya."

Tears welled in Abigail's eyes. She'd tasted whiskey only once before—with much the same result.

Last summer, her brother, Oliver, had returned to their house with two visitors. The men were dressed in worn, tattered breeches and frayed waistcoats over soiled shirts, the cuffs browned with dirt. Oliver had introduced the strangers as members of the Continental Army under the command of none other than George Washington himself.

The colonial soldiers—who looked nothing like soldiers—had brought American whiskey, and they'd all drunk. She'd choked then, too, just as she had today.

Molly broke Abigail's reverie, turning to Jamie. "Fine, let's see it. How'd ya do today?"

Jamie glanced around and then emptied his pockets, one at a time. Onto the carved and splintered surface, he dumped an assortment of coins, a fine gold watch, a worn leather wallet with paper bills sticking out the edge, and a woman's bag, intact but with its strings neatly cut. Taking his time, he emptied the wallet and bag, putting the silver and gold coins in one pile and laying the paper money in a stack. He counted it up, adding the figures aloud as he went. When he finished, he announced the total, and Molly squealed, her green eyes going wide. She stretched across the table and kissed him, and he fondled her breasts.

She giggled, and when they both slid back to their seats she said, "We should celebrate."

Abigail stared at the two of them. "You mean you're a—" She had trouble getting the words out.

Molly grinned. "He's a knuckler." She grabbed his hand. "One of the best pickpockets around, and he's mine." She kissed him.

A pickpocket? Abigail tried to wrap her head around it, her gaze moving from one to the other. She didn't know what to say.

One arm still around Molly, Jamie said, "Ya new here? Ya come to New York alone?"

Abigail shook her head. "No. Me and my father." Then she corrected herself. "My father and I came here together."

Molly frowned. "Well, my father *and I*," she repeated. "Ain't we fancy."

Abigail offered a sad smile. "No, it's not like that. I'm a teacher . . . or used to be, until a few weeks ago. I taught at a small school on, uh, Long Island." Her voice trailed off.

Molly asked, "What happened?"

Abigail couldn't tell them about the rape. She couldn't. But she could tell them the rest. "Three men came to the farmhouse. Claimed to be soldiers. They said they needed to 'commandeer' our goats and chickens for the regulars. Said they'd give us a note for the animals. My father said no, told them we couldn't farm if they took our livestock."

She glanced at them, and their faces showed concern, so she went on.

"When my father tried to stop them, one brute—I think he was the leader—a man with an ugly pockmarked face and a scar across his left cheek, knocked down my father and held a blade to his throat. Then I tried to reason with him, even cajole him to leave us some animals, but—" She stopped again and gulped, staring at her lap. "Let's just say it didn't do any good."

Molly whispered, "Bastards."

"Later, we found out they'd taken livestock from all the farms around. Almost everyone had to give up farming and move somewhere they could get some food. So no children, no school."

Jamie asked, "Were these British or rebels?"

Abigail shook her head. "The ugly one, they called him left-tenant, said they were scouting for the British, but none of them wore any uniforms."

After a bit, Molly asked, "Ya goin' to teach at a school here?"

Abigail shrugged. "That was the idea, but so far, no luck. Today I was planning on knocking on some doors on Water Street to see if any of the families need a tutor." She glanced at her soiled frock. "I don't think I can go like this, so I'll go back, wash it, and try again tomorrow."

Molly exchanged a look with Jamie and finally said, "Jamie knows how to read and do figures good." She gazed at the young man with admiration. "He's really smart." Then she turned back to Abigail. "Ya think ya could teach me to read . . . a lit'l maybe? We could pay. At least a lit'l."

Abigail nodded. "Of course I can teach you to read *and* write *and* do figures. I taught students much younger than you. You don't need to pay me. Did you go to a charity school here?"

Molly shook her head. "Never had much time fer school."

Abigail looked from Jamie to Molly. "You both alone?"

Molly grabbed Jamie's arm again. "We ain't alone. We got each other."

Abigail looked down. "I mean, you don't have any family? Any parents or brothers and sisters?"

Jamie answered first, shaking his head. "My mum and dad died two years ago. Burning fever. Took my lit'l brother too."

"It was only my mum and me," Molly said. "Never knew my dad." She hung her head. "Mum died last winter. Consumption." She brightened and added, "Now Jamie and me are family. We look after each other."

Abigail studied the girl and boy—they looked too young to be man and woman. Maybe her own situation wasn't so bad. She'd lost her mother, but at least she still had Father . . . and Oliver somewhere. She gave them both a wide smile. "Thanks so much for helping me today . . . um, understand what was going on." She glanced at Molly. "Of course I'll teach you. We can start tomorrow after I knock on a few doors."

The young girl beamed. "I'd like that."

Abigail asked, "Where do you live?" When Molly hesitated, she went on, "Where do you want to meet me to begin?"

Jamie pointed to the ceiling. "Right here. We got ourselves a lit'l room upstairs—at least fer now."

Abigail rose. "I need to get home, get this"—she indicated her outfit—"presentable for tomorrow. I'll come by in the afternoon, after I've had a chance to look for work."

Molly jumped up and hugged Abigail, catching her off guard. "Thank ya." Abigail saw the young girl had tears in her eyes.

4

"Certainly not," the lady screeched in the center of the tall foyer. "We're a genteel family. We can't have young Master William tutored by someone who looks like, like some street urchin. And take your *references* with you."

She threw the two wrinkled papers at Abigail, who didn't snatch them in time. They fluttered to the floor, and Abigail tried to keep her composure as she bent to pick up the sheets. They were standing in a lofty foyer, a crystal chandelier holding twenty-four candles overhead. She'd counted them while she waited.

When Abigail had knocked on the tall wooden door and requested to see the woman of the house, the Black footman had examined her from head to toe and, after a hesitation, allowed her in—but only as far as the foyer. She'd stood—paced—on the stone floor until a few minutes ago, when the footman had announced, "Mistress Harriet." The woman had appeared in a bright green dress of fine silk with ruffles and layers of petticoats underneath.

Under the woman's stern stare, Abigail's right hand flew to her hair, and she tugged a lock behind her ear, a nervous habit she'd developed. Dropping her hand, she curtsied and, after inquiring about children in the household, gave her best pitch, explaining her background and knowledge of the classics, rhetoric, and mathematics. She handed her references to the woman, who had barely glanced at the papers before tossing them back.

After retrieving the pages, Abigail straightened and made one final attempt. "I taught in a common school in London and was headmistress of a school here in the colonies."

That last was a stretch at best, but Abigail figured if she were the only teacher, she was also the headmistress. She held her head up and met the other woman's gaze.

Mistress Harriet's eyebrows arched. "Headmistress. Where?"

Abigail tried a reassuring smile. "Queens County, Long Island. My father and I have only recently arrived in New York."

"Long Island?" The woman's lips pursed. "The country. No, certainly not." She whirled and ordered, "Abraham, see this woman out."

The heels of the footman's black boots cracked on the limestone floor as he crossed the foyer and opened the large wooden door. Sixty seconds later, Abigail stood at the bottom of the stone steps, staring back at the mansion and shaking her head.

So it had gone all day.

Several doors had been slammed in her face even before she got a few words out. And this place—she took another glance at the symmetrical glass windows and the four tall stone pillars across the front porch—had at least admitted her into the inner sanctum. Twice today she'd been told by some kind of fancy butler to inquire at the servants' entrance around back. There they dismissed her as effectively as Mistress Harriet, though not all were as rude. At one house, when she walked around to the rear courtyard and found the small door next to the stable, she stepped in a pile of dung from the animals and had to use a leaf from a nearby maple tree to wipe the disgusting mess off her shoes.

Exhausted, discouraged, and unnerved, she headed back to the Pelican. At least she could start teaching Molly to read. The day would not be a total waste.

The late afternoon sun baked the cobblestones of Water Street, and the tall houses blocked any breeze. Sweat ran down inside her bedgown, and Abigail noted how much hotter the city felt. New York seemed hotter even than summers in London. Once again, she wished she were back on Long Island, in the country with the open fields and gentle summer winds.

She reached the green and crossed the open space, grateful even for the slight breeze stirring off the river. She tried not to look but couldn't keep her gaze away. Just as Molly had said, the dead boy still hung there, his body bloating, flies swarming around the corpse. Abigail shivered and hurried past.

Stepping onto the wooden planks, she headed down the narrow road bordering the water, the smell of rotting fish heavy in the air. Ahead, she could see a long stretch of the road as it curved to parallel the snaking East River. All along the river, ramshackle wooden buildings faced the water, two and three stories tall, the structures crammed close together. Most appeared to house businesses and warehouses below and living quarters above. The wood that held these buildings up was not like the stout logs of most of the cabins on Long Island. This wood looked warped and badly weathered, as if it had been salvaged from old ships and broken crates, giving the impression the structures might collapse in a strong wind. Above, most second and third stories had a window facing the water, some flanked by two slatted shutters. In the heat, every window seemed to gape open, flies buzzing in and out.

All kinds of people dotted the waterfront—rough sailors from the ships; dockworkers, shirtless in their worn breeches; merchants in linen shirts and brown waistcoats. Even a few gentlemen, with their long-striped breeches, white stockings, and full linen suits, made the trip from ship to warehouse.

Farther down the row, she heard squealing, and a moment later a large hog erupted out a stable door. The animal turned and charged down the sidewalk. Snorting, its hooves clattered on the wooden planks. Abigail tried to flatten herself against the building but didn't move fast enough. As it whizzed by, the animal bumped her, and she stumbled to the ground. Hot on its tail, two young boys ran after the creature, bare feet clambering on the slats past her head. By the time she pulled herself up, the fat hog and its pursuers had disappeared around the corner. She brushed off her frock and checked that her precious papers were unharmed. Then she continued on.

She pondered where she'd start with Molly, since the girl was so eager to learn. The alphabet, maybe, and some part of a broadsheet, if one had been left in the tavern. Lost in her thoughts, Abigail almost missed the shout.

"Hail below," a woman hollered from above.

A few feet ahead of her, a pile of waste dumped from a second-story window plopped down, half onto the timbers and half into the mud, the odors of human feces and rotting food overwhelming in the humid air. Coughing, Abigail covered her nose and hurried to the other side of the street, closer to the river. She glanced back up at the woman, who still held the bucket out the window, dumping the last of its contents onto the street below. Abigail shook her head. And these city people liked to think they were more advanced than those in the country.

She missed her time on Long Island—just Father, Oliver, and her. After her mother's death from whooping cough in London, the three of them had taken the *Friendship* to the colonies in search of a new life. Originally, it had been her parents' dream to start over in America. On her deathbed, Mother had made Father promise not to give up on that dream. She had wanted a new start for her children as much as for herself and Father. So when Abigail applied to teach in the country school and was accepted, they'd decided on Long Island for their new home. Father managed to purchase some acres there, and they settled in their new world in May 1773, just in time to start their work on the land.

The first two years passed quickly, Father and Oliver taking to farming. And Abigail loved teaching the children in her school. When she arrived at the school building—little more than a converted barn—none of the twelve boys and girls could read or write. Her students learned quickly under her care, and their progress convinced her they had made the right choice. The new land seemed so full of promise.

That was before the plundering . . . and the incident.

She pushed that from her mind and turned her attention to the harbor and the busy wharf, searching for Father. Down the road and around the first bend, she watched a ship being unloaded, shirtless men straining to lift barrels and heavy crates onto waiting wagons, their torsos gleaming with perspiration. She scanned the figures emerging from the hold into the bright sunlight, their muscles bulging with effort, trying to catch a glimpse of Father. She wondered how much dock work he'd managed to find. She knew they had little money left, though he'd told her not to worry. Still, it shouldn't all be on Father. He was old, almost fifty, and the dock work was hard. That was why she wanted—no, needed—to find some employment.

Between watching the unloading ahead and keeping an eye out for more second- and third-story dumps, Abigail almost missed the signboard. Out of the corner of her eye, she caught the crude image of the bird and the word PELICAN burned into the wooden sign. She crossed the street and stepped inside the tavern and out of the bright sun, the heat, and the putrid odors.

5

As yesterday, it took a while for her eyes to adjust to the gloomy interior of the tavern, and she paused just inside, her gaze sweeping the darkened space. Several patrons sat at tables, and two men stood at the bar. Her eyes found the table in the rear where she'd huddled with Molly and Jamie, but it sat empty. Glancing around, she didn't see either of them and froze, nervous and uncomfortable. The other six patrons were all men. She was the only female in the room. They all turned toward her when she came through the doorway. A slight prickle crawled up her neck.

She recognized the man behind the bar—same darker skin, same scraggly beard, same wild black hair—and stepped over to him. Before she had a chance to speak, the barkeep said, "Ain't ya that friend of lit'l Molly and Jamie?"

Abigail hesitated and choked out, "Yes. I was supposed to meet Molly here . . . to tutor her."

The bearded man said, "She told me she had to do a quick one and, if ya showed up, I was to git ya a drink. What'll it be?" He smiled, revealing a mouth of blackened and broken teeth.

"Um, rum, I guess," she said.

The barman nodded, one hairy arm pointing to the rear. "Go on to their table, and I'll bring ya a nip."

Glancing left and right, Abigail made her way to the rear table and took one of the benches, glad to be off her feet. She figured she'd been walking on cobblestones and pounding on doors for more than six hours. She sat there, watching and listening, wondering how long she should wait for Molly.

At the table next to her, two men argued, though both strained to keep their voices low. Still, Abigail could make out most of what they were saying.

"Ya gotta be crazy, talkin' like that around here," said the man with his back to her.

The man facing her replied, "I'm not crazy, just committed. I'd rather be teaching and working with children, but I gave that up to help with the fight. I don't think our people can take much more of the *king's justice.*"

She caught the word *teacher.* Another teacher. Maybe *he* would have an idea for a job as a tutor.

She studied the man facing her. He looked to be tall, though she couldn't be sure as he was sitting. He had golden hair and, even in the dim light, she could tell his eyes were blue. His head was turned slightly so she caught only part of his face, but it was a rugged, almost handsome face.

The man continued, "Men and women." He paused, and his eyes came up and met hers. "Men *and* women need to decide if they are willing to knuckle under to the crown's tyranny or . . . do something about it."

The man with his back to Abigail twisted his head. As he turned, all she could see was a profile, a full head of long, stringy brown hair, a broken nose, and one bushy eyebrow. He swiveled his head left and right, as if looking for eavesdroppers.

The man whispered, "Keep your voice down. All these taverns have Redcoat ears."

The barkeep arrived, diverting her attention. Placing a tankard down, he leaned in. "Miss Molly should be here directly." Next to the drink, he set a small loaf of bread. "She thought ya might be a wee bit hungry."

Abigail reached to pull out a coin, but the barkeep said, "Miss Molly already paid for ya." He straightened and slid back behind the bar.

Abigail *was* famished. She hadn't eaten anything since that morning. She bit off a chunk of the hard bread and washed it down with some of the watery rum.

Her attention returned to the pair of men and their conversation. After the soldiers' theft of their livestock, Father had insisted she needed to keep her opinions about those ugly Redcoat thieves to herself. The wrong talk, he said, could put their lives in danger, especially in the city. But Father didn't know about the attack in the barn. She'd never told him.

God knew she had her own reason for hating the British. At least, some British. She wanted to hear more of what this man had to say.

The man facing her reached into his pocket and handed the other man a small money bag. The one with his back to her leaned over the small table and slid something across, though Abigail couldn't see what it was. "Nathan, keep your head down and be careful who ya talk to." He gulped down what was left of his drink, slamming the mug onto the wood. Tossing a few coins on the table, he got up and headed out the door.

Abigail watched the young man named Nathan, who now raised his own tankard, nodded to her, and took a long drink. She glanced around at the other men in the tavern. None appeared to have paid the pair any attention.

Nathan stood up—he was tall—and stepped over to her table, hat in hand. He gave a slight bow and said in a low voice, "Ma'am." He turned to leave.

Abigail stared up at him and decided she might as well take a chance. "Sir, could I ask you something?"

"For a lady as charming as you, anything," he said, a broad smile on his face. "How can I help?"

"I heard you mention you were a teacher."

"Nathan Hale, from Connecticut, ma'am." He gave another slight bow. "Was a teacher *in* Connecticut until recently."

Abigail stayed seated, not quite sure of the protocol here. "Abigail Trench, teacher of late on Long Island . . . until the British came and claimed all livestock for their army. People had to give up farming and move away. So no school to teach in."

Nathan Hale's face darkened. "I am distressed to hear that."

Abigail noticed he stood over her and turned his head slightly so she saw him almost in profile. She said, "If you're from Connecticut, you must be new here, like me. But I still want to ask." She took a quick breath. "I wondered if you knew anyone who might be looking for a tutor. I need to earn a living, and . . ." She glanced around the tavern and lowered her voice. "And I was hoping to do some work other than a barmaid."

His smile broadened. "I completely understand." He rotated the tricorn hat in his hand. "Well, I went to Yale, so I know several families here in New York. I will be most happy to ask around. For you."

Abigail took his offered hand. "That would be most generous."

Holding her hand in his, Nathan leaned down and kissed it. His curly blond locks dropped around his head, and she saw a shadow on the right side of his face. When he straightened, he asked, "If I learn anything, where can I find you?" He gently released her hand.

"Right now, we have temporary lodgings by the wharf. How about here at the Pelican?" When she saw the question in his face, she added, "I'm tutoring a young woman here, Molly. Teaching her to read and write. She lives upstairs."

"How progressive," Nathan said. "I love it." He offered his wide smile again and turned his tricorn hat another full revolution. "May I be so bold as to ask, did you come to New York alone? Do you have any family here?"

Abigail caught his drift. "I moved here with my father, Caleb Trench. He's trying to pick up work on the docks."

Nathan glanced at the floor. "Then, when I return with news of any family in need of a tutor, could I be so bold as to offer to take you to see a few sights of New York?" His head came up, his features expectant, though still in a slight profile.

Abigail felt her face flush. Mister Hale *was* handsome enough, in a rough sort of way. He seemed courteous and willing to help her. She flashed a smile. "That would be quite nice."

Nathan gave another slight bow. "Until then."

Replacing the hat on his head, he turned and headed out, almost bumping into a pretty lady in a yellow dress who swooped in through the door. The other men turned to glance at her, then went back to their drinks. The woman stood for a moment, silhouetted in the doorway, turning as if examining the interior. She stepped over to Abigail's table.

Abigail stared at the lady, whom she didn't recognize. The woman wore a pale yellow dress of thin silk with white lace cuffs. Another set of frilly lace lined the V neckline, which swooped low to reveal two generous breasts. The pretty face held rosy cheeks and bright red lips. A small brown beauty mark spotted her right chin. When the woman spoke, Abigail almost jumped.

"Good. Levi took care of ya."

"Molly?" Abigail squeaked.

"In the flesh." Molly did a full turn, followed by a small curtsy.

Abigail stared. She didn't look like any child. She looked like . . .

"Grab your drink and bread," Molly said. "I need to get outta this before it gets dirty. Well, more dirty." She smirked and crossed the tavern.

Abigail followed her to a ladder she'd not noticed before, tucked behind the bar. Molly gathered up the dress and climbed. Abigail stuffed the bread in a pocket, held the mug in one hand, and used the other to grab the side of the ladder. Climbing one rung after another, she looked up and noticed Molly wore nothing under the fancy dress—no petticoats, no undergarments. Inside the scoop of the lace-trimmed yellow dress, two rosy cheeks of Molly's bare ass seemed to float overhead.

6

Shrugging, Abigail followed Molly up the ladder. She climbed through the opening and stepped into a small room, dimly lit by a narrow slit in the outer wall covered by a rag. Abigail examined the cramped space. Dust swam in the thin beam of light. On the warped wooden floor stood a narrow bed, a stool, an upturned crate serving as a makeshift table, and, in the corner, a wooden chest.

"It ain't much, but it works fer us." Molly kicked off her shoes and yanked the dress over her head, standing naked in the center of the room, facing Abigail. "Why don't ya have a seat, and I'll join ya as soon as I git into somethin' else."

The stool hardly looked comfortable, so Abigail made her way to the bed and sat, trying not to stare—and failing. Molly was certainly a pretty girl, with bright green eyes, the smooth skin of youth, and the full breasts of a woman. Her hips were slim, not yet widened by childbirth. When that thought struck, Abigail whispered another prayer that she hadn't had to suffer that indignity after . . . after her encounter with scar face.

She forced her thoughts back to the girl. Seeing Molly nude and close made Abigail realize how thin the girl truly was, the faint outline of ribs testifying to sporadic meals at best.

Unsure what to do with her rum, Abigail swallowed the last of it and set the tankard on the floor. Standing there nude in front of her, unembarrassed, Molly folded the yellow dress atop the chest, then bent to lift the lid. She laid the fabric carefully inside. Her hands fumbled around until she found and withdrew the bed dress and flock Abigail had seen her in yesterday. Molly stepped into them, then crossed to the bed and plopped down beside her.

"I hope ya wasn't waitin' long," Molly said, taking a quick breath. "I wanted to be here when ya got back, but one of my regulars came by." She held up two silver coins.

The thump of feet on the ladder sounded through the opening. A few seconds later, Jamie's head popped up, messy brown hair crowning his grinning face.

"Hey, Miss Abigail," he said as he climbed onto the floor. "And me love." He crossed the room and gave Molly a passionate kiss, smudging her red lips. When he broke away, he asked, "Levi said ya got a late one. How'd ya do?"

Molly held out her hand with the coins and beamed. "Not bad fer a half hour's work."

Watching them, Abigail couldn't hide her surprise.

Jamie grinned. "Oh, ya didn't know Molly was on the loose?"

"On the loose?" Abigail echoed.

Molly laid a hand on Abigail's arm. "He means I, uh . . . take care 'a men."

Abigail didn't want to judge. She'd learned the hard way that this land could be a tough place, especially for women. You did what you had to do to get by. Still, she was curious.

"That yellow dress?" She pointed to the chest.

Molly giggled. "The dress was Jamie's idea."

Jamie smirked. "Molly's quite the looker, but the blokes pay more if they can pretend they're doin' it to *a lady*."

Abigail studied the girl's face. "What about the red and the beauty mark?"

"Ah, the red is jus' a bit o' beet juice—tarts me up." Molly took a rag and wiped her lips and cheeks. Pointing to the mole, she giggled. "And this is jus' a bit o' grease." With her fingertip she first smudged, then wiped away the brown spot.

"We got two dresses, a yellow and a green one," Molly went on. "Jamie bought 'em with his coins." She shot him a sly look. "And we don't have t' bother with no petticoats."

Abigail grinned with them. Then a thought struck her. Could *that* be her only option if she failed to find a family needing a tutor? Please God, she hoped not. Her gaze flicked from Molly's lithe body to her own. How far would she go if she were hungry . . . or if Father needed something?

"I hope I didn't shock ya," Molly said, interrupting her thoughts. Her gaze went to the closed chest. "Not that many ways fer a woman to earn coin . . . in New York. 'Specially if ya can't read or write or do numbers."

"We're about to change that," Abigail said.

As Abigail watched, Jamie took the two coins. "Miss Abigail, could I ask ya to close them pretty green eyes o' yers?"

She stared at him and, seeing his fist close around the coins, understood. "Uh . . . sure." She covered her eyes with one hand and squeezed them shut. She heard a creak—likely the chest, though it might have been a feint—then the rustle of fabric. Of course they were careful. Living as these two did, you had to guard every coin. In this new land, it was hard to know whom to trust.

"Ya can open 'em again," he said.

When she did, Jamie was standing beside the bed. Her gaze went from Molly to him, and she marveled that her first friends in the city were a pickpocket and a . . . strumpet. And perhaps, a man named Nathan Hale.

Molly looked at her. "How did *your* day go?"

Abigail shook her head. "No success. I must've spent all day knocking on doors, but no luck." She glanced down at her drab bedgown. "Several took one look at what I was wearing and wouldn't even speak to me. I never even got to show my references."

"Rich folk put a lotta stock in appearances," Jamie said.

"They do. That they do," Molly agreed, shaking her head. She exchanged a look with Jamie. "I got an idea. How about I lend ya one o' my fancy dresses? Jus' to git ya in the door of one o' them mansions."

Abigail hesitated. "That's very kind, but—"

"'Course, you'll wanna take it and maybe wash it," Molly cut in, giggling. "And you might need t' git a petticoat or two."

Abigail glanced from Molly to Jamie.

"Consider it a loan in exchange for learnin' me," Molly said.

"It's teaching you—"

"Teachin'?" Molly squinted at her.

"I *teach* and you *learn*," Abigail said.

"Al' righ'." Molly nodded, then pointed at her. "With that nice brown hair and those beautiful green eyes, I think you'd look grand in the green one." She looked up at Jamie. "What ya think?"

Jamie flashed his wide smile, crossed to the chest, and drew out another dress, this one the hue of a shimmering emerald. Facing Molly, he said, "I think Abigail'll show up them fancy ladies when she knocks at the mansions in this."

Abigail eyed the second dress and saw it had the same plunging, risqué neckline as the yellow. Not a style she would normally choose. Her gaze went from Molly's bosom to her own. She might not be as young and perky as Molly, but she'd fill the bodice well enough.

Oh, Father would *not* approve. What would Mother say, if she were here? After a moment's thought, Abigail decided Mother would advise her to do what she needed to gain an advantage . . . and perhaps secure a teaching position. Besides, she could always throw a shawl over the top, to be discreet. She pictured how she might drape a white shawl just so—if she happened to meet Nathan.

She rose and took the offered garment. "You're both very kind. Thank you. I'll accept it only until I can get a position . . . and buy my own dress." She laid the green silk-and-lace creation carefully on the bed beside her. "Now, I suppose I'd better start earning it."

Molly commanded Jamie. "Sit over there and don't bother us, so Abigail can learn me—er, I mean, *teach* me."

Obediently, Jamie crossed to the stool and sat, keeping his eyes on them. Abigail ignored him and turned to Molly. "You ready?"

"As ever." Molly smiled, her eyes going wide.

7

The next day was Sunday, which meant church. It also meant Abigail couldn't knock on any doors looking for work. No respectable family would receive her today.

So she and Father attended service at an Anglican church called St. Paul's Chapel. Father argued it would help to be seen as faithful Anglicans and loyal subjects, even though they'd attended a Methodist chapel in England. Abigail did not argue. When she donned the green silk-and-lace dress, he frowned but relented when she draped a discreet shawl around the top of the revealing bodice. On her way home yesterday, she'd used a bit of her savings and purchased the shawl and a pair of petticoats. That night she'd gone over the shimmering fabric, cleaning and brushing it until it looked almost new.

When they walked the few blocks to the church, she had to lift the hem so the lace wouldn't drag on the ground. She stared speechless when they passed between the tall stone columns and through the heavy wooden doors. The structure was as grand as any church she'd seen in London—and the tallest building she'd yet seen in New York City. The place was packed, noisy worshippers nearly filling the interior. All kinds of people crowded inside. Rich gentlemen and ladies in fine silks, powdered wigs, and fancy hats sat in the central box pews. Around them pressed everyone else—merchants in waistcoats and breeches, the poor in whatever clothes they had, and soldiers. British soldiers. Redcoats dotted the nave from front to back, some even occupying the box pews. At the sight of scarlet coats, Abigail's gut clenched. She scanned their faces for that ugly scarred one, then scolded herself she was being silly. Long Island was a long way off. None of these men matched her haunted memory.

During the service, her mind wandered. All she remembered afterward was a sermon on what the vicar called the "Caesar passage" in Matthew—"Render therefore unto Caesar the things that are Caesar's and give unto God the things that are God's." Somehow, the priest turned this into a command to be loyal to the king.

Afterward, telling Father she had plans to tutor Molly, she kept on the dress. But, after she kissed Father on both cheeks, sending him on his way, she tucked the shawl into a hidden pocket. She hoped her—well—outfit might catch a certain young man's eye. Along the way to the Pelican she drew a few leers, whistles, and catcalls from men lounging near the wharf.

"Well, aren't ya a toffer, Miss Abigail," Levi said when she stepped through the tavern doorway. The barman grinned, showing his blackened teeth. "Ya certainly fill out that green dress o' Molly's." His gaze dropped straight to her nearly exposed breasts.

Abigail felt heat rise in her cheeks and turned away from his stare. Spotting Molly at a table near the back, she hurried toward her.

"Get her a drink, ya rake," Molly hollered. When Abigail reached the table, Molly's eyes looked her up and down. "He ain't wrong. Ya got what it takes to wear that thing."

Sliding onto the bench beside her, Abigail tugged at the silk, smoothing it over her lap. She gave the room a quick sweep. Molly was not the only one she'd hoped to see, but her student sat alone, back in her plain bedgown.

Eyeing the fancy outfit, Molly said, "I'm a bit surprised ya wearin' it today."

"I came straight from church."

Molly's eyebrows shot up. "You wore *that* to church?"

Abigail grinned. “With a nice shawl, of course.” She took one more look around. “Well, let’s get started. As long as it doesn’t get too loud, we can work in here. We should get a little light at this table.”

From a pocket sewn into the dress, Abigail drew out what she’d brought from Long Island in the hopes of finding a tutoring position.

“What’s that?” Molly asked.

“It’s a hornbook.” She produced a piece of white chalk. “You write on this sheet laid over the wooden paddle.” She made a quick squiggle. “Then we wipe it off and use it again and again.” She swept her fingers across the surface, and the mark vanished. Molly nodded slowly.

“Well, I’ll be,” Molly said.

“We might as well start at the beginning.” Abigail sketched a letter. “This is an A.” She put the chalk in Molly’s hand. “Now you copy.”

Molly beamed and bent over the board.

Abigail soon found her an enthusiastic, quick learner. They worked side by side at the worn table for more than two hours. A few men drifted in over the course of the afternoon, one at a time, and Abigail glanced up to study each new face. No Nathan. Disappointed, she tried not to let it show and kept her focus on Molly.

The girl struggled, as anyone would, but she was patient and refused to tire. One step at a time, Abigail moved her from the alphabet and a few words to parsing an actual sentence.

Molly stared at the chalked line and sounded out, slowly, “The . . . man . . . ate . . . an . . . apple.” When she finished, she looked at her teacher, eyes bright with delight.

“Well done,” Abigail said, smiling. She patted Molly’s hand. “This is a very good start.”

Abigail took one more look around and, sighing, made a decision. She needed to get back to fix supper for Father. Nathan wasn’t coming after all. She felt a pang of regret, not sure whether she mourned the missed opportunity for work or the absence of the handsome young man himself.

As she scanned the tavern, something on the bar caught her eye. She crossed to it and picked up a tattered page of a broadsheet someone had left behind. She skimmed the lines. The piece reported a gathering of representatives from all the colonies in Philadelphia—or part of the report, at least. The page was torn, brown splotches from spilled ale freckling the print, and the ending was missing. Not a problem for what she had in mind. She brought the broadsheet back to Molly.

"When Jamie gets back, here's what I want the two of you to do," Abigail said. "Sit together, close." She scooted in tight beside Molly. "Close enough so you both can see the words." Leaning over the paper, she waited until Molly did the same. "I want Jamie to read some of the sentences aloud, and I want you to follow along. Like this." She demonstrated, pointing to each word as she read, one at a time. "The . . . date . . . for . . . the . . . meeting . . . is . . . not . . . yet . . . set . . . but . . . will . . . likely . . . be . . . early . . . next . . . month."

She glanced up to see if Molly was tracking her finger. She was.

"That way, you get used to seeing the words while he reads, even if you can't read them yet," Abigail said. "It'll help." She leaned back. "Will Jamie do that for you?"

Molly grinned. "Jamie'll do perty much anything for me."

Abigail pushed herself up from the bench. "I need to go. Father'll wonder what's keeping me." She gave the open door one last look. No Nathan. "We can have another lesson tomorrow, after I do some more door knocking—in my new frock." She twirled the lacey dress once and nearly collided with a tall blond figure coming through the open door. She staggered back a step.

The man stepped into the tavern. "Abigail Trench? You look quite . . . fetching." He took off his hat and did a slight bow. "I was delayed and feared I might miss you. I am pleased I did not."

Abigail tried to compose herself, tucking a loose lock of hair behind her ear. Through his bow, his eyes landed on her, caught sight of her neckline, and then he hurriedly brought his gaze up to meet hers.

"Mr. Hale. I'd almost given up on you," she said.

"I pray you do not do that," Nathan replied. "At least not yet."

Molly came to stand beside her, and Abigail said, "Mr. Hale, this is my friend Molly—" then faltered, suddenly realizing she didn't know Molly's surname.

"Molly Brighton, sir," Molly supplied smoothly, her lashes fluttering.

Nathan gave another slight bow. Abigail noticed he wore his Sunday best—for her?—a formal brown waistcoat and matching breeches trimmed with ornamental buttons. Ruffled white cuffs peeked from his sleeves and matched his crisp collar. His blond hair had been brushed and tamed. Once again, she noticed the darkened skin along the right side of his face.

"Molly, this is Nathan Hale," Abigail said. "We met yesterday."

Nathan turned back to her. "I am relieved to find you still here. I have two things for you." He drew a folded paper from an inner pocket of his waistcoat and held it out. "Here is the name and address of a family friend, Mr. Lionel Hampton. He has two children very much in need of a tutor. I took the liberty of telling Mr. Hampton about you, and you are expected to call on them tomorrow at their home on Water Street."

Abigail stared at the writing, stunned. A tutoring position. At last. She lifted her gaze from the paper to Nathan's face, reading the faint anxiety in his dark blue eyes.

"Thank you. I am . . . most grateful," she said. With care, she folded the paper and slid it into the dress's hidden pocket, straightening her shoulders. "I'll go there first thing tomorrow." She looked back up. "You said two things."

Nathan turned the brim of his hat between his fingers and grinned. "Now that I have granted your request, I was hoping you would grant me mine."

II

MAJOR PARKER MONTEITH

PARKER

8

Major Parker Monteith rolled over in bed, unable to sleep. Again. He had arrived in the colonies two months before and had yet to settle into his new posting.

Of course, as a soldier, he went where he was sent. As the second son of the Earl of Stanton, he would inherit neither title nor land, so the most logical course had been the army—and travel. After his studies at Cambridge, his father had purchased him a commission. Parker had already served a few years in the West Indies and done a stint in Ireland. Then came the trouble at Lexington and Concord last year, and he had been ordered to the colonies along with other officers and more than two thousand fresh troops. His new orders had arrived on March 15—his son's fifth birthday. He had not liked leaving his family, but he was not unhappy either. For the first time, he was to command a company of men in the colonies. One hundred soldiers would report to *him*. He would at last see the America he had read so much about, all on His Majesty's halfpenny.

Though he did miss his young family.

Parker turned and glanced at the empty bed beside him. In his mind's eye Louisa lay there, warm body curled in his arms. He inhaled, imagining the jasmine scent of her hair. If he concentrated, he could conjure the faces of his children as well—Elizabeth and Henry. He drew a long breath and let it out slowly.

He was proud to serve. Most of the time he enjoyed the status and deference that came with an officer's rank. But the long absences from home weighed on him. He had been away when Henry took his first steps. He had missed Elizabeth's first ball, even if she had attended only as a very young girl. At least, for this posting, they would be joining him soon.

Rising from the bed, he padded down the hall. Snores and grunts from the other rooms accompanied his quiet footsteps. Like the other new officers, he had been given a billet in the officers' quarters. The place was fine enough—bedrooms with fireplaces and chamber pots, a grand hall for meals, drink, and smoke. Officially, the mansion belonged to a Tory businessman, delighted to open his home to His Majesty's soldiers. Rumor said the owner feared war was imminent and had fled with his family to the country.

Still in his nightshirt, Parker went down the stairs and out onto the rear porch. At the edge of the wooden platform, he paused and gazed into the valley below. The rich smells of earth and grass hung heavy in the air. Beyond lay the city of New York, huddled in darkness, only a scatter of lights blinking like fireflies in the distance. The only sounds came from insects in the grass.

A few weeks into his posting he had reached a decision. This new land was so vast and so beautiful that he decided to stay on once his family arrived—after this small rebellion was settled, of course. He recalled the letter he had written and rewritten before finally sending it to Louisa.

> Dearest Louisa, I hope this letter finds you and the children well. I know they are in good hands with you and our staff. I am safe here in my new posting. All is quiet here, at least for now. I have had time to think.
>
> This land is even more beautiful than I had been told. The rolling hills and lush valleys extend as far as the eye can see. New York is the largest city in America, even though it is quite

small compared to London. The city bustles with all kinds of people in its streets and alleys. I have seen dockmen and sailors, merchants and businessmen, lords and landowners, Negroes and even some savages. With your inquisitive nature and curiosity, I think you will love it here. I cannot wait for you to join me.

He had left other things out. He did not mention the rude reception British soldiers received. He had been told there were only small bands of unruly, rebellious militia and that most people remained loyal to the king, eager to embrace British officers as protectors. Now that he was here, he did not know if his superiors had been deluded or deceitful.

They had been quite wrong.

True, he found that some merchants and landowners were sympathetic. They wanted nothing more than to prosper within the empire. But most New Yorkers treated British soldiers with disdain or outright contempt. Parker had been here long enough to grasp how wide and deep the colonists' discontent ran.

He watched a thin slice of light push over the horizon, igniting the far hills in crimson.

Parker grasped the colonists' situation, but he was a soldier. A soldier followed orders. Even so, the assignment had not been what he had imagined. Most days he marched the men through the same mind-numbing drills over and over, or he bailed soldiers out of jail because of some drunken brawl.

He did not crave battle but found the constant waiting and marching stupefying. Word and rumor of distant actions reached them—the British victory at Fort Ticonderoga to the north and the disastrous withdrawal from Boston after the shocking fight at Bunker Hill.

But as yet, no fighting had erupted in New York.

Naturally, he had not burdened Louisa with any of this. Picking a small stone off the porch, he flicked it into the valley and watched the tiny object get swallowed up by the darkness. Louisa's arrival—and the children's—would change everything.

Still, Parker wanted out. Not out of the army, but out of the officers' quarters. He was tired of the endless bickering and sniping among his peers. He could no longer stomach the contempt many in the upper ranks expressed for the colonials in general and the American fighting forces in particular. He did not believe the colonials were all backward, lazy, and untrained, but most of his fellow officers refused to listen. More than once he had been forced to leave the grand hall to avoid quarreling with Hollister or one of the others.

To escape, he had his eye on a house in one of the better neighborhoods, on Water Street. With funds from his father, he had engaged a solicitor to negotiate. He planned to move there as soon as his family's ship arrived.

He could not wait.

9

Parker heard a noise behind him and turned to see a stooped figure filling the doorway. Lieutenant Colonel Theodore Cain. The man's red waistcoat hung open, white buttons undone. He stepped out onto the wooden planks, gait slightly unsteady. Straightening to his full height, he ran a hand through unruly red hair streaked with gray and offered a wry, tired smile. A half-lit cigar drooped beneath his red-and-gray mustache.

"Ah, Monteith, you're up early," Cain muttered.

"And you are up late?" Parker asked.

Cain chuckled. "Guilty. Just got in from a night at Martha's Place." He grinned. "I'm partial to that Caroline. She cuts quite a figure, in and out of clothes. I just hope she doesn't give me the clap."

Parker had heard plenty about the knocking shops in the Holy Ground, the district of ill repute that lay in the shadow of Trinity Church. Other officers, and more than a few of his men, sought "relief" there. Parker had thus far resisted the temptation. He did not think himself a prude, but he believed such establishments unfit for a British officer, whatever his superiors might think. More important than that, he shuddered at the possibility of carrying some vile disease home to Louisa.

"Come now, Monteith, don't be such a prig," Cain said, scowling. "I've found such places are good for more than a little roll. Those girls become privy to the most *private* of secrets. Pillow talk and all." He laughed at his own joke.

The foul smells of cheap tobacco and stale alcohol drifted across the porch, and Parker frowned.

"Well, have *you* heard the latest rumor?" Cain asked.

Parker drew himself up, trying to look properly serious—no small feat in his nightshirt. "You mean about representatives from all the colonies meeting next month in—" He broke off as Cain shook his head.

"Naw, that's common knowledge. There was even a piece in *The Tattler* about it." He straightened, tugging his coat closed, and flicked the cigar into the dark. "No, I'm talking about the assassination plot."

"You mean a plot to assassinate Governor Tryon?" Parker asked. The governor was beloved of the Tories and despised by the colonials. Rumors circulated that rebels meant to do away with him.

Cain shook his head again. "No. That's mostly foul gossip. Besides, Tryon'd be hard t' reach, hidin'. No, the talented Caroline's heard talk of a plot to assassinate the rebel leaders—maybe even their King George."

"General Washington?" In the two months since his arrival, Parker had heard plenty about the man from Virginia. Most British officers considered him a joke as a general, but Parker had learned that the rebels—especially their soldiers—held Washington in high esteem. He stepped closer. He did not want his words to carry on the morning air. "We are going to assassinate Washington?"

The lieutenant colonel looked at him as if at a slow child. "Not us. Them."

Parker flinched. "The rebels? Why would they assassinate their own leader?"

Cain laid a hand on his shoulder. As both were about the same height, the lieutenant colonel stared straight at the major. "I'm only a mere soldier, but if I were to speculate, I'd guess there are many in their so-called rebel army who would like it all to be over. They just want peace. And, according to the delightful Caroline, some friends of ours have given the rebels a little push." He smiled thinly. "I'd guess His Majesty's peace offer has given the conspirators their opportunity. Caroline says she doesn't know which day, but it should be soon."

"But Washington?" Parker said. "That would be very good for us."

Cain's eyes crinkled. "It might . . . or it might not. It could be very good . . . or it could all go to hell. Depends which way it falls." He gave Parker a once-over, perhaps only now noticing he was in his nightshirt. "You'd better get down there with your men. Get them ready and keep them ready. In the meantime, make sure they don't do anything t' light some damn fire or start something. At least not till we're ready."

"Yes, sir." Parker saluted, though it felt weird in his nightclothes. He suspected there was more to the story, more intrigue at work. But then, he was "a mere soldier."

Still, it presented an interesting scenario.

The first rays of morning crept over the far bank of the East River, spearing through the trees and setting the blue water alight. Parker turned and went inside.

With General Washington removed, would the British army face only token resistance? Would the rebellion simply collapse? By the time his family arrived, would there be peace? He might even be able to travel with Louisa and the children, to see some of the wonders of this new country he'd read about.

He did not intend to be the officer responsible for soldiers who blundered into some incident at precisely the wrong moment. He pounded up the stairs to his room, mind already ticking through a list of which soldiers to watch. And he knew exactly who would top that list.

10

Half an hour later, Parker was dressed and on his horse, riding down to the garrison. He had taken care with his appearance, bright white shirt and waistcoat beneath his long redcoat, the blue edging that marked his regiment turned smartly out. His spotless white breeches were tucked into polished black boots, and he wore a black tricorn hat trimmed in gold.

When he arrived at the garrison just outside the city limits, he swung down from the saddle and handed the reins of the black stallion to a waiting sergeant. Several men lounged on the ground, their backs against the tent wall, dressed as he had been earlier—in nightshirts or shirts only. He guessed they had moved outside to escape the stifling heat inside. He used his boot to nudge the foot of each man.

"Men, look lively." He got a few grunts in return. "Go rouse the rest of the men. I want to see every soldier out here in parade dress in five minutes." When no one moved, he shouted, "All right, make that four minutes."

He saw the sergeant returning. "Sergeant Fagan, would you show them how it is done in His Majesty's army?"

The small Black man with short-cropped hair and the beginning of a goatee at least had his breeches on. He gave a quick salute. "Yes, sir."

With a few shouts and strangled encouragements, Fagan herded the men into the tents. Parker stared at the stone-and-wood buildings of the town beyond. Since the rebel militia controlled New York City, his company had been ordered to camp outside town. They were to remain visible but not threatening. The soldiers could travel through the city in small groups, as long as they caused no commotions. His men went to taverns, attended services at St. Paul's Chapel, and frequented the knocking houses in the Holy Ground. All these forays were tolerated by the militia and the locals—as long as the soldiers did not cause trouble.

That last part had been Parker's greatest problem so far. He had a few soldiers he needed to keep under tight rein. All the men in his command were volunteers, but that did not mean they were all the same. Their inclination toward and interest in soldiering differed greatly. Some men came seeking adventure. Some served out of real duty to their country. Others joined to escape a jail sentence or worse. A few simply wanted to fight anyone, anytime, anywhere, with no real battles. These men often created their own conflicts.

Waiting, he paced out front, ignoring the grumbling and groaning within. The wind shifted and the stink from the latrine drifted around one side. Parker turned his back on the putrid draft and strode the other way, toward the parade ground—a nearly flat expanse. Marching feet had beaten down the grass and weeds, but a few stray wildflowers still swayed in the slight breeze, green stalks tipped with bright white and yellow blooms struggling through the dirt.

The men started to emerge, dressed and ready, sleep still in their eyes. The company continued to file out until the whole group had exited their tents. They assembled in what passed for dress uniforms, standing in ranks of ten as they had been trained. Parker strode between the lines, inspecting and checking off individual soldiers. About half wore the bright red waistcoat notable for British soldiers. The rest were in some patchwork of brown and white.

He completed his sweep and returned to the front. The men stood at strict attention. The sun had climbed higher, and with it the humidity. The temperature was not yet torrid, but the clamminess grew quickly oppressive. He could feel sweat gathering beneath his shirt but ignored it.

"Men, I know we have been here drilling for quite a while, and I know we have all found it tiring." He got nods of agreement and murmurs of assent. "However, today I have learned that our training may soon come to an end."

Heads came up all along the line, and Parker marched in front, meeting their gazes. "Now, according to military protocol, I am not at liberty to share the details." He paused. "Let me just say we may all soon see some real battles."

The men answered with loud cheers and whoops, raising their muskets and shaking them.

"I cannot say any more now, but for the time being we have to stay vigilant and continue our training. And it is vitally important that we do nothing to call attention to ourselves as British soldiers until the command is given and we are ready to act." Parker stopped at the head of one of the lines. "Sergeant Jenkins, I want your group to lead the drills today."

A large man with broad shoulders and a brown beard stepped up. "Yes, sir, I can do that." He turned to face the men, his eyes hard. "All right, lads, let's look sharp for the major."

Parker took a few strides to the right to allow Jenkins to lead the company and called, "And, Sergeant Fagan, I want to see you over here."

The small sergeant stepped forward, head bowed, refusing to meet Parker's gaze. "I can guess why ya want to see me, sir."

All Parker could see was the top of his black mop of hair. "Three of your men did not respond to roll call. Where are Garrick, Langham, and Reeves?"

Fagan shook his head, still looking down. "I dunno, sir. They took off for town last night and hadn't come back. Checked their cots. Don't look slept in, sir."

"All right." Parker drew a deep breath, thinking. "Do you have any idea where they were headed?"

"When I asked the fellows, they say Reeves said somethin' about goin' to one o' the taverns by the wharf." Fagan lifted his face at last. "Sorry I don't know more than that."

Parker shrugged. "It is a start. Get Davis in here."

"Sir?" Fagan asked.

"You two need to go find those soldiers. And maybe keep us all out of trouble."

11

"Pound that pole in harder," Major Parker Monteith barked to his men. "It needs to be solid and sturdy."

He strode several paces down the row. Another set of men wrestled a second ten-foot wooden pole into the hole dug in the ground. "This has to hold a writhing man."

He gripped the post, trying to rattle it with his gloved hand. It did not budge. He turned toward the man holding the hammer. "Davis, give this a few more blows and then move on to the next one."

The sergeant, with his massive, powerful arms, nodded. He raised the huge hammer and swung it in a wide arc, the effect echoing across the field. Parker marched farther down the line to where a third hole had been dug. Straining under the weight, two men lifted a third pole and set it into the cavity.

"The same with this post." Parker nodded at the group. "I don't want it to move an inch."

The soldiers nodded, but no one spoke. The men went about their tasks in eerie silence. Their earlier excitement had been snuffed out as soon as the three missing soldiers were brought back in shackles.

While the two sergeants had gone to search for the absentees, Parker had begun issuing orders for the construction of the posts. The exercise was new to the young recruits, but a few veterans knew what was coming. Whispered gossip flared through the company. In no time, the mood had shifted from excitement to dread. Rather than assign the duty, Parker had asked for volunteers. He had no difficulty finding them. The men were more than willing to work. That meant they would not be the ones tied to the poles.

Normally, Parker Monteith was proud of his steely composure. He strove to remain calm and unflappable even under trying circumstances. Today, Reeves and his companions had shattered that resolve.

Before the construction was finished, Davis and Fagan returned with the three. Fagan reported what they had found. Reeves and the others had been doing exactly what Parker feared—causing the sort of disturbance Cain had warned about. The three of them had been taking turns with a young girl, perhaps thirteen years old, all of them drunk and trying to rape her. With Davis's help, Fagan had pulled Reeves off the girl and paid her with the money Parker had given him. Then they had bound the men and marched them back to camp.

Ever since Lieutenant Colonel Cain had told him of the assassination plot, Parker had let his hopes rise. He believed the crown and the colonists could reach a compromise if both sides would bend. And if the plot unfolded as Cain had intimated, the colonists—minus a few key rebel leaders—might agree to the latest proposal. New York and the other colonies could be at peace by the time his family arrived in a few weeks. That could save hundreds, perhaps thousands, of British and colonials.

All this Reeves and his friends had put in jeopardy.

Parker needed to maintain discipline. That meant he had to use the punishment as a cruel example for the rest of the men, one they would not soon forget.

He did not truly like this version of military justice. When he had seen it meted out during his short stint in His Majesty's navy, he had argued with the commander that the practice was barbaric. Yet here he was, ready to administer the same punishment. He could still hear Commander Wilson aboard the *Majestic*. Reeves and the others "needed to be taught a lesson," and the rest of the men needed to learn it as well.

He hoped this would do it.

He turned to the men guarding the barracks where Reeves, Garrick, and Langham waited. "Bring the three out." He could not bring himself to call these miscreants soldiers.

They were led out with their hands tied together in front of them. Garrick and Langham looked wary and terrified. Reeves wore the same angry scowl. The guards marched each man to one of the posts, face to the wood. In unison, each guard untied his prisoner's wrists, yanked the arms up, and retied the hands to a peg nailed high on the post. The men's arms were stretched over their heads, their backs exposed. The guards stepped away and joined the rest of the company standing at silent attention.

Their backs bare, Reeves, Garrick, and Langham straddled the posts. Their feet pushed off the ground, trying to brace themselves for what was coming. The first two swiveled their heads, trying to see Parker. Reeves stared straight ahead.

Major Monteith walked between the posts, checking each set of bindings. When he reached the third, Reeves spat at him. The phlegm struck the right side of Parker's bright red coat. Parker drew out a handkerchief, wiped the spittle off, and never once looked at Reeves.

Turning his back on the three, he faced his company. "Men, I told you we may be close to seeing some action." He paced in front of the columns and met the gaze of each soldier. "That was only half true. A battle, and soon, is one very real possibility. Another possibility is that we make an end to this conflict and we all go home."

This time there were no cheers, no whoops. Instead, he watched recognition dawn on the soldiers' faces. "You have probably heard that His Majesty's government has made a new peace proposal and it may receive serious consideration from the colonials." He purposely did not say rebels.

He gestured toward the three men lashed to the posts and glanced at his company. "These things take time. There is no exact timetable. But one thing is certain. We cannot have British soldiers raping local women, especially young girls. Misconduct by His Majesty's troops could be used to sabotage any peace effort. And even if peace is not in the offing, we cannot, *cannot* start trouble before the rest of our forces arrive. Word is that new companies will land soon. Until then, the rebels have us at a serious disadvantage."

He nodded toward the poles without looking at them. "These three have put all that in jeopardy. Not only were their actions reprehensible, they could well have foiled any hope of peace. For that reason, these three men, *three British soldiers*, must be disciplined. Were we in England, their behavior might have earned them a three-moon stay in the Steel. Here in the colonies, that is not possible. Instead, under the Code of Military Justice, they are to be publicly flogged with you as witnesses. After questioning each of them about last night's events, I have determined that Garrick and Langham were not the instigators and merely went along. As a result, they will receive only four lashes. Since Private Reeves made no bones about being the ringleader, he will receive the maximum—twelve lashes."

Several soldiers uttered quiet gasps.

"Patterson, bring me the cat-o'-nine-tails," Parker said, never taking his eyes off his men.

When the private brought the whip, Parker removed his long red coat, folded it carefully in half, and handed it over. He gripped the wooden handle and snapped the cotton cords through the air, hearing them crack. Several of the younger men flinched. He worked to show no reaction. This had to be done. He took a deep breath and turned.

He strode to Garrick, the first man. Raising the whip, he lashed out at the man's corpulent back. The tips bit and drew blood, and Garrick screamed. Parker took another deep breath, steeled himself, and repeated the action once, twice, three times. He did not pause or think. Garrick's screams cascaded one upon another, echoing across the landscape. When he finished, Parker forced himself to stare at the man's back—a mess of red welts oozing blood, angry rivulets dripping down his skin and onto the ground.

Parker stepped to Langham. The man's spindly legs quivered in anticipation. Without a word, Parker flogged him in much the same way. All four lashes came one after another. Because the man was so thin and his back so narrow, Parker had to aim the cat-o'-nine-tails at nearly the same spot each time. Langham's back ended in a far bloodier state, his skin a mass of scarlet. Rather than scream, he sobbed aloud with each strike, blubbering like a child.

Parker strode down the row. Sweat dripped from his face and arms. He set the whip on the ground and rolled up the sleeves of his white linen shirt, now soaked and streaked. Picking up the cat-o'-nine-tails again, he stepped to Reeves's post and stared at the man. Reeves had insisted on keeping the orange scarf or handkerchief at his neck, and Parker had allowed it. Without waiting or thinking, he raised the whip and brought it down. One lash followed another. As he flicked the cords, he heard some of the men behind him counting—"Five, six, seven . . ." His motions with the whip rapid, he wanted to get this all over. Before his eyes, the light pink skin of Reeves's back turned into an ugly patchwork of red stripes and welts, blood dripping down his sides. Twice, Parker saw the tips catch and tear flesh.

"Ten, eleven, twelve."

Parker stopped and lowered the whip. He heaved several heavy breaths, sweat stinging his eyes. Pulling out his handkerchief, he mopped his brow and face. He studied Reeves—that stupid orange rag around his neck almost blended into the red cuts below. The coppery smell of fresh blood filled the humid air.

Throughout the ordeal, Reeves uttered only grunts and curses. At the end he twisted his head and glared at Parker with furious brown eyes, the two facial scars livid.

Parker met his gaze and did not look away. Then he turned back to the men, still standing at stiff attention. "These three are to be left here until sundown. After that, I will have Corporal White see to their wounds." He swept his eyes across the ranks. "In the meantime, no one is to give these men aid. Is that understood?"

The company answered in unison, "Yes, sir."

His gaze found Fagan. "Sergeant, you have the first guard duty. See that these men have water to drink, but that is all."

Sergeant Fagan saluted. "Yes, sir."

"Let this be a lesson for all," Parker said.

He retrieved his coat from Patterson and walked toward his horse. The wind carried Garrick's cries and Langham's sobbing behind him. He needed to get out of his drenched clothes. He could not stand another minute beside the men he had just disciplined.

God, he hoped he had done the right thing.

ABIGAIL

12

Considerate.

That was the word that came to mind when Abigail thought of Nathan Hale. Or perhaps earnest . . . and caring. Oh, he was ruggedly handsome, even with the scar, but what endeared him to her was his honesty and civility. But she wasn't sure how he felt about *her*.

The family he'd referred her to, the Hamptons, welcomed her with an enthusiasm she hadn't experienced since the parents on Long Island. The Hamptons' two children, Christina and James, ten and eight, proved to be rascals who loved mischief and pranks—but none Abigail hadn't experienced. She discovered both children possessed an insatiable curiosity, so she designed lessons to feed it. Excursions outside and explorations of the creek behind the house fascinated them and quickly won them over.

"I didn't think girls were that smart," eight-year-old James had exclaimed when Abigail held a salamander they'd captured—and then released—explaining how the creature could grow his own legs back after losing them. He was disappointed when she would not let him "pull off one leg and watch." His comment earned him a punch on the shoulder from his sister.

When the Hamptons learned she had newly arrived in New York, they advanced her a month's salary, allowing her to purchase two proper outfits, complete with petticoats. Isabel Hampton had even given her the name of a seamstress. That meant Abigail could return Molly's flamboyant green dress.

Because of the Hamptons' generosity, she and Father could breathe a little easier, with money for food and rent. Abigail tried to prevail upon him not to work so hard, but he waved her off with his customary caution.

"I'm right proud of you for landing this fine tutoring job," Father said when she told him, "and I'm thankful to this Nathan fellow for his help. But this new land is unpredictable. You never know what's around the next corner, especially with all the politics goin' on. I'll keep my nose to the grindstone, and you do the same. It's what your mother would tell us."

Nathan had made all of this possible, so, true to her word, a week later she let him show her some of the city's sights—though that was hardly a sacrifice. His "sights" were not quite what she'd expected.

For their first outing, she had agreed to meet him again at the Pelican after one of her afternoon reading lessons with Molly. When Nathan stepped through the doorway with that impish grin, she rose and went with him.

As soon as they were out of earshot of the tavern, Nathan said, "My, Miss Abigail, you look fetching in that dress. Is it new?"

She stopped, smiled, and gave a small twirl, displaying the outfit she'd chosen—a cotton dress of pale yellow with white bows. She hoped the color set off her brown tresses, which Molly had helped her pin up. Her fingers slid a stray lock behind her right ear. Because she meant to wear the dress while tutoring, she had chosen a modest neckline, revealing a few inches of skin but little else. In deference to the summer heat, she'd decided on a single sand-colored petticoat. The hem of the frock, trimmed in white, ended just above her laced leather shoes.

"Why, thank you, Mr. Hale. Thanks to the generosity of your friends, the Hamptons, who gave me an advance, I was able to purchase a few suitable outfits. I'm glad you approve."

"I most certainly do," Nathan said. "Not that you didn't look scrumptious in that green one you wore last week."

Abigail felt her cheeks redden and chose to change the subject. "I can't thank you enough for connecting me with the Hamptons. They're wonderful people, and I simply love Christina and James."

"Their children? Lionel confided in me the children can be quite a handful. You're not finding them a bit much?"

"Not at all," Abigail said, grinning. "They're merely curious and crave attention."

She took in her handsome companion. Nathan looked particularly sharp in a white linen shirt beneath a long brown waistcoat that only emphasized his height. His tan breeches were brushed and clean, ending in black shoes with shiny silver buckles. His blue eyes sparkled when he mentioned the two children.

"You know Rousseau believes we should not put society's restrictions on children too soon," she said. "I'm trying that philosophy with the Hampton children."

Nathan met her gaze and grinned, one corner of his mouth disappearing into the darkened skin. "Rousseau also believes nature makes us happy and good, and only society makes us wicked."

Abigail stared up at him. He stood a head taller than she, with a full head of blond hair. "Nathan Hale, you know Jean-Jacques Rousseau?"

He gave a courteous nod. "*Emile, or On Education*. You know, those of us educated in the colonies have learned a thing or two."

"I didn't mean that." She blushed and started walking again, realizing she had meant it, though not unkindly. She resumed walking. Nathan fell in beside her, and she added, "I apologize. By the way, where *did* you attend school?"

"Yale College, of course, class of '73."

"I'm confident your training at Yale was quite good, but I'm a bit surprised they'd teach Rousseau there."

He chuckled. "The masters didn't. They're a bit stuffy. I've read Rousseau on my own."

"As have I," Abigail said, surprised at the common ground. Considerate and well-educated.

"But going to Yale—and succeeding there—was important in the Hale household." He counted off three fingers. "In my family, hard work, integrity, and education are the three principles we learned early on."

"Sounds like a fine family," Abigail said, suddenly conscious of his other hand resting lightly on her arm.

Nathan shrugged. "Like many families, I'd guess. Mostly good. Father's a deacon in the church."

"Sir, can you spare anythin'? My mum and me is starvin'," cried a young boy who emerged from a dark doorway. His clothes were dirty and ragged, and he was shoeless, his bare feet brown with grime.

With a slight tug on her arm, Nathan stopped, and Abigail did the same. He reached into a hip pocket and drew out two halfpennies. Without hesitation he dropped them into the filthy, outstretched palm. When the boy closed his fingers around the coins, Nathan wrapped his hand over the smaller one.

"Now, you take this straight back to your mum," Nathan whispered. "And tell your mum she can get some fresh bread at Wappings on Williams."

The boy's deep-sunk eyes widened, and a broad smile crossed his face. "Yes, sir."

Nathan let go, and the lad scampered along the walkway, disappearing into a doorway.

Nathan's hand returned to Abigail's arm. It felt . . . right there.

"That was kind of you. Many men would simply walk by."

A trickle of sweat rolled slowly down the roughened side of his face and he flushed. "I was taught to be kind to those less fortunate. One of my father's favorite lessons is from Matthew twenty-four: 'Whatever you do for the least of them, you do for me.'"

She held his gaze. "Nathan Hale, you are an interesting man."

As they walked on, he said, "Tell me about *your* family. What are they like?"

So, as they strolled along the wooden walkway bordering King Street, she told him. Father's promise to Mother on her deathbed, their voyage to the new country, and then their uprooting to New York City. She even shared that her younger brother had joined the Continental Army, watching Nathan's eyebrows rise. As she spoke, she noticed he seemed genuinely interested, not merely polite the way suitors in London had been. It was so easy to talk to him that she did not realize they had turned a corner onto a different walkway, this one more worn and dirty.

Nathan looked down at her and grinned. "So it is only your father and you. You mean to tell me no beau has won your hand? With one as pretty as you, I find that hard to believe."

Abigail felt herself blush again and kept her gaze straight ahead. "I had a few men court me in London, and one who almost proposed. But after my mother died and we decided to come to America . . . well, I had Father and Oliver to care for, and my suitor was hardly keen on leaving England."

"Then I would say that was his loss—missing out on your charming company *and* this beautiful country."

She glanced at his face and couldn't help being curious. He seemed comfortable talking with her. Still, she didn't know if she should ask what she wanted to. She decided to risk it.

"Do you mind if I ask about your . . . face?"

He halted, and she stopped with him. He looked away. For a moment he said nothing, and she feared she had blundered.

His left hand rose to the right side of his face and he rubbed it gently. Raising his head, he smiled. "I've had it so long I almost forget it's there. When I was a boy, a shell exploded near me and I got burned. Back then other boys made fun of it and I was embarrassed." He dropped his hand and shrugged. "Now I realize it's simply a part of me."

Thinking it might help, Abigail said what she'd been thinking all along. "I like it. I believe it makes you . . . distinctive. Ruggedly handsome."

"I'm glad you do not find it offensive."

Abigail looked into his roughly handsome face and smiled. She loved teaching, loved watching children's faces light when some new knowledge opened up to them. She had enjoyed teaching, and tutoring Christina and James had only sharpened that joy. But was teaching all she wanted?

Many people said she was already too old to think otherwise. Besides, she had Father, and she could take care of herself. Did she truly want a partner to share this new life? Looking into Nathan's kind blue eyes, she wondered whether life might be better with a man like him.

13

They started back up. Beyond him, Abigail saw the buildings rise to three and four stories, packed tightly together. Off to the west the tall steeple of Trinity Church rose above everything else. The buildings looked much like those near the wharf, though these seemed more solidly built. As with the riverfront structures, the ground floors held mostly stables, and as they passed, the odors of horses and other animals drifted out, and she saw heads bobbing over stall doors. Looking ahead, she spotted the corner of a wider road.

When they made the turn, Nathan's pace quickened and she hurried to match it. In less than a minute, she saw why.

"Fine sir, I do things to your body the pretty lady wouldn't even try," called a raspy female voice from a doorway.

A woman stepped out of the shadows and planted herself before them. She had dirty, unkempt black hair, deep sunken brown eyes, and a soiled, torn bedgown. She swayed back, and as Abigail passed, the woman jabbed a sharp elbow into her, making Abigail flinch.

Up close, the woman reeked of sweat, animal dung, and fetid breath. Abigail clapped a hand over her nose. Elbowing past her, the harlot stepped in front of Nathan and yanked her top over her head, exposing discolored breasts veined in blue and dotted with small yellow pustules beneath one mound.

"And you can squeeze 'em and do whatever you want." She made her eyebrows bounce, and her leer revealed rows of crooked teeth.

Nathan seized the woman by both arms, lifted her aside, and set her out of the way so they could pass. He released her and again took Abigail's arm, urging her forward. Together they hurried along the walkway.

Abigail had seen such women in London's alleys and on street corners, but never this close. When the woman first lurched from the doorway, Abigail had taken her for an old crone. Yet her hair was dark, with no trace of gray. The years had not been kind. She earned her living the same way Molly did. Men, weary from war and far from home, came to such women for comfort.

Is that what fate awaited Molly in years to come? Holy God, Abigail hoped not. Not if she could help her. She glanced around, her head on a swivel now, and saw several more women and girls. She hadn't noticed them at first. They seemed part of the very walls. Bodies leaned from doorways, faces peered from open windows. Some women looked old and worn while others seemed younger than Molly.

"There seemed to be quite a few," she said to Nathan, lifting her eyes to indicate the women who appeared like wraiths in every opening. He didn't respond at first.

After they'd walked the length of the block and crossed another street onto a different wooden walkway, Nathan shot a glance back and spoke. "I'm sorry. That was not something a lady should have to experience. I'm embarrassed to tell you this, but after nightfall there will be scores of such women lining this route. It will be nigh impossible to get by them." His cheeks burned crimson. That was one of the things she liked about him—he did not hide his true feelings.

Without breaking stride, he swept his free hand to the left. "Even though this was shorter, I should have taken a different route, brought you over Williams Street instead. This area is what they call the Holy Ground. It's lined with knocking houses."

Puzzled, she glanced around as they kept up their pace. Two- and three-story wooden buildings faced the street, doors and windows flung open to the hot summer afternoon. Some structures were in serious disrepair, with rotten siding and crooked doorways, while others looked well kept. Different odors drifted across the stagnant air—cooking, damp animals, and some kind of perfume—layered one atop another. Her eyes were drawn to one door painted a deep red. Above it a sign read MARTHA'S PLACE.

"Holy Ground?" she asked. "Wasn't that a—"

Nathan nodded. "Yes, the woman's a jack. This place is full of them."

"Why do they call it the Holy Ground, then?"

"Well, it's bordered by Trinity Church on one end and King's College on the other—hence Holy Ground. The middle is where the tippling houses, taverns, gambling dens, and disorderly houses are."

He kept hold of her arm as they stepped off the planks onto a muddy street, guiding her around puddles. As she had noticed earlier along the wharf, all classes were represented. Laborers in soiled work clothes hurried in and out of doorways while women of varying ages, in revealing gowns, tried to draw them in. Couples walked together, including a Negro woman with a white man. There were even gentlemen in fine coats and top hats.

After surveying the scene, she turned and looked up at Nathan. "All right, I've been patient enough. Where are we headed?"

"I want to show you something I find inspiring," he said as they started along another strip of sidewalk, their feet echoing down the row. "It's much like this new country, but it carries more meaning than it first appears." He nodded. "The Commons is not much farther."

After another block they turned a corner and stopped at the edge of a green, a much larger space than the patch by the river where they had hanged the boy. A slight breeze drifted across the open ground—the first she'd felt since they left the water. People milled about, some cutting across the grass, others sitting and basking in the sun. At the far end she saw men in military garb.

Nathan pointed toward the center of the common. "*That* is what I wanted you to see."

In the middle of the broad space rose a towering pole, perhaps forty feet high, bearing a single red flag that fluttered in the breeze. A metal fence about the height of a man encircled its base.

With his hand still on her arm, Nathan guided her over and stopped at the fence. "This is called the Liberty Pole. The Sons of Liberty have held demonstrations and protests against British oppression at its foot for ten years now—like the demonstrations last year against the Intolerable Acts."

He pointed upward and her gaze followed, her hand shading her eyes. "It looks like a ship's mast," she said. "I think the mast on the *Friendship*, the ship we came over on, was about that tall."

"That's exactly right," he said, grinning. "In fact, this is the third Liberty Pole. The first was the mast we cut from the deck of the HMS *Diana*, a British warship we captured. I wasn't here, but I heard there was quite a celebration. The Redcoats were so angered they tore that one down, so the Sons put up a second. The British did the same to that pole. So the patriots erected this huge one and built the fence around the bottom. It stands as a symbol of resistance against British tyranny and—"

Across the green a voice shouted, cutting him off and drawing Abigail's attention. At the far edge of the space, three lines of colonial militia in formation marched across the grass toward them. As they neared, she saw a few men in bright blue coats she recognized as Continental Army uniforms, though most wore common brown and white. One soldier in a long blue waistcoat marched backward in front of the first line, barking orders. Only a few words reached them across the open space, but Abigail caught the tone.

She turned to Nathan. "It looks as if they're preparing for battle. Are the British getting ready to attack New York?"

14

Abigail and Nathan stood side by side, watching the lines of soldiers file across the Commons. When the men had marched halfway across the green, she glanced up at Nathan. His face bore the look of a proud father. She waited for him to answer her question, but he only watched the formation, the soldiers' feet pounding in unison.

When the militia passed, Nathan turned and set his hand on her arm again. "Let's head back."

Without another word, he led her across the grass and onto a different sidewalk. Hurrying her steps to keep up with his long strides, she said, "Nathan, your silence is unnerving. You serve under Washington's command, so I assume you know something of what's coming—or have heard something."

They continued down the walk as a carriage rattled past in the road, raising a trail of dust, making any conversation impossible. The silence from her usually talkative companion unsettled her. He guided her past a man selling sheep's feet and did not speak again until they were out of earshot of anyone else.

"Yes, I've been a soldier in Washington's army, but I am no longer. Like you, I am now . . . a teacher looking for work." He looked down the street and said no more.

Abigail stopped. Being the gentleman she knew him to be, Nathan halted beside her, his hand slipping from her arm. She sensed he was keeping something from her. She glanced around. This street was more narrow and less busy than Broadway, and small knots of people dotted the walk and hurried in and out of buildings. A few doors ahead, men stumbled through an opening, and from their condition she guessed it was another pub. No one seemed to pay the two of them any attention.

She looked up into his blue eyes. "The day we met, I overheard you in the Pelican . . . talking with that other man." When he still made no response, she went on, "I am not a child, Nathan. I can read between the lines."

He cast a cautious look around, his gaze sweeping the street both behind and ahead. Then he met her eyes, laid his hand on her arm again, and urged her forward. He set a brisk pace and she kept up.

When they had passed well beyond the public house and no one was within earshot, he spoke again in a low voice. "I cannot say much. And I don't want to place you in any danger."

They stepped off the walk into the dusty street, crossed at the next corner, and climbed back onto the boards on the far side. As they moved, his posture stiffened and his gaze made a full circle before returning to her. A couple passed—a tall white man in workman's clothes hand in hand with a short, pretty Black woman. For a moment, Abigail was distracted. Before New York, she'd never seen a mixed couple, not in London and certainly not on Long Island.

Nathan nodded to the pair as they moved aside, edging closer to the building's wooden siding. When no one else was nearby, he spoke in a whisper. "All I can tell you is that I will be assuming a different role—for the army, for General Washington. I can say no more."

They walked on, their footsteps echoing on the planks as snatches of other people's conversations drifted through the humid air. They passed a pair of Redcoats heading the other way, waistcoats open, laughing and jostling one another. Abigail and Nathan gave them room. Nathan offered the same nod. Both soldiers returned it, grinning and reeking of alcohol. A minute later, he spoke again in a quiet voice.

"To answer your question about a British attack, we know it is coming, though we don't know how soon. We know the British plan to take New York, but we haven't yet learned their timetable."

Abigail kept her voice low. "With the soldiers in the garrison up on the hill, they must have plenty of men."

Nathan shook his head. "Oh, Washington's troops far outnumber the British—for now. The king will have to send many more soldiers, and we believe they are on their way. It's only a matter of time. New York is simply too great a prize. We don't know if it'll be one month or one year." After a pause he added, "We're doing all we can to prepare."

He must have seen something in her expression, because he added, "Keep your head about you and I don't think you have anything to worry about. At least, not yet. But yes, the war is coming to New York."

Together, his hand on her arm again, they followed the walkway down toward the water. Staring straight ahead, Nathan said in a more conversational tone, "The officers are hosting a dinner party next Saturday evening, and I have managed to get an invitation. I'd love to have you accompany me."

"Officers?" she asked, glancing up at him.

He smiled. "Yes. General Washington and the officers of the Continental Army are hosting the party."

She returned his smile. "I'd love to."

15

As the carriage rolled up to the grand house, the horses slowed and stopped, the rhythmic clatter of hooves dying away. Through the window, Abigail saw only sand-colored siding and four steps leading to a black door. When she descended, her gaze took in the immense structure. Twelve windows spanning the front, six on each floor, every one flanked by black shutters. She stood staring in amazement—this place was even grander than the Hamptons' estate—while the carriage wheels rattled on the gravel drive as the horses trotted away.

Their journey had taken a while, as the promised event was held at an estate in the country—for security reasons, Nathan had explained. Abigail had been jostled inside the coach as they traveled over rutted, muddy roads, waves of dust clogging her nose and eyes. Inside the compartment, conversation had been nearly impossible over the racket of wheels and hooves, but Abigail figured it a small sacrifice. Her insides felt as jumbled as her body, battered by the coach's bouncing progress.

Abigail expected to enter through the front door, hoping to inspect the mansion. Instead, Nathan took her arm and led her to the right. As they rounded the corner, the sound of musical instruments floated through the air, intermingled with conversation and laughter.

The backyard extended left and right, a grassy meadow running perhaps two hundred feet deep. Beyond, the yard fell away in a gentle slope into a sunlit valley bordering a winding river, its water sparkling in the afternoon sun like scattered diamonds. At the far end of the vista rose a line of majestic hills, their forested peaks disappearing into white, gauzy clouds. The scent of grass and fresh water filled the air, a refreshing change from the noxious odors of the city and the dust of the ride.

Nathan guided her across the lawn. In the center of the vast yard, a long canvas tent had been erected, its flaps open on all sides. Around it, men in full colonial uniforms stood, long blue greatcoats festooned with shiny brass buttons. Others wore civilian dress, white silk shirts beneath brown and tan waistcoats, ending in brushed black shoes with shiny buckles. The women's attire matched the grandeur of their partners, dresses of pale yellow, green, and pink trimmed with white lace, each more ostentatious than the last.

Abigail was glad she'd selected her new green dress with its generous amount of fleecy lace—Nathan said the color brought out the emerald of her eyes. He looked just as dashing as any of the men, wearing a white shirt inside a pressed, long brown waistcoat. Unlike the others, he didn't tie the collar, leaving the lapel of his linen shirt open. Abigail liked it that way.

A Negro servant appeared beside them, dressed in formal livery. "Would you care for a drink?" he asked, holding out a tray of crystal glasses.

"Why, thank you," Nathan said.

He took two drinks, handing one to Abigail. Side by side, they strolled among the crowd, their gazes shifting from the partygoers to the ground. A few animals roamed the lush green lawn—two chickens pecked the earth, searching for crumbs, and a small hog ambled lazily among the guests. When the chickens roamed close enough, their pungent odor wafted up.

Nathan had confided this was to be a relaxed affair, and she saw the guests were hardly standing on formalities. Several men approached and greeted Nathan, slapping his back and shaking his hand with exchanges of frivolity.

Nodding and chatting, they wandered toward the tent. Beneath the canvas stood a quartet of musicians. One member played a brass instrument Abigail hadn't seen before. The musician blew into a metal tube shaped into a coil, ending in a wide, circular, mouth-like opening.

Nathan noticed her staring. He leaned close and whispered, "That's called a French horn. All the rage in Paris." He grinned.

She slapped his arm playfully.

"Well, Nathan Hale, as I live and breathe," said a high-pitched voice.

Abigail turned to find a handsome young man, short in stature with a rosy, boyish face and a head of curly blond hair. Nathan switched his glass to his other fist and grabbed the offered palm. "Alexander. You look well." Then he turned. "Alexander, *this* is Miss Abigail Trench." He nodded to her. "Abigail, meet Captain Alexander Hamilton."

She performed a small curtsy, careful to balance her drink. Just then, another server came by with a tray, and she set her glass on the silver platter. "I'm quite pleased to meet you, sir," Abigail managed, returning the young man's smile.

Nathan said, "Alexander has already distinguished himself in the battle at the Battery."

The young officer gave a slight bow. "One of many to come, I fear."

Like several others, the young man wore full military garb, a blue waistcoat that looked too long for his short frame, the material dotted with silver buttons. He looked impossibly young—*Only a little older than my brother*, she thought—to be a captain.

"Captain, what regiment are you with?" she asked.

The young man's grin broadened. "Please call me Alexander. I command the New York Provincial Company of Artillery, though now we serve as part of the Continental Army under General Washington."

"Could I beg a favor, Captain, er, I mean, Alexander?" she asked.

Hamilton nodded. "What is it? I'll be happy to grant it if I can."

"It's about my brother, Oliver Trench. He joined the fight last summer. Father and I, um, had to move from Long Island somewhat suddenly, and we haven't been able to get word to him that we are in New York."

The captain said, "Many companies are now stationed in and around New York. He could be close by. What regiment did your brother join?"

"The 3rd Pennsylvania Regiment."

"3rd Pennsylvania." Hamilton nodded. "The army is a big place, but that helps. I'll be happy to ask around. Tell me again your brother's name."

"Oliver Trench."

The handsome captain and Nathan shook hands once more, and then Hamilton took her hand. He bent and kissed her fingers. "I will go right now to find quill and paper and write down, Oliver Trench, 3rd Pennsylvania Regiment.' If I learn anything, I'll pass it on to Nathan."

"Thank you so much, Alexander."

Cherubic face smiling, Hamilton headed out, mumbling to himself.

Abigail had no idea where Oliver was. Neither Father nor she had heard from him for months, though with the Continental Army, that was hardly unusual. And Oliver was not one for writing letters. Perhaps, thanks to Nathan's friend, she'd get to exchange letters with Oliver soon, or maybe even see him.

Nathan led and they sauntered farther into the crowd. Several more men stopped to greet him and bow to Abigail. She was surprised Nathan knew so many of the men—and more than a few of the women.

It felt quite good to be here on Nathan's arm. Today, he'd gone out of his way to introduce her to all his friends and acquaintances, lavishing praise on her she wasn't sure she deserved.

What would it be like to have him as a husband? She realized she didn't know that much about him. Yet how could she complain Nathan was not completely forthcoming when she had shared only the barest details of their forced departure from Long Island?

She shoved the thoughts aside and returned her attention to the crowd. Scattered among the knots of soldiers, gentlemen, and ladies, Negroes in formal livery scurried about, heads bowed, offering drinks and food or collecting empty plates and glasses. She wondered if they were slaves, here at a gathering of officers fighting for independence.

Under the tent, the musical group struck up another tune, this one with a faster beat. Her gaze wandered to the rear of the yard and the majestic view beyond. To the left of the white canvas, she caught sight of a tall, blond-haired man in a blue military uniform different from the other officers. Across the front, a large, pale blue sash ran from shoulder to belt. He stood conferring with two other officers, one round and pudgy with a serious expression, the other thinner, though both a head shorter. The tall man looked up, his blue eyes seeming to catch hers. He nodded, smiled, and returned to his conversations with the men.

Abigail looked toward her companion and found Nathan watching her. "Is that . . . ?"

He grinned. "Yes, *that* is General Washington."

Her gaze went back to Washington. Around him stood four other soldiers at attention, their eyes alert. Their uniforms, though clearly colonial, looked different—blue coats with white facings decked out with silver buttons. And their hats looked unusual, round rather than tricorn, with a blue and white feather.

Nathan must have read her mind again. He nodded toward the soldiers surrounding the general. "And those are Washington's Life Guards. His bodyguards."

Abigail studied Washington, fascinated. With his short blond hair, aristocratic nose, and oval face, Washington cut an attractive figure, made more so by his height—even taller than Nathan. But as she watched, she saw he possessed a certain quiet composure. While others around him became animated, talking quickly with hands flying, Washington stood tall and remained calm, his expression changing little.

Nathan leaned in so close she could smell the wine on his breath. "Would you like to meet him?"

She stared. "You know General Washington . . . personally?"

"Well enough to introduce you." Nathan's smile broadened like a proud schoolboy's.

She caught her breath. "I'd be thrilled."

Nathan placed his hand on her arm, and together they weaved between the guests to the queue waiting to speak with the general. Abigail couldn't believe her good fortune. Weeks ago, she and Father had arrived in New York City with little money, no destination, and few prospects. Now, she had a great tutoring job—making far more money than she had on Long Island—had made friends, and was about to meet the most important man in the colonies' fight for independence. She brushed a stray hair behind her ear.

To steady herself, she examined Washington and the four men flanking him. Two hens meandered between the legs of the bodyguards, picking at bits of food dropped on the ground, though the men appeared to take no notice. She watched the chickens weave in and out, then lifted her gaze to study the guards. Three of the four stood still and quiet, eyes roving the crowd. The fourth, the soldier on Washington's immediate right, looked different. His posture was erect, but his eyes jerked left and right, then settled on something—or someone—in the distance. Abigail studied him, puzzled. He looked . . . nervous. Did he sense a threat?

Abigail scanned the crowd. At first, she saw nothing unusual. Then she caught sight of one man dressed in a fine brushed waistcoat and brown breeches, a white wig atop his head with a few stray black hairs sticking out beneath.

The man stared at Washington, and she thought he was probably watching the general like most of the crowd. Then she flicked her gaze from the well-dressed man to the fourth bodyguard. She could've sworn she saw a reaction. The well-dressed man nodded once. In response, the soldier's head dipped—just the slightest movement.

Something seemed off.

16

Abigail didn't have time to ponder what she observed. Nathan tugged on her arm and pulled her attention back. He strode forward, and Abigail matched his steps.

"Well, if it isn't Nathan Hale," said a low voice.

Nathan released her arm and executed a deep bow. Beside him, Abigail performed a quick curtsy. "General Washington," Nathan said, "I'd like to introduce you to a friend of mine, Abigail Trench."

Eyes on her, Washington smiled. "And quite a *lovely* friend, Mr. Hale. Where did you find such a gem?"

Abigail spoke up. "My father and I came to New York from Long Island. I'm a teacher, and Nathan has been good enough to help me find employment here."

"Welcome to New York City." Washington leaned his tall frame toward her, his smile widening. "I hope you are finding it to your liking."

Abigail liked his smile. For a man so important, his warm countenance was reassuring. It calmed her nerves. "We're finding our way . . . in part thanks to Nathan." She nodded toward her companion. "We were forced to abandon our farm on Long Island when the British took Woodmere and looted the whole countryside. I was teaching at a small school there, but the families left, taking their children with them."

Washington looked pained, as if *he* personally were responsible for the defeat. "I am so sorry. Even though our cause is worthy, this conflict has already exacted far too many hardships upon good people."

She found herself nodding, and the general met her gaze. "We *are* working on plans to retake Long Island."

"My brother will be glad to hear that."

"Your brother?" Washington looked puzzled.

"Yes, sir. My brother, Oliver Trench. He enlisted in the 3rd Pennsylvania Regiment last August. He'll be anxious to fight to get our land back, as well as for this country."

"We are fortunate to have brave men like your brother volunteer for the cause of liberty."

A long, shrill blast from the horn interrupted all conversation, silencing the crowd.

When it finished, Washington continued, "Ah, it seems they are ready to serve the meal. I'm told the chef has prepared one of my favorites—sweet peas." He gave a short bow. "Very good to meet you, Miss Trench. Perhaps we can talk more later."

"I'd like that, sir," Abigail said, feeling like a lovesick schoolgirl.

Washington turned away. Behind him, servants had placed tables under the tent, chairs lining both sides. Each table bore a pristine white tablecloth and a centerpiece of native flowers bursting with red, pink, and gold. Silver dishes overflowing with meat and vegetables covered the surfaces.

She faced Nathan, who winked. She had just met General Washington, the head of the rebel cause. Abigail felt heady.

She watched Washington stride to the end of the first table, looking confident and . . . almost regal. All the other guests followed, taking seats, chattering and laughing again. Not wanting to be left out, she and Nathan found seats at the next table. Even the animals trailed behind the humans, scurrying underneath the tables in hope of scraps. Only the bodyguards remained aloof, standing at attention in a semicircle around Washington's chair.

The dishes on their table—venison, chicken, a savory potato dish, a stew in dark gravy, and fresh mixed greens—gave off such tempting aromas Abigail heard her stomach growl. Until that moment, she hadn't realized how hungry she was.

After a minister pronounced a prayer, the guests turned and watched Washington, who smiled and reached for a dish. Using a large spoon, the general ladled a serving onto his plate. Leaning back in her chair, Abigail saw that Washington had indeed reached for his peas first. She liked peas well enough but thought, with turkey and duck available, they would not be her first choice.

"Stop!" someone yelled from near the house. "General, stop!"

Abigail turned to see a figure sprint across the lawn. The man, dressed in military garb, ran full-out across the grass, arms flailing, the lapels of his blue waistcoat flapping with his hurried steps. The features on his face stretched tight, he leaped over the hog settled in the grass. Two bodyguards grabbed for him, but he was too quick. In seconds, he reached Washington's table. Rather than stopping, the man kept running and slid across the table, knocking the plate in front of Washington to the ground. Three other platters clattered down, fine porcelain cracking in the collision. The white tablecloth slid into the dirt beside the food.

Washington stood. "See here. What is the meaning of this?" he asked, not raising his voice.

Two bodyguards seized the man off the table and held him, arms pinned behind his back. The intruder's face was red, his breath coming in ragged pants.

Washington glared down at the shorter figure. "Well, what do you have to say for yourself?"

The intruder tried to catch his breath. "General, sir." He gasped. "We just, uh, learned they were poisoned." Another quick breath. "The peas."

Several ladies gasped. Everyone stood, staring down at the chickens now pecking at the peas, swallowing one after another.

Taking in the scene, Washington said, "The chickens would seem to disagree."

Several guests laughed at his jest, Abigail joining them.

As the crowd watched, one hen finished with the peas and waddled toward the spilled stew vegetables. Her small head lowered, and she seemed to convulse. Then she dropped on her side and stopped moving. Thirty seconds later, the second chicken repeated the sequence—another fat, lifeless bird.

Washington stepped back from the table, gaping at the scene.

One of the bodyguards yelled, "Stephen, Jeremiah, get the general to safety. Now."

17

"Thomas Hickey, you have been found guilty of mutiny, conspiracy, and treachery and have been sentenced to hang from the neck until dead," a gravelly voice announced over the murmurs of the crowd. All quieted.

Abigail stood a few rows back, staring ahead like everyone else. She couldn't believe she was here again, witnessing her *second* hanging in a few short weeks. Nathan had asked her to accompany him, insisting they needed to be here. Only three days ago she'd been attending a dinner party, eating and drinking with the officers of the Continental Army and General Washington. Now, she simply prayed the biscuits she'd eaten this morning would stay down.

Minutes earlier, Nathan's carriage had brought her to this field north of the city. After sending the carriage away, he led her by the elbow through the knots of people, stopping to talk with several men, each wearing an expression more severe than the last. He maneuvered around soldiers and civilians, women and Negroes, merchants and servants, most dressed in their Sunday best. Young children scurried about the adults' legs.

As they moved closer to the front, Abigail remembered thinking the crowd at the earlier hanging had been considerable—maybe a hundred. But this? She glanced around, trying to take in the sheer mass of people waiting to watch this execution. She'd never seen so many people assembled in one place, not even in London. There must be thousands.

Across the open field, she saw rows upon rows of Continental Army soldiers marching into position, standing at attention, their officers alongside them. They stood in precise lines, full military dress—bold blue waistcoats over white linen shirts, black breeches, and shoes. Row after row.

When she and Nathan finally stopped, edging their way to the third row, she caught her breath. "Why are so many people here?"

Nathan lowered his head. "General Washington put the word out he wanted everyone to witness this hanging, especially the soldiers." He gestured to the lines of blue coats. "He directed every soldier to attend, and they spread the word."

His explanation did little to ease her anxiety. It was another hot summer day, though overcast, and by midmorning, the press of bodies made it stifling. She felt no breeze, and beads of perspiration rolled down the inside of her gown, the same green dress she'd worn to the dinner.

Studying the faces around her, she noticed a difference in temperament from the first hanging. No smiles, no gaiety, no jesting.

Back a ways and to the right, she saw a gaggle of girls and women in revealing dresses, their somber faces garishly made up, muttering among themselves. Abigail realized even the inhabitants of the Holy Ground had shown up, one or more perhaps familiar with Hickey. Seeing their gaudy face paint, she wondered about Molly . . . and Jamie. Jamie wouldn't miss such an opportunity, a huge crowd huddled together for his "work." She shuddered to think what might happen if he were caught here.

"By virtue of and in obedience to this warrant," the rough voice called, "the accused has been ordered to suffer death in the manner prescribed."

The speaker, dressed in a pressed military uniform, stood stiff to the side of the accused. The condemned man was bound and bracketed by lines of guards. From this group, four men stepped up, two on each side. They escorted the prisoner to the small wooden gallows—two steps up to a platform supporting two posts. A board lay across the posts, and a rope dangled over it, ending in a noose.

Abigail understood the execution was necessary, but her insides roiled. She wanted to look away.

Beside the speaker stood a line of six military men in formal dress. Abigail recognized Washington—it was hard not to notice him towering over the others—as well as some of the men from the party. She was close enough to see Washington's face bore a stern, hard look, but his eyes seemed pained.

At the dinner, Nathan had explained the men beside Washington were officers in the Continental Army. On Washington's left, she recognized the handsome face of Alexander Hamilton, his expression troubled.

"Does the accused have anything to say before the sentence is carried out?" the speaker asked.

The man croaked, "I knew we'd lose." The shouted words pulled her attention back to the bound figure some twenty feet away. He pinched his face as if speaking hurt. The accused was a fireplug of a man, sturdy with a dark complexion. He scowled at the crowd. "I knew we was doomed and was tryin' to give meself a chance to live."

She recognized the countenance, though bruised and beaten, eyes swollen and bloodshot. She examined his clothes—the distinct blue uniform, though soiled and torn. All that was missing was the round blue hat with the feather. He was one of Washington's bodyguards, the one she saw making eye contact with the man in the crowd.

She nudged Nathan. "Isn't that one of General Washington's Life Guards? I remember him from the dinner party."

Nathan gave a quick nod. "He was one of the general's inner circle. That's why the attempt so unnerved Washington."

"But he wasn't working alone. In fact, I saw him signaling another man in the crowd, a tall, distinguished fellow in a white wig."

Nathan lowered his voice. "You're probably right. From what I heard, Washington has sorted out most of those guilty. They interrogated Hickey for three days. Hickey gave up the others. The conspiracy goes all the way up to Governor Tryon."

Governor Tryon. Even though she'd been in New York City only a few weeks, she'd heard much about the governor—appointed by the crown, loved by Tories, hated by rebels. Since the Colonial Army held the city, he'd been forced to take refuge aboard the *Halifax*, a British ship anchored in the harbor. Of course, he'd be behind any effort to cripple the rebellion.

Abigail kept her question to a whisper. "Then what about the others?"

"Word is he's using Hickey as an example."

The speaker cleared his throat loudly. "Thomas Hickey. While others have fought and died for the cause of liberty and independence, you have chosen to betray your new country and everything others have sacrificed for." Straightening, the older man faced the crowd and yelled, "Let this be a lesson to all. We will root out anyone who supports tyranny and threatens our noble cause." Turning back to Hickey, he pronounced, "May the Almighty have mercy on your soul."

The judge nodded to the soldiers. They pushed Hickey forward, the condemned man stumbling in his leg bindings. One soldier forced Hickey to climb the steps and stand atop the platform. Another slipped the noose around his neck.

The judge stared at General Washington, who nodded once. The raspy voice announced, "Let it be done."

Abigail gulped. She couldn't make herself watch.

Shutting her eyes did not block out the horror. She heard the jerk of the rope, the man gurgling, struggling for breath and failing. Gasps and cries erupted from the women around her. She realized this was war, *and* yes, Hickey deserved his fate, but . . .

She glanced at Nathan, who remained focused on the dying man. She couldn't take it. Sliding her hand off his arm, she turned away. She weaved a path to the edge of the crowd. Behind her, Nathan called her name, and she heard quick footsteps. She kept going, lurching past the onlookers until she stepped onto the grass, barely in time.

18

Abigail glanced at the clock on the building. Five o'clock. Father had said he'd be done by then, and she'd decided to come down to the dock to meet him. He shouldn't have been working today, a Sunday, but after the assassination attempt on Washington, the atmosphere in the city had changed. Residents seemed to move a little faster, hurrying to stay out of harm's way. Whenever she spotted soldiers anywhere in the city—Redcoats or men in blue—they looked more nervous, on alert. Father had decided it was no longer safe for them to attend services at St. Paul's Chapel, even to keep up appearances. Instead, he had taken work at the dock on Sundays.

Staring out into the harbor, Abigail didn't see the two lads whose bare feet hammered down the wooden walkway behind her. As she turned, a round wooden ring bounced past, chased by two boys. The first, bare-chested and wearing only a tattered pair of dirty breeches, brushed her as he passed. Stumbling a bit, she managed to catch herself as the second ran by, his deeply tanned back glistening with sweat. Both boys wielded slim wooden sticks, using them to propel the ring as they ran, laughing. She envied their innocence.

After they passed, she stepped from the wooden walkway into the dusty street and glanced across at the East River. Her gaze went first not to the piers where the ships were docked but to the outer harbor. She wasn't certain, but there seemed to be *more* ships in the water farther out, riding at anchor with their masts furled. None of them flew flags—except for the *Halifax,* the British man-of-war that housed Governor Tryon—but rumors flew that the new ships were all British, carrying more men and munitions. Word had it they were waiting for even more to arrive before they raised their Union Jacks and sailed into the harbor to take New York City.

She watched as small groups of men and women ambled along the wharf in the hazy sunshine, wearing everything from fancy Sunday dress to plain breeches and frocks. Some stared out at the water while others huddled outside one of the tavern doors, talking.

Nearby, three ships sat anchored at the piers, their sails collapsed, their gray hulls rocking in the gentle waves. The first two lay empty and abandoned, their gangplanks pulled. Atop the third, a few men moved about. She headed that way. Here, close to the water, the tang of salt mingled with the odor of dead fish.

As she approached the third vessel, two Negroes emerged from the hold, crossed the gangplank, and stepped onto the dock. They nodded at her as they passed, their teeth bright white against their dark-brown faces. Both were stripped to the waist and their skin glistened with perspiration. Once past her, they exchanged words in a tongue Abigail couldn't make out, but the tone was clear. They were complaining. They looked much younger than Father, perhaps in their twenties. If these strong men were exhausted, how hard must it have been on him?

When Father emerged through the opening, he saw her on the dock and gave her a wave and a tired smile. Stripped to the waist, his skin wet with sweat, he moved slowly, shoulders drooping. Since he'd been working here at the docks, he'd tanned considerably until his skin approached the shade of the men before him. His large gray eyes blinked behind his spectacles in the late-afternoon sun. Untying his cotton shirt from his waist, he wiped his torso and head. In the weeks since coming to New York, Father had let his whiskers grow and now had the beginnings of a nice beard and mustache, both a russet color. Most days she thought they gave him a distinguished look, but today the whiskers, soaked with heavy drops of perspiration, made Father look tired . . . and old. She caught the lines etched around his eyes, and her heart ached.

As he came up to her, he smiled. “Ah, my beautiful Abigail! Come to meet your father as he comes off the boat, hey?” He chuckled, eyes crinkling. “Seeing you as I came out of the hold, I had a vision of your mother when she and I were quite a bit younger. For many reasons, I’m sorry she’s not here—not the least of which to see what a beautiful young woman you’ve become.”

Abigail blushed. “Come on, you old flick. Let’s head home. Supper’s waiting.” She slipped her arm through his as they started down the dock. “You look exhausted.”

Caleb nodded. “Backbreaking work today. Unloading barrels of rum. I swear we carried enough to float all of New York City, the captain in a hurry to unload. He thought the inns were going to be in great need of refreshment.”

“On Sunday?”

Caleb shrugged. “Or maybe first thing tomorrow. He was convinced residents would be doing a good deal of drinking, and soon.”

“You know you don’t have to work like this. At least not today.”

He patted her arm inside his. “My daughter, we don’t know what tomorrow will bring. This life has taught me nothing is certain, and it’s best to prepare for the worst.”

She smiled at him. “And hope for the best?”

“Yes, and hope for the best. Speaking of hoping, why are you not with young Nathan? I haven’t seen him around lately.”

Abigail was glad he didn’t press her to marry like most parents who expected their daughters to have a husband and a house. Even though she was past twenty, he never pushed her. In this new city, how likely was she to find a man—the right man? Could Nathan be him?

Glancing around, Abigail lowered her voice. “If you must know, when I last spoke with him, he said he was preparing for a special mission for the army. For General Washington himself.”

A lad burst out the door of a warehouse at the end of the block and clambered across the walkway, his bare feet making hollow sounds on the planks. "Hail all. I have the ticket. Big news, the biggest!" he yelled, loud enough for those on the ships in the harbor to hear. Eyes bright, the boy struggled to hold a pile of broadsheets that tried to slide out of his grip. "News from Philadelphia. A new declaration!"

His hawking worked, and several bystanders ambled over to him.

Abigail caught only bits of the exchanges.

"What's this about a declaration?"

"Ya mean from the Continental Congress?"

The lad announced, "Read for yourself. Only a ha'penny!"

People crowded around, coins exchanging for papers. One older man, bald, and wrinkled, scanned the print. Halfway through, he said to the woman next to him, "Walker! I'll be damned. I never thought I'd see this."

Another man jumped up and threw his sheet into the air. "They did it. They really did it! We're free from Britain!"

A young man in fine garments and a stiff posture read with spectacles perched on his nose. He raised his gaze to a smartly dressed woman in a yellow dress. "Oh God. There's no turning back now. They're all going to hang."

When the boy with the papers made his way over to Abigail and Caleb, she stuffed a coin into his dirty palm and took a copy. She scanned the print, her eyes running down the page.

"Well, what is it?" Father asked impatiently.

She read a bit and then stopped and met Father's gaze. "The Continental Congress has declared independence from Great Britain."

Behind the lenses, Father's eyes grew huge.

She read aloud, "We hold these truths to be self-evident—that all men are created equal."

19

"All right, now for a little math," Abigail said to her two students.

Young James Hampton protested, "I hate math."

Christina, her small pink lips in a pout, added, "I don't see why I need to learn all this math." She batted her eyes. "Mother says I'm going to be quite the beauty. She says before I know it, boys will be flocking over me. I'll have them to do the math."

Abigail chuckled. Only ten years old and Christina was already figuring on capturing a man. She turned to the girl first. "Look, while I certainly agree with your mother—you will be a real beauty—"

Christina giggled. "Thank you."

"That doesn't mean you don't need to know math." Christina frowned, but Abigail plowed on. "Even the best man will appreciate a partner who can assist him in his livelihood—who can help him with the budget, with planning expenses. And in most households, the woman is in charge of purchasing food and other necessities for the family and paying house staff. You need math for all that."

Abigail turned toward the eight-year-old. "And, Mr. James. A man who knows his numbers can't be cheated by merchants and is able to figure out pay for his workers. Didn't you say you plan to own a shipping company when you're older?"

James frowned, blue eyes looking through dangling rust-colored hair. "Yes-s-s," the boy said, as if sensing a trap.

"Well, a ship owner needs to know all kinds of math—from how to calculate how much cargo a ship can hold, to how to estimate the time of passage, to how to determine which seller is offering you the best price for his goods. You need math for all of that and more."

"You do?" James's eyes went wide.

"So, how about we jump into a little math?"

Both children sighed in unison and said together, "All right."

"Good," Abigail said. "I've planned something a little different for today's math lesson. I'm going to teach you a new game."

"A game?" James's eyes went wide again.

"Yes. It's called Nine Man Morris." She looked at them both. "People have been playing this game for hundreds of years. In fact, no one knows how old it is. I think you're going to like it."

From the worn canvas bag that held her hornbook, schoolbooks, and other tools, Abigail took out a large broadsheet she'd wrestled from a printer earlier in the week. One side had lines of text printed on it, covered by several large black ink stains. The printer had ruined the piece and was discarding it when Abigail rescued it. The flip side was mostly blank except for small dark splotches where the ink had bled through, but she figured it would work for her purpose.

She unrolled the paper and laid it on the table, pointing to the design. "This is the grid you use to play the game. If you'll look, I've drawn three squares, one inside the other."

Both children leaned over the drawing.

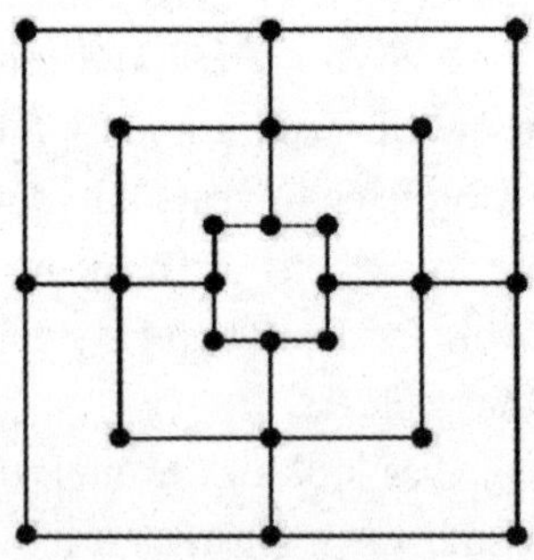

Abigail pointed to the three spots along the top where the lines met. "Each place where the lines intersect—remember that word?" She glanced at their faces, seeing confusion. "Where two lines run into each other, like here." She pointed to each location. "To make it easy, I've drawn a large dot at each intersection." Both small heads nodded. "All right, to play the game, you first place your markers at any of these intersections."

She reached into her bag, extracted a handful of pebbles, and set them on the table in small piles. "The brown stones are your markers, James, and the gray ones are yours, Christina."

Both children picked up their stash of pebbles and Abigail explained how to play, placing markers at the intersections until they got three in a row, horizontally, vertically, or diagonally. It took a few fits and starts, but in a few minutes, both caught on, taking turns leaning over the board, faces scrunched in concentration.

Leaning back, Abigail studied her two students. Little did they realize they were learning geometry, planning, counting, and strategy. Later, after a few rounds, she would take the time to demonstrate some of the math they were—

She felt a tap on her shoulder and turned to see Isabel Hampton standing next to their table. The mother's hazel eyes took in the children hovering over the paper, intent and concentrating, and her red lips parted in a sad smile. She turned and met Abigail's gaze.

Gesturing with her fingers, Isabel indicated for Abigail to come with her. She took a few steps away from the table and Abigail followed. She sensed something was wrong. When they were a little bit away, Isabel said in a low voice, "When you have a minute, Lionel would like a few words with you." She said no more and headed back the way she'd come.

Turning, Abigail watched her two charges sliding stones across the paper. She returned to the table.

"You're doing great." Both kids beamed at her praise. "Your father wants to see me, so you go ahead, and I'll be back to check on you in a few minutes."

Abigail headed down the hallway, not wanting to keep Lionel Hampton waiting. Her stomach turning, she pondered what he might want. She hoped she hadn't upset the Hamptons somehow.

As she approached the doorway of the library, she saw Lionel Hampton pacing back and forth across the pattern of red and brown leaves woven into the rug. When he saw her, he stopped.

"Ah, there you are, Miss Abigail. Come in, please." Lionel held a tight smile on his face.

Taking a deep breath, Abigail crossed the threshold and stood across from the man. For a moment neither spoke, and Abigail shot a quick glance around the room. Isabel sat on the couch, small hands in her lap and head of blond hair bent down. Against three walls stood shelves stacked with books from floor to ceiling, their spines glistening. Abigail had only been in the library a few times and couldn't help but envy it. One day a few weeks ago, she'd taken time after the children's lesson to browse the shelves. All these books—some authors she recognized, like Jonathan Swift, John Locke, and even Voltaire, and others she'd never heard of. Isabel had said she could borrow any she wanted and Abigail had taken two home to read.

Abigail's gaze returned to Lionel, who still wouldn't meet hers. He stared at the pattern at his feet. Finally, he cleared his throat. "I don't know how to tell you this."

Abigail swallowed again.

In a solemn voice, Lionel Hampton announced, "We have to let you go."

20

Abigail struggled to find her voice. "I'm sorry," she squeaked. "I thought you were pleased with my work, um . . . with your children."

Several fears struck her at once. She wouldn't get to see Christina and James anymore. She had come to love the two imps. She wouldn't be able to help Christina see there was more to being a woman than getting a man. She'd disappoint Nathan, who'd been kind enough to help her secure this position. And, oh God, she'd lose her income. Father would have to take on even more grueling work on the docks. She'd be forced to do . . . what?

Lionel shook his head, his loose red curls flipping exactly like his son's. "No, Abigail, it's not you."

Isabel rose from the couch and stood next to her husband. She pushed one stray blond curl back in place. "You've done wonders with our children. They get excited whenever you come. Christina adores you." She reached a small, cool hand across and patted Abigail's arm. "Losing you will be hardest on them."

Abigail's glance shifted between them. "I don't understand. If you're not unhappy, why are you letting me go?"

Isabel turned to her husband, who met her gaze and then faced Abigail again. "We have little choice. We've decided to leave New York. I, uh, I believe it will soon not be safe for us . . . and anyone who holds our view."

Abigail knew the Hamptons sympathized with the rebels, even if they weren't vocal about their beliefs.

"You don't think the Continental Army can hold New York?" she asked.

He shook his head slowly.

Before he answered, Abigail added, "I thought with the new Declaration of Independence the colonies would stop their bickering and unite. I thought the Declaration would rally all the militias and would convince the colonies to provide the men and money needed to defend us." She had heard of the loud arguments between the colonies, especially between those in the South and those like New York in the North. Like many others, she'd clung to the belief the new Declaration would change that.

A look flashed over Lionel Hampton's face—the same one she used on Christina and James when she was about to deliver a lecture. Then his countenance softened and he nodded, his red hair bobbing this time. "You're right. The fact that all thirteen colonies signed the Declaration of Independence will probably help. It will, as you say, rally the militias. And the southern colonies, led by Virginia, have agreed to provide more help, especially with the costs of fighting."

Abigail said, "Then Washington and his men will have what they need to maintain control of the city."

The look of disappointment reappeared on the man's face. "It won't matter. There are thousands more British troops on their way. Our little colonies against the greatest fighting force the world's ever known—we don't stand a chance."

Abigail glanced from Isabel to Lionel. "I don't understand. I thought, as a businessman, you needed to do business in a place like New York. If it was inevitable, why did you set up shop here?"

Again Lionel looked at her as if she were a child. "Even though we want our freedoms, none of us wanted war. It's bad for business. We'd hoped that Britain would let us alone and let us do our own thing. Or we hoped that one of the negotiation efforts, maybe the one by

Ben Franklin, would result in peace." He shook his head again. "With this *Declaration*, all that is lost. The radicals have won. By now, King George and his cabinet will be furious with 'the upstart colonies.' They will throw everything at us."

Abigail stood there, dumbfounded, not knowing what to say.

Lionel pointed out the window, past the fancy mauve drapes, in the direction of the East River. "There are more British ships in the harbor every day. It's simply a matter of time. When they strike, New York will be their first prize. I can't put Isabel and the children in that kind of danger."

"Where will you go? Back to England?"

Isabel finally spoke up. "No. We love America. Lionel has found us a place in Richmond . . . Virginia. He thinks things will be safer there, and he has found a nice home there for us."

Lionel added, "And I plan to take what I can with me and start business over again."

Gesturing to the library and the marble floor complete with the expensive rug, Abigail asked, "What about the Reserve?" She'd learned from Nathan that the Hamptons had this expensive place built, including imported marble, glass windows, and rugs from Europe. "What's going to happen to your beautiful home?"

Lionel glanced at his wife and then at Abigail. "I've arranged for the house and the grounds to be leased . . . by another family." He dropped his gaze to the floor and added, "To a British officer and his family."

"Oh." Abigail's voice got small. "When? When do you plan to leave?"

"By the end of the week," Lionel said, his voice crisp again.

Isabel Hampton brightened. "I know. Why don't you come with us? We'll be happy to pay for your passage. You could even board with us. We'll have plenty of room, won't we, Lionel?" She turned to her husband, who nodded. She grasped Abigail's hand, staring into her face. "That way you could continue to work your magic with our children."

Abigail met the mother's gaze. "That is most generous of you. But I can't." She shook her head a few times. "I have Father to consider as well, and we think my brother, Oliver, is somewhere around the city with the army."

Isabel said, "We were afraid you would say that . . . and we understand. Family is very important."

She released Abigail's hand and extended her own toward her husband. Lionel reached inside his waistcoat and pulled out an envelope, handing it to his wife. Isabel offered it to Abigail.

"You've done a remarkable job with the children, you really have. They've learned more in the past few months than they have in the last few years. We hate to lose you. This is your pay for this month and wages for two more. That should hold you until you secure another position, which we have no doubt you will."

When Abigail accepted the envelope, Isabel's hands closed around hers and she felt the smooth skin of the woman's fingers. They stood so close Abigail could even smell the faint scent of herbal soap she used. She met the woman's gaze and saw tears in the corners of her eyes. "I don't know what to say. Thank you very much. Again, this is very generous." She felt her own tears trying to squeeze out. "Do the children know?"

Lionel said, "Not yet. We wanted to tell you first. We didn't want to give them the heartache any sooner than we have to."

"I'd better tell them, then," Abigail said.

When she turned to leave, Isabel reached out and stopped her. "Why don't you wait? They sound as if they are having quite the time with that new game you taught them." As if on cue, the children's laughter floated through the house. "It's our decision, so we need to tell them ourselves. Why don't you just finish your lessons for today? You can handle the difficult task of saying goodbye when you return tomorrow."

Tomorrow? Abigail nodded and stepped away. Clutching the envelope, she thought, *At least we won't starve. Not yet.* She kept walking, drawn by another peal of laughter, this time from Christina. She tried to figure how she was going to explain *this* harsh lesson to children ages eight and ten when she said goodbye tomorrow.

PARKER

21

From a pocket in his waistcoat, Parker Monteith pulled out the folded broadsheet and scanned the words he had read several times already.

We hold these Truths to be self-evident.

He recalled when he first read the document, its portent dawning on him. It was common knowledge the Continental Congress had been meeting in Philadelphia. Rumor had it that the representatives were haggling over what to do next. Cain thought the colonies would break into groups or maybe accept the latest peace proposal, not take so brazen a step as this Declaration. Not only had the rebel leaders gotten all thirteen colonies to come to agreement, but their representatives had actually signed their names beneath the document.

He decided to take the copy to Lieutenant Colonel Cain. The man was lounging in the grand room, feet propped on a chair. Next to him, Colonel Hollister reclined on a sofa, red waistcoat unbuttoned and open, half-smoked cigar dangling from his lips.

"Sirs, I got this from one of my men. I thought you should see it." Parker handed Cain the broadsheet.

Cain nodded. "We heard about the rebels' supposed Declaration, but I haven't seen a copy." He started reading, his voice in a singsong taunt. "'When in the course of human events, it becomes necessary for one people to dissolve the political bands—'"

Hollister launched himself off the sofa, not without some difficulty. He snatched the paper from Cain's hand. His cigar bobbed between fat lips, its burnt ash dropping onto the red and orange woven rug. His bloodshot eyes narrowed as he scanned the wording, his bushy eyebrows crawling together like two black caterpillars. He struck the paper with his fist. "I heard about this. Listen to this tripe. 'But when a long Train of Abuses and Usurpations, pursuing invariably the same Object, evinces a Design to reduce them under absolute Despotism, it is their Right, it is their Duty, to throw off such Government.'"

His brown eyes raised from the paper, staring past his bulbous nose. He looked first at Cain, then at Parker. Two fat lips broke into a leer. "These rebels are such flats. Are they such buffleheads they don't realize they have no chance, no chance at all? And this will incense the king. Once His Majesty releases us, we will march through this city and crush this little . . . *rebellion*."

His flabby hand released the paper and sent it fluttering to the floor. He collapsed onto the sofa again.

Parker studied Hollister's obese form on the couch, massive belly straining the few remaining buttons still fastened, the blue feather now lying across his wide waist. He had heard Hollister's story about the feather. The man claimed he had taken it off a great Indian warrior he killed. Parker doubted it. He tried to picture Hollister leading men across this country, even on horseback. He failed.

Hollister continued, "What a bunch of snots. Cain, what do you think?"

Cain hesitated, one finger smoothing his small mustache. "Well. It's something we should keep an eye on. No telling how this might stir up the locals."

"Nonsense," barked Hollister. "This little . . . *Declaration*." He grabbed up the broadsheet. "This is going to amount to nothing. Years from now, no one will even remember this. Except that they'll all be hanged, those who signed, every last one of them." One fat finger poked the place on the paper where the names were listed.

Parker thought Hollister wrong. When he visited the taverns—out of uniform, of course—he noticed the locals seemed to become more excited every week. The Declaration had united the people from different colonies, even the rich landowners from the South like Jefferson.

He had also learned the assassination attempt on Washington had failed. That plan had had exactly the opposite effect intended. Since word of the failed plot circulated in the taverns, the locals had become more resolute. They felt free to cast even more rancor at their mother country. As he completed his nightly reconnaissance, he noticed fewer and fewer loyalists willing to speak up in defense of Britain. When the people were roiled up like this, they forgot they had no chance against the greatest fighting force in the world.

Then this "Declaration of Independence" had followed on the heels of the failed conspiracy. It might as well have been called the Declaration of War.

Of course Hollister, lazy duffer that he was, was right about one thing. Once the full might of the British army and navy descended on these shores, it would be a bloodbath. The war would sacrifice many of his men, but far more rebels. His soldiers were spoiling for a fight, drilling day in and day out. They would get it, but for now they waited. The colonials still held too great an advantage here in the city.

More merchant ships and men-of-war had been arriving almost daily, anchoring in the East River. Every trip into town, he studied the harbor, spotting more ships, sails furled, bobbing in the water.

He had been told they had to wait. Even more ships were coming. Including the ship carrying his family. He offered another anguished prayer for their safety. Clearly, New York would *not* be the tranquil place he had hoped for when they arrived. The way things were going, Louisa and his two little ones would be landing in the middle of the maelstrom.

22

Weeks passed and Parker heard no more. Nothing more about the rebels' plans or the arrival of more troops. Cain had trusted him, though, with inside information from Washington's camp, information few in the command knew.

While he and the lieutenant colonel stood alone on the deck one morning, looking down at the city below, Cain had said, "We've received word that Washington is grooming a spy."

"A spy? How do you know that? From your, uh, friend Caroline?"

The lieutenant colonel laughed, a deep belly hoot that echoed across the open field. When the laugh died down, Cain said, "Not everything we know comes through Martha's Place."

When the lieutenant colonel said no more, Parker asked, "You still have people inside Washington's camp? Even after the assassination attempt? And the hanging of Hickey?"

"According to our sources, Washington learned just how far the conspiracy went, all the way to Governor Tryon. Actually, a pretty good job of investigating." Cain pulled a cigar and match out of a pocket of his waistcoat. He lit it and blew the smoke out over the deck railing. "But Washington is soft. He was afraid to wipe out everyone who was involved with the plot. Thought it would make him look weak if people learned how many of the rebels were willing to turn on him. Instead, he decided to make an example of Hickey."

Parker said, "I am surprised anyone is still willing to talk. Hickey's hanging was quite the spectacle. I heard half the city was there. After that, I am amazed you still have people inside Washington's camp who will give you secrets."

Cain shook his head. "Not give. Sell. It's a sad commentary on humanity, but you can always find someone—rebel or loyal—who will sell out their own mother . . . for the right coin."

Parker had been buoyed by Cain's willingness to bring him into his confidence, but it did little to stave off his loneliness or personal anxiety. What was most frustrating was that he had received no further details about his wife and children. His last letter from Louisa had arrived almost six weeks earlier, giving him the name of the ship, *Matilda,* as well as the captain's name. The last sentence had been seared into his brain.

We are in good hands, loving husband, and will be with you in America before you know it.

Not hardly.

All he received were Cain's vague assurances that their ship was traveling in the safe company of a group of British war vessels. In his tortured nightmares, his imagination ran wild, conjuring up storms and catastrophes at sea and terrifying images of his two young children floundering in monstrous waves. Hardly rational. Still, Parker had trouble shaking these visions. And the longer the wait, the more his fears haunted him.

He did not know what else to do, so he kept busy with training his troops during the day and with clandestine trips to the taverns at night. Each day he watched as more and more ships arrived in the harbor, now all flying the Union Jack, exactly as Cain had predicted. When he used the spyglass from the deck of the officers' quarters, he could now count more than fifty ships in the harbor. Every day he prayed the *Matilda*—the one carrying his lovely Louisa and his two young ones—would float into view of the scope.

Thus far, his prayers went unanswered.

With the arrival of more and more British ships, he became less concerned about traveling in his uniform, at least during the day. Cutthroats still roamed the streets at night searching for a fresh Redcoat victim, so he found some excuse to visit the harbor every day. He wanted to be there when their ship did come in.

He had already inspected the house he had arranged, and he could not wait to show Louisa and the children. Located on a promontory on Water Street, the two-story stone structure was truly impressive. He felt certain his family would love it there.

Of course, there was still much to do. Knowing his Louisa, she would want to do her own decorating, and he was glad to have the funds to give her free rein. Also, they would need a small staff and a tutor for the children.

But Louisa and his children had to arrive first.

After his men completed their drills and training for the day, he released them to brad-faking and throwing bones. The gambling would distract them, at least. He headed down to the city. On his way into town, he caught glimpses of the harbor, snatches of the curves of the river. Cain was right. So many ships now crowded into the watery expanse it looked as if the vessels sat so close together sailors could almost jump from one to the other. And most now flew the Union Jack.

The hot August sun glared down on him as he trudged his way through the noisy streets. The heat and humidity assaulted him again. By the time he reached Water Street and a little cooling breeze off the water, dark red sweat stains marked the creases of his uniform. He had to unbutton his waistcoat just to get a little air. He used his kerchief to blot the perspiration off his face, squinting against the water's glare.

There, at the dock below him, sat three ships, bobbing in the rocking waves of the harbor. He recognized the two closest to him as merchant ships. The first, *Experiment,* a huge brown ship with a broad keel, banged against the pier with the slap of a wave. He watched men scurry about on board. A deafening boom resounded as the gangplank was dropped from the ship to the dock. Two Black men disappeared into the hull. A few minutes later, they reemerged, hoisting huge barrels on their massive shoulders, their feet scurrying down the gangplank.

His gaze moved to the second, and he read *Dolphin* painted along the side. The smaller cargo ship was only now settling into its berth. Deckhands ran about, securing the ropes to the posts on the dock. Mopping his brow, Parker continued his route, and beyond, he saw the third ship. He caught his breath. He was afraid to hope but could not control himself. He kept walking, picking up his pace. When he got around the warehouse that fronted the harbor, he read the name across the bow, *Matilda*. It was *their* ship. His Louisa and Elizabeth and Henry. Whooping like a boy, he ran down the length of Water Street and cut toward the pier. He jumped from the road to the dock, his feet slamming onto the wooden planks. He watched as the mates set the gangplank down.

The first people emerged from below, shielding their eyes in the sun, and walked across the board—two men and an older woman. Not Louisa or Henry or Elizabeth. He held his breath. His heart raced. He blinked and looked again.

Then he saw Louisa's head duck through the opening and emerge, her blond curls glistening in the brilliant sunlight. Eyes blinking, she glanced around but must not have seen him yet.

He went to call her name and found his throat had gone dry. Louisa ducked back down into the hold and came up again, holding Elizabeth's small hand. Mother and daughter stepped onto the deck. And right behind them both skipped Henry, his brown hair flopping back and forth with each movement.

It was the best sight Parker had ever seen.

23

The carriage came to an abrupt stop. Parker jumped down, extending his hand to his wife. Using the long platform and grasping her husband's hand, Louisa stepped down, blue-gray eyes wide. She helped little Elizabeth navigate the rung, and seconds later, Henry exploded from the cab, vaulting to the ground and bounding up the stone steps.

Louisa stared at the mansion. Her gaze took in the limestone structure, two floors tall. Two giant white pillars stood like sentries at the top of five stone steps leading to an ornate carved door. A narrow garden of greens, dark reds, and yellows bordered the front.

Elizabeth stood by her mother's side, mimicking her awe. At the top of the entry, Henry tugged on the door handle.

"Henry, leave the door alone and come down here," Parker called.

His son turned and clambered down, pulling up short next to his father.

Parker continued, "Elizabeth and Henry"—he looked at each of his children in turn—"there is much to see here. First, Elizabeth, I would like for you take your brother around back and check out the yard."

Henry started running. "Come on, Liz!" He disappeared around the building. Elizabeth followed, legs churning.

Parker called after them, "Stay out of the creek!"

"Creek?" Louisa asked.

He grinned. "Yes, a lovely stream runs along the edge of the property, only a little trickle of water. Enough for the children to enjoy, but not enough to get into trouble."

"You can never tell with Henry." Louisa giggled, cheeks reddening.

He'd missed that laugh.

Taking her arm, he guided her up the steps and opened the heavy door. Louisa stepped inside, gaze lighting on the black-and-white tile floor, the vase of cut flowers, and the crystal chandelier. He extracted a rose from the bouquet and handed it to her. Louisa wove it into her hair.

"You like the place?"

"It's beautiful. After weeks in the cabin, I would've been content with a hut. But yes, it's wonderful." She turned to him. "And it's ours?"

"The place is owned by a family named Hampton. They have left the area. I have leased it . . . for the foreseeable future."

Louisa stared. "Will it be safe here? New York, I mean? I saw rebel militia on the streets."

Parker placed his hands on her shoulders. "I am confident it will be fine soon. Cain told me our mass landing will happen any day. Once the new troops are here, the colonials will come to their senses." He kissed her. "I have missed you so."

She pulled his face toward hers. "Not as much as we have missed you."

"What would you like to see first?"

Louisa batted her eyelashes. "I trust this mansion comes with a master bedroom?"

"Complete with fireplace and a view of the meadow. Perhaps I should offer a private tour."

"I like the private part."

They started up the staircase, grinning. A hollow knock sounded at the front door.

Louisa looked up, concerned. "Expecting anyone?"

"No." Parker turned. "Who is it?"

Silence, then the shuffle of feet.

"Stay here," Parker whispered. He descended the stairs, looking for a weapon.

A woman's voice stopped him. "My name is Abigail Trench. I apologize for the intrusion. I saw your carriage and thought I'd knock."

Parker opened the door to find a young woman in a light green dress. She curtsied, bowing a brown-haired head. When she straightened, he saw she looked to be in her early twenties, well cared for and with manners. Her cheeks reddened with obvious awkwardness.

"Sir, I'm sorry. It's a little embarrassing."

From inside, Louisa said, "For heaven's sake, Parker, invite her in."

Parker stepped aside.

Louisa came down the steps, extending a hand. "Miss Trench, I'm Louisa Monteith, and this is my husband, Parker."

"Good to meet you both." The young woman's green eyes roamed the interior. "Do you own this house now?"

"We have leased it from the Hamptons," Parker said.

The visitor glanced toward the second floor. "As I said, I'm embarrassed. I can explain."

"Take your time," Louisa said. "I'm guessing you were in the service of the Hamptons?"

The woman reddened. "I'm a teacher. I couldn't find a teaching job in New York, so I was tutoring the children until—"

"The Hampton children?" Parker asked.

"Yes, James and Christina."

Louisa asked, "How old are they?"

"Eight and ten." She took a breath. "I've misplaced my bag . . . with my schoolbooks. I'm hoping it might be in the nursery."

Louisa glanced at her husband, who nodded. "We've just arrived. You probably know where the nursery is better than us. Why don't you look?"

"If you don't mind?"

"Please." Parker extended a hand.

"Thanks." The woman hurried up the stairs, hand on the railing, feet flying as if she knew exactly where she was going.

Louisa turned to her husband. "Have you secured a tutor?"

Parker shook his head. "I thought I would leave that to you."

"I think I may have found a perfect candidate."

Parker's eyes narrowed. "This young woman? We do not know her." He had imagined an Oxford scholar, though he had no idea how to find one in New York.

"If the Hamptons thought her right, and they could obviously afford who they wanted . . ." Louisa looked at him. "I'll check references, but I'd like to give her a try."

The visitor returned holding a brown canvas bag, beaming. Parker conceded she might be good with Henry and Elizabeth.

"Bless the Lord. It was right where I left it." She pulled out items. "*Arithmetic Primer*, *New England Primer*, biology book. Oh, and the new algebra book by Euler." She showed them a sketchbook and a hornbook.

She knows reading, algebra, and science, Parker thought.

The woman showed them a yellow paper. "Mrs. Hampton left me a note." She stuffed it back into the bag. "Thank you for your kindness."

She headed for the door, and Parker opened it.

"Before you go," Louisa called, "I may have a proposition for you."

ABIGAIL

24

When the knock echoed, Abigail froze. She glanced at Father, whose eyes widened behind his lenses. It was late, and the only light came from her oil lamp. The weak beam made the creases of Father's face look haggard.

Rumors ran rampant. Each day she walked past the harbor, she counted more ships. The East River looked like it sprouted a forest of wooden poles, the ships so close together. Everyone said they were British, biding their time.

The Continental Army held New York, but for how long? Soldiers stepped briskly, and locals grew restless. Paranoia filled the conversations she overheard.

Father raised a crooked finger to his lips and motioned for her to move into the back room. He approached the door. "Who's there?"

"It's me, Nathan."

Abigail ran into the front room.

Father opened the door. "Come in, boy. Abigail has missed your company."

In the shadowy light, he looked the same—tall stature, handsome face with the scar, blond curls—yet something had changed.

Father glanced from Nathan to her. "I'll leave you to it." He ambled into the back room, leaving the door ajar.

Conflicted feelings rushed at her. Thrilled to see him, she was concerned by his long silent absence. Not a word in weeks. She wanted to tell him everything, like a lovesick schoolgirl, about the Hamptons leaving and her getting a new post with a *British* officer, no less. But one look told her this was not the time for trivialities.

Nathan held his tricorn hat, fingers twirling the brim. "I apologize that I haven't been around. Much has been happening."

"A few things have happened with me as well."

"I heard about the Hamptons. I'm sorry you lost your income."

"The Hamptons were generous. And I've already found another position." She told him about forgetting her bag and meeting the Monteiths.

Nathan looked her up and down, smiling. "Well look at you, Miss Abigail Trench."

"I'm glad for the work, but I haven't decided how I feel about working for a British officer."

"What's he like?"

"I've only met him a few times. I usually work with Louisa, Mrs. Major Monteith. He seems like a decent fellow."

"A British officer . . . With what's coming, it could help protect you. And you'll continue to have an income."

"The Monteiths aren't as generous as the Hamptons, but the pay is fine. And I get to teach." She grinned. "I miss James and Christina. The Monteiths have two as well, Elizabeth and Henry."

She found it was easy to share with Nathan, but she felt he was holding back. Like he was keeping some secret.

She broke the silence. "So what's happening with you?"

He straightened. Even in the dim light, she saw he wore the clothes of a commoner—plain brown waistcoat, dark breeches. No scarf, no ruffles. Even his hat looked frayed.

"You remember I told you I'd been given an important mission by General Washington."

"I remember."

"I can't tell you much, except I'm on the . . . assignment."

Abigail looked into his eyes. Her heart fluttered at the sight of his rugged face, but something felt off.

His gaze dropped. “I’ll be traveling and didn’t know when I’d see you.” He stopped and stared off to the side, then brought his gaze back to hers. “My new role will require me to do things . . . things I wouldn’t normally do.” Nathan glanced up this time, as if he were searching for divine inspiration. “All I can say is that my role will involve a good deal of . . . deception.”

“Deception?”

One hand released the hat and grabbed hers. “When you hear about it, I didn’t want you to think less of me. To think I was *that* kind of man.” He tugged her hand and stared into her face. “I’ve always tried to be honest and forthright with you.”

She cringed hearing the word. Deception? Was this what she had sensed? What he’d been holding back? She didn’t understand what he was trying to tell her.

Abigail hurried to ask, “Will it be dangerous?”

He chuckled. “Is there any role in this war that isn’t? Still, I prefer liberty with danger than peace with chains.”

“I’m worried about you, and you’re quoting Rousseau?” She scowled. “This isn’t an academic discussion.”

He gave a small smile. “It’s dangerous but important. Right now, life in the colonies is dangerous. Especially here.”

Abigail asked, “Do Father and I need to get out of the city?”

Nathan glanced around the room. He lowered his voice. “Keep your heads down. And it won’t hurt that you’re tutoring the children of a British officer.”

The British were getting ready to take the city.

“I’m going to be traveling. It will probably be safer for you if we are not seen together.”

“What kind of role is Washington asking you to take?”

“Washington said what I’m doing could change the fate of the war.” He looked into her eyes. “If anyone asks, tell them you knew me because I’m a teacher like you.”

“Knew you?” Stunned, she said, “What are you telling me?”

He didn't answer.

"It's late. I should take my leave." Nathan placed his hands on her shoulders, leaned in, and kissed her cheek. "Everything about this fight is uncertain. If anything happens to me, I want you to know you have brightened my days."

Her stomach lurched, and tears fought their way out.

He stepped away. "Good night, Mr. Trench . . . goodbye, Miss Abigail." He turned and headed out, closing the door softly.

Father appeared next to her. "Are you all right?"

She moved to the window, watching Nathan's figure swallowed by the dark. "I'm not certain."

"It was good to see him, yes?"

"I don't know." She faced Father. "I have a bad feeling. Like I might never see him again."

25

SEPTEMBER 14

Abigail remembered the date. Her mother's birthday. Although after 1776, she'd remember it for a different reason.

This morning, she and Father honored her mother with blueberry biscuits made from her special recipe.

"Last night I was thinking about how she read to me and Oliver," Abigail said. "No matter how busy she was. We must have read every page of the few books we owned a hundred times." She patted the Bible on the table.

"Her Bible." Father fingered his red and gray beard.

"She taught me to read and convinced me I could help others. When I'm teaching, I often think how Mother would have helped them learn."

"She'd be so proud of you." He wiped his eyes.

When they finished, Abigail headed to the Pelican for another lesson with Molly. It was Saturday, so she had no duties at the Monteiths'. Traveling the few blocks, Abigail noticed a strange quiet in the city. Usually on Saturdays, vendors hawked and people bustled, but today the streets were practically deserted. Those she did see hurried past her and into a store or tavern. The harbor felt different. She recalled Nathan's warning.

At the tavern, Molly waited at their usual table. The young woman brightened when Abigail entered, giving a little wave. Today she wore a plain frock. She sat hunched over a stack of stained broadsheets.

Molly must've seen something in Abigail's face. "Are you well? Ya look . . . perplexed?"

"You remembered that word. Very good." Abigail patted the girl's arm. "Yes, I guess I am *perplexed.* The streets were practically deserted."

Molly nodded. "Sumpin's up. Jamie went to check with some other buzzers to see if he can learn sumpin'. We might as well do a little teachin' and learnin' while we wait."

"Let's try this." Abigail pointed to a column on a broadsheet.

Molly squinted. "De-serted, from the Ranger armed, vef—"

Abigail pointed. "Remember they sometimes use *f*'s for *s*'s. The word is *vessel.*"

Molly nodded. "Armed vessel, the eleventh of September, THOMAS WARD, seaman, born in Dublin . . . fair com-plex-ion, frefh—fresh colored, little pitted with the pox." She smiled.

"You're doing great."

Molly blushed. "It's only because of you."

"You're doing the hard work."

Molly continued reading. Abigail watched the girl's finger crawl along the lines. She suspected the young woman was quite smart.

Molly finished, "shall have four dollars reward for each." She looked up. "They each worth four dollars."

Abigail corrected, "They *are* each worth—"

Thunderous hoofbeats resounded outside, drowning her out.

Abigail and Molly headed for the door. Scores of horses trotted by, crowded so tight they pushed onlookers to the edge. Riders in blue waistcoats and tricorn hats bobbed up and down.

The horses kicked up dust, wrapping the riders in a tan fog. Abigail stared west. All she saw were more men on horseback. Then she caught sight of General Washington in the center of the throng. He wore the same blue waistcoat and sash. Riding high, erect, his gaze swiveled. He nodded to her, but his acknowledgment showed no recognition.

Behind the horses came the clatter of metal wheels. Cannons rolled through the street, teams of mules pulling each piece. Abigail started counting and stopped somewhere north of thirty. Behind the artillery marched lines of soldiers. The first line carried drums—they looked so young she had trouble calling them soldiers. They beat a rhythm, and the others behind marched to the cadence.

She stared west and saw hundreds more soldiers in all stages of uniform. Most wore plain brown waistcoats. Others carried rifles—sometimes balanced on a shoulder, other times the gun swinging in a hand—or homemade weapons.

Abigail scanned the faces, hoping to glimpse her brother. She'd heard nothing from Alexander Hamilton, and Nathan was gone.

Twice she thought she recognized Oliver, the long brown hair, thin face with pimples, and cocky stride. Excited, she ran down the walkway to stay even with the soldier as he marched in line. Each time, when the young man noticed her movement on the side, they turned as a group and grinned. But each time, she'd been mistaken. Not Oliver.

Abigail watched as the Continental Army climbed the hills to the northeast, becoming tiny figures disappearing over the rise. The rebel army moved to higher ground. And they left the city of New York defenseless.

As the last of the army climbed the hill, Abigail heard shooting and cannon fire. She turned west and saw advancing British troops, rifles and a cannon rolling down the street. None of the ammunition hit its mark, but the rear soldiers picked up their pace. Shots whizzed by.

Abigail and Molly headed inside, brushing dust from their frocks.

As soon as they sat down, Molly said, "Levi, bring us two new mugs. We need to wash the dirt outta our throats."

"Make that three," called a voice.

Jamie stood in the doorway. He joined them, pulling another stool and placing his bowler hat on the table.

Molly squeezed his hand. “Did ya see them soldiers?”

“Yep. Crept around the city, up and down the harbor, and talked to a few. Passed the buggin’ line of ’em. Had to use back alleys.” He took a swallow of ale.

“What did ya find out?” Molly asked.

“He took me to this place downriver, where it curls like a cat’s tail. Billie knew right where, and he took me back of the waters. We had t’ creep behind these bushes so we wasn’t spotted and we could look out at the water without bein’ seen. And I seen it with my own two eyes.” He drank again, as if needing fortification.

“What?” Molly asked.

“I saw ’em. Thousands. Redcoats on barges, just waitin’. So frigging many the water looked like a field of bloomin’ red poppies!”

26

The next few days were some of the most unnerving in her life—well, besides that nightmare of a day on Long Island. Just hours after the Continental Army retreated, cannons from warships upriver began firing on the heights, explosions sounding like constant thunder in the distance. No one had any idea whether they were hitting the positions of the Continental Army. The barrage seemed to go on forever.

Fearing the worst, Abigail abandoned the lesson with Molly. Neither could concentrate on reading anyway. She wound her way to their flat, hearing explosions erupt not that far away. As she scurried from building to building, she feared the next cannonball might land beside her. Hurrying, she kept her head on a swivel, scared she'd encounter a hostile Redcoat around the next corner. What would she say if one stopped her? What if they asked if she knew Nathan? Or General Washington? Her heart only stopped racing when she made it inside and found Father already there, safe and staring out the window.

Then came the stream of Redcoats. For two days, ships dislodged men, horses, and cannons. The flow of red flooded the streets. The first British hustled down the roads and fired upon the flank of the colonials as the last of the militia retreated to the heights. She could hear the echo of gunfire and the screams, though she could see little from their second-story room. But as more Redcoats came, she feared the worst for the Continental Army, for New York.

Most of all, she anguished for her brother. Was Oliver in the middle of the fighting? Was he hurt or wounded or captured? She would not let herself believe he could be killed. Though, from the tortured cries of pain that reached her ears, some colonial soldiers had paid with their lives. And what about Nathan and his *special* mission? Was he involved in the battle or was he somewhere else?

When the fighting died down, she heard the echo of marching cadence. As if to taunt her, British soldiers recited songs she'd loved as a child, like "God Save the King," now carrying a forbidding portent.

For days, Father and she never left their flat. Thankfully, they had a little bread to eat. Rumors flew of British authorities commandeering houses of rebel sympathizers and evicting suspected collaborators to find space to house all the officers. There were stories of locals being stopped, beaten, and questioned by Redcoats and of residents going missing. Abigail knew all this was gossip but figured there was enough truth in the whispers to warrant her paranoia anyway. With red-coated soldiers everywhere, she had no desire to cross town, even though they would soon run out of money.

On the evening of the fourth day, she received a note.

Miss Abigail Trench,

We hope you are well and have come through the current difficulties unhurt.

Abigail stared at the words.

Current difficulties. That sounded so mundane and routine. That's all this was to the Monteiths?

Major Monteith assures me the worst is past and our troops have secured the peace in New York. We are most desirous for things to return to normal for our children. At your earliest convenience, we would ask you to return to resume their lessons.

I am assured you will have no trouble crossing through the city but, if you are stopped and questioned, please show them this letter and the Major has warranted you will be free to pass.

Louisa Monteith, wife of Major Parker Monteith

Below the mother's neat script was another line in a different hand.

This woman, Miss Abigail Trench, is in my employ and under my protection. If she is stopped for any reason, she is to be allowed to pass to fulfill her duties.

Major Parker Monteith, Royal Regiment of Artillery

Abigail had little choice. The following morning, she packed up her books and walked through the eerie streets, keeping her head down. Besides the knots of red-coated soldiers on every corner, she encountered few people on the streets. A desperate half hour later, she arrived at the house on Water Street without incident, though it took quite a while for her heart to stop thumping.

"Oh, you don't know how happy I am to see you!" Louisa cooed. "I love my children but, by George, Elizabeth and Henry have been driving me *crazy.* Like everyone else, we've been stuck inside the last few days, and the children have been *so* demanding. I'm at my wit's end." A broad smile on her lips, she patted Abigail's arm. "You are a true godsend."

"Current difficulties" meant cannonballs blowing up buildings and killing young men, but this woman was stressed because her children had been demanding. Abigail struggled to keep a neutral countenance.

Louisa did not look "at her wit's end." Her golden blond hair hung in perfect curls around her heart-shaped face, and she even had a red carnation woven in. Abigail smelled the hint of floral cologne Louisa wore and realized she didn't remember when she'd last bathed. But the older woman's blue-gray eyes were kind and her relief seemed genuine. Louisa turned and hollered up the stairs, "Children, Miss Trench is here." Without waiting for a response, she walked across the foyer and opened the door on the right. "The last few days at least gave me time to arrange the library the way you requested, with the servants' help, of course." She pointed inside the room. "We set up two tables with chairs just like you asked."

Standing there in the foyer, Abigail glanced to her left into the parlor, which they had converted to an office. Major Monteith sat in an armchair next to two other men in British officer uniforms. The major met her gaze and nodded, smiling, then returned his attention to his guests. Abigail walked over to the library doorway and examined the interior. The leather chair and couch had been removed, and in their place sat two small tables, each sitting on one side of the room, with a chair and a stool. Surrounding them on three sides stood the tall shelves of leather-bound books, all left behind by the Hamptons.

"Having your children surrounded by all those beautiful books will help inspire them, don't you think?" she'd suggested.

Louisa had agreed. "God knows my children could use the inspiration."

So the tutoring lessons were moved from the nursery to the library.

"Why don't you read the second chapter in the *New England Primer* while I work with your brother?" Abigail suggested once the children were settled at their tables.

She drew letters on the hornbook for Henry. "Can you draw *f*, *g*, *h*?"

Henry glared.

"You can do this, Henry."

With a glance at his sister, he accepted the chalk.

Henry and Elizabeth worked, mostly quietly, and Abigail took in the library, scanning the titles she could make out. The smell of leather, the neatly stacked rows of books, the polished colors of the spines—all helped calm Abigail's anxiety. She needed to ask if she could borrow another volume or two.

When she examined Henry's work, she saw he was drawing stick figure animals.

"Those are pretty good. What are they, dogs?"

Henry looked at her as if she were crazy. "No, horses."

"Of course, but we're not supposed to be drawing horses, are we?"

The boy looked sheepish.

"How about I promise we will do some drawing lessons tomorrow? Okay?"

The brown head of hair nodded.

"Doesn't horse begin with *h*?"

Henry's eyes went expectant. "Yes."

"Very good." Abigail erased the board. "Let's try the letters again. Maybe draw three of each letter this time." She drew a clear *f*, *g*, and *h* and handed the hornbook back to the boy along with the chalk.

Abigail moved to the second table to check on Elizabeth, whose finger slid across the lines in the primer, her lips moving with each word. Abigail waited until the girl got to the end of the page and looked up.

"Finished," Elizabeth announced.

"Good," Abigail said. "Now, tell me what you just read."

A frown crossed the very pretty face, a more petite version of her mother's, hair the same golden tint and eyes a bit bluer, closer to the hue of the sky. "I didn't know I had to remember what I read."

Abigail chuckled. "Well, that's the whole point of reading, isn't it? To learn about something you don't know."

When the girl released a sigh, Abigail asked, "What can you remember?"

And so the lesson went, commanding Abigail's full attention and pushing her concerns aside, at least for a time. Toward the end of the session, Louisa knocked on the opened door and came in.

"You *are* a godsend." She handed Abigail an envelope. "Here is your next month's wages. I thought, with the times as they are, you might need the money."

"Thank you."

"I'm afraid I've neglected their lessons. I'm glad we have you."

Abigail took in both children. "We're almost finished for the day. If you'd like, I can come back tomorrow."

Louisa nodded. "That would be great. The children will be glad for the attention."

Abigail chuckled. "I'm not certain about that."

Abigail heard the front door open. Parker Monteith said, "Thank you for the information." Before he closed the door, a few stray red leaves were blown in by the wind. "Oh, good, Louisa, you are here. I have news." Then, noticing Abigail, he said. "Good afternoon, Miss Trench. Thank you for returning. I trust you had no trouble getting here."

Abigail did a small curtsy. "No, sir, but I appreciate the note, just in case."

"Good—keep it. For any future problems."

"Thank you, sir."

Louisa said, "Thank you again. We'll see you tomorrow, then." She stepped over to her husband, pacing in the foyer. "You said you have news. Good news, I hope."

Abigail walked over to the children, dismissing them. Elizabeth and Henry broke out in wide grins and dashed from the room. As she collected her things, Abigail heard the major talking excitedly.

"We got a name today from our source in Washington's camp," Parker said. "We learned old George's spy is a man from an old Connecticut family. Cain told me the name. What was it?"

Abigail moved to the side of the doorframe, intrigued. She was out of sight of the door, but not out of earshot. She pulled a book at random from a shelf.

Parker whispered loudly, "Oh, I remember. Hale. Nathan Hale."

Abigail dropped the book, making a loud slap on the tile floor.

27

"I still cannot believe it." Abigail's hands shook as she lifted the mug. "Nathan a spy? The man is a gentleman. His father is a deacon. Why would he do something so loathsome? So dishonest?"

Molly reached across the table. "Ya got it right? Nathan Hale a spy for the rebels?"

Abigail set the tankard down hard. "Nathan told me he had a *special* mission. I wasn't supposed to tell anyone. Not that my discretion matters now."

Molly looked at her sideways. "Ya think a special mission means spyin'?"

"I never would have thought so. But the British believe Nathan to be a spy, and they got their information from someone inside Washington's camp. So Nathan must be a spy." She felt her chest tighten. "I only hope Jamie can get word to Nathan that the British are on to him."

A few hours ago, Abigail had arrived at the Pelican in tears. In fits and starts, she told them about the overheard conversation and how she dropped the book and almost fainted. Louisa heard the noise and came in to check on her. Abigail said she was lightheaded. She hadn't eaten much in the last few days. The Monteiths had made her sit and had a servant bring some bread and figs. Not knowing what else to do, Abigail ran to the Pelican, and Jamie had taken off to spread the word. No news yet.

"Maybe Nathan got word of the leak, too, and he'll be careful," Molly offered.

Abigail shook her head. "Nathan is not good at dissembling. He's not good at pretending he is someone he's not."

Molly brightened. "Like I do when I pretend to be a lady?"

"Something like that. Nathan wears his feelings on his sleeve. I doubt that quality will serve him as a spy."

Abigail recalled Nathan's features at their last meeting. He seemed moody, serious. *I didn't want you to think less of me. To think I was that kind of man.* It all made terrible sense now.

Damn this war.

Molly signaled Levi for a refill. Abigail used her sleeve to brush tears away and took another swig.

A silhouette blocked the doorway light. Jamie strode in.

He called out, "Levi, bring me a tall one." He sat next to Molly.

Abigail's heart caught. "Did you have any luck? Did you hear where Nathan is?"

Jamie took a long drink. "No one has seen 'm. I checked with all me contacts and got nothing."

Molly said, "Mebbe he's around but keepin' out of sight?"

Jamie shook his head. "With that scar, if he was around, someone would take notice."

Abigail asked the question she dreaded. "Maybe he's been captured?"

"If the Redcoats had him, they'd be crowin' like a rooster. I don't think so." He drank again. "Mebbe now he'll get word he's a wanted man and be careful."

"Maybe," Abigail muttered.

What else could she do? She felt helpless. And angry at Nathan for being so reckless. Then she remembered his words: *I prefer liberty with danger over peace with chains.*

But spying? She shuddered. What about liberty gained at the end of a rope?

Oh Nathan, where are you?

28

Nothing.

Two days, and they'd heard nothing from Nathan.

Abigail didn't even know if he'd gotten the warning. Jamie had done his best to spread the word, asking his fellows to keep a lookout and pass on the alert discreetly, *if* they were able to make contact. But Jamie had heard nothing back. He warned Abigail they needed to be careful. Now that the British controlled the city, alliances were shifting.

"Most of them fellows are only out fer themselves," Jamie said. "If they think they can make a quick coin or two from the Redcoats, they'll sell out their mum. If'n the Brits put a price on Nathan's head, all bets are off."

So the next night, uncertain what else to do, she returned to the places around the city she had visited with Nathan. She knew it was likely useless, but she could not sit idle while worry gnawed at her. They weren't exactly a couple, were they? She didn't know what they were. She only knew she cared about him.

In the fading daylight, she stumped along Broadway, doing her best to ignore the Holy Ground. Watching British soldiers stagger in and out of the dilapidated buildings lining the street, she thought this was one sight Nathan could have left off his tour. One burly Redcoat tried to stop and proposition her, but she moved quickly out of his grasping arms, leaving him to stumble onto the wooden walkway. She hurried all the way to the Green, then to a small café they had visited. No sign of Nathan. The season had begun to change, and with it the temperature, now almost brisk. The wind picked up, sending swirls of debris through the streets, flinging dust and dirt. Pulling a shawl around her shoulders, she walked to the edge of Manhattan, to a river overlook where she and Nathan had stood close together, watching leaves flutter in the breeze and the waters bubble over the rocks below.

Was that only last month?

None of her searching bore fruit. Her efforts garnered only suspicious looks or leers from the soldiers who seemed to infest every corner. She was at a loss.

During the days, she tried to stay busy. She did her best to hide her anxiety as she conducted her tutoring sessions with the Monteiths. As usual, the children were demanding—their mother was right about that—and keeping Henry and Elizabeth on track required her full concentration. Abigail even hoped, or rather feared, she'd overhear something about Nathan at the Monteiths', but the major had not been home either day. At the end of each session, dread consumed her anew.

Today her lessons seemed to stretch for hours, her attention claimed first by one child, then the other, the cycle repeating endlessly. At times, it felt as though Henry and Elizabeth were using her in a tug-of-war. By the time she left for home, she was spent. After her exploration the previous evening, her stamina waned. She trudged on, twisting her way through streets and alleys, keeping her head down and the major's letter close—just in case. The winds had intensified, blowing harder now, and she used her shawl to cover her face.

Along her way, she noticed the city had begun to return to some semblance of normalcy, even in the grip of British occupation. On the second and third floors of buildings, windows were flung open. A few more locals traveled the walkways, doing business in and out of storefronts. On Water Street, brave vendors hawked their wares again. Abigail figured they had to make a living, regardless what colors the soldiers wore.

When she came down Queen Street on the edge of Manhattan, she spotted a small crowd gathering in front of a house—an unusual sight lately. She'd noticed the house a few times on her trips to and from the Monteiths'. It was a handsome two-story structure with white clapboard siding and two chimneys, set back from the road, a small open meadow between it and the other buildings. While nowhere near as grand as the Hamptons' mansion, this house stood out, far finer than most homes in Manhattan. Its most noticeable feature was a long porch running across the front. In the center sat two wooden chairs, perfect for rocking and taking in the view of the city and harbor beyond. Some days, as she passed, she'd daydreamed about sitting in those cozy chairs, rocking in the sunset.

Seeing the gaggle of people—locals, women and children, a few older men, and two Negroes standing next to young toughs who were likely dock workers—Abigail moved to cross the street. Exhausted, she did not want to get caught up in whatever was happening. Halfway across the dusty road, she heard a familiar voice.

"Respectfully, sir, this is a really bad idea."

She recognized the bass tone of Major Parker Monteith, though he kept his voice low. Her curiosity now greater than her fatigue, she turned and headed toward the onlookers, stopping at the edge of the group to get a better look.

Major Monteith said, "Sir, we only took control of the city a few days ago. Is *this* how we want the locals to view us?"

Abigail's gaze went from the major to the house. On the porch, two figures sat in those rocking chairs she coveted—a middle-aged man and woman. No. She stared. The two were tied to the chairs, hands and feet bound to the wood, and were guarded by a pair of Redcoats, rifles at the ready.

On the walkway running along the street, a third soldier was painting two crude letters on the wood. As he finished and stood, Abigail looked past him. She recognized *R* and *C*. A clang drew her attention back to the structure. Two more soldiers, glass bottles in hand, banged them against the siding. The men sloshed dark liquid onto the clapboards. When they finished, they dumped more onto the porch floor and down the steps to the street.

The major stood close to another man in uniform, a smaller, obese officer whose large belly strained the silver buttons of his red greatcoat. As she stared at the second officer, she noticed a long blue feather dangling from a coat button. A gust blew across the porch, making the feather flutter—a delicate motion so out of place in the grim scene.

Abigail watched Monteith, posture stiff, sweep his gaze over the crowd. He gestured toward the house. "Colonel Hollister, I suggest *this* is far too drastic a measure," he uttered through tight lips, obviously struggling to keep his voice under control. "This will only enrage the locals. It will give them more powder."

"Nonsense," the older officer bellowed.

Abigail supposed the man was Major Monteith's superior. The obese man turned and glanced at the crowd. Abigail caught bloodshot brown eyes above a bulbous nose, a cigar dangling between puffy lips. The fingers of one hand played with the feather, flipping it over and over.

Pulling the cigar from his mouth, the man used it to point at the house. "*This* will strike fear into their disloyal hearts. They'll see what happens to those who collaborate with the rebels."

Abigail glanced again at the two sloppy letters painted in red on the walkway. R. C. Rebel Collaborator.

Monteith asked, "Are we certain these two are collaborators? Colonel Hollister, what about a trial? Isn't that what English justice calls for?"

"Trial! Huh!" The colonel puffed on his cigar and pulled it out again. "We caught these two red-handed. They were getting ready to pass information to the rebels." He stabbed the cigar toward the major. "Your troops, Monteith. Caught them trying to pass details on troop placement to the damn rebels. You think we should allow that to happen?"

"Of course not," Monteith said. "But there has to be a better option than this."

"For these spies, this is precisely what they deserve," the senior officer announced.

Abigail stared across at Major Parker Monteith. As if he could feel her eyes on him, the major met her gaze. Though he made no move at first, Monteith's eyes seemed to acknowledge her, his face a mask of disgrace. He shook his head slowly, his gaze shifting from his superior to the house, then finally back to Abigail. He took a few quick steps and stopped next to her.

"Miss Trench, this is not something you will want to see." His head jerked back toward the prisoners. "This is not fit for a young woman to witness."

Abigail looked at Monteith, then nodded past him to the activity on the porch. "No one should witness this. I certainly don't want to," she said, steel in her voice. "But if British soldiers are going to commit such a heinous act, someone needs to witness it."

"War is *ugly*." He shifted his feet, glancing back toward the house. "This is not my idea of war, but I am not in charge."

The fat colonel hollered, "Are you two about finished?" Abigail turned to see the portly man gesture at the soldiers pouring liquid on the house.

Shaking his head, Monteith retraced his steps and returned to his position flanking the structure.

Hollister harrumphed. "Hurry up. I have a supper to get to. I understand the cook is preparing lamb for tonight." He puffed one more time on the cigar. Indicating the two sentries standing behind the prisoners, he bellowed, "All right, you two men, better get off there."

Relief flooding their faces, the two Redcoats scurried off the porch.

The brown liquid oozed down the walls and onto the floorboards. More of it lay in ugly pools on the wooden steps. Abigail swept her gaze from the officer holding the burning cigar to the porch drenched in fluid. A breeze carried a familiar, fishy odor from the house. It hit her—whale oil. The same oil used to light lamps at night.

This British officer, this colonel, was going to execute these two right here, in plain daylight. No, not merely execute them. He was going to torture them. Burn them. A modern version of burning at the stake. And Major Monteith was simply going to watch?

What could she do? She glanced around but saw no one she recognized. Nathan would have stepped forward, but . . .

Others in the crowd must've realized what was happening. One of the dockworkers asked, "Ya gonna burn 'em? Right here?"

An older man protested, "You can't do that. You need a trial or somethin'."

A young woman yelled, "This ain't right."

Grumbling erupted from the crowd. Men and women faced each other, gesturing wildly. Abigail shot a glance at the soldiers, who no doubt heard the rumblings. They looked at each other, then at Hollister, then back at the crowd.

Abigail prayed some colonial marksman would fire from a building and kill Hollister. With this ugly fat man eliminated, the other Redcoats might see how evil this was and do *something*. If Major Monteith were in charge, he would handle the affair in a more humane manner, wouldn't he?

But the last of the colonial militia had left the city days ago.

Would all these British soldiers simply stand there and watch this couple burn alive? What would they do if she or someone in the crowd rushed them? Would they fire? They were all following orders. Including the major. And these soldiers were her countrymen—or had been a few years ago. Now, they had become savages. No, worse than savages.

Abigail studied the couple tied to the chairs. She didn't recognize either of them. Both looked terrified, eyes wide, mouths gaping like beached fish. The man struggled against his bonds, yanking and bucking in the chair. A sheen of tears covered the woman's face, and Abigail could hear her sobbing even from the street.

Holding the burning cigar aloft, Hollister stepped to the front stair, its surface an oily mess.

"Wait!" the man on the porch pleaded. "This is some kind of terrible mistake. We *are* loyal subjects of the king. We only wish to serve His Majesty."

The colonel bellowed, "Oh, you *will* serve His Majesty, all right." He turned to stare at the crowd, a triumphant sneer on his pudgy face. "You'll serve as perfect examples. This is what happens to traitors to king and country." He turned back toward the house.

"I tell you, this is barbaric!" yelled the young Negro man. "God will punish ya for this."

Hollister whipped around. "Who said that?"

No one gave the man away. Still holding the cigar, Hollister's gaze went from the suddenly silent crowd to his soldiers. The five men shuffled their feet, casting anxious glances at the officer, then at the crowd.

Hollister shot an angry look at Monteith, then stared at his men. "Buck up, men. You have the rifles and bayonets. Stand ready to use them if *anyone* starts anything." He stabbed his cigar toward the onlookers. Then, he puffed once more and dropped it onto the wood.

The burning tip hit the oil.

Someone in the crowd screamed, "Oh my God."

A woman next to Abigail covered her child's eyes. Abigail didn't want to look, didn't want to see this, in spite of what she'd told the major. But she couldn't look away. The whoosh of fire riveted her vision to the house and the desperate victims.

The woman screamed, "Someone help us, please!"

Before Abigail or anyone could act, Hollister yelled at the group, "Don't even think about it. Sergeant Davis, shoot the first person who moves."

The soldier turned his rifle toward the crowd, though he didn't look happy about it. His glance flitted from the onlookers to the couple being executed, his features betraying confusion and hesitation. After a moment, the other soldiers joined him, facing the crowd, faces pinched, eyes nervous.

The man on the porch screamed, "Is *this* the justice you want?" The woman shrieked, her cries loud and pitiful.

Even as she stared at the scene, horrified, Abigail couldn't believe the speed of the fire. Within minutes, the wood of the house was being devoured, boards cracking and breaking. The woman tied to the chair screamed, and the man bellowed in pain as flames climbed their legs.

The wind shifted, blowing black smoke into the faces of the onlookers, bringing with it a sweet, sickening smell. This was so much worse than hanging. She choked on the smell, bile rising in her throat. Turning away, she spat and coughed, again and again. Pulling out a handkerchief, she held it to her nose and mouth, trying to screen the stench and fumes. It did little good.

Soon, the soldiers started coughing as well. Using sleeves to wipe their eyes, they let their rifle barrels droop, but it mattered little. The fire was too far along. Others in the crowd hacked uncontrollably. A child wailed, screaming at the top of his lungs until his mother pulled him away and down the street, glancing back over her shoulder at the inferno. More watchers broke from the group, hurrying away as if the flames might chase them.

Abigail had wanted to do something, anything, but it was too late. She felt helpless and ashamed. First Nathan, and now this godforsaken man and woman she didn't even know. Tears running down her cheeks, Abigail couldn't believe her eyes. The sight was too horrific, too barbaric to be real. She turned away.

How could the British, her British, commit such atrocities? She shook her head. No, not her British . . . not anymore. How could those in charge tolerate such heinous behavior by this pompous officer? How could Major Monteith simply stand there? The civilized Britain she knew in London a few years ago seemed like a distant, fading memory.

Witnessing this was changing her. Her white-hot fury at the British army, ignited by the ugly rapist last year, was crystallizing into hard granite, forged by this gruesome inferno. She would never be able to unsee this.

She had to get away. To get safe. To get home. She wanted to run, but her feet felt like stones. As she pushed herself down Queen Street toward the wharf, the dying screams of the tortured man and woman followed her, carried by the wind along with that sickening stench.

She knew those horrid cries would haunt her nightmares.

29

"Fire! Help!"

In her tortured slumber, the plea sounded plaintive and distant. Still, the nightmare felt vivid, her mind grasping the image of the desperate couple as the inferno whipped around them, imprisoned in their chairs, licked by flames. Abigail could taste burning ash on her tongue. She turned on her mat, trying to shake the gripping tendrils of the horrid dream. But even in her semi-conscious state, the stench of blackened wood assailed her nostrils.

Dragging herself from the nightmare, she shook her head, then curled her legs to stand. She would get no more rest tonight. She shot a glance at the open window and the darkness beyond. When she and Father had lain down, he'd convinced her to leave the window open, saying the cool fall temperatures made for better sleeping. She stared at the night and saw—or thought she saw—a glow to the south.

Was it almost morning?

She had no idea how long she had lain gripped by the nightmare, but she didn't think it had been long. She glanced at Father, who still lay curled on the too-small cot, snoring softly.

"Fire! Please, someone help!" The cries came again, still distant but fiercer now, terror squeezed into the syllables. The pleas were *not* from her dreams. They came from outside. She ran to the window, knocking a mug to the floor, its dented metal clanging on the wooden slats.

"Wh-a-t? What's wrong?" croaked Father as he turned in bed. His gaze settled on her, and he reached for his wire-rimmed glasses on the crate beside him. Putting them on, he peered at Abigail. "Daughter, what is it?"

Abigail pointed into the night. "Fire," she said, hearing the hysteria in her voice. To the south, above the two- and three-story buildings, she spotted a red glow in the distance, the glare pulsing in the dark. The odor of burning wood drifted through the open window.

Father slid his legs to the floor and came up beside her. Together they stared, watching the edges of the black night consumed by waves of orange and red. Buildings were on fire, likely near the wharf. She pictured the rows of flimsy wooden structures—perfect kindling for a raging fire.

Father said, "We need to see if we can help."

What time was it? She wondered as they both slipped into their clothes—Father into trousers, her pulling a cover over her bed dress. She didn't think she had slept long, though with her tortured dreams she couldn't be sure.

Together, they hurried down the stairs and out into the street. As they made their way toward the harbor, others joined them, a small stream of people flowing out of buildings. No one spoke, faces filled with dread. It took the group only minutes to cross the two blocks.

When they rounded the corner onto Water Street, the wind whipped at them, carrying smoke and ash. Father coughed first, then Abigail, their lungs struggling against the debris. Soon the others were coughing and hacking, using their arms to block the smoke. Abigail pulled a handkerchief from a pocket and handed it to Father, then pulled a second for herself. They stared down the road to where the wharf bent along the curve of the river. There, a row of one-, two-, and three-story buildings were alight.

Covering their noses and mouths, eyes blinking against the sting, they led the way down Water Street. Hurrying, their footfalls clattered on the wooden walkway, while echoes from the others behind followed them. Their pace took them past one open door after another, sleepy occupants emerging. Several doors down, she glanced at the entrance to the Pelican. Levi stood there, mouth agape, staring down the wharf. She gave a quick nod but, keeping up with Father, had no time to ask about Molly and Jamie.

As they rounded the bend, the heat from the inferno struck them, sudden and intense. Father stopped, Abigail halting beside him. Ahead, the row of structures was engulfed. Abigail counted five—no, seven—buildings belching smoke and flames. The farthest looked nearly consumed, its upper floors caving into the first. She watched as the wooden structure collapsed upon itself, sending a huge pillar of angry red and gold up the skeleton of the building and hurling debris into the air. Within seconds, the wind grabbed the burning splinters and shingles, and deposited them onto nearby buildings. In less than a minute, that wood was ablaze as well.

The other buildings in the row, though not yet consumed, weren't far behind. The next two had flames erupting from windows, while the ones closest to Abigail belched black smoke.

"Can someone help me?" called a feeble voice from above.

Abigail glanced up to the second floor of the first building in the row. An older woman stretched a skinny arm out an open window, her pale face staring down with abject fear. Without a word, Father hustled through the door, disappearing into the black cloud.

"Father!" Abigail cried to his back, but he was gone, swallowed by the dark fumes. Before she could decide whether to follow, another cry stopped her.

"Someone help me, *please*. Help me and my baby," screamed a voice.

Abigail scanned the windows, peering through the gathering smoke. Then she saw her, a woman in the second-story window of the third rowhouse.

"Hold on, I'm coming!" she called.

Abigail ran down the walkway, then stepped into the street to get a better look. Mother and child were framed in the window, blackness behind them. She saw no fire yet, but it was only a matter of time. The building beside it spouted flames, the third floor fully ablaze.

The first floor of this structure housed a stable or warehouse, but she saw no livestock. She could make out nothing inside the wide, dark opening but figured there had to be stairs or a ladder. She bounded onto the walkway and heard someone following a beat behind. Running through the opening, she peered around, coughing into her handkerchief. The space was filling with smoke, nearly blinding her. She blinked, trying to pierce the darkness. Then she saw it, a door in the back. She ran to it and threw it open.

Her gaze went up the steep steps. The top of the stairs glowed, hot tongues of fire racing across the floor. Behind her, the wind whooshed through the open door and whipped up the stairs. The rushing air acted like a bellows, engorging the flames and sucking them down toward her. She slammed the door shut.

"What are we going to do now?" someone asked. She turned to see a man with disheveled hair and anxious eyes.

She pointed at the door. "We can't go that way." She turned, studying the stable, searching for anything that might help. There wasn't much. No ladders, no rope. Then she saw them—a row of wooden casks stacked against the wall. She ran to them. "Here, help me."

With some tugging and dragging, aided by the stranger, she managed to get the first barrel moving, rolling it on its bottom rim out to the walkway. When she turned back, the young man was rolling a second barrel right behind her.

"Good. Set it alongside." She pointed to her barrel. "Now we need more. We can set one atop and use it to climb."

Without waiting for a response, she rushed back inside. In seconds, she had another barrel rolling out. Abigail lined it up next to the first two, making a triangle. By the time she set it in place, the stranger had rolled a fourth barrel up.

Abigail turned to look at the young man. His face was blackened from smoke, sweat making rivulets in the soot, hair plastered to his head. She must look the same.

She coughed, trying to clear her throat. "We need to get this barrel balanced atop the others. Then we should be able to reach them. Help me lift."

He nodded. She bent to grab the cask by the bottom, watching him mimic her actions. When they lifted the metal-rimmed bottom, they found it wasn't too heavy, maybe only half full. Together they maneuvered the fourth container into place, balanced on the rims of the three below. Abigail hoped it would hold.

She used the handkerchief to wipe her smeared face, then handed it to her partner. He made a few quick swipes and handed it back.

She said, "I need you to hold it steady while I climb up. Can you do that?"

"Why don't you let me go up?" the man's voice rasped.

Abigail shook her head hard. "No. I need you to keep this thing steady so it doesn't collapse. I'm not sure I'll be able to do that."

The man studied the arrangement, then looked at Abigail. Nodding, he placed his hands around the bottom rim of the top barrel. "I'll do my best."

She climbed onto the barrel closest to her, standing on its edge. Then she pulled herself, one arm and leg at a time, to stand on the higher barrel. It shifted slightly as she rose, and she glanced down. Her partner had both arms encircling the bottom of the barrel, his blackened face turned up to her. Abigail looked at the open window.

"Hand me your baby. I'll be careful," she called to the distraught mother.

The mother's hair was plastered to her skin, smeary blond curls over her forehead. Huge eyes stared at Abigail's outstretched arms, then down at the contraption they'd built.

Trying to keep the fear out of her voice, Abigail said, "It'll be all right. What's your baby's name?"

Fear etched in her features, the mother managed, "Olivia."

"Olivia. That's a beautiful name. My name's Abigail." She coughed. "What's yours?"

The woman's gaze jerked from the baby to Abigail. "Dorothy," she croaked.

"Wonderful, Dorothy. Hand me Olivia, and then we can get you down from there."

The mother hesitated a second longer, then lowered a wrapped bundle. Abigail grabbed it with both hands. As soon as the baby left her mother's arms, she started crying—loud, frantic wails audible over the roar of the fire.

Abigail cooed, "Shh. It's going to be all well."

Fighting for balance, Abigail handed the baby down the length of the barrel. As the man took the bundle, he had to release his hold, and Abigail felt the container under her shift. She froze, waiting until the makeshift structure steadied. Slowly, she raised herself back to a standing position. She studied the mother, who never took her eyes off the child.

Abigail watched as the young man below handed the bawling bundle to a nearby woman, then returned to his post, grasping the barrel again. A number of people had gathered below—men and women in bedclothes, dock workers, even a few Redcoats, waistcoats unbuttoned. Ignoring the audience, she turned to the mother. "Now it's your turn. You need to lower yourself out the window onto this barrel next to me."

Face white, the young mother looked at her daughter, then at the barrels, then at Abigail. "I don't think I can." She shook her head. "What if I stumble and make it fall?"

The baby gave a harrowing cry, and the mother's eyes widened.

Abigail said, "Your daughter needs you." She pointed to the ground. "You can do this. Come on." She stretched a hand out.

The mother turned and disappeared for a few seconds. Abigail stared with rising anxiety. The heat was ratcheting up, and streams of sweat rolled down her back, drenching her bed dress. Her gaze went to the burning structures only two doors down. She turned back as the woman backed out the window.

"Please," the mother gasped. "Don't let me fall."

As the legs came closer, Abigail reached out, grabbed both, and guided the woman onto the rickety top of the barrel. The mother wrapped both arms around Abigail and hugged tightly, tears flowing down her cheeks.

Crack. The structure two doors down shuddered. Sounds of boards splintering and snapping echoed down the walkway. In their awkward embrace, Abigail and the mother watched as geysers of red and yellow flame shot into the sky. A few seconds later, that building groaned and collapsed, pulling down the wall of the structure next to them. Below, bystanders gasped and screamed.

Abigail stared into the mother's terrified eyes. "We need to get down. Now." She pointed down the impromptu structure. "He'll help you."

The mother's gaze went from the ground to the erupting columns of fire, to Abigail, and then back to the window. She pleaded, "But Rufus is still up there." Her head jerked toward the opening. "He'll burn up." The mother's eyes fixed on the second story.

Abigail stared at the window. She saw nothing. "Someone is still up there?"

Dorothy nodded hard. "Rufus is up there, shaking in the corner." She looked at Abigail. "I didn't want to leave him, but my baby . . . Olivia." Tears flowed.

Abigail shot another look at the window, then leveled her gaze on the woman. "Let's get you down to your baby, and I'll go get Rufus."

As if on cue, the baby below wailed anew. The mother nodded, and Abigail steadied her as she lowered one leg after the other until she found her footing on the lower tier. After the young man helped her to the ground, the mother ran over, took the baby, and cradled her. Olivia stopped crying the moment her mother grabbed her.

Abigail thought about the mysterious bond between mother and child, pining for the mother she missed. She returned her attention to the window. Smoke was spreading to the upper floor, tendrils of gray curling out the opening. *Rufus, I'm coming.* She stretched to her full height, raising her arms above her head.

"What are you doing?" called a hoarse voice from below.

She turned to see the young man gesturing with one hand, the other still clinging to the rim.

He said, "The fire is spreading fast. You need to come down. Now."

Abigail shook her head. "The mother says there is someone still trapped. Rufus. I'm going to find him."

She turned back toward the window and stretched. Her fingers grasped the sill and pulled. The wood was warm, but not yet hot. Using all her strength, she dragged her body up until she could get her elbows on the ledge. She hoisted herself up and rolled inside, landing hard on the floorboards. When she placed her hands flat on the wood, they came away hot. Without using the boards to push off, she raised herself. The space around her was dark, nearly black.

"Rufus? Rufus, where are you? It's time to go," she hollered, coughing.

She thought she heard movement in a corner and stepped toward the noise. Halfway across the room, the darkness swallowed her. She turned, trying to get her bearings, but could no longer locate the window, the smoke so thick. Coughing and hacking, she felt her breathing labor. Time was running out.

Desperate, she tried again. "Rufus? Where are you?"

30

A sharp crack split the silence, close by. Abigail guessed the boards were splitting in the structure next door. The fire had almost reached this room.

Squinting through the haze, she could make out only the barest outline of a small, quivering gray body in the darkness. "Rufus?" she croaked, her throat raw. A coughing fit seized her. Smoke was getting into her lungs. She would not last long.

A frightened yip erupted from the darkness. A dog? She stretched out a hand and grabbed a fistful of fur.

The mother sent her back up to rescue a dog?

Well, she was here now. Might as well take the dog with her . . . if she could figure how to get out. She peered into the inkiness and swiveled her head. Coughing again, she thought she saw a change in the light to the right. Gathering the pet under one arm, she reached out with the other, trying to grab something, anything. Her fingers scrabbled across the warm floor as she half-crawled, half-walked toward where she hoped the opening was.

Her hand landed on something hard. The window ledge? No, a table. Moving her fingers around the edge, she dragged herself to a standing position, the quivering animal tucked under her arm. She blinked rapidly against the smoke.

Then she felt it.

A warm breeze blew past her on the left. She edged that way, arm outstretched, fingers grasping for a perch at the height she thought the bottom of the window ledge would be. As she moved, the draft struck her face—a hot breath carrying the stench of fire. She choked but leaned forward. Her hand hit something. Fingers scrabbling along the edge, she made sure it was the windowsill, though she had to yank them off the overheated wood. Praying, she thrust her head out and found air. She stared down. She could make out figures below, moving and gesturing. She heard voices carried on the hot wind.

"Are you all right?" a male voice hollered.

She tried to yell, but the answer only squawked in her throat. She waved her free arm instead. She turned her face toward the shivering creature at her side. "You ready, Rufus?" she gasped. "Let's do this."

Rather than go backward like the mother, she decided to go forward to see where to land. She climbed up, one leg at a time, sitting on the ledge, legs dangling. Even through her clothes, the wooden frame seared her skin. This place was going to go up any second.

She stared below and caught sight of the top barrel. The rim looked impossibly small. No wonder the mother had shaken with fear. She didn't think she'd be able to steady herself with only one hand, but what choice did she have? The dog wouldn't survive the drop, and neither would she.

She eased the left side of her body—the one not clutching the squirmy animal—off the ledge, stretching her leg down to touch the rim. At the very end of her reach, her toes brushed the wood. She shifted her weight on the ledge and lowered her second leg. By some miracle, she came down squarely on the center of the barrel. She released a breath. The barrel wiggled under her weight, but she stood still, and after a few anguished seconds, it settled.

She glanced down. Her partner still grasped the bottom barrel, arms encircling the lower metal rim. He looked up, face darkened with soot, eyes large and white.

"Looks like you made it," he called.

Abigail gave a quick nod. "Perhaps." She couldn't help but smile.

"You saved our Rufus! Thank you so much. May God bless you," an anxious voice called from below.

Abigail assumed it was the mother. She turned back to her partner. "Let me lower this guy down." She reached with her left hand to grab the dog. When her hand touched his side, Rufus yelped and squirmed. Abigail adjusted her stance, trying to cradle him with both hands, but Rufus kicked, wiggling to jump. As she shifted to keep hold of the flailing dog, she lost her balance. One arm clutching the animal, she reached out with the other, but there was nothing to grab. She toppled. Somewhere on the way down, the dog sprang from her arms. Abigail shut her eyes, bracing for the impact.

Instead, two arms grabbed her in midair, and she collapsed on top of someone. They finished the fall together, hitting the solid ground, his body breaking her fall. When she opened her eyes, she stared into the soot-covered face of her partner.

"Thank you," she managed through a parched throat.

They untangled, she somewhat clumsily, and rose to their feet. The young man reached out a hand. "Are you all right?"

Abigail glanced down at her torn dress, legs and arms filthy with ash. Her bones ached from hitting the packed dirt, and her throat hurt, but she didn't think there was long-term damage. Her eyes met his. "I think I'm mostly unhurt . . . thanks to you."

The young man shifted his weight and thrust his hand at her. "I'm Robert Townsend."

She shook the offered hand. "Abigail Trench."

31

From behind, Abigail heard feet pounding and felt strong arms surround her, squeezing with abandon.

"You're all right. You made it out." Father turned her, put hands on her shoulders, and studied her. When he pulled back, hebrushed her arm, and his hand came away red. "You're bleeding."

She raised a hand to her shoulder. "Must've happened when I fell." Her fingers probed the cut. Not much bleeding, at least. "Probably cut myself trying to rescue Rufus."

"Rufus?" Father asked.

"The dog," she said, glancing around, searching for the mongrel.

"You went into a burning building to rescue a dog?" Father's tone morphed from anxiety to annoyance.

"Well, I didn't know—"

"I don't know how I can ever thank you. God bless you!" Yelling, the mother ran up to her, baby in one arm, Rufus trotting beside her, tongue lolling. The young woman gave Abigail a one-armed squeeze. Tears flooded her face, and she wiped them with her sleeve. Rufus gave a short yip.

Dorothy turned to Father. "This woman is the bravest person I know. She saved me and my daughter." She sniffed. "And she saved our Rufus." She glanced down at the dog. "She's a real hero."

Abigail saw Robert standing behind them, and she gestured to him. "And this is Robert Townsend. I couldn't have rescued you without his help." Her gaze met the young man's. "He caught me when I fell."

"Well, thank you, then," Father said, shaking Robert's hand.

Behind them, the building shuddered. The siding cracked open, a tongue of fire spitting through.

Father grabbed Abigail's arm. "We need to get away from here *now*."

Abigail, Father, Robert, Dorothy, and the child hustled across the dirt road, stopping at the river's edge. The dog trotted behind. As one, the group turned to stare back at the row of structures, the entire section now engulfed. Spouts of red, yellow, and orange erupted from every opening like evil spirits escaping hell. The wall of another rowhouse collapsed, raining fiery shards onto the walkway where they had stood moments ago. Swells of heat undulated across the road like boiling waves.

Sweat ran down her back, dripping off her forehead. Standing near the water, Abigail pulled her filthy handkerchief and wiped her neck and face. She studied the tableau, watching flames jump from one structure to the next. The first seven buildings were consumed, little more than fiery skeletons. The wild wind whipped through the ruins, making the flames dance and blowing sparks onto the next group of houses. The dry wood ignited like kindling. The fire cast an eerie light in the waning night.

Up and down the wharf, onlookers backed away, mesmerized by horror. Farther down Water Street, two men ran from door to door.

"Fire's comin'! Git what ya ken and git out!" one man hollered.

The second, younger and smaller, used a large branch to pound on doors and upper window ledges.

"Not much time!" the first screamed over the roar. "Fire's got a mind of its own!"

More and more people poured out of buildings, scurrying down steps. Half-dressed or in bedclothes, men, women, and children ran onto the dusty road, grasping what few items they could carry. Several women clutched babies close, the wails of infants mingling with the roar of the fire. Abigail noticed there were no fat merchants or fancy lords here. These were poor, working people with little to their names.

The crowd swelled to a hundred or more. Spectators peered across the road, weeping and panicked, watching their lives go up in flames. Twice, the swirling winds grabbed a burning board and threw it toward the crowd as if taunting them. Women screamed, and men spat curses and stomped on smoldering embers. When another wall fell, sounds of desperation rippled through the crowd—angry curses, quiet weeping, terrified cries.

Abigail's sense of helplessness deepened. First, on Long Island, the robbery and the assault by the disgusting soldiers. Then, yesterday, the ghastly torture of the couple. Now she could only stand by and watch this raging inferno destroy so much.

She wondered how the fire had taken such hold. Where were the fire wardens? Then she remembered. The colonial government was gone. Since the Continental Army fled, those responsible had left or gone into hiding. The British had controlled the city for less than a week—not enough time to set up a fire watch, or perhaps they simply hadn't cared to.

Behind her, the sky began to change, migrating from inky dark to the gray of dawn, layered with smoke. It must be later than she thought. Suddenly, Abigail felt exhausted. Her body ached from the collision with the ground. Her head throbbed. She wanted nothing more than to lie down, but that wouldn't happen for hours.

With the graying sky, she could see beyond the burning buildings. Outlines of the city came into view. To the north, the spire of Trinity Church. Beyond it, the Liberty Pole poked through the gloom. All seemed quiet there.

She brought her gaze back to the fire. Studying the flames arching across the roofs, she tried to trace the path backward. At first, she could make out little through the dark cloud. Then a gust of wind parted the grayness. She stared down beyond the bend and saw it. On a rise, across a small meadow, sat the burnt remains of a single house. Even from this distance, embers glowed like fireflies in the rubble. Among the blackened timbers, she could just make out parts of the white rail of the porch.

That house.

Her mind jerked back. She recognized the place where she'd witnessed the execution. Her stomach lurched. Could the fire have traveled that far? The wind picked up again, hot on her face, and she *knew*. Sometime during the night, smoldering bits of that fire must have been carried on a gust.

First, that horrid little colonel ordered the barbaric torture . . . and now he had ignited this inferno. She peered at the fire reaching the next set of buildings. He paraded his cruelty yesterday, and now his ruthlessness had cost these people everything.

Father broke her concentration. "They're going to burn down half of Manhattan," he grumbled.

"Do you live near here?" Robert asked.

"We used to," Father answered. "When we first moved to New York, we lived right there." He pointed to a structure now engulfed. "We moved a few weeks ago. Now we have a small place a few streets back. We're safe . . . for now."

"What about you?" Abigail asked Robert. "Do you live nearby?"

"I have a store on Broadway, a dry goods store. I live in the flat behind it."

"Abigail!" a girl's voice screamed.

Turning, Abigail watched the crowd part. A fancy yellow dress came at her—or rather, the girl carrying it.

"Can you help me here?" Molly squealed, dropping the yellow frock into Abigail's arms. She hauled up a green gown, balled it up, then retrieved the yellow dress. "I had to git out so fast, these were all I had time to grab. And one more thing." She nodded at Abigail, eyes darting to her own bosom.

Abigail glanced at the girl, then turned. "Father, Robert, this is Molly. I'm tutoring Molly in reading and math."

Molly beamed. "Abigail is a great teacher. I learned a lot already."

Abigail decided not to share Molly's current occupation. Instead, she asked, "Where's Jamie?" She scanned the burning rowhouses. "He's not still in your room?"

Molly shook her head. "Naw. He ain't there."

"Where *is* Jamie?"

Molly's eyes dampened, and she looked like a little girl rather than a woman. "I don't know." She shook her head again. "He ain't back from searching . . . fer our, er . . . friend."

32

"Move! Outta the way!" called a voice.

Abigail turned to see a soldier staring at the inferno. He yelled over his shoulder, "Hurry, men. It's going to take a lot of water. We'll have to be at sixty to even make a dent."

Only then did Abigail notice a line of Redcoats trudging up the hill, each toting a pail, water spilling over the rims. The men passed the buckets up the makeshift line. When the soldier at the front got a pail, he tossed its contents at the fire and handed it back. In a few minutes, the line established a rhythm, scooping water from the East River and sending it up the row.

Abigail watched as the men attacked the flames, one group on the south end and another on the north. It made little difference. The conflagration had a life of its own. Every time the bucket brigade doused a small part of the fire, the flames fought back. The inferno acted like a primordial beast, its fiery breath reigniting splintered boards the moment they dried.

Catching a soldier who passed, Abigail asked, "Can we do something? Help in some way?"

"We don't need no help from any stinkin' rebels," yelled the Redcoat, handing a bucket up the line. He pointed an angry finger at her. "You locals started this damn fire. Let us try to put it out afore ya burn the whole damn city down."

Abigail wanted to scream that she knew how this fire started and rebels had nothing to do with it, but she held her tongue.

The fiery beast huffed, and another gust ripped through the inferno, raining flaming debris onto the brigade. The line broke as soldiers dove out of the way, dropping buckets. Then an officer barked commands, and in less than a minute, the men re-formed.

"You made it. You're safe," Molly squealed when a short figure parted the crowd. Abigail turned to see the girl practically jump into Jamie's arms, squishing the fancy dresses between them.

"Easy, girl, or y'all knock me down," Jamie called, a tired frown on his face. His blond hair was filthy, plastered to his head, clothes soot-covered. Like the rest, Jamie fixed his gaze on the flames.

Molly buried her head in his chest. "I was so worried about ya. I mean with the fire and all. I'm just so happy ya made it back."

Abigail was glad to see the pickpocket too. Though anxious for news, she didn't want to interrupt the reunion. Jamie's careless, easygoing manner had vanished. He held his shoulders stiff, and his trademark smirk had vanished. Abigail felt the pit in her stomach wrench tighter.

She stepped closer. "Jamie, are you well? Did something happen? Were you caught—" she realized what she was saying and added, "in the fire?"

Jamie shook his head. "Naw, it ain't me. I'm all' righ'. I was headed this way and saw the glow. Ran all the way. Was worried 'bout ya." He held Molly at arm's length.

Molly brushed tears away. "I'm all' righ' too." She held up the dresses. "Our place is gone, but I managed to save these." She grabbed Jamie's hand and placed it on her breast—or rather, between her breasts. "And I saved one more thing." She managed a weak smile.

Jamie met it with a thin one of his own. "You're a keeper, Miss Molly." He reached down her dress and retrieved the bag, palming it smoothly, then hugged her again. They stood in an awkward clinch, a bundle of lace and cotton between them, smeared faces lit by the growing daylight and the arching flames.

Abigail couldn't wait any longer. Even with the misery surrounding her, she hadn't forgotten the purpose of Jamie's roaming. She said, throat tight, "How'd your *travels* go?"

Jamie looked nervous, checking for eavesdroppers. When his gaze finished the sweep, it met Abigail's, and he lowered his voice to a whisper.

"My travels were . . . fruitful. I have news of"—he glanced at the Redcoats working the fire—"our friend."

Abigail squeaked, "What?"

"The British got 'im."

33

Abigail stood at their small window, watching the sun climb above the hills beyond the river, its rays filtered by the pall of gray smoke hanging heavy in the air. At least the fire was out. This morning, the breeze blew the stench of burned wood and ash into the second-floor room, a reminder of yesterday's horrors.

Last night they had stayed—she and Father, Molly and Jamie, Dorothy and her daughter, Rufus, and even Robert Townsend—on the edge of the crowd, watching in helpless dread. The conflagration spread from house to house, structure to structure, a raging monster on a rampage. Nothing could stop it.

The soldiers battled for hours, but their efforts made little difference. Each time the crew seemed to make a dent, the wind would pick up flaming debris and deposit it on a new building. It looked like the beast was playing with mere mortals. Twice the regiment moved and set up lines anew, to no avail. Eventually, exhausted, they gave up and joined the crowd to witness the flaming monster devour the city.

Abigail remembered standing there, mesmerized, as the steeple of Trinity Church—the tallest structure in New York—became a huge flaming pyramid and collapsed.

Then, just when it looked like the entire city would be engulfed, the wind died to a whisper. Without the gusts, the beast lost its breath, consumed the buildings still ablaze, and burnt itself out.

The waiting had been interminable. She wanted to pull Jamie aside, to demand everything he'd learned about Nathan. But they couldn't chance it. With so many people packed together, the risk of being overheard by a Tory or a Redcoat was too great. So they waited.

Thankfully, the fire spread toward the Battery, leaving their simple neighborhood unscathed. She and Father dragged themselves home after dark, inviting Molly and Jamie since they had nowhere to go. Once in the flat, the four shared what little bread remained and surrendered to slumber.

First up, Abigail checked on Father, still asleep on the cot. On the floor, the young couple huddled together under one cover. Then Abigail looked again. The thin blanket showed the outline of only one figure.

Molly stirred and turned her face toward the window. "Jamie's gone out. Tryin' to find a new place for us. He's checkin' with his friends. Said he'd be back—"

She was stopped by an angry exchange from downstairs. A man's voice was arguing with a younger, higher-pitched one. Through the floor, the words were hard to make out, but the intent was clear. The older voice wanted something, and the younger one was trying to stop him. A shuffle, a door slam. Abigail glanced at Molly, who shrugged.

Their door opened, and Jamie slid through, carrying a wrapped bundle. "I know ya shared all ya had last night, so I got us some bread and jerky."

Abigail said, "Thanks." She pulled a knife and metal plate from a box, cutting the loaf.

Molly sat up, folding the cover. "Did ya have any trouble?" Before Jamie could answer, she added, "What was all that uproar downstairs?"

Father asked, "Something about a new law?"

Abigail hadn't noticed Father wake. He had put on his spectacles and sat up on his cot.

Jamie said, "There's a sentry downstairs. A British regular, pimple-faced kid with a musket. Thinks he's some general. He's inspectin' everyone who comes and goes. Said he's quartered here now. As of this morning."

"Quartered here? Why?" Father asked, wary.

Jamie shrugged. "From what I overheard, there's too many British soldiers and not enough places to put them, 'specially after the fire. So they're quartering men in houses still standing. And the locals are required to house and feed them. Damn Redcoats are inspectin' packages too."

Abigail thought, first the British take the city, now they invade homes. This was not the England they'd left.

Molly said, "I didn't hear ya arguin' with any Redcoat."

"Let's just say some of us know how to avoid pryin' eyes." Jamie grinned. "I wasn't running the chance he'd confiscate my package."

"What's it like out there?" Father asked.

"Bloomin' lobsters everywhere," Jamie answered. "And they's mad as hornets. Overheard a few blamin' the rebels fer the fire. Said they wanted to burn the city down since the British took it."

"They're spreading lies," Abigail said, "to cover up what really started it."

"What?" Jamie and Molly asked in unison.

"They burned a couple alive in their house yesterday," Abigail spat. "An execution. Just down the road from where the fire started. That's how this whole inferno started."

Molly's pretty face went white. "What execution?" Jamie asked.

Abigail caught the look in Father's eyes, so she kept her explanation brief.

For a while, no one spoke. Then another muffled argument from downstairs broke the spell—this time a woman and the high-pitched Redcoat. Sharp words, a scream, then silence.

Abigail decided she couldn't wait any longer. "Do you know what happened with Nathan? The details?"

Jamie gave a slight nod and hung his head. "Yep . . . well. Most of 'em." He paused. "Slide—he's a friend I asked to keep an eye out—he hangs out at the Ox and Ass, over by Trinity Church." Jamie glanced out the window. "Criminy, that place is prob'ly gone now too."

Abigail reined in her exasperation. "What happened?"

Jamie brought his gaze back to Abigail. "Slide heard about a man asking about British troops and thought it might be Nathan. So he went over there."

Abigail fought to keep the anger from her voice. "Why didn't he warn him? I thought that's what your friends were supposed to do."

Jamie nodded hard. "He was goin' to. But he got there too late. According to Slide, some Redcoat turd pretended to be a rebel sympathizer with information. When Nathan arrived, a couple of lobsters came outta the back room and grabbed 'im." He shook his head, face a mask of failure. "I'm sorry. I tried."

Abigail stepped over and placed a hand on his arm. "I know you did. And I'm grateful." She fought the tears threatening to fall. "What will happen now?"

Father's low voice answered, "They'll hang him. For treason."

Abigail lost the fight. Tears rolled down her cheeks. The ugly images of the hangings she'd already witnessed flashed in her mind—the young lad accused of rape, the Life Guard, Hickey. Then she thought of Nathan—gentle, considerate Nathan—at the end of a rope. The sobs came harder.

For a while, the only sound was Abigail's quiet weeping. When she managed to stop, sniffling back the last of the tears, she said, "I want to be there."

Father came to her, placing a strong arm around her shoulders. "No, Abigail. You shouldn't. You don't need to watch that."

Jamie said, “It’ll be dangerous. I expect they’ll hang him at British headquarters.”

Their exchange was interrupted by another argument from the first floor. Raising her gaze, Abigail stared at the others. “I don’t care if it is dangerous. I don’t want Nathan to die alone.”

Jamie and Father exchanged looks. Finally, Father shrugged, and Jamie said, “I’ll see what I can do.”

34

"It ain't great, but it's the best I can do," Jamie said as they turned the corner down the alleyway. "Them Redcoats are perty particular about who they let into their camps." He eyed Abigail, gaze stopping on her nearly exposed breasts. Then he deliberately looked away as they walked. "At least, the way ya look, the lobsters won't have no suspicions."

Abigail felt her face redden. She had to tug on the front of the dress to keep her breasts from popping out. Not an easy task. She almost tripped over a rock but caught herself. She was anxious, embarrassed. How did Molly manage this?

Her young friend had lent her the green frock with the white lace trim. Jamie had found a way to get inside the British camp, but it required scheming. Nathan's sentence was set for the next morning. After finding out where Nathan was held, Jamie greased a palm, claiming he had a beauty who'd be a great poll to "ease the soldiers' burdens." Abigail agreed she needed to look the part, and Molly had been quick to offer the revealing dress.

Jamie turned another corner and stopped. Twenty feet ahead, two British soldiers flanked the entrance. The rising sun at their backs, both men stood erect, red coats buttoned tight, rifles resting on the ground. The man on the right was older, gray whiskers peppering his chin, and the one on the left looked no older than sixteen, face erupting with pimples, eyes bloodshot.

"Halt! What business do you have here?" the older soldier called.

Stepping up to the sentries, Jamie pulled Abigail next to him, a bit roughly. "I's supposed to deliver this here for Sergeant Dickson."

He reached across and pulled Abigail's breasts further out of the bodice. The eyes of both sentries went right where Jamie wanted them. The man on the right leaned his rifle against his side and reached for her.

Jamie slapped the soldier's arm. "Sergeant Dickson wouldn't like that." The sentry pulled back in a huff.

Jamie grinned. "Nice, ain't she? I promised I'd git her to Dickson, and that's what I aim to do."

The older man took a step toward Abigail. "I'll deliver her to him."

Jamie blocked his path. "I ain't doin' this fer free. Now, if ya want to pay me . . ."

The sentry glanced at his partner, whose gaze stayed riveted on Abigail, then relented. He pointed to his left. "You'll probably find Sergeant Dickson in the kitchen."

Jamie nodded. "Thank ya kindly."

He escorted Abigail into the camp. As soon as they were out of view, Abigail worked to stuff herself back into the dress. The ruse was necessary, but the lechery made her feel dirty. She had insisted on being here, but now that she was here, her stomach knotted.

Jamie handed her a tan cloak. She slipped it over the dress and pulled the hood up. As the two made their way across the camp, she swept her glance around the compound, examining the faces of every Redcoat she could see. Rows of tents dotted the grass, more than thirty of them. At the north end stood a two-story house, commandeered by officers. In the yard on the left, she saw it—a wooden platform with a plank attached to two vertical boards. A rope and noose dangled from the center.

She stopped and gaped.

Jamie yanked her arm, pulling her past the kitchen tent and several canvas shelters. They stopped behind the third tent in the last row.

"I think we'll be fine here," he whispered.

Their entrance had gone unnoticed. Soldiers crisscrossed the space, carrying food or filling canteens. At one end, two men used both hands to cradle the black iron balls and waddled from the end of the wagon to the next pile, before lowering it on top of the others. Beside small fires, soldiers huddled, waistcoats open.

She and Jamie weren't the only civilians. Men and women carried wood or crates in and out of the larger tents. She watched a young girl climb down the steps from the house, closing her dress as a guard leered. Hopefully, she and Jamie looked like just two more camp followers.

Abigail stared at the empty gallows. Did she really want to do this? Watching the last two hangings had made her stomach crawl. But she owed Nathan this. Perhaps he would recognize her and know she was there.

It was all so senseless. Senseless the British would not treat the colonists as if they were . . . British, which they were. Senseless that the king sent these lads to kill their fellow Britons. Senseless that Nathan had to spy, and senseless that he had been caught.

"Good morning, Miss Abigail," called a quiet voice behind her.

She jumped.

35

She and Jamie jerked backward. Abigail peered over Jamie's shoulder, then relaxed. A tall civilian in a brown waistcoat stood there, a sad smile on his face.

"Robert?" she asked.

Jamie's glance lurched from Abigail to the intruder. "Ya know this guy?"

Abigail said, "Jamie, you remember Robert Townsend, from the fire?"

Robert offered his hand. "You probably don't recognize me without the soot."

Jamie shook it. "Molly told me 'bout that."

"Robert, what are you doing here?"

He shrugged. "Same as you, I suspect. I heard about Nathan's sentence. Had to see for myself."

Jamie said, "This is a little late to ask but I thought British law required a trial."

Robert shook his head. "It seems our king has decided we colonials don't deserve such rights. They claim they can simply hang him as a spy."

Movement at the north end of the camp halted their conversation. An officer came down the steps of the house. Older, clean-shaven, wearing a long red greatcoat fringed in dark blue, the officer adjusted his tricorn hat. His gaze swept the camp. On reflex, Abigail shrank back, as did Nathan and Robert.

Standing there, cringing behind a tent, helplessness swept over her again. Back on Long Island, her efforts were useless against the rapist. At the execution of the couple, she was powerless. Now Nathan was going to be hanged, and she was simply going to watch.

"Bring out the prisoner," the officer demanded.

Everyone in the camp stopped what they were doing and stared. The soldiers stood and faced the gallows. The boys with the cannonballs froze. Silence fell.

The sentry by the greenhouse stepped through a small door and reemerged with a tall, blond man. Oh God, Nathan. Hands bound, he walked erect and unbowed. He didn't look beaten. His face was unbloodied, clothes intact. Even from the distance, she could make out the scar on his face. He stopped in front of the officer. Nathan's gaze moved across the camp, stopping on her side.

Very deliberately, Abigail slid off the hood of the cloak and shook out her hair. She stared and thought she saw recognition dawn in Nathan's eyes. And concern.

"Does the convicted have any last request?" the officer announced in a formal manner.

Nathan's voice was quiet but carried over the hushed camp. "If I'm going to meet my Maker, could I have a few minutes with a minister first?"

Abigail hoped this might give him precious minutes, perhaps enough for a miracle.

The officer's response was quick. "Spies are not entitled to last rites." He cleared his throat, but his next words came out phlegmy anyway. "Escort the prisoner to the gallows."

The guard poked Nathan, and he stepped up onto the platform. The guard set his rifle down and placed the noose over his neck, cinching the knot tight. Abigail closed her eyes and swallowed hard.

Remembering she asked to be here, she opened them. Oh, kind, considerate man. She bit her lip.

The officer marched to the platform. "Nathan Hale, you have been convicted of high treason and spying against His Majesty and sentenced to death. Do you have any final words?"

Nathan looked out at the crowd, his glance sweeping slowly and stopping where Abigail, Jamie, and Robert stood. His eyes were bright, his stature proud. When he spoke, his voice boomed. "I regret that I have but one life to lose for my country."

So like Nathan. Patriot to the end. But damn, this was no academic exercise.

The officer nodded. The guard pulled the plank. Nathan dropped. Abigail heard the sick tug of the rope and the choke of breath. She closed her eyes, tears rushing down. From all over the camp, soldiers hollered jeers and catcalls, peppered with nervous laughter. A commotion drew her attention back. A soldier climbed onto the platform, hung something next to Nathan's dangling body, and ran off laughing.

"Take that, Herr General!"

"You're next, you maggoty coward!"

"We got another noose ready for ya!"

Robert whispered, "I think it would be prudent if we made our exit now."

Jamie said, "Agreed. Follow my lead."

Tears blurring her vision, Abigail followed the men. As she turned, she saw what hung next to Nathan—a wooden plank with a crude painting of a soldier and the word "Washington" scrawled above it. She pulled her eyes away.

Jamie paused by the kitchen tent. "Grab one." He pointed to empty food crates sitting in the grass. He hoisted one, and Robert picked up another and handed a smaller one to Abigail. The three walked right between the guards, faces hidden by the containers. As they turned the corner, Abigail shot a glance back and saw a soldier poke Nathan's body with a bayonet. She jerked her head forward, the world blurred with tears.

III

FALL AND WINTER, 1776–77

PARKER

36

Parker Monteith watched a plume of dust rise in the still October air, horse and rider coming down the hill in an easy trot. Lieutenant Colonel Cain slid off his mount and approached. Parker called, "At ease, men."

Cain muttered, "We need to talk."

Parker followed Cain into a nearby tent. He figured it must be important, maybe even battle preparations, as the lieutenant colonel had never ridden down to the company camp. Parker glanced at his uniform, glad he had polished the brass buttons.

"Monteith, I have an assignment for you," Cain began without preamble. The unlit cigar bounced in his mouth. "I want you to take a detachment to the Commons, over by St. Paul's Chapel. You know where that is?"

Parker nodded. The Commons was where locals gathered for relaxation and sometimes demonstrations. He had taken Louisa and the children on a picnic there, and Henry had played tag with a local boy.

"Yes, sir. I have been there with my family."

Cain looked surprised, then smiled. "Of course. How are Louisa and the children taking to your posting?"

"Quite well, sir. Louisa is redecorating our place on Water Street. You are welcome to come by any time, sir."

"I may just do that, Parker. I suppose you're glad to have your family with you. So you're happy with your posting here?"

"All in all, sir, we are quite well."

"Good. Anyway, Parker, I suppose you've seen that tall monstrosity on the Commons the rebels call the Liberty Pole?"

"Of course, sir."

"Governor Tryon has decided it needs to come down. Says now that we've chased those bastards out, we don't need a symbol of rebellion in the center of the city. I want you to chop the thing down and bring back the wood. We'll use it for firewood."

Parker asked, "How many men do you recommend I take?"

"Hell, I don't know. Take a detachment with a wagon."

"Do you anticipate any resistance, sir?"

"I don't think the locals are going to throw you a welcome party." He gestured with the cigar. "Maybe take the whole company. Show of force."

"When would you like this done, sir?"

"Today. The governor is hot on this." He started through the tent flap and turned back. "And try not to make an international incident out of it."

"I understand, sir."

After Cain rode off, it took Parker the better part of an hour to organize his unit.

"Men, I need to warn you," Parker concluded, pacing in front of his troops. "The task is straightforward—cut the pole down and bring back the wood. But that does not mean it is without peril. We are likely to encounter resistance. Act like British soldiers. Do your job, stand guard, but *do not engage*. Is that clear?"

"Yes, sir!" a hundred soldiers answered.

It took another hour to march his company down Broadway. As they passed the burnt-out skeletons of buildings, Parker felt a bit of pride in their formation. The men didn't break ranks when locals hollered lewd comments or epithets.

When they reached the Commons, he halted them. The Liberty Pole erupted from the center like a giant tree trunk, flags fluttering, a small fence surrounding it.

Residents gathered around the edges of the green, arguing and pointing. Couples stopped to stare. More men and women poured out of taverns on Broadway and Franklin, heading their way. The gossip pipeline in New York was fast.

Studying the crowd—women with babies, hard-looking men, merchants—he saw few friendly faces. The army had seized the city but not the hearts of the locals. The fire had only made it worse. He saw no weapons, but he feared the worst. He knew it took only one incident to spark a riot, like the one in Boston years ago. It would have been far better, and safer, to complete this assignment in the dark of night, but he had not been given that option. Governor Tryon no doubt wanted to make a bold political statement. He wanted the pole destroyed in front of these very locals and damn the consequences.

The crowd swelled, numbers now greater than his complement of soldiers. Major Parker Monteith was glad to have his full company. He feared he might need them.

37

"Attention, men," Parker called. "I want every man *not* assigned to the cutting crew to fan out. Form a circle around the perimeter. Face the locals, guns at rest. Remember your training. No matter what they do or say, *do not engage*."

"Yes, sir!"

Parker searched the front row. "Sergeant Davis, you take your detachment and the wagon and head to the pole. Everyone else to your positions."

He watched as the soldiers fanned out, forming a ring of red coats. He scanned the crowd and saw anxiety and anger, but no movement yet.

Perhaps this assignment would not end in disaster.

Then, a commotion. Four locals burst from the onlookers and sprinted toward the Liberty Pole. Two men and two teens sat on the ground, locking hands around the fence, creating a human chain.

They began shouting, "Give me liberty or give me death!" Soon, the crowd picked up the chant.

Sergeant Davis led his detachment and the wagon to the pole. He strode back to Parker, balancing a long axe on his shoulder.

"Major, what are your orders here?" Davis stroked his unruly black beard.

Parker studied the scene. "Have the men back away a few paces. Remind them *not* to engage."

"We're jus' gonna let them sit there?"

"For the moment." Parker touched the axe blade. "Then I want you to approach the pole, step over that fence, and start chopping. Once you begin, stay at it."

"What if they try to stop me?"

Parker shook his head. "You're bigger than any of them. But swing that axe high. Don't come close to their heads. Understand?"

"Yessir."

Anxious murmurs rippled through the spectators. Davis returned to the pole and stepped over the barrier, pulled the axe off his shoulder, and waited. Then, with one quick motion, he swung. A mighty crack echoed through the Commons.

Snap.

The crowd quieted, then erupted.

"Hey, leave our Liberty Pole alone!"

"You red-bellied cowards! Ain't you Redcoats learned yet? You cut it down afore and another magically grows in its place."

A tomato struck the pole, splattering pulp on Davis's arm. He wiped it off and glanced at Parker.

Parker moved closer to Davis's group and yelled, "We do not have any complaint with any of you. Our orders are to take down this pole. We do not want any trouble. When this is done, we will return to camp, and you can all go home."

The taunts stopped, at least for now. Parker nodded to Davis.

Davis chopped furiously, powerful arms swinging in arcs. From where he stood, Parker could see the blond wood inside the gash. The four locals leaned their heads together, then backed away, scuttling until they were clear. They ran back to the line of onlookers.

Smack. Smack. Smack.

Perhaps Parker's ploy might work.

Crack. Crack. The sounds of the chopping carried across the Commons, the more subdued crowd doing little more than angry grumbling.

Raised voices pierced the calm. Parker turned. At the other end of the Commons, a local was yelling. To his horror, Parker saw one of his soldiers advancing, bayonet outstretched. Parker took off running. He kept his eyes on the confrontation and halfway there saw the orange scarf around the soldier's neck.

Reeves. Oh God.

38

"Soldier, lower that rifle!" Parker yelled.

He raced across the grass, sword flapping, slipping slightly before stopping on top of the two men. Reeves pointed his rifle at a local. Parker laid a hand on the barrel, the metal cool.

"Reeves, at ease," he spat between breaths.

Reeves did not flinch.

Parker needed to do something. He studied the face of the rebellious soldier. Reeves's eyes narrowed above that rat nose. A scowl slashed across his lips. The scars on the right and left sides of his face looked inflamed, scarlet. Whitened knuckles gripped the rifle.

Reeves growled, "Mebbe I jus' run you through."

"At. Ease. Soldier," Parker barked. Reeves glanced at Parker briefly, then returned his gaze to the civilian.

The bayonet tip was inches from the man's forehead. The civilian, young with reddish-brown hair, stood stiff, refusing to budge. Parker realized he knew him.

"Robert Townsend, right?" Parker asked. "Sir, you own that dry goods store on Broadway?"

Townsend averted his gaze from the bayonet, though he did not back down. "Yes, Major, I remember you."

Then Parker recognized the woman standing next to Townsend. Abigail Trench, face white, clutching Townsend's sleeve. She focused her stare on Reeves, eyes huge with panic.

"Miss . . . Abigail, surprising to meet you here," Parker managed.

Abigail's gaze shifted to Parker. "Major," she started. "Not as surprised as we were to see your men."

"Miss Abigail, would you tell me what is going on here?"

She took a breath. "Robert and I were enjoying quiet time when your company arrived. Your . . . soldier here ran up and started yelling for us to move. I guess I didn't move fast enough, so he poked me with his bayonet." Her lips trembled.

Abigail looked like she was trying to be brave and failing. This was nothing like the calm woman who handled his demanding children.

"Robert was kind enough to step in," she continued, eyes narrowing on Reeves. "Then *he* came at Robert. Stuck his bayonet in Robert's face."

Parker asked, "Private Reeves, what do you have to say for—"

A giant boom echoed through the park. Abigail squealed.

Parker knew what had happened. It was only a matter of time. Davis had cut through the tall pole and it collapsed, making the ground shudder. Parker whipped around, using the distraction to knock Reeves's rifle to the ground. In one motion, he snatched the gun.

Reeves whipped back, face beet red, scars pulsing.

Parker barked, "Private, not one word." He set the rifle at rest. "I will hold onto this. Head over to Davis's group and help load the wood."

Reeves stood stiff, fists clenched. Finally, he muttered, "Yes . . . sir," venom in the words. He stomped away.

Satisfied the man was no longer a threat, Parker turned to Townsend and Abigail. "Private Reeves was totally out of line. I sincerely apologize. I promise he will cause you no further trouble."

Townsend wiped sweat from his forehead. "We're fine now."

But Miss Abigail did not look fine. Her eyes looked hard with anger . . . or fear. Her body stood rigid.

Parker tried one more approach. "I am aware of the residents' affinity for that post. If it were my choice, I would have left it standing. We are merely following orders."

Townsend said only, "I understand the importance of following orders."

In truth, Parker really did not understand the locals' attachment to the tall piece of wood. Liberty Pole, indeed. The colonial militia had been routed over a month ago, abandoning the city. All but Fort Washington on the north end and, from what Cain had shared, the rebels would not control that point for long.

He studied Townsend and Miss Abigail. With one more nod, the young man turned and gently laid a hand on Abigail's arm. At first, she did not seem to notice, her attention still riveted on Reeves's lanky figure making his way to the felled post.

"Abigail?" Townsend said quietly and that seemed to break the spell.

She glanced up, eyes still hard. She let him turn her away from the departing soldier.

Reeves had been a problem since he joined the company. God, what would Parker have told his children if Reeves had shot Robert Townsend or Miss Abigail?

ABIGAIL

39

The same damn British soldier. Not only in New York, but in her face. Abigail couldn't believe it. She couldn't stop shaking. This time, he nearly ran Robert through. She couldn't get the image of the razor edge of the bayonet out of her head. She'd seen it before, up close.

As soon as Major Monteith headed back to his men, Robert escorted her to a tavern. A banged-up cup of rum sat on the scarred table, untouched. She hadn't uttered a word. Inside her, fury battled fear, and she wasn't sure what would come out of her mouth.

Robert had been kind. As they left the Commons, he greeted people calmly, keeping one hand firmly on her arm. It had been a comfort.

Now, sitting at the table, Robert slid his hand to her arm again. She stared into his somber brown eyes and heaved. The tears burst out, coming in torrents down her cheeks. She shook and sobbed.

Robert wrapped an arm around her. "It's over now. If you need to cry, go right ahead."

She buried her face in his shoulder, tears wetting his waistcoat. It took several minutes to halt the sobbing. Sniffling, she noticed few patrons—only two men across the room.

Robert asked quietly, "Are you going to be all right?"

Was she? How much could she tell him?

She used the sleeve of her dress to wipe her nose. She stared into his eyes, noticing the brown iris in his right one had a streak of gold down the center. Had it always looked that way and she hadn't noticed? In the weeks since Nathan's execution, Robert had been exceptionally kind. He knew she and Nathan had been close, and he simply wanted to be there to support her, if she needed it. Last week, they had taken an evening stroll. When they walked through the quiet city street, neither spoke at first, the only sounds their footfalls on the wooden walkways and the murmur of voices inside a tavern they passed.

While on the walk, he'd asked, "You mentioned you were a teacher in London. How did you get to New York?"

Abigail had told him her tale, from England to Long Island to New York, though in abbreviated fashion and without all the sordid details.

"What about you?" she'd asked.

Robert had drawn figures in the dirt with a stick. "Grew up in Oyster Bay. Father was an active politician and a Quaker. Mum was Episcopalian. Father got me an apprenticeship at Templeton and Stewart. Dry goods store on Broadway near the Holy Ground."

"I've been past the Holy Ground."

Robert's face had reddened. "It's not like that. Broadway gets a lot of traffic, you know, because of—Anyway, I run things now."

Abigail smiled. "I'll have to come by and check out your store."

"I'd like that."

She appreciated Robert's calm presence. He was different from Nathan—more reserved, harder to read—but a good listener. Nathan's death formed a bond between them.

He broke the silence now. "I didn't know you knew Major Monteith."

"I teach his two children."

"That explains it. I know what happened today shook you up. That ugly Redcoat was menacing, but I didn't think he would try something right there."

Abigail said, "With that bastard, I wouldn't be so sure."

Robert's eyebrows went up. "Do you know that soldier?"

She gulped. This was it. Abigail stared at the dented mug. Bruised and dented—just like her. She took a long drink. But still serviceable. She set the mug down, wiped her lips, and stared at Robert.

"I've run into him before . . . on Long Island."

"He was one of the soldiers at the farms?"

She nodded. "He was the one . . . who came to our place." Tears forced their way out.

"After all this time, you're certain?"

She gazed into his eyes. "Hell yes. And he had that putrid orange scarf. You saw it."

Robert nodded. "Maybe it's a symbol of something."

She sniffed, voice quivering. "Did you see the scars on his face?"

"Made him bloody ugly."

"I gave him the one on the right."

Robert met her stare and didn't speak for a while, realization dawning on him, she guessed. He wrapped his fingers around her hand. "I'm so sorry, Abigail."

Hearing him speak those words in his calm, considerate voice helped, but it also started her quivering inside.

Robert took a drink, giving her time. He set down the mug and reached his arm around her. She tried to keep still but felt her body trembling.

In a voice so soft she barely heard, he whispered, "If you want to tell me, I'm here. If it's too painful, I understand."

She started, voice cracking. "Father tried to reason with him. Said, 'We're all Englishmen here, son.' Reeves snarled, 'I ain't your son, old man, and this ain't England. I can take whatever I want.' He hit Father with the butt of his rifle."

She stopped, looking into Robert's face. He held her gaze. She shook her head and tried to say the next part but found her throat so dry she couldn't get the words out. Pulling her hand from his grasp, she picked up the mug and drank again, another long, slow swallow, letting the rum slide down her throat. She set down her drink and tried again, peering into the mug and seeing the ripples of the crooked metal.

"I followed him into the barn. I tried to *plead* with him." She let out a sarcastic laugh. "A lot of good that did. He grabbed me and threw me down." Tears returned. "When I didn't cooperate . . ." She shook her head.

She wiped her eyes. "I snarled at him. He slapped me hard. He stood over me . . . grabbed the bayonet. Put the blade right next to my throat."

She turned her face away. Her shoulders shook. Her chest felt so tight she could barely breathe. Gently, Robert pulled her into him. For several minutes, neither moved.

"I'm going to kill that lobster bastard," he muttered. "Don't know how, but I'll find a way."

40

She certainly hadn't planned to tell Robert everything that had happened on Long Island. It had simply spilled out, no doubt because seeing that ugly, scarred face again had terrified her. She couldn't help herself. Then, after she confided in Robert, she dreaded his reaction. Would he see her as damaged goods? But when she finished and was able to stop her weeping, all she saw in his features was kindness and compassion. Abigail felt as if a weight had been lifted.

She appreciated Robert's chivalry and his willingness to shield her, and she envied his resolve to do something—or at least his belief that he could. Now she had a name—Reeves. And he was in Major Monteith's company. Maybe she could ask the major to make Reeves keep his distance. But what excuse could she give? She certainly wasn't about to tell him the whole story.

Between the tears, the fears, and the fury, her insides roiled through the rest of the day and into the next.

Abigail knocked on the black door of the large mansion and waited. After everything that had happened yesterday, she'd almost canceled. She figured the major would've told Louisa, and they'd probably understand. But Abigail thought it best to stay busy, and Elizabeth and Henry would demand so much attention she'd have little left for anything else. Not to mention, they needed the money.

After the Negro servant Ruth opened the door, Louisa Monteith met Abigail in the foyer. "Miss Abigail, we're so glad you were able to make it." She glanced toward the parlor, where the major sat with another officer, and turned back to Abigail. "Parker told me about the incident, uh . . . with one of his soldiers. I'm so sorry that happened." She looked once more toward her husband, who gave a slight wave. "Anyway, Parker asked if he could have a word with you after you finish with the children's lessons."

Before Abigail could answer, Louisa rolled her eyes and whispered, "He had planned to talk with you first, but then Lieutenant Colonel Cain came over and said he needed to meet with Parker."

Abigail's gaze traveled into the parlor and took in the other officer. Thank God it was not the portly one who'd ordered the burning of the couple. This man was taller and wirier, with a head of red hair going gray. He laughed, a cigar bobbing in his mouth, and smiled at Abigail. She nodded.

To Louisa she said, "Of course. I'll go see him after I've finished their lessons."

Louisa patted her arm. "That would be fine." She raised her voice toward the stairs. "Elizabeth and Henry, Miss Abigail is here!"

The two children raced each other down the steps, pounding along until they skidded to a stop in front of their mother.

Louisa said, "No need to run, dears."

Henry looked up at Abigail. "You said we could do our lesson by the creek today if the weather was fair." He pointed to the sunshine pouring through the tall windows. "Well?"

Abigail had forgotten her promise. Friday seemed like forever ago. She stared at their eager faces. An outdoor lesson would be even more demanding than sitting at the table with books and pencils, but she put on her teacher's smile. "All right. Let me set my things down in the library and we can head out."

Two hours later, teacher and students came in through the kitchen door, the children's voices exultant. It had worked. The children's eager curiosity about frogs and fish had lifted Abigail's spirits. Helping them learn and seeing the excitement in their faces was a tonic.

Stomping together on the wooden floor, they tried to shake off the mud and dirt from their shoes. Abigail shooed them upstairs and glanced at her own dress. Some dirt here and there, but not too bad for a conversation with the major.

She did not know exactly what Major Monteith wanted to tell her, but she suspected it had to do with yesterday's encounter. She had no desire to relive the whole thing.

"Miss Abigail. Good, you are back," the major called. "When you can, could you see me in the parlor?"

"I just need to wash up a bit and I'll be right there," she answered.

Five minutes later, she stood in the doorway to the parlor, feeling oddly like a schoolgirl summoned by the headmaster. The major sat at the desk at the far end, concentrating intently on whatever he was writing. After a moment she said, "Major?"

Parker Monteith looked up and saw her. Setting down his quill, he crossed the room. "Thank you for coming. Henry and Elizabeth surely sounded happy, coming in from their lessons. Louisa tells me you work magic with my children, and I tend to believe her."

Abigail shrugged. "I enjoy working with both Henry and Elizabeth. They can be a little strong-willed, but they have great curiosity. I can work with that."

"I can see that." The major nodded toward the yellow upholstered love seat. "You may sit if you wish."

Abigail indicated a few stains on the front of her dress. "I can't see the back, but I suspect it might look even worse. I don't want to soil your fine furniture. I'll stand."

Major Monteith hesitated, as if unsure how to respond. "Very well." He remained standing and cleared his throat. "Miss Abigail, I simply wanted to apologize again for the behavior of my man."

"Thank you, sir, for stepping in when you did. I fear what might've happened if you hadn't arrived in time."

"You are quite welcome. There is no excuse for Private Reeves's actions, and he has been dealt with. He's been in my company only a few months, and this is *not* his first infraction."

"Thank you for sharing that, sir."

"Miss Abigail, I do not wish to pry, but I noticed you looked extremely distressed yesterday."

"Well, sir, your soldier threatened us, and I thought he was about to stab my companion."

"Even after I disarmed Reeves, you still looked troubled." The major cleared his throat again and shifted his weight. "What I mean to ask is, did something more take place? Before I arrived?"

Abigail stared at him and worked to keep her voice even. "I told you yesterday what happened. Reeves accosted me, then Robert, and threatened to kill him."

The major nodded slowly. "Yes, that was bad enough. But I know Reeves. I would not be surprised if there were more trouble." When she didn't respond, he continued, "Have you or Robert encountered Private Reeves before?"

Abigail felt tears welling and forced them back. "Unfortunately, yes, sir. Last spring Private Reeves came to our farm on Long Island. He made off with all our livestock and ransacked our pantry. Said he needed them for the army. When we tried to stop him, he assaulted my father and me."

For a moment Major Monteith was speechless. He stared at Abigail, his dark green eyes blinking, then looked down. At last he said, "I am so sorry, Miss Abigail. Last spring Reeves was not under my command, but I have no trouble believing you." He shook his head. "I had heard some divisions in the country were raiding farms, but I will have you know my company had no part in it. Besides, knowing Reeves, I am not sure how much of what he stole ever made it back to the army."

"I'm not sure I care. Reeves wiped out our farm, and we were forced to move to New York."

Parker Monteith looked embarrassed and uncomfortable. When she said no more, he shook his head. "Private Reeves is a poor example of the British army. All I can do at this point is apologize. If there is anything I can do for you, please let me know."

Abigail thought of telling him Reeves was hardly alone. She had heard plenty of tales about other Redcoats crossing the line, plundering and raping here in New York. And she and the major had witnessed the inhuman torture of that couple. Instead she said, "If you can, I'd simply ask you to keep Private Reeves away from me."

The major took a step toward her and nodded. "I will do what I can. As much as I would like to, I can make no promises. It is war."

"So you have said, Major. I don't believe war is any excuse for atrocities by Reeves and men like him. Good day, sir." Abigail turned and headed out the front door.

41

"Don't you think you've done enough today?" Father frowned at Abigail. "After that scary encounter with that hideous soldier on the Commons yesterday, and then working all day with the Monteith children, why don't you stay home tonight? I'd love the company. Molly would understand."

Yesterday, when she'd come through the door in rough shape, Abigail had told Father about the Redcoats invading the Commons and chopping down the Liberty Pole. When he pressed, she shared the confrontation with Reeves and Robert stepping between her and the vicious Redcoat. She also told how Major Monteith had intervened and defused the situation. But she hadn't told Father about breaking down in front of Robert and, of course, she said nothing about the rape months earlier.

Abigail mustered a brave smile. "I'm well, Father, I really am." She wrapped her fingers around his hand. His skin felt rough and his fingers gnarled. "Working with Henry and Elizabeth today helped. Seeing their faces light up learning about fish hibernating in winter banished all my other cares. I think tutoring Molly tonight will do me good the same way. Besides, she's doing so well. Did I tell you she's reading sentences now? And she's learned her sums up to eighteen."

Father's frown eased into a reluctant grin. "You were certainly made to teach. You have the gift." Undoing her fingers, he wrapped his hand around hers. “I know it’s not far, but I want you to be careful. It’s already dark out there.” He glanced toward the small window.

“I promise I will. But I’m not about to let some stupid Redcoats keep me from helping Molly.”

Her own words surprised her. When she’d come across the ocean, she had thought of herself as an Englishwoman, but events in this country had pushed her farther from that belief than she would’ve thought possible. The confrontation with Reeves had flipped a switch in her. Since that dark afternoon on Long Island, she realized, she had been running away, trying to avoid more trouble—for herself and Father. She was tired of running. And the clash yesterday had shown her that running was futile anyway. It had made clear who the real enemy was.

Father gave her a hug and held on, perhaps a little longer than usual. She kissed his forehead, grabbed her schoolbag, and gave him one more look before heading out. She pounded down the stairs. As her foot hit the final step and she reached for the outside door, a hand clamped around her arm.

“Hold up there,” a male voice squeaked. “Where ya headed?”

Abigail stared at the red sleeve gripping her. Slowly she let her gaze travel up to a youthful face dotted with angry pimples. Tufts of matted brown hair jutted out beneath the brim of a black tricorn hat. The young soldier scowled, wrinkling his upper lip beneath a few scraggly tan bristles.

After all she’d been through in the past few days, she was not about to let this boy playing soldier intimidate her. She was through being pushed around.

“Private, I understand the Quartering Act gives you the right to be housed here. But you have no right to detain me or anyone else.”

The soldier’s eyes flashed and his mouth hung open, as if he did not know how to respond. Abigail knew she was hardly the first to quarrel with him. In the last few days she’d overheard several arguments between other boarders and the quartered soldier. Perhaps no other women had dared to challenge him.

"Kindly release my arm." She stared at his hand.

The youth only managed to stammer, "I-I-I've been told to search everyone comin' and goin'." He tried to put some bravado in his voice, but Abigail saw the panic in his eyes. "There are traitorous rebel spies afoot and we've been ordered to inspect all packages." He pointed a shaky finger at her worn schoolbag dangling from her left arm.

She felt the bag ripped from her grasp.

"Hey!" she cried, reaching to snatch it back.

Setting his rifle in the corner, the soldier turned away from her and began pawing through the contents. Pulling out the *New England Primer,* he swiveled back and thrust the book at her. "What's this?"

"It is what it says it is." She pointed to the words printed across the leather cover. She glanced at the young man, expecting suspicion. Instead, she saw only confusion. When he didn't respond, she added, "It's the *New England Primer.*" Her finger traced the raised letters.

He stared at the book in his hand and then back at her. He opened it and flipped through a few pages, but no recognition dawned. Abigail studied him. Looking from his face to the book and back, she understood. She had seen the same look of incomprehension on Molly's face when she first put the book in the girl's hands.

This Redcoat—this young soldier—could not read.

Of course, it was not uncommon. Many young people in Britain, both in and out of the military, could not read or write. They had little time for school and had to work to support their families. From her work at the charity school in London, she knew many boys had never attended school at all. But leave it to the British army to post an illiterate soldier to stand guard, searching for clandestine messages. He'd have no idea whether he was looking at notes about military formations or a recipe for plum pudding.

Her thoughts were interrupted. "Ha! What's this?" he cried. His hand still trembled, but it held a sheet of paper with a handwritten note. "I found this hidden in the back of the book." His tone was triumphant as he waved the page.

This time she snatched it from his fingers before he could react. "It wasn't hidden. That's simply where I keep it. How about I read it to you?"

His face turned an even deeper red. He opened his mouth, but no sound came out.

She read only the last line aloud: "'This woman, Miss Abigail Trench, is in my employ and under my protection. If she is stopped for any reason, she is to be allowed to pass to fulfill her duties. Major Parker Monteith, Royal Regiment of Artillery.'" She grinned.

If possible, the young soldier's face grew redder still. With a quick motion, he shoved the primer back at her. She took it, folded the paper into the back cover again, and dropped the book into her bag. His gaze never left her. "Ya know Major Monteith?" he asked.

Schoolbag back on her arm, Abigail straightened. "As a matter of fact, Private, I do. Quite well. I've just spent the day at his house."

The young Redcoat only stared, slack-jawed.

"What is your name, Private?"

The teen gulped. "Private Hutchinson, miss. Private Thomas Hutchinson. I'm sorry to offend you." He glanced around as if searching for eavesdroppers. "Please don't report me to the major."

Abigail studied him a moment longer. "Private Hutchinson, how about I strike a bargain with you?"

"Anything, miss." Now he looked every bit the teenager he was, blue eyes beseeching.

"If you have to be stationed in this house, I want you to show a little dignity and courtesy toward the people here. These are decent people, doing their jobs just like you. Not everyone is a rebel spy."

Private Hutchinson looked pained. "But, miss, I was given orders to search anyone who looked suspicious."

"Private, did you really think I looked suspicious?"

"No'm. I just saw the bag and thought . . ." He trailed off and dropped his head.

"You can still do your job and be civil. People will resent you less and will cooperate more."

"I'll try to remember that, miss." He stepped back, picked up his rifle, and nodded toward the door. "Of course, you can go."

"Thank you, Private."

After she exited the boardinghouse and strolled a little way down the dusty avenue, she turned and looked back toward the entryway. She was proud of herself. Not only had she refused to let that Redcoat push her around—she had pushed back. For once she didn't feel helpless or powerless. The young soldier's reaction to the major's letter had been something. She had received the letter several weeks earlier and had almost forgotten it. She wondered just how far that piece of paper might carry her.

42

"We are lost! Lost, I tell ya!" a voice shouted from outside.

Jamie burst through the door of the Gooseneck Inn, glanced around, and then yanked another fellow hobbling in behind him. Once both were inside, he slammed the heavy wooden door, shutting out the cold November wind. As soon as the other young man entered—wearing what looked like a tattered shirt—he started babbling again. "We are lost. There was too many of 'em. Redcoats everywhere. And the damn Hessians!"

"Get 'im sumpin' to drink," Jamie called.

After the Pelican had burned down, Jamie had found this tavern on Queen Street, and he and Molly had set up shop much as they had at the Pelican, with a small room above—for a piece of Jamie's take. A few days later Levi, the bristly bartender from the Pelican, had arrived and been hired—probably with a little help from Jamie. Since their new quarters had no window and only a few slats for light, there was too little illumination for reading or study, so Abigail tutored Molly downstairs in the tavern. In the two months since, teacher and pupil had settled into a routine, meeting in the late afternoons before most men got off work, when business was light and distractions few. This afternoon they had been alone in the tavern—until Jamie showed up.

Jamie hurried the disoriented man over to the table and sat him next to Abigail. He was no man at all, but a boy with a shock of bright red hair, maybe fifteen or sixteen, about the same age as her brother.

When Abigail looked him over, she saw one pant leg darker than the other and realized it was soaked in blood.

"You're hurt," she said. Leaving her book on the scarred tabletop, she crouched beside the lad. His body trembled as she reached for the leg. "Let me take a look."

"Wait," Jamie said. "Benjamin, drink this first. It'll help." He handed him a dented metal mug.

The boy took it with shaking hands, rum sloshing over the rim. He managed to get it to his mouth and drained it, getting most of it down. Hands still trembling, he set the empty mug on the table. Abigail squatted and took hold of his leg with both hands, examining it. Blood still ran down the torn tan breeches from a hole in the fabric.

"Looks like you've been shot," she said, glancing up into his frightened face.

"I-I-I know," he stammered. "Don't know how bad. I been so scared runnin' and hidin'. I ain't stopped to look."

"We need to get those breeches off so we can see how bad it is," Abigail said. She glanced at Levi. "And I'm going to need some fresh water to clean that wound. Can you get me some?"

The teenaged soldier shot an embarrassed look at her and Molly, and his face turned red.

"Don't worry about it," Abigail said. "I've got a brother about your age and I've seen him naked." She glanced over her shoulder at Molly, who blessed their young visitor with a coquettish smile. "And she's seen men wearing a lot less."

Jamie came to the boy's rescue. "Here, I'll help ya."

Between the two of them, they got the breeches off, though the lad cried out whenever they moved the leg. Molly brought over another stool so he could sit and extend his leg. Levi returned from the well with a basin of water. As Abigail worked on the injury, the soldier told his story in fits and starts.

"I was in the middle of all the fightin'," Benjamin said.

"What fightin'?" Molly asked, standing beside Jamie.

"Didn't ya hear the cannons? Fort Washington, o' course," the young soldier said. "Ow-ow-ow."

Abigail chuckled. "Settle down. That was only water." She knelt over the bared leg and dabbed at the wound. "Looks like the bullet just grazed you. You're lucky."

The boy winced and tried to move his leg, but Abigail held it fast. "Ow, it don't feel lucky." His breathing quickened.

"Benjamin was in 3rd Connecticut," Jamie said. "They were sent to defend Fort Washington."

Pulling a clean cloth from a pocket of her frock, Abigail pressed it against the cut, trying to staunch the bleeding. "I've seen it," she said.

"You have?" Molly and Jamie asked together.

Hand still on the wound, Abigail looked up and nodded. "Nathan and I took a carriage ride up there. One of our excursions around town. It didn't look like much of a fort to me."

"That's what I sez when we marched up there two weeks ago," Benjamin said. "Jus' a bunch o' mounds piled up to form this shape. Don't remember what they called it."

"Pentagon," Abigail said. "Nathan told me." Using her teeth, she tore off two strips of white cloth. "They were supposed to be earthworks that would protect from attacks on all sides." She wrapped each strip around the wounded leg and tied them into firm knots. "There."

"'Sposed to. Didn't work." Benjamin lowered his leg to the floor and gritted his teeth. He tried to stand and stumbled.

"Sit your butt down," Jamie said, "before ya fall down."

Benjamin obeyed and asked, "Could I have some more rum?"

Jamie nodded. Levi went to the bar and returned with the tankard half full, handing it over.

"Tell 'em what happened," Jamie said after the young soldier drank.

Finishing the second mug in a gulp, Benjamin wiped his mouth with a dirty hand. "Like Jamie said, I was with 3rd Connecticut, and we were ordered to guard the south flank of the fort. Other regiments had the east and north sides. Ya know Fort Washington was the last bit o' New York City the army held. Well, we did 'til today." He shook his head. "We had to retreat into the fort and were holed up in there. Them Redcoats poured cannon shot on us for two hours. Hell, they was firin' cannons into the fort from a ship in the harbor. So many cannon balls exploded inside, you was jus' waitin' fer one to get ya. Then them Redcoat rifles started firin'. I heard men all around me cryin' out and screamin'. And there was so much smoke, ya couldn't see much."

He shivered at the memory. "Still, we kept firin'. But there was just too many damn Lobsterbacks. No matter how much we fired, they jus' kept comin'. Must've been three for every one of us. And that ain't countin' the damn Hessians."

Benjamin went quiet and stared down at the mug in his hands. "Then I sees Harry. Ya see, he joined up with me—said he wanted a little excitement. Our enlistments were up next month." He stopped and shook his head. "Well, at least mine is. Harry was firin' next to me and laughin'. He hollered sumpin' about gettin' himself a Lobsterback. It was hard to hear with all the explosions. Then he stopped yappin', jus' like that. When I looked over at him, I see a hole in the middle of his head." He pointed to his forehead and sucked back tears. "Then he collapsed on the ground next to me. Dead jus' like that. I leaned down and yelled, 'Harry.' Next thing I know I feel sumpin' hit my leg and I think I passed out."

No one spoke at first. In a quiet voice, Molly said, "At least ya got out. Ya here now."

Abigail felt tension climb her spine. She was afraid she knew where this was going. "It sounds horrible. Did many get away?"

Benjamin shook his head. "Naw. I think mos' ever'body was killed or captured." His blue eyes widened. "When I came to, I was on the ground and my leg hurt like hell. There was men everywhere lyin' on the ground, either dead or screamin' in pain. I saw this Redcoat general or sumpin' say, 'Check on the wounded. If they're alive, take 'em prisoner. If not, leave 'em.' So when one o' them Lobsters comes up to me, I keep my eyes closed and lay still. This soldier pokes me with his bayonet in the hurt leg. It hurt like hell and I wanted to scream, but I squeezed my eyes shut and forced my lips together. The Redcoat must've thought I was dead 'cause I heard him walk away, poke Harry, and then the next body."

"How'd ya get away, then?" Jamie asked.

Benjamin nodded. "I waited till the Redcoats moved outta the fort. Took a long time. I had to stay there, not movin' the whole time. I heard 'em herdin' everybody left. I dunno. Then I gets up, look around, and see all these dead bodies everywhere—men with arms blown off, one guy with his whole face gone." He shut his eyes hard as if trying to erase the image, then opened them. "Then I sneaked out o' the fort, threw away my blue coat, and hobbled off, hidin' every time I heard someone."

"I saw Benjamin shiverin' in an alley off Brewery and helped him get here," Jamie added.

Abigail listened to the whole tale, dread building in her chest. "Did you say all of our troops were killed or taken prisoner?"

"I can't be sure," Benjamin said, "but I think so. I didn't see anyone left . . . 'cept dead bodies. I think the rest were marched off with the Redcoats."

Abigail started to ask her next question, but her throat closed. She cleared it and tried again. "Do you know which regiments were there, defending the fort? Besides 3rd Connecticut?"

Benjamin cast his gaze down, as if searching his memory. "There was the Maryland and Virginia Riflemen regiment. They were defendin' the north, where the Hessians attacked." He took a breath. "Harry said the ones shootin' next to us were from the Bucks County Militia." His eyes brightened. "Oh, and there were two regiments protectin' the east flank—regiments from Pennsylvania, the 5th and—"

"The 3rd," Abigail whispered.

Molly stared at her. "Isn't that the regiment your brother joined?"

"Yes. Oliver signed up with the 3rd Pennsylvania Regiment."

Molly gasped. "So your brother is either dead or taken prisoner!"

PARKER

43

One arm around his wife, Parker leaned close so she could hear him over the racket of the coach as the wheels bounced across the rutted streets. He had to raise his voice, but he did not worry about being overheard by the footmen. He would be lucky if Louisa could make out half of what he said.

"I really wish we did not have to go to this *party*."

"Not like we had much choice," Louisa said. "What were Cain's words?"

He intoned, "Governor Tryon is celebrating the success of the mighty British army. He expects all His Majesty's fine officers to attend. 'Parker, you are certainly a fine officer.'"

Louisa patted her husband's bright red greatcoat and brushed her fingers along the polished brass buttons. "At least that much is true."

It was a cold January afternoon, a stiff wind whipping from the East River through the tunnels made by the buildings—or what was left of them. They were both dressed for the weather, he in his heavy woolen uniform and Louisa wrapped in a warm shawl. Still, they shivered.

The carriage clattered over the rutted street and the horses whinnied as the footman turned off Water Street onto Bennett. Parker had instructed his servants to steer clear of the wharf, hoping to avoid crowds and, more importantly, trouble. They had never traveled to this mansion called Incleberg, but he understood the trip would not be long, only about four miles. Still, they had to pass through the part of the city still in ruins, devastated by the fire months earlier. As the horses' hoofs struck the frozen, hard-packed earth, his wife stared at the jagged remains of the buildings they passed. He had been through here numerous times with his men but had managed to keep Louisa and the children away from this part of the city—until today.

The structures on both sides of the street had been ravaged by fire, leaving little more than skeletons of charred timbers and scarred boards. Residents had tried to survive by using broken and burnt wood as supports and torn pieces of ships' sails to create lean-tos, part hut and part tent. The bitter winter wind jerked at the soiled cloths as if it meant to rip the fragile shelters apart. Garbage and human excrement lay in heaps beside many of the lean-tos, the rotten odors impossible to ignore even inside the carriage.

The coach made an abrupt stop. When Parker leaned out the open window, he saw two men in ragged clothes staggering across the road, drunk no doubt. The carriage had halted so as not to run them down and now stood in the middle of what was called Canvas-town. The two footmen hurled curses at the drunken men, ordering them to move. The drunks looked back with blank stares.

Pulling himself inside again, Parker offered Louisa a brave smile. He swept his gaze from one side of the road to the other. Men, women, and children stood in small clusters, hunching over weak fires and glaring at his expensive carriage. The locals appeared thin and emaciated, with hollow eyes and pale skin. Their faces were set in angry frowns.

He regretted choosing this route, even though another would have added several uncomfortable miles in the freezing temperatures.

Leaning out his window once more, he checked the front of the coach. The two men were still there, one stumbling and collapsing in front of the horses. Normally, he would have one of his footmen get down and move the man, but he hesitated. Today he might need both men in position to defend the coach.

Parker settled back and shot a quick glance out Louisa's window. He saw only desperate stares. No one looked ready to rush the carriage.

Scanning the knots of people gathered on his side, though, he noticed two blackguards. The toughs looked menacing, scowling at the coach. Both men leered at Parker, mouths full of brown, broken teeth. Their clothes were tattered and torn—dirty brown breeches and ugly stained shirts. Their matching green waistcoats, however, were of better quality, though each had a large rip on one side. Had they robbed others and stolen the coats? He was about to call a warning to his servants when he caught a sudden movement.

The two toughs rushed the carriage. One ran straight at the door, yanking on the handle. Parker reached down to draw his sword, but the hilt snagged in his heavy coat. He let it go, drew back his arm, and shot his fist through the open window. His knuckles smashed into the man's face. The attacker screamed and grabbed his bleeding nose. Losing his grip, the man fell to the ground, groaning.

Shaking his fingers, Parker did a quick check out Louisa's side. No movement. He stuck his head out his own window again and watched the second attacker rush the footman. Then the two drunkards in the middle of the street suddenly straightened up. As one, they lunged for the driver's seat.

"Israel, go, man! Whip the horses!" Parker shouted.

The Black servant flicked the crop, the snap echoing off the dilapidated buildings. The horses jumped and broke into a trot. The coach rocked violently from side to side. For a few seconds, Parker feared it might topple. Then the carriage bounced hard on its wheels and began to roll faster.

Israel shot a desperate glance back. Parker saw the panic in his eyes. "Just keep going!" he yelled. "Get us out of here!"

Turning, the Negro whipped the horses again and they leapt forward, their hoofs pounding on the hard-packed earth. One attacker fell to the ground. Parker watched the horses' strong forelegs stomping dangerously close yet somehow missing the man. Then the carriage wheels bumped over the body and the coach rocked again. The man screamed.

The second blackguard tried to grab onto the driver's seat. Seeing him, Israel turned from the horses long enough to slash at the man three times with the crop. The tough let go, cursing as he tumbled into the road. Seeing what had happened to his fellows, the fourth man gave up, and the coach rattled away, the horses not slowing. When they were clear, Parker heard Israel call to the team and felt the carriage ease into a gentler rock. Satisfied they were out of danger—for now—Parker relaxed in his seat.

As they passed more burned-out buildings, he again scanned both sides of the road but saw no further threats. Turning to Louisa, he saw her flushed face. "Are you all right?"

She gave a slow nod but said nothing.

He worked to keep the anxiety from his voice. "It will be all right now. I believe we are out of danger." He pulled her close and hugged her, feeling her shudder against him.

When he released her, Louisa took out a handkerchief and blotted her forehead. "By George, that was frightening. You assured us it would be safe here. In New York. What is going on?" She pointed back the way they had come. "Who were those attackers? Rebels?"

"I think not. I am not sure there are that many rebels left in the city." Parker shook his head. "Those were just desperate, angry people—many of them loyalists. Or they used to be."

"Didn't you tell me the army promised to rebuild all this? After the fire?" She pointed out the window as they rolled past more hollowed-out structures, knots of desperate people huddling over pitifully small fires. But no one else tried to approach the moving carriage.

He nodded. "They did. General Howe made a grand speech about making the city whole again."

Louisa's gaze followed the passing skeletons of buildings and returned to Parker. "The fire was, what, three months ago?"

"Almost four now."

"Well, it doesn't look like they've done anything."

The carriage rolled past a huge pile of garbage on the left, its contents rotten and ripe, the odor flooding into the cramped interior.

She covered her nose with the handkerchief. "And it looks like the army hasn't even picked up the rubbish for months."

Parker wished more than ever that he had not agreed to attend this foolish party. He could not meet his wife's fierce gaze. Without looking up, he shrugged. "They have not done anything about cleaning up this part of town."

"But why has nothing been done? We have all these soldiers here with nothing to do most of the time. How many times have you come home and told me your men are bored and need something to do? It seems a simple task to put them to work cleaning up this mess." She waved a hand toward the window.

Parker heaved a long sigh. How much should he tell her? Well, she was his wife. "Those at the top—General Howe and his staff—continue to quarrel among themselves. One group blames the rebels for starting the fire. They say the rebels created this wretched mess so they can live in it. They have not moved past that."

She raised her eyebrows. "But we know that's not true. You told me how the fire really started—from that house where Hollister ordered that horrid execution by burning that couple and their home."

"We know how the fire *probably* started." The afternoon he had come home from the fiery execution of the rebel collaborators, he had indeed told her everything, including how he had tried to persuade Hollister against such an inhuman act. In any case, she could smell it on his clothes the moment he stepped in the door. It had taken Ruth days to clean the greatcoat and purge the stench.

"Still," he said, "you are correct, but there is little I can do. I am only a major. I have no choice but to follow orders."

"Yes, but it's not right . . . to treat people like that."

Meeting his wife's stern gaze, he drew another slow breath. "I cannot disagree." He looked past Louisa and saw more wretched, desperate people lining the route. "We have not kept our word. Now I fear that because the army has not taken care of this, those residents who had been loyal and welcomed us when we took the city are now desperate and angry. I am not sure how loyal they will remain."

"Can you blame them?" Louisa said. "I can't imagine what it must be like living in those conditions for months."

Parker shook his head. "You are right, of course. I do not blame them. In fact, I am afraid we are fomenting a new crop of rebels—rebels Washington will be only too glad to make use of when the time comes."

44

It took some time to travel through the swath of the city devastated by the fire, but when the footmen turned the coach onto Hester Road, both Parker and Louisa breathed a little easier. He watched his wife compose herself, arranging her hair and using her handkerchief to wipe her face before tucking it away. Now that the danger had passed, he, too, tried to recover his composure.

As they turned west, the setting sun broke through the clouds. The air, though still cold, held the crisp feel of a late winter afternoon. The horses trotted along a gravel path as the road sloped upward, the carriage passing through an avenue lined on both sides with tall trees and hunched magnolia bushes, their branches stark and bare in the harsh January light. In spring and summer, the view would be stunning.

When they topped the rise and rounded a bend, Incleberg came into view. The magnificent estate stood on the crest of the hill, a large stone-and-wood structure with eight tall glass windows and black shutters. Chiseled fieldstones wrapped the lower level of the massive house, while the second story was painted a dark red, the color burnished by the sinking sun. Smoke billowed from five chimneys, promising warmth inside. A set of stone steps led up to a wide porch, two towering columns supporting a slate roof.

The driveway curved in front of a broad portico, where several other coaches waited in line, drivers holding their teams. At the bottom of the steps a pair of lanterns welcomed guests, and lights glowed from every window. While they waited, Parker checked his appearance. He brushed the red fabric, satisfied his greatcoat looked none the worse for the recent scuffle. He had not lost any buttons. He straightened his sword in its scabbard and glanced at Louisa, who flashed him a brave smile.

When their turn came and the coach rolled up to the entrance, he alighted first and helped her down. His hand on her arm, they ascended the six stone steps together and, as a Black porter held the door open, they stepped inside a huge foyer. Music drifted in from a ballroom—the strains of violins and the brassy blare of a horn. They paused at the entrance, their gazes scanning the massive hall. At one end, a quartet played on, though the guests seemed to pay little attention.

The ballroom was a sea of red uniforms and white powdered wigs, most of the men paired with at least one woman. The ladies wore expensive, flowing gowns over layers of petticoats, in shades of pale green, yellow, and cream, a sharp contrast to the scarlet coats and black breeches. Seeing the display, Parker was glad Louisa had insisted he wear his best dress uniform, newly cleaned and polished. And he was thrilled his wife's peach-colored dress stood out, looking stunning. It did not hurt that her attractive face still held a smile that could melt his heart. He noticed she had even laced a small posy into her hair, the color matching her dress. He had no idea what flower it was but supposed she had grown it in the greenhouse behind their home.

Couples strolled about the room and among them he recognized a number of officers, each with a woman on his arm—a few with a woman on each arm. Parker knew few of the ladies present were their wives. Most of their wives were safely tucked back in England. Not many women were willing to brave the voyage to the colonies as Louisa had.

A huge stone hearth dominated the far wall, carefully laid fieldstones framing a roaring fire. Above the fireplace, two flags hung at cross angles, the first the Union Jack. The second held the family crest of General Howe—a gold shield bearing three wolf heads, surrounded by blue feathers, the name HOWE printed in bold letters across the center. Several couples gravitated toward the fireplace, no doubt for the warmth, chatting and laughing.

In the center of the room sat a massive table set with more food than Parker had ever seen. Tureens of stew sat beside roasted quarters of animals—deer, hog, and turkey. Two Black servants stood behind the meats, carving knives at the ready. Platters of cooked vegetables—white potatoes, orange squash, yellow turnips, bright carrots—added color to the arrangement. Two overweight officers stood at the table, laughing and piling food onto their plates. Parker recognized Hollister but not the other. The men thrust their plates toward the carvers, who layered slices of meat on top. When the stewards finished, the officers heaped vegetables and ladled stew beside the meat, overflowing their dishes and spilling meat and vegetables onto the floor. Hollister laughed, the stub of a cigar bouncing between his lips.

Staring at the display of excess, Parker thought of the locals they had just passed—their pale, emaciated faces. He recalled a black-haired boy, gaunt and thin with dirty face and hands, who stared open-mouthed as the carriage rolled by. Parker wondered when the lad had last eaten.

He and Louisa made their way farther into the room. Formally dressed waiters circulated with trays of ale, rum, and wine. One stopped and extended his tray. Parker took two crystal glasses and handed one to Louisa. From her expression, he guessed she was harboring similar thoughts about the unrestrained extravagance.

Eyebrows raised, she whispered, "Whose estate is this?"

He kept his voice low as well. "I believe a family named Murray owns all this and offered it to General Howe."

"This"—she waved a hand—"is a bit much to take . . . after what we just witnessed."

"I know," he said quietly.

Louisa's gaze roamed the room again. "What did you tell me he's calling this *celebration*?"

"Toujours de la *gaieté*."

"Always cheerful?" she translated. She harrumphed, so loudly he worried others might hear. He shot a glance around. No one had.

"Haven't our forces suffered some military setbacks of late?" she asked. "That one at Christmas?"

Parker nodded but kept his voice low. "Yes. Washington took Trenton on Christmas Eve. Caught the Hessians drunk and reveling. Hardly fired a shot. The first blow was a surprise, but a week later Washington's army took Princeton."

Louisa's eyebrows shot up. "I hadn't heard about that." She glanced toward the laden table, where two drunken soldiers were pretending to duel with turkey legs. "Then why are we celebrating?"

"Major Monteith!" a voice bellowed from behind.

Parker turned to the speaker—a puffy face with two bloodshot eyes.

Oh God. Hollister. He felt Louisa squeeze his arm and tried to summon a smile. "Good evening, Colonel Hollister."

"So glad to have one o' my finest majors 'ere at the party," the man called, louder than necessary, words slurring.

"Colonel, I do not believe you have met my wife, Louisa."

Balancing her wineglass, Louisa executed a perfect curtsy, a polite smile fixed on her face.

An overstuffed plate in one hand and a tankard in the other, Hollister attempted a bow in return but had to stop as food slid off his plate. "Oops," he giggled as a slab of meat landed on the polished floor. In seconds a young Black woman scurried over, scooped up the food, and wiped the floor clean with a rag.

Hollister leered at Louisa. "Cain hath tol' me you have a beautiful home."

"Thank you, Colonel," Louisa said. Then, before Parker could stop her, she added, "We'd be delighted to have you visit whenever it's convenient, sir."

Inwardly, Parker cursed his wife's courtesy and social grace, but now the damage was done. He added, "We will be glad to welcome you any time you would like to visit."

Hollister's gaze flicked from Louisa to Parker, delight brightening his features. "Splendid. Splendid." Bringing the tankard to his mouth, he drained it, brown ale dribbling from his puffy lips. With a belch, he set the mug on a passing waiter's tray and wiped his mouth with the back of his hand. Flicking the blue feather, he grabbed Louisa's free arm. "I simply must introduce you to General Howe. He's goin' t' love you." Hollister turned and glanced at Parker. "And you, too, Monteith."

Parker and Louisa set their glasses on the waiter's tray, and Hollister led her across the room, Parker only a step behind. As they threaded through clusters of guests, several officers hailed Hollister, who paused to exchange a few loud words. Hollister escorted Louisa to the far side of the room and stopped before a grouping of upholstered couches and chairs, covered in pale blue fabric. An older man sat in the center of the sofa with a pretty, much younger woman off to the side. In front of them, two officers were straightening from bows, muttering, "Thank you, General," as they turned toward the food.

Parker had never seen General Howe in person, but he had heard much about him. The general had commandeered his own mansion in town and had not visited the officers' quarters—at least not while Parker had been there. Howe had been promoted and replaced General Gage as commander in chief a few weeks after the fire ravaged the city. Parker knew Howe was generally well liked among the officers, but *he* had seen little promise in the man's leadership so far. Of course, he kept his own counsel.

The man before him was tall, long legs splayed across the settee. Unlike most other ranking officers, General Howe wore no white wig—his brown-and-gray hair protruded in bulbous curls from beneath a blue tricorn hat with gold trim. He had fleshy jowls, a straight nose, and deep-set brown eyes. Gold epaulets graced his red greatcoat, and blue trim lined the center of the jacket. The general held a mug in one hand and his eyes lingered on the woman sitting close—but not too close.

"General Howe, I'd like you to meet Major Parker Monteith," Hollister announced, trying for formality though his voice squeaked. "Major Monteith commands a company of the Second King's Regiment—the company that took down the Liberty Pole on the Commons last fall."

Parker gave a small bow and General Howe nodded. "It is good to meet you, Major. Your men did a fine job dispossessing the locals of their rebellious symbol—and without incident. Governor Tryon was pleased, and I commend you."

"Sir, my men and I were simply doing our duty," Parker said.

Hollister nudged him aside and pushed Louisa forward. "And this, sir, is the major's lovely wife, Louisa."

Parker watched Louisa perform another flawless curtsy and extend her hand. General Howe sat up, took her hand, and kissed it, lingering a moment too long. Parker knew the general was not married and was rumored to be a rake.

Sliding his arm through his wife's, Parker said, "General, this is a fine celebration. Thank you for inviting us. We are truly looking forward to partaking of your charming presentation of food. Everything looks delicious."

"Of course. It was good to meet you, Major and Mrs. Monteith." Howe waved them off with long fingers, two of them glittering with jeweled rings.

Parker gave another quick bow and led Louisa toward the buffet.

Halfway there, Louisa tugged on his arm and steered him to a quieter spot before one of the long windows. "After what we saw on the way over here, I don't have much of an appetite."

"I understand. I just wanted to get us away."

She squeezed his arm and leaned close. "But I'm dying to know who the other woman is—the one sitting with General Howe. He didn't introduce her. Is that his wife?"

Parker glanced around to be sure they would not be overheard, then shook his head. "The general is not married. The woman is Mrs. Betty Loring. She is, uh . . . a friend of General Howe's."

"A friend?"

He sighed, rolling his eyes. "According to the gossip, General Howe has appointed Joshua Loring"—he gave a slight nod toward the couch—"Betty Loring's husband, commissioner of prisoners, in exchange for, uh, certain *favors* from his wife."

While still keeping her posture erect, Louisa's gaze drifted to the pair on the blue couch and back. "I don't understand."

Parker leaned close to her ear. He wanted any onlookers to assume he was merely flirting with his wife. "After I tell you the rest, I want you to giggle—even though you will not feel like it."

Louisa's eyes swept the ballroom and returned to his. She gave a tiny nod and pasted on a smile.

"The commissioner of prisoners is a highly paid position," Parker said softly, "and I have heard Joshua Loring is selling off much of the rations intended for the prisoners, making himself quite wealthy in the process."

She gave the requested little giggle, but her eyes went wide. "Um, yes," she chuckled, "but isn't that dangerous? What if the rebels do the same thing? Our men who are captured could starve."

"As usual, you have hit on it precisely. Other officers have voiced the same concern—but only among those of us who are junior, the ones who really know the men." His gaze slid to General Howe and Betty Loring. "But because of this special liaison, no one dares question the arrangement."

"What despicable behavior," Louisa whispered, her false smile frozen in place.

"I could not agree more." Parker slipped his arm through hers and led her across the hall.

He had seen plenty of prisoners of war, and as he watched Betty Loring flirt with General Howe, he wondered how much the captured soldiers of the Continental Army would pay for the general's dalliance. A price even he could not calculate.

45

Abigail Trench stood in the doorway of his study, shoulders slumped, hands clasped in front of her.

Parker had heard her arrive hours earlier for her tutoring session with his children. Today she had worked with them in the library, their voices drifting across the foyer through the open office door. Miss Trench's voice had sometimes alternated with the children's, but it lacked its usual bouncy timbre. He had grown accustomed to the excited murmur from Henry and Elizabeth when they were engaged in their lessons. They reminded him of the future he was fighting for. Today, the murmurs had been quieter, and their teacher's voice barely audible.

He glanced up now and saw her there, silent and unmoving. He had no idea how long she had been standing there, quietly waiting. She had stepped into his study only once before, when he invited her the day after the encounter with Reeves on the Commons.

"Miss Trench, is there something wrong?" He saw her face pale. "Is it something to do with the children?"

She relaxed a bit. "No, they're both fine. Did you know Elizabeth can now read whole paragraphs and has memorized all her sums and minuses? Oh, and Henry can draw almost every letter in the alphabet. Your son has quite an interest in drawing."

Parker eased back in his chair. "My wife has tried to keep me apprised, but I did not know all that. Henry an artist, huh?" He tried to imagine boisterous, loud Henry as a moody artist and failed. Then again, the boy was only six. Much would happen in the next years. "I will have to think about that. Anyway, I know Louisa is quite pleased with your work, as am I."

He studied her hunched posture and drawn features. The time before, when he asked to see her about Reeves, Miss Trench looked nervous and anxious. Today, though, she looked worse—distraught.

"Thank you for the fine report about my children, but I suspect something else brought you to my office door. Please come in and tell me what is on your mind." He gestured to an upholstered chair next to his desk. "You are not here to give notice, I hope."

She gave a weak smile as she stepped to the offered chair. "No, I love working with Elizabeth and Henry. They give me hope for the future."

"I feel the same way." As she crossed in front of him, he caught the whiff of paper and pencil lead. "So, what can I do for you, Miss Abigail?"

She perched on the edge of the seat, staring at her folded hands in her lap. Several moments passed before she spoke, and when she did, she did not look at him. "I've come to ask for a favor."

"Is this about Private Reeves? He has not been bothering you, has he?"

She shook her head and finally looked up. "It has nothing to do with Reeves."

"Well, what is it, then?"

Miss Trench simply stared at him, as if she did not know how to begin. When she said no more, he added, "I have no idea if I can help unless you tell me what favor you need."

She heaved a long sigh. "It concerns my brother."

He sat up. "Your brother?"

She nodded. "I shared with Mrs. Monteith that my brother, Oliver, joined the Continental Army last year. He was only sixteen and quite impressionable. Some militiamen visited our farm, and he wanted to join them."

Parker knew. Louisa had told him about the brother fighting for the other side, and it had worried him. But his wife had convinced him it did not disqualify Abigail as a tutor. In the months since, Abigail had given them no reason for concern. He wondered if that was about to change. "Yes, Louisa told me about your brother. What about him?"

"Your wife mentioned you and your company were part of the force that captured Fort Washington last November." She paused and dropped her gaze again. "My brother . . . was fighting on the other side."

"I am sorry to hear that."

"The rumors I've heard indicate you dealt the Continental Army quite a defeat—killing and capturing a good many men."

He guessed where she was going and did not like it. There was only so much he would be able to do. He started to say so, but she hurried on.

"I was told he was one of more than a thousand soldiers taken prisoner at Fort Washington."

His eyebrows went up. "Actually, we took almost three thousand men prisoner at the fort."

Her face paled again. "Well, what I ask might be quite the favor, then."

He hoped she did not expect him to pull strings he did not have. "What is it—this favor?"

She raised both palms in mock surrender. "Oh, I'm not asking for any special treatment for Oliver."

"I do not understand. What is it you ask, Miss Trench?"

"I've learned prisoners are allowed visitors at times."

"Yes, from time to time."

She looked up at him, her expression earnest. "I have no idea what condition Oliver is in. Was he hurt in the battle? I'd just like to visit him, to see if he is all right. He is only sixteen." She stopped, corrected herself. "Well, seventeen now." She paused again and glanced up at him, deep green eyes wide. "And he's my brother."

"I understand."

"But I have no idea where he is being held prisoner. I'm asking if you can find out where Oliver is and see whether it'd be possible for me to visit him."

Parker held her gaze before answering. With what he had learned about how prisoners were being treated, he did not want to raise false hopes. She sat there on the edge of the chair, waiting. Finally he said, "I will see what I can do."

"Oh, thank you, sir," she breathed, relief softening her features.

"What regiment was your brother serving in?" He pulled out a sheet of paper.

"Oliver Trench. The 3rd Pennsylvania."

"Understand I can make no promises, but I will see what I can learn about your brother's disposition. After all you have done for my children, it is the least I can do."

As she rose, she managed a small smile and thanked him again. Watching her leave, he feared he had given her false hope. He dreaded what she might find when she saw her brother again.

46

"Private, I need you to row us over to the *Jersey,*" Major Parker Monteith ordered the young man standing beside a rowboat.

The lad glanced out into the fog-shrouded harbor. "The prison ship? I-I-I don't think ya want to go there."

Parker watched the white puffs of the boy's breath blow away in the brisk February wind. "That is precisely what we intend. My name is Major Monteith, Second King's Artillery. Now, Private, hop to it." He pointed at the small boat tied to the pier and turned to his companion. "Miss Trench, please go first. Mind your step."

Abigail Trench stepped into the bottom of the boat, water sloshing over her shoes. She said nothing, simply maneuvered around and sat on the wooden slat in the bow. Clutching the bundle in front of her, she maintained the same stoic expression and stared straight ahead.

It had taken Parker four days and three exchanges of letters to reach the correct officer with the log of prisoners from Fort Washington. In the process he had learned Miss Trench's brother was confined to the HMS *Jersey*—and little more. Not his condition, not his health. Only that the young man was to be detained there with more than a thousand other prisoners until the end of the conflict.

But his inquiries had revealed a good deal more about the state of the prison ship, and none of it good. What he learned confirmed the rumors. Not only was Joshua Loring, commissioner of prisoners, diverting almost all of the money allocated for food and the prisoners' upkeep—and becoming quite rich as their numbers grew—he had denied the men and boys even basic medical care. Parker feared what Miss Trench would find and decided he needed to accompany her.

He had shared only the barest details, cautioning her about what they might encounter on the ship, but she had remained resolute. When he finished, she asked if she could bring a few things for her brother. She now clung to her pitiful bundle—some hardtack and biscuits and a note from their father, all wrapped in an old woolen blanket. On the carriage ride to the harbor, he had her unwrap everything on the seat. He felt indebted to Miss Trench for the care of his children, but he was not about to risk bringing any weapon onto a prison ship. When he completed the inspection, she carefully arranged the items again inside the worn cloth, her movements meticulous.

Parker climbed into the small boat, feeling the craft rock as he shifted his weight, and settled onto the forward seat, facing the harbor. Behind him he felt the private push the dinghy off the sand and heard the soldier wade into the water before climbing onto the center bench, causing the boat to pitch so sharply Parker feared it might tip. Then the lad went to work, the only sound the repetitive *splash, splash, splash* of the oars dipping in and out of the water. As they moved farther out, the little craft steadied.

Parker exhaled and watched his breath erupt in a small white cloud. The East River was shrouded in fog, wisps of it swirling in the wind like wild, menacing wraiths. As the oars pushed them out into the harbor, Parker watched small chunks of ice float by, some bumping the boat before drifting past. They steered around a piece of ice nearly as large as the rowboat itself.

He did not want to be out here. It had been a frightfully cold few weeks, with temperatures hovering well below freezing since mid-January. When the fog thinned enough to reveal the surface, he saw waves forming small whitecaps before smacking against their fragile craft. He did not fear the water. He had been at sea for months at a stretch, often sailing for weeks without any sighting of land. But these waters looked frigid and treacherous. They would not survive long if a wave swamped the dinghy.

The young soldier rowed and groaned from the effort in the strong waves but said nothing. Against the powerful current, progress was slow and it seemed to take forever. Then, ahead of them, a vessel emerged slowly from the fog like some grotesque phantom, a brown-and-black hulk materializing out of the gray mist.

It was not large by ship standards, perhaps one hundred fifty feet long, and did not look much like a sailing ship. Only one mast remained, stripped of sails, and on her starboard side, where gunports had been, two black holes stared back, like lifeless eyes. The anchor chain had been dropped forward and the ship rocked only slightly in the swell.

Then he spied one feature that made him relax a bit. A long, narrow gangplank had been attached to a floating platform moored by another anchor. He had feared he and Miss Trench would have to climb a rope ladder to come aboard—no easy feat in rolling waters. Now he realized the army had wanted an easier way to load prisoners, especially those ill or wounded. The gangplank was still narrow, and crossing it would not be simple, but he was glad he did not have to watch Miss Trench climb a rope ladder above him in a dress and petticoats.

The rowboat bumped against the wooden platform and the private stowed the oars, then stood and jumped onto the planks in one swift motion. Kneeling, he caught the hull. He turned first to his female passenger. "Miss, if ya hand me the package, I'll hold it while ya step up here." He extended his other hand to her.

Miss Trench looked down at her bundle, then passed it to the young man. She rose and, taking a few seconds to steady herself, stepped up onto the platform beside the soldier. She retrieved her package and waited. With the boat now empty but for him, Parker took his time to rise, widening his stance for balance, and then climbed up onto the boards.

"Ye want me to keep my boat here 'n wait fer ye, sir?"

"Yes, Private." Parker glanced at Miss Abigail, shivering in the wind off the water, and realized for the first time all she wore over her dress was a thin shawl. He turned to her. "I will precede you so I can address the man in charge."

When she nodded, he started up the gangplank. Stepping onto the narrow footbridge, he looked down, surprised to see slats broken and missing in the walkway. Through the gaps in the wood he could see the waves slapping against the hull of the HMS *Jersey*. Without turning around, he called back, "Watch where you step, Miss Trench."

He pushed on, feeling the gangway rock with the motion of ship, platform, and water. At the top he stepped over the rail and onto the swaying deck. Hearing her behind him, he turned and reached for the bundle as Miss Trench stepped aboard. Once she was settled, he handed it back to her.

A short man bustled out of a small cabin and hurried up to Parker, a large belly protruding between the lapels of an unbuttoned red waistcoat. He pointed a filthy finger at Miss Trench. "Hey, she can't be here."

The man had not shaved in some time. Stubbly black whiskers bristled along his chin and upper lip. Reaching up, he tried to straighten the tricorn hat that sat crooked on a mop of unruly black hair. He reeked of alcohol but tried to force his features into a stern grimace. "This here's a prison ship. No 'ladies' allowed. She needs to get right back on that there dinghy."

47

Parker studied the pudgy man and recognized the insignia on his coat. "Sergeant, what is your name?" he barked.

"Um, what business is it to you?" the man muttered.

Parker's temper flared and he started to raise his voice, but before he could get another word out, an even higher-pitched voice cut across the deck.

"Com'on and bring 'im over here, boys, and drop 'im over by the rail."

It sounded like it came from a boy, but a tall, skinny man backed out of a cabin door midship and walked to the port side. Behind him two lads who could be no older than ten carried a limp, nude figure. Grunting under the weight, the boys lugged the long body, which sagged in the middle, and dropped it onto the wooden deck with a thud.

"Go on and git the other one and bring 'im up and put 'im in the same place," the tall man ordered, his voice squeaking. He turned and noticed the visitors, ambling over to them. He wore a clean blue waistcoat Parker recognized as the uniform dress of a Continental officer, though it hung several sizes too large on his slim frame.

The tall man said, "Sarge, I didn't know we had visitors." His eyes took in Miss Trench in her drab cotton dress and worn shawl. "And a *pretty* one at that." He grinned through blackened teeth.

Parker caught the leer in his tone. He turned back to the portly sergeant. “I am *Major* Monteith. Sergeant, what is your name?”

The man tried to straighten. “Beggin’ your pardon, sir. My name is Harmsworth. Sergeant Harmsworth.”

Parker reeled toward the other man. “And your name, Private?”

The skinny fellow’s face turned red and he gulped. “Colins . . . sir.”

Parker glared at the men’s appearances. “And *this* is how you dress as members of the British army?” He pointed to the sergeant’s open coat. “Fasten those buttons.” Then he wheeled on the other man. “Colins, why are you wearing that? And where did you get it?”

The tall man gulped. Parker saw a scar on his neck pulse and guessed the reason for the high, squeaky voice.

“Sir, it’s warm . . . and I figures he don’t need it no more.” Colins jerked his head toward the body lying naked, face down on the deck.

“Get out of that rebel uniform and into your own, unless you want to be court-martialed.”

“Yes, sir,” the man called, his voice climbing another octave. He took off toward the cabin door, long legs hammering across the planks, and disappeared inside. The door slammed behind him.

Within seconds it banged open again and the pair of boys frog-stepped out, another figure sagging between them. This body was shorter and they had less struggle with it. In a few steps they repeated the process, depositing the second naked body with a clunk, face up this time, and then vanished back into the cabin.

Parker’s gaze went from the sprawled bodies to the fat man in front of him. “Sergeant, what is going on here?” He pointed at the naked figures.

The sergeant started, his voice quavering. “Well, sir, th-th-they’s dead.”

“I can see that. Who are they? Prisoners, I assume.”

“Damned if I know.” He threw both short arms in the air. “Some captured Continentals.” Then he added, “Or they might’ve been privateers.”

Parker looked from the dead men back to Harmsworth. "What are you going to do with the bodies?"

Harmsworth shrugged. "We dump 'em in the drink. After all, they's just stinkin' rebels, and they don't care."

Parker noticed Miss Trench studying the bodies. Horror registered on her features, but no recognition. At least not her brother. He brought his attention back to the sergeant. "Is this how you would want your fellow soldiers to be treated?"

"No, sir." Harmsworth swallowed. "But we's jus' followin' orders."

"I *suggest* you take time to give them a decent burial. It's not as if you have a great deal else to do around here. Then perhaps the colonials will be more likely to do the same for British prisoners." Parker glanced toward the cabin door. "We are here to see a prisoner—a Private Oliver Trench. I want you to take us to him."

"Sir, I-I-I can't do that." Harmsworth's voice sounded desperate. He flicked another glance at Miss Trench. "Women ain't allowed on this ship." His cheeks flushed. "Believe me, I tried. My major will skin me alive."

Parker looked at Miss Trench, then at the corpses on the deck, then finally back at the sergeant. "Well, how about this: Miss Trench and I will climb back into the transport and I'll have the private row me over to headquarters." He gestured toward the rail. "Then I will call on Major Barnes and share with him what I've found on this prison ship. He would be quite interested. He might even want to join me on my return visit."

Parker turned as if to start toward the gangplank and nodded toward his companion. "Miss Trench?"

As surprise bloomed on the woman's face, Harmsworth sputtered, "Well, n-n-no need to be hasty . . . sir." He swallowed hard. "When Major Barnes gave them orders, he probably didn't mean another major like you." His gaze went to Miss Trench. "And since the lady is with you, she'll be fine too."

Parker shot a glance at Miss Trench and gave her a slight nod. "Now. Private Oliver Trench. He was with the Pennsylvania 3rd Regiment."

Harmsworth still looked hesitant and shook his head. "Well, I think them boys is in the aft hold . . . but I have no idea if he's there." When Parker started to object, the sergeant added quickly, "Them prisoners ain't chained er nothin'. They can get up and walk around."

Parker's eyes narrowed. "Show us."

Harmsworth led them through the cabin door and down a ladder to the lower deck and then deeper into the hold. Parker followed and glanced up to be sure Miss Trench could manage the steps while balancing her bundle. She had no trouble.

Before his boots even touched the floor of the hold, it hit him—a stench so powerful it assaulted his nostrils and he had to fight the urge to cover his nose. The reek of human sweat and excrement, and, far worse, diseased, rotting flesh, hung heavy in the air. After Miss Trench descended behind him, she pulled out her handkerchief and pressed it over her nose.

It took a while for his eyes to adjust to the gloom. He heard them before he could see them. All around, men and boys groaned, raved, cried, and prayed. The murmur rose—hurried words and syllables barely audible at first, bouncing around the space. The sound swelled as the mumbling spread across the hold. At first Parker could make out little, but as he listened, the tone shifted from fear to anxiety to anger. Though the prisoners vastly outnumbered them, he judged there was little real threat here. Even so, he put a hand on the hilt of his sword.

Harmsworth yanked a pistol from his belt and waved it at the horde of men. "Go on, back off, unless'n ya want a little lead." He tried to sound brave, but Parker could hear the tremor in his words.

"God will strike you all dead!" someone screamed from within the throng. "His sword will smite the wicked!"

"Who said that?" Harmsworth growled, wheeling, his gun swinging. "I'll send you to meet your God right now." He shoved the barrel toward several faces and the men shrank back.

As the mumbling quieted, Parker peered into the dimness, his eyes slowly adjusting, and realized they stood in the middle of a huge horde of prisoners—lying, sitting, standing, pacing. Many of the men were nude, or nearly so, with no coats or blankets to ward off the cold. Knots of naked bodies huddled together, limbs intertwined, no doubt trying to preserve what little warmth they had. Everyone he could see—man or boy—looked gaunt and emaciated, some prisoners' skin so pale they resembled ghosts with hollow eyes staring back.

Though no wind cut through the hold, the cold here was still palpable. The chill had a different quality below decks, cloying and inescapable. In only a few minutes, Parker felt it invade his body, the cold pricking his skin and face. And he had on his heavy wool greatcoat and overcoat. These men had little or nothing to wear or cover themselves. How long could they survive in these frigid conditions?

Being a soldier for years, Parker had witnessed distressing human suffering all too common in war. Still, these conditions were far worse than anything he had encountered. The prisoners were treated no better than animals and, thanks to Loring's greed, too many would fall victim to disease and starvation. He wondered how many could possibly survive. If he was repulsed by what he saw, how much worse must it be for Miss Trench, her brother somewhere amid this brutal degradation? He began to question the wisdom of agreeing to bring her.

He turned to see her scanning the crowd of prisoners, her face taut with anxiety. Her gaze swept the space in slow arcs, turning where she stood so she could catch every face. Shaking her head, she frowned and started forward, heading toward the rear of the ship. Parker put a hand on her arm and she paused. He turned to Harmsworth. "All right. Where do we find Private Trench?"

The sergeant's gaze flitted around the room. "We's lookin' for an Oliver Trench. He's in Pennsylvania 3rd. Which of you's knows him?"

A skinny boy with thin blond hair spoke up. "I remember Ollie. He got wounded in the leg. They stowed 'im in the back with the other ones hurt." He shook his head. "Haven't seen 'im in a while. How 'bout I take ya to 'im?"

He started off and Miss Trench followed, bundle tucked in the crook of her arm. She moved so quickly it took Parker a few seconds to react. Up ahead, the boy threaded his way around a clutch of men, Miss Trench only a step behind. Parker had to hurry to keep up. Several prisoners reached out toward her, their grasps feeble, and she fended them off easily with her free hand. Together, the boy and she stepped over men lying on the floor, and Parker followed in their path, glancing down at the injured prisoners they passed.

Behind him he heard Harmsworth forcing his way through the throng, shoving and even kicking men out of his path. Parker longed to knock the sadistic bastard senseless but kept his focus on Miss Trench.

He looked around at the men and boys they passed. All stared back with the dead eyes of hopelessness. Many had skin covered with lesions and pustules, the odor of rotting flesh inescapable. Twice he watched large rats scamper over bodies, nosing at exposed flesh, and the men did not even react. One rat bolted toward Parker's boot, and he kicked it across the room, the animal bouncing off the hull. Again he checked on Miss Trench, but she seemed oblivious to him, intent only on finding her brother. Perhaps she had shut out everything else.

Up ahead, he saw the boy and Miss Trench cross into an area where men and boys lay in crooked rows. Some sat propped against the back wall, though most lay face up on the floor. Few moved when the group entered the space.

The lad said, "Las' I saw 'im, he was over here." He walked to the port-side wall, where two boys lay on the planks, eyes closed.

Placing a hand on Miss Trench's arm, Parker stepped ahead of her and approached the pair. Both had wounds on their legs, each bandaged with a filthy rag. The edges of the red-and-black gashes had turned an ugly green. From the sight and the smell, he knew the wounds had gone gangrenous. The boys would have to lose their legs—or worse. Both looked impossibly young.

Unable to wait any longer, Miss Trench stepped around him to the second boy. He had a shock of brown hair plastered to his head, a small nose, and sunken cheeks. All he wore was a thin tunic and, below it, Parker saw that his bare feet had turned blue.

She set the bundle aside and knelt next to the lad. "Oliver, I'm here," she whispered, hovering over his face. "It's Abigail."

The boy did not stir or open his eyes. Parker felt his gut clench.

Miss Trench reached down and grabbed his hand. "It's so cold," she cried, anguish roughening each syllable. Her hand went to the lad's cherubic face and then fell away.

"Oh, no. No. No." Her voice rose to a scream. She leaned close to his face. "No, no. It can't be."

Her fists pounded on the boy's chest, and Parker watched the dull, unresponsive bounce of a corpse.

"He's dead." She glared at Parker and then at Sergeant Harmsworth. "You killed him! You all killed him!"

ABIGAIL

48

"The Lord is my shepherd. I shall not want," the minister intoned, his voice rising and falling with the familiar phrases.

Abigail took little notice. She fixed her eyes on the plain wooden box lowered into the freshly dug hole. Oliver lay in that coffin, dead. But as she stared at the rough lid, she could still see his pale skin, almost white tinged with blue. She could still feel the icy chill of his cheek beneath her fingers. Rage and a fierce helplessness seethed through her. The reverend's words did little to ease her pain.

Two days earlier, aboard the dreaded prison ship where she'd gone to give her brother a little comfort and warmth, she'd found only his corpse. While she raged, pounding her fists on his lifeless body, she felt Major Monteith lifting her off Oliver and heard his voice.

"Miss Abigail, he is gone now. There is nothing more you can do for him here."

Not much after that was clear. She remembered it had taken both Major Monteith and the sergeant to pull her off Oliver. The major had half carried, half led her up the ladder, onto the deck, and down to the rowboat. After some argument with the sergeant, Major Monteith had arranged to have her brother wrapped in the blanket she'd brought and carried out to the transport. The two young lads had laid the bundle on the bottom in front of her. Once they were rowed ashore, the major and the private placed the body in the carriage. Major Monteith had even carried Oliver up the stairs to their flat and laid him gently on the floor.

She'd tried to tell Father what had happened but found no words would come. Instead, the major had given a brief explanation, offered his condolences, and taken his leave. After he left, Father sat for hours staring at the wrapped figure that had been Oliver, but refused to touch it. He didn't even pull back the cloth to look at his son's face. Watching pain carve deeper lines into Father's features only increased Abigail's anger and sense of vulnerability. She knew she ought to rail and scream for vengeance. Instead, all she felt was numb.

Who knew what would have happened had it not been for Robert Townsend? Later that evening, Robert arrived, saying he'd heard about Oliver's death. He held her, and his embrace released another torrent of weeping she had no will to resist. With Father's silence and her own acquiescence, Robert took charge of her brother's body and made the arrangements for a decent burial—casket, minister, and service. He found a place for Oliver in a small cemetery a few miles out in the country and even commandeered a wagon to transport coffin, Father, and her.

Now she stood over the grave, shivering in the cruel, cold wind, and glanced at the faces of the few mourners. Jamie and Molly had come, wrapped in layers of old clothes, their faces stripped of their usual frivolity. Father stood beside her, one arm around her shoulders. He remained silent, though she could feel his body quivering. Across the raw wound in the earth, close but still at a discreet distance, Robert stood with his head bowed, staring at the coffin. At the foot of the grave, the blond head of Louisa Monteith was bowed in prayer. Louisa had bundled herself in a heavy coat against the wind. Abigail had been surprised by the kindness of the major's wife, who had said, "You've done so much for my children. I want to be there for your family."

Abigail was grateful for the woman's support, especially since she hadn't yet decided whether she could continue her tutoring work.

Though what else would she do? Father and she still needed the money.

When the minister finished, he expressed his condolences for Oliver's death, mumbling something about the horrors of war. Then he mounted his horse and trotted down the road. For a few minutes no one moved or spoke, as if they were all frozen in place. At last Louisa Monteith broke the silence.

"I had better get back to the children. They will be giving Ruth fits by now." She walked around to where Abigail stood beside the grave. "Miss Abigail, the children have sorely missed you these last few days, but I know you're grieving something terrible. You take as long as you need, and we'll be glad to welcome you back in our home when you're ready."

She pressed an envelope into Abigail's hand. Abigail accepted it without even looking down.

Louisa glanced around at the others. "I'm happy to give anyone a ride back into town."

Jamie spoke up. "That'd be most kindly, ma'am. Molly and me be forever in your debt." He reached to take Molly's arm, but she gently pushed his hand aside.

Instead she went to Abigail and hugged her, thin arms squeezing tight. "I's so sorry, Abigail. We're here for ya, if ya need anythin'." She kissed her friend on the cheek and then took Jamie's arm. Together they walked toward the waiting Monteith carriage.

Abigail gazed at Father. He looked old, the lines on his face more deeply etched than she remembered. Releasing the arm that circled her shoulders, he slumped down and threw a handful of dirt onto the wooden lid of the coffin, the soil landing with a quiet plop. When he straightened, his posture remained bent, as if the world were pressing down on him. One hand smoothed his black hair and he wiped his fingers across his beard. He adjusted his glasses, pushing them farther up his nose. Then he squeezed his eyes shut.

She knew Father, and she knew his heart was being torn apart, perhaps even more than hers. First he'd lost Mother in London, then Oliver had slipped away from him in this dreadful war. He was probably blaming himself—for bringing them to America, for settling on Long Island, for allowing Oliver to join the Continental Army.

Abigail reached out and hugged him, feeling the bony thinness beneath his coat. Seeing the three others making their way to the carriage, she said, "Why don't you go with them?" She met his gaze.

He started to object. "But what about Oliver's grave? I need to finish burying him. He was my son." The ache showed in his sorrowful eyes.

Abigail started to answer, but Robert laid a hand on her arm, stopping her. In a quiet voice he said, "I'll take care of it, sir. I'll make sure everything is done right." He extended his hand to Father, who stared a moment, then took it.

"Thank you, son," Father said. He turned to Abigail. "What about you?" His glanced from the gravesite to his daughter.

"I'd like a little time alone with Oliver . . . to say goodbye." She held his gaze, feeling the tears gathering again.

Robert spoke once more. "I'll take care of her too. I'll bring her home safe."

Father simply nodded and turned toward the carriage, where the Black servant waited. After Father climbed aboard, the servant closed the door, took his place up front, and shook the reins once. The pair of horses neighed and started trotting, the sound of their hooves soft on the green pasture. Abigail watched until the coach traveled over the hill and down, slipping out of view.

When she turned back, tears dripping from both cheeks, Robert was standing beside her. Neither spoke as he wrapped her in his strong arms and she wept. She had no idea how long they stood there, her body heaving against his chest, but Robert waited, holding her.

At last she managed to sniff twice and look up at him. Then she nodded. He didn't speak, only released her and went to the head of the grave.

Right then it began to snow, large fluffy flakes drifting down, dotting the green pasture with white. Abigail watched a few float down and land on the top of the blond-wood coffin. Robert glanced up at the falling snow, then picked up the wooden shovel. He dug it into the pile of fresh soil, the tip making a slushing sound in the dirt. Shovel full, he began refilling the raw scar in the earth before the snow did.

49

"Take another drink. You need it," Robert said, his tone conveying only compassion and concern.

They sat in another tavern, the Phoenix, one she'd never visited. It looked much like the others—scarred wooden bar on one side and old, mismatched tables scattered around the room, two oil lamps casting shaky shadows across the dirt floor. In the midafternoon they were alone, the other tables vacant, waiting for dockworkers or warehouse men to saunter in after a day's labor.

The only other person about was the barkeep, whom Robert hailed as Harry, an older man with most of his teeth missing and hair sprouting from a mole on the side of his nose. When Abigail peered over the rim of her mug, Harry appeared to be asleep on his stool behind the bar. She did as instructed, feeling the watery rum slide down her throat.

It would take more than a few mugs to make a dent in her crushing grief. She took another long swallow and studied her companion. "I haven't told you how grateful I am that you took care of the funeral arrangements for Oliver. I'm not sure how Father or I would've coped."

"I was happy to be of service." Robert reached over and gave her hand a gentle squeeze.

"But you didn't even know my brother."

"I've known other brave men like Oliver," he said, his voice quiet.

She looked up at him, into soulful brown eyes, again noticing the unusual gold stripe in his left one. Feeling her own eyes well again, she brushed her free hand across them. "You know what the worst part of it is—at least for me?"

Robert simply breathed in and out, never taking his eyes from her face.

"I feel like Oliver died for nothing. I want to rage and seek revenge, but I can't. I feel absolutely . . . impotent."

Robert tilted his head, his words a whisper. "Why do you think Oliver died for nothing?"

"Look at us. We're completely surrounded by the British army." Her arms flailed about the air. "There was a time I would have thought that a good thing. How ridiculous that sounds now. They've even invaded our damn homes."

Robert started to say something, but she cut him off. "Then Oliver and his regiment *and three other regiments* tried to hold off the British at Fort Washington, and all that happens is the whole lot get killed or captured—which, it turns out, *is* the same thing!"

She barked a bitter laugh that collapsed into sobbing, the sound loud in the quiet inn.

She needed to get it all out. Before, in the numbness after she'd found her brother, she'd felt pent up, her silence an appropriate penance for the deaths around her. Now she wanted to scream, right through her tears. She glanced toward the barkeep. Still asleep.

In the time she'd known him, Robert had never been loquacious. Like Nathan, he was a good listener. More than that, he had a quiet composure that made her feel she could confide in him. He looked comfortable in his silence, content to wait for her to unload, argue, or cry. He no doubt knew she needed this.

The memory of Nathan triggered another thought, which erupted from her mouth before she had time to stop it. "And, worst of all, I feel so incredibly helpless. I told you about Reeves and what he did to me, his filthy breeches around his ankles and his ugly . . . thing hanging there. I wanted to cut it off, but I couldn't do *anything*."

She kept going. "And then Reeves attacked us when we were simply sitting on the Commons. We had to stand there and do nothing. God, I thought he was going to run you through."

Her voice rose. "Oh, and that poor couple they burned in their own house. I stood there in that crowd, watching while that fat colonel had the house doused with oil and set it on fire. Blast, we *all* stood around and watched it . . . helpless."

She realized she was almost shrieking and glanced over to see if her tantrum had awakened the bartender. His snores said otherwise.

In the brief pause, Robert said in a quiet, controlled voice, "I wasn't there, but I heard about that."

She stabbed a finger at him. "And you're the one who told me about the British army pillaging your home *to teach the rebels a lesson*. And your family had to stand around and watch. There was nothing they could do."

"I did." His voice stayed calm, his eyes on her face, and his hand returned to hers.

"And then they hanged Nathan . . . without even a trial. The man who was so kind to me, who secured my first tutoring position. If he hadn't helped me, I might've had to work the streets like Molly."

She felt her face redden at the very idea. "I thought nothing could be worse than that, watching the life drain out of Nathan at the end of a rope." She shook her head hard, as if warding off some evil. "I was wrong. When my hand went to Oliver's cheek and felt the icy coldness of his skin, *I* wanted to die. I thought, what's the point?"

The sobbing came now in full force, her chest heaving and her cries loud inside the tavern. Through her tears, she managed, "I wanted to do something, strike out at someone, even kill someone, but I realized it was all useless. How in the world did the colonists think they could take on the British army—the greatest fighting force in the world—and think they could have any success?"

She took a quick breath and finished, "You know what the worst part of it is? There is *nothing* someone like you or me can do about it."

Robert kept his gaze fixed on her. He wrapped his hands around both of hers. His question came almost in a whisper. "What if there *is* something you and I can do about it?"

50

Abigail fought to rein in her weeping so she could understand what Robert meant. He was not one for fantasy or even exaggeration.

She pulled a handkerchief out of her pocket, wiped both eyes, and then used it to blow her nose, the sound like a goose honking. She looked across the tavern to see the barkeep stir, his gaze traveling around the place. After glancing at Robert and her, Harry shifted his position on his stool, laid his head back on the wooden bar, and shut his eyes again. In a few seconds, the snoring resumed.

Cloth in her hand, Abigail sniffled a few more times until her breathing evened out. "I don't understand. What are you talking about?"

Robert's gaze swept the tavern, paused on Harry, and came back to her. "I'm saying everything is *not* hopeless. *We* are not helpless. There *are* things we can do." His words dropped to a whisper, and she leaned closer to hear. "There are things that I . . . do."

Abigail said, "You told me you served as a logistics officer for Washington. I can see how—" She stopped when she saw him shaking his head.

"I'm not talking about that."

"Then what?" When he didn't answer, she pressed, "I don't understand. How can one person do much of anything against twenty thousand British soldiers stomping around New York, looking to kill or capture any rebel they find?"

He eased back on his stool and peered at her, saying nothing at first. She studied him, reddish-brown hair falling partly across his forehead. The gold streak in his left eye seemed to shimmer. For the funeral, he'd dressed the part today and looked somber in a new green waistcoat and black breeches, white cravat around his neck.

When he spoke, he leaned over and whispered directly in her ear. "If I'm going to share this with you, you cannot tell a soul. Ever. Not your father. Not Molly or Jamie. No one. Understand?"

She nodded but couldn't get a word out. Robert wasn't satisfied. He inched away from her ear but kept his voice quiet. "Abigail, I have really come to enjoy your company . . . even if some of our times together have been over very sad events."

She turned and looked at him, giving him a weak smile. "As have I."

"But if I'm going to share this with you, I'm taking quite a chance. I need to know."

Robert's enigmatic manner captured her, pulling her out of her grief-induced misery. She said, "Need to know what?"

"I need to know for certain you will not divulge what I'm about to share with you, that you will go to your grave . . . with my secret." She started to nod but he interrupted her. "Say it."

She stared into his deep eyes. "I promise I will not tell a soul."

For a minute, neither spoke, each one sitting, staring, waiting. Then Robert said, in a voice little above a whisper, "Several months ago, I gave up my position as logistics officer for the army. I had my shop to run, and I decided I could better serve the cause in a different role." He paused, and his gaze once again swept the empty tavern before returning to her. "After the Continental Army fled New York and the British took the city, I decided I could best help Washington by . . . getting him information about the British army here in New York."

Abigail felt her eyes go wide. She whispered, "You're a, a, a spy?" When Robert didn't answer, she added, "Like Nathan? It got him hanged." The clench returned to her gut.

Robert shrugged and offered a small smile. "I hope not like Nathan, rest his soul."

"But why take that chance? Isn't it dangerous?"

"I think it would be obvious by now. I believe in the cause of liberty." He gave a small chuckle. "Any role in the fight is dangerous. Just look at your brother and the thousands of other soldiers. Besides, I'm tired of the British treating us like second-class citizens." He gave her fingers a gentle squeeze. "I decided the Redcoats had to be stopped and I refused to believe I was powerless."

"But spying?" Abigail shook her head. "It's so, so . . . devious."

His eyes went hard. "No more devious than burning a couple in their house or letting men like your brother starve and freeze to death."

The reminder of her brother stung her. She asked, "But how?"

His features softened. "I think it best if I leave out most of the details." He patted her hand. "I told you I have a shop by the Holy Ground."

"Yes, you told me you do a lot of business with Redcoats, from officers all the way down. You said you don't mind making money off the British."

He smiled. "There's that. Well, let's say soldiers talk . . . and I pretend to have a sympathetic ear. It's not that hard. Many of the successful merchants are loyalists. They want to keep the British happy, so trade and money keeps rolling in."

Abigail took it all in, her mind reeling. Then she remembered Nathan, on his last visit to their flat, so excited about his new role, which turned out to be spying as well. "But they'll catch you just like they caught Nathan."

Robert squeezed both her hands again. "No, they won't. I'm being *much* more careful. From what I've learned, Nathan was a good man and very committed, but he was way too cavalier. He let his secret out to too many people. It only takes one to betray you. And I have a better cover than Nathan. My shop. Most important, no one else knows. No one." He looked up at her. "Except you and my contact in the Ring."

"The Ring?"

He whispered, "The Culper Ring. It's what we're called."

Abigail pulled her hands free and eased back on her stool. "But why me? Why are you telling me? Why would you share this secret with me?"

Sitting together, their faces inches apart, she caught his scent—musk and alcohol. Instead of answering, he reached his hand to her chin, leaned in, and kissed her, the touch soft and gentle. Abigail was stunned, but it felt right. Or maybe she was merely clutching onto something in her grief.

When they broke the kiss, Robert adjusted his posture on the stool. His gaze roamed the dim interior of the tavern again. Harry continued snoring away on the bar. Robert looked back at her and leaned in again. "That's why."

IV

SPRING–FALL, 1777

51

The change in Father shocked Abigail. He looked like he'd aged twenty years. He was listless, ate little, and frightened her. Father had taken Oliver's death so hard, he hadn't left their flat for weeks. When she broached the subject of his returning to work, he simply growled at her.

She was not much better. With neither of them earning any money, their funds dwindled quickly, even with the advance Louisa had pressed into her hands at the funeral. Abigail decided *she* had to do something . . . or they would starve. She had little choice but to return to her tutoring position. For a British officer.

As soon as she stepped onto the black-and-white floor of the foyer, Louisa Monteith hugged her and held her close. "You've been sorely missed. You have no idea," the woman whispered in Abigail's ear. When she released her, Abigail could see genuine relief in the mother's blue-gray eyes. Today Louisa wore a lovely canary yellow dress drawn at the waist with white ribbons and a gold flower in her hair.

Louisa called up to the second floor, "Children, look who's come to see you."

The stairs echoed with footfalls bounding down the steps. "Miss Abigail!" the two children yelled together. Elizabeth's normally demure smile exploded, and Henry jumped up and down with glee. Both children were dressed smartly, the girl in a yellow dress similar to her mother's and Henry in a pressed white shirt and black breeches.

Eyeing some British officers in the parlor next door, Abigail thanked Louisa and scooted the two out of the foyer and into the library. After they settled into their chairs, Elizabeth confessed in a conspiratorial tone, "It was so bor-r-ring around here without you."

Abigail couldn't help herself. A little laugh escaped and she patted the girl on the sleeve. It was a short, quick chuckle, but Abigail realized it was the first time she had laughed in weeks.

Once she had both students working, the whole process felt natural again. It took only a few minutes for all three of them to return to their routine, almost as if Abigail hadn't been absent from their lives for two months. She stared at Henry, perched over his paper, laboring over drawing his letters. His brown eyes squinted, then shone with each crude letter accomplished. At the other table, Elizabeth sat back in her chair, golden curls falling down each side of her head and the tip of a pencil poised in her mouth as she contemplated her next subtraction problem.

Abigail took a slow, deep breath. In spite of everything, this felt . . . good. For a few minutes, all the horrors and fears of the war retreated, and she reveled in the simple task of teaching. These were not Tories or rebels. They were simply children, children who needed her. And, in the details of helping them learn, watching their eyes light up with each tiny achievement, Abigail felt some sense of accomplishment. She was doing something.

But even this relief proved short-lived. A few loud exchanges from the parlor across the hall brought the reality of war back. Some shouting about troops and artillery.

Outside the walls of the Monteith home, things had not been good. In the intervening months, she had watched the British army tighten its grip on the city, each week bringing more stories of ruthless tactics by the Redcoats. The soldiers were everywhere—in the taverns, in the shops, on the wharf, patrolling the streets. Hundreds, maybe thousands, roamed the city, waiting to capture or kill any Continental soldiers or rebel collaborators they caught.

In quiet, secretive voices, residents shared tales of British soldiers rampaging through neighborhoods, ravaging the homes of suspected rebels or "rebel collaborators"—Abigail could still picture the ugly "RC" painted on the steps of the house engulfed in the inferno last fall. On each of the tutoring visits to Molly that Abigail had managed, Jamie had word of another home ransacked and another "RC" taken away. As the Redcoats' stranglehold on the city tightened, Abigail couldn't help but feel the colonials had little chance . . . regardless of Robert's faith.

"Is this right?" Henry asked, derailing Abigail's unsettling thoughts. He held up his paper with a crude drawing of an apple and a few scratches that were supposed to approximate a capital *A*.

Abigail gave him her best teacher smile. "You're getting better." She took the sheet from him, used her pencil to correct one line, and handed it back. "Why don't you try to do a few more?"

While Henry hovered over the paper and worked on his next attempts, Abigail rose and, strolling across the room, checked on Elizabeth. Standing and leaning over the table, she reviewed the girl's work.

Elizabeth, who was on the last line of numbers, glanced up at her teacher. Face beaming, she asked, "How am I doing, Miss Abigail?"

Abigail nodded and smiled. "Quite good overall. I see an error on this one." She reached down and pointed to a problem in the first row and then moved her finger to one in the third row. "And this one."

Elizabeth glanced up, her blond curls swinging with the motion, and scrunched her nose. "What did I do wrong?"

"See if you can figure it out. I'll give you a chance first, but if you don't see the mistake, I'll show you." Abigail patted her on the shoulder and winked. "I bet you can find your errors and fix them."

Elizabeth returned her gaze to the page, her attention on the rows of numbers again. Abigail glanced from one student to the other, pleased and surprised—pleased her absence had sharpened the children's enthusiasm for learning, surprised at how far both students had progressed under her tutoring, even with the months-long break. Besides the math progress, Elizabeth had made her way through most of the *New England Primer.* Henry could now recognize all the letters of the alphabet and could even read a few words. And his drawings looked pretty good for a six-year-old, as far as Abigail knew. She hadn't lost her gift for teaching.

Both children again intent on their tasks, Abigail's mind wandered.

Between her grief over Oliver's death and her fear about British cruelty, she had not allowed herself time to process the perplexing thing that had happened in that moment with Robert. His kiss.

That kiss had been so unexpected.

Since Oliver's funeral, Robert had continued to call on her, when she allowed him—though he hadn't tried to kiss her again. Still, Abigail couldn't forget the feel of it, the gentle touch of his lips on hers. Even here in the hushed library, she remembered it, one finger running gently over her lips. At the time, she'd been so stunned by the romantic gesture, she didn't know how to react. When they had parted, she felt a bit awkward, but Robert's smile was warm and inviting. Still, neither had mentioned it again.

She was not sure what she felt. At the time, she doubted herself—she was dealing with the crushing grief of her brother's death, after all. Still, she had to acknowledge she felt something. Abigail was hesitant to admit it but, when they were together, she couldn't ignore it. Still, her fears held her back. Nathan and she had been only friends. Then he died . . . so horribly.

And what about Robert's revelation about being a spy? In their times together since, he hadn't mentioned that either. In the haze of her grief and confusion, sometimes she wondered if she had imagined his bold admission. Was he really a spy? Maybe Robert only told her that at the time so she wouldn't feel so useless. And if he did spy and she let herself feel for him, she might see Robert swing at the end of a rope.

"Hell, with twenty thousand men, we own this city. We can do whatever we want!" a voice bellowed from across the hall—a voice Abigail recognized, a voice she wished she could forget. She froze. Images of the inferno of the house flashed through her mind, the nauseating stench once again in her nostrils. That fat, horrible British officer roaring at the crowd.

Glancing at the two children, Abigail noticed both had stopped, pencils paused in midair, eyes turned toward the parlor. She rose and went to the door. As she pulled it closed, she saw Major Monteith across the hall, rolling his eyes. When she shut the door, quieting the blabber some, Elizabeth nodded her thanks and returned to her subtraction. Drawing on her memory, Abigail tried to recall the horrible officer's name. Louisa had told her once, in passing, how disagreeable the man was. Hollister, that was it. Colonel Hollister.

When they finished the lessons, Abigail dismissed the students, Henry and Elizabeth as happy about being released as they had been to see her.

"You're coming back tomorrow?" Henry asked before he left.

Abigail grinned as she collected books and papers. "Of course. I want to see what you'll draw for me."

The boy's smile broadened as he skipped into the foyer, passing his mother. Louisa stepped into the library and glanced back at the boy bounding up the stairs. "Those two sure left happy. Did they behave themselves?"

"They were great."

Her features turning serious, Louisa asked, "How are *you* doing?"

Abigail took a deep breath, realizing for the first time how weary she felt. She collapsed into a chair, lowered her head, and then looked up. "What can I say? It's been really hard." Then she managed a small smile. "But being back here with your two children certainly helped. Their bright eyes do."

Louisa walked over and took the chair her daughter had occupied a few minutes earlier, ruffling the yellow fabric as it gathered around her legs. Staring across, she laid a hand on Abigail's arm. "I'm so sorry for what you've had to go through. I pressed him and Parker finally shared with me what he found inside that prison ship. Shocking." She shook her head. "No one should be treated like that . . . even in war."

Abigail nodded. "Mrs. Monteith, I can't tell you how grateful I am for your generosity. If it hadn't been for your advance, I'm not sure how we would've survived the past—"

"None of that." Louisa patted Abigail's arm. "We can afford it. And after everything, please call me Louisa."

"Well, thank you, then, Louisa." Abigail felt her eyes tear up.

Releasing her arm, Louisa reached into a pocket of her flowing dress, pulled out another envelope, and pressed it into Abigail's palm. When Abigail started to shake her head, Louisa said, "This is for this month's work. We can afford it . . . and I'm sure you need it."

"Then, thank you. Again."

Excited voices from the parlor interrupted them. "We control all of New York, soon the northern colonies."

Louisa sighed, looking at Abigail. "Now that the British have regained control, maybe the war will end soon." She rose. "And we can all devote our attention to important things." Her gaze drifted toward the stairs. "Like educating the next generation." She paused, then asked, "We'll see you tomorrow?"

"Of course, Mrs. Monteith—er, Louisa."

Abigail was rewarded with the mother's broad smile as the yellow dress disappeared through the doorway. Collecting the few remaining papers, she stuffed them into her worn bag.

From across the foyer, Hollister's ugly voice announced, "It won't be long now. Mark my words. Come Christmas, we'll all be celebrating in our club in London, toasting another victorious campaign by His Majesty's great army."

Dragging her weary body from the chair, Abigail walked out of the library, through the foyer, and out the front door, closing it softly behind her. She stared back at the closed door, almost as if she could see through the wood.

The Monteiths *and* Colonel Hollister.

She shook her head. The couple brought back memories of London, of warm friends and neighbors concerned about them and celebrating with them, all before Mother passed. Hollister, on the other hand, seemed to be the essence of Britain in the colonies—brutish, arrogant, and oppressive.

What a horror if Hollister's kind were to rule afterward.

52

After another draining tutoring session, Abigail figured she had enough energy to check on Molly. She hadn't seen her young friend for two weeks and decided her own spirit could use an injection of Molly's vitality. When Abigail stepped through the dusty doorway of the Gooseneck Inn, she spied Molly perched on a stool at the bar. As the girl raised a tankard to her mouth, she turned, saw Abigail in the doorway, and let out a high-pitched squeal. Slamming the mug down on the worn wood, she slid off the stool, ran over, and wrapped Abigail in a hug that made her stagger.

Despite her weariness, Abigail couldn't help grinning. "Easy, girl. You're going to knock this tired teacher down."

Molly released her grip and flashed an embarrassed smile. "I's sorry. I'm jus' so happy to see ya. I been workin' real hard and want to show ya." She took Abigail's hand and practically dragged her to a table in the rear, yelling at the bar, "Levi, bring Miss Abigail a drink and bring mine over here, would ya?"

By the time the bartender delivered two dented tankards to the table, Molly and Abigail had settled onto the hard wooden stools. Both women took slow swallows and set the mugs down, then Molly carefully pushed them back. "Don't wanna mess up the paper." She pulled a bundle of printed pages out of a pocket of her gray bed dress.

Molly flattened the curved pages onto the wood as best she could. Without waiting, she started reading, the words sometimes smooth, sometimes halting. "These are . . . the times that try men's . . . s-s-souls. The summer soldier and sun-shine pa-tri-ot, patriot will, in this cri-sis, shr-ink shrink from the ser-vice of their country." Molly glanced up at her teacher, emerald eyes shining.

Abigail recognized the words immediately. She shot a glance around the small bar, relieved to see she and Molly were alone except for the barkeep, who appeared to have fallen asleep, one side of his bushy black hair flattened on the wooden counter. Abigail brought her attention back to her student, who looked at her expectantly.

"How'd I do?"

"You did . . . incredible." Abigail's gaze swept the room again. She picked the bundled pages off the table and flipped to the front. No cover page. That was good. Fighting not to betray her apprehension, she indicated the papers. "Where'd you get this?"

"Your friend, Robert." Molly's words betrayed concern, her excitement waning. "Is somethin' wrong?" Her own glance mimicked Abigail's, darting around the room. "Anyway, he told Jamie and me we shouldn't leave it lying around, ya know, with the Redcoats comin' in and outta this place."

Abigail nodded.

"So we ask Levi to keep it hidden behind the bar. And when I git a chance and the coast is clear, I get it out and work on my readin'. There ain't much readin' stuff around here. Is that all right?"

Abigail nodded again and patted Molly's hand. "It's just that with the British controlling New York, we can't be too careful."

Abigail recognized Molly's halting words as the beginning of the rebel pamphlet *The American Crisis* by Thomas Paine. She'd heard about it, and Robert had even quoted a few lines from it on one of his visits, but she hadn't seen an actual copy. Hardly surprising with the British in control and hell-bent on shutting down any "rebel" printers. However, she was not surprised Robert had managed to procure one.

"This is a very famous pamphlet about the rebel cause," Abigail said. "Like Robert said, we need to be careful. I haven't read it either, only heard about it. Let me take a look." She scanned the first page.

> *THESE are the times that try men's souls. The summer soldier and the sunshine patriot will, in this crisis, shrink from the service of their country; but he that stands by it now, deserves the love and thanks of man and woman. Tyranny, like hell, is not easily conquered; yet we have this consolation with us, that the harder the conflict, the more glorious the triumph.*

Abigail stopped and looked back at Molly, who was staring at her with something approaching awe. "Did ya jus' read all them words?" Molly asked.

"Those words, and yes."

"And ya know what ya read?"

"Pretty much. It's easy because Paine is such a good writer."

"Do ya think I could ever read like that? I mean easy like that."

"Look how far you've come." Abigail glanced around to make certain no Tories were lurking in the shadows. She had a premonition they needed to use extra caution—ever since her brother's death, her paranoia ran rampant. "Just to be on the safe side, let's try reading something else." Pulling up her worn schoolbag, she slid the pamphlet inside the pages of the *New England Primer* and pulled out a soiled, folded broadsheet. She slid the worn brown bag back underneath the table.

Molly flattened the large paper atop the table and studied the block letters across the top. "Roy—al Gaz?" She glanced up.

Abigail kept her voice quiet. "*Royal Gazette.* It's a paper supporting Britain. The Monteiths had a few copies, and this is an older edition. Mrs. Monteith said I could use it for your lessons." She gave Molly a reassuring smile. "Let's try the first article." Her finger pointed to a piece on the right side of the broadsheet.

Molly started on the title. "George Washington wants to be a dic-ta-tor." She kept staring at the paper but asked, "What's a dic-ta-tor?"

Abigail frowned. “It’s like a king. One person who rules everyone.”

Molly’s gaze came up from the sheet, anxiety in her eyes. “Is that true?”

Abigail placed a hand on Molly’s arm. “Of course not. It’s only British propaganda.”

A commotion at the tavern doorway interrupted them. Two British soldiers stomped into the inn and pounded on the bar, yelling at Levi. “Two ales and make it quick,” the first one hollered. Both men wore red coats, though their waistcoats had seen better days. The scarlet wool was faded on both, and one had a few holes in the fabric. The two men were short and stocky and . . . neither one was Reeves. Abigail checked and, once confirmed, felt her heart rate ease. Both were too short, a little over five feet tall, and neither bore the parallel scars on their faces.

But that didn’t mean they weren’t like him.

The leader—at least, he looked a decade older and had done the talking—glanced toward the table where Abigail and Molly sat. He strode over, his gaze shifting from them to the broadsheet on the table. Voice thick with sarcasm, he said, “Well, look at this, Gaines. These two *ladies* are doing a little reading.”

The second soldier approached and glanced at the newspaper. He demanded, his voice tinny, “Let’s have a look. We’ve been told to bring in anyone caught with rebel propaganda.”

Abigail shot a furtive glance at her schoolbag on the floor.

53

Thinking quickly, Abigail reached out her hand to the second soldier and tried her best plaintive voice. “Sir, my name is Abigail Trench and, like the two of you”—she pointed to the Redcoats—“I’m British. From London.” She wore a fake smile and worked to keep her voice steady.

The two soldiers exchanged glances, and Abigail thought she read hesitation on their faces, so she plowed on. “I was a teacher in a charity school in London before I came over, and now I’m a tutor. In fact, I’m teaching this young woman to read.” Her hand brushed Molly’s shoulder and then picked up the broadsheet. She extended it to the older soldier. “And, gentlemen, as you can see, this is no rebel paper. It’s the *Royal Gazette*.”

The leader guzzled his entire mug and set it on the table. “Tastes like piss but at least it’s wet.” When he wiped his mouth with his red sleeve, Abigail noticed two buttons missing from the fabric. He snatched up the paper with a large hand covered in dark hair and tossed it to his partner. He turned to Abigail, his features stern. “Ma’am, Gaines and me ain’t no gentlemen and this here ain’t England. These here are the stinkin’ colonies and we’re at war. We got a job to do and that’s what we goin’ do.”

Waving the newspaper, the second soldier chortled, swiveling his head on a thick neck. He squeaked, “Why’s a woman need to know how to read anyway?” He elbowed his partner. “Women only need to know how to do two things, be a good mummy and take care of the kids. What d'ya think, Harrison?"

The older soldier—Harrison, Abigail now knew—glanced around the tavern, his brown eyes hard. Then he broke into a smirk and leered at the two women sitting alone. "Women are good for fadoodlin' and keepin' the kids quiet so a man can sleep. That's about it."

Both men convulsed in laughter. The second one handed back the newspaper. He released an ugly belch in Abigail's face, the stench fouling the air. She ignored it. He muttered, "Just a copy of the *Royal Gazette*."

Right then, Jamie appeared behind the men. "Well, if it ain't two of His Majesty's fighting men. Can we get ya another drink?"

Jamie must've come down the ladder behind the bar, because Abigail hadn't seen him walk in the door. He just appeared. She remembered his ability to slip in and out unnoticed in a crowd and figured the talent came in handy for more than mere pickpocketing.

Most likely, Jamie had heard the soldiers and figured Abigail and Molly might need rescuing. The young man stood about the same height as the two soldiers, but while he was wiry and quick, the two Redcoats looked like short, solid tree trunks. Jamie would have no chance against either one, much less two.

Surprised, both soldiers rounded to face Jamie. He didn't flinch. "Welcome to the Gooseneck Inn. Home to the finest whiskey around."

Jamie turned and threw a quick glance at Levi. "Levi, give these two fine British soldiers some of that great corn whiskey you keep hidden under the bar."

The bushy black beard masked any expression, though Levi studied the two soldiers with hard gray eyes. Without taking his gaze off the visitors, he reached underneath, brought up a bottle, and poured the golden liquid into two chipped glasses. He slid them to the edge of the bar.

Both soldiers stepped over, snatched up the glasses, and chugged them down. By the time they set the glasses back down, both men were grinning and coughing hard hacks. "That's more like it," Gaines managed in a tight voice.

"Glad you enjoyed it," Jamie said, grinning himself. "We believe in treatin' our brave defenders from across the water w' respect. You're always welcome at the Gooseneck." He turned to the barkeep. "Right, Levi?"

"Yup," Levi said, his face still expressionless.

Still keeping the grin on his face, Jamie asked, "What brings ya to our little pub?"

Harrison said, "We're huntin' rebel collaborators. Been sent to check out each crib on this street. Supposed t' arrest anyone suspected of supportin' the damn rebels. And we're lookin' for readin' materials that are—" He turned to his fellow. "What'd the major call them materials?"

Gaines chirped, "Subversive."

Harrison nodded. "That's it, subversive. Ya know, paper arguin' independence and such." He indicated the bar. "Gaines, check behind there. See if they're not hiding anythin'—"

"Subversive," finished Gaines again, grinning through broken teeth. He handed his rifle to Harrison and walked around behind the bar. He tried to shove Levi aside, but the big man wouldn't budge. Abigail read fury in the bartender's eyes, but then she watched a brief look exchanged between Levi and Jamie. In stiff silence, the bartender stepped aside. Gaines stooped down and slid bottles around, the sound of metal and glass clinking.

Harrison returned his attention to Jamie and pointed to the two women. "Either of these yours?"

Jamie sidled next to Molly and placed a hand on her shoulder. "This is Molly, the love of me life." Molly leaned her head against his hand.

"A pretty tart," the older soldier said, lust thick in his voice.

"Look-ee what I found," called Gaines in his shrill voice.

Abigail's heart jumped. She knew they hadn't stashed the pamphlet under the bar but wondered if Levi had hidden some other rebel literature there.

Gaines pulled another whiskey bottle from underneath and slammed it on the bar. "I think we need to examine this a little more closely." He smirked and filled the glasses to the brim, some of the amber liquid spilling onto the wood. Harrison stepped over and laid the rifles against the bar. In quick fashion, both soldiers repeated their earlier drinking performance, complete with more coughing and grinning.

With both men's attention elsewhere, Abigail used her leg to slide her schoolbag farther underneath the small table. The older Redcoat shook his head as if trying to clear the effect of the booze, and his eyes landed on Abigail.

Had he seen her furtive movement?

Harrison released another loud belch and stared at Abigail. "What's the deal with you?"

Her insides churning, Abigail struggled to keep an innocent smile plastered on her lips and her voice calm. "Like I told you, I'm a tutor. I teach the children from important families here in the city. I—"

"So what are ya doin' tutorin' this harlot? She ain't from some important family," Harrison managed, his words slightly slurred.

His gaze swiveled between the two women, and Abigail thought his eyes were clouding. She guessed the Gooseneck was probably not the first tavern on their trip today. She glanced at the two guns lying against the wood and the two tipsy soldiers. Would Molly, Jamie, Levi, and she have any chance against them?

She decided to continue her subterfuge. Still smiling, Abigail turned toward the intruders, doing her best to block their view of the table behind her. "Molly's a friend and wants to better herself. I'm just trying to help."

The ruse didn't work. Harrison looked at the two women and, turning his head sideways, tried to peer at the table behind them. A bit wobbly on his feet, he stared as if trying to focus. "Well, what have we here?" He pointed beneath the table. He took two uneven steps, bent over, and reached down. When he came up, he was holding her brown bag.

Abigail's voice caught in her throat. "That's my . . . schoolbag. Please be careful. It's got my schoolbooks I use in my work. The ones I use with Henry and Elizabeth, Major Monteith's children."

Pawing through the bag, Harrison stopped, his glare on Abigail. "Ya tryin' to tell us ya teachin' this jack *and* ya also tutorin' Major Monteith's children?" He shot a glance at his companion. "Jus' how dumb do ya think we are?"

Leaning against the table, the Redcoat held the bag open with one hand while the second fished around. Abigail held her breath. No one spoke in the room, the soft rattle of paper the only sound. When his hand came up, rather than the pamphlet, he held the note from Major Monteith. Out of habit, Abigail had always kept it on top. Right now, she was glad she did.

Harrison stared at it, trying to make out the writing. He called, "Gaines, git over here and read this."

The younger soldier came up beside his partner and took the paper. Squinting, he read aloud in his tinny voice, "This woman, Miss Abigail Trench, is in my employ and under my protection. If she is stopped for any reason, she is to be allowed to pass to fulfill her duties. Major Parker Monteith, Royal Regiment of Artillery."

When Gaines tried to reach inside the pack again, Abigail yanked it back, pulling it away from the soldier. She held it close. The younger soldier tried to grab it, but Harrison stopped him. Placing a hand on Gaines's arm, he muttered, "Better let the major sort this out. Hand me my gun. I'll stay here and ya go fetch him."

The two British soldiers' eyes met, and Abigail read some war of wills. After a moment, the younger man shrugged. He offered one rifle to Harrison and shot an ugly glance at Abigail that made her squirm. Gaines turned and sauntered through the door outside.

Abigail and Harrison stared at each other, and she refused to blink. Eventually, Harrison relented and walked over to the bar to pour himself another drink. With his attention diverted, she shot a surreptitious glance inside the schoolbag, working hard to keep her breathing even. Could she pull the pamphlet and hide it somewhere without the Redcoat noticing? A bead of sweat rolled down the side of her face, and she used her sleeve to wipe it. A glass to his lips, Harrison downed it, grinning at her.

54

As Abigail watched, the soldier kept busy downing more whiskey but at least stayed away from her some. Ten minutes later, the heavy door squeaked open, and she heard the voices before she saw anyone emerge through the doorway.

"She claims t' tutor your youngin's, sir. Even has a note supposed to be from ya," Gaines's reedy voice announced.

Then she heard the major's hearty baritone. "Her name, Private? What did she say her name was?"

Two men were silhouetted in the doorframe, then Gaines entered, followed closely by Major Monteith. Abigail hesitated. Did the major know she was tutoring Molly? Abigail had shared with his wife about teaching the young woman to read, trying to help her better herself, and Louisa had approved. But Abigail had no idea if the wife had confided any of this to her husband.

Gaines said, "Don't rightly 'member. Well, there she is." The squat young soldier pointed at Abigail.

She held her breath, trying to decipher the look on Monteith's stoic features. Then, beyond the first two soldiers, she saw a sight that made her choke.

Behind Gaines and Monteith, two more Redcoats strode into the pub carrying rifles with bayonets affixed. She had no idea who the first soldier was—older, darker-skinned with a shaved head and bushy black beard—but she recognized the next soldier. She stifled her gasp.

Reeves. Here. Her gaze fixed on the twin scars bracketing his face, one he'd had and one she gave him. She raised the schoolbag up in front of her as if to use it as a barrier.

Her eyes flashed to Major Monteith, whose attention fell on Harrison slouched next to the bar. Recognizing his superior, Harrison tried to stand up straight but had little success. Ignoring Abigail, the major stepped over to Harrison and addressed him in a firm, quiet voice. Abigail couldn't hear much of what was said, but she could tell Major Monteith was not happy.

Her glance went from Monteith to Reeves, ambling to the other side of the tavern, then to Jamie and Molly. After Gaines left, Molly rose from the table and joined Jamie in the far corner. Jamie kept a protective arm around the young woman's shoulders. Her green eyes were wide. Last fall, Abigail had confided in Molly about Reeves and the confrontation on the Green. She had described Reeves's scars, and she wondered if Molly recognized him too.

Abigail took a step toward the bar to be closer to Major Monteith . . . and to ask for his help if she needed it. Her heart thumped in her chest.

Apparently finished with Harrison, Monteith turned his eyes toward her. The major must have seen the stricken expression on her face because his first words were, "Miss Trench, are you all right?" His gaze jerked to Harrison, then Gaines. "Have my men been disrespectful?"

Abigail tried to respond but found her throat dry. She swallowed and managed, "I'm . . . fine." Monteith eyed her up and down, his face still impassive. Feeling his gaze on her, she tried to get out more. "I was tutoring . . . Molly, the young woman." Her glance went to Molly and then returned to Monteith. She struggled to find the right words. "These . . . these soldiers came in and demanded drinks."

Gaines squealed, "That ain't right, sir—"

Abigail cut him off. "They laughed at me for helping a . . . you know." She glanced over at Molly again. "Then they started rat-ting through my school things, and I was afraid they'd damage the books I use with Henry and Elizabeth." Abigail raised the worn schoolbag she'd clutched in her hands, working hard to keep it from shaking.

Monteith turned to the pair of soldiers and glared. Harrison must've had more sense because he withered. But Gaines argued, "When she said she taught this harlot"—one finger jutted toward Molly—"and then tried to tell us she tutored your chillins." He took a quick breath. "Well, ya gotta admit it's kinda hard to swaller."

"Gaines." Monteith uttered the single word in a way that froze Abigail, but the young soldier obviously didn't get nuance.

Pointing to the table where Abigail and Molly had been seated, Gaines stumbled on, "Then she said they was readin' that broadsheet. And ya told us to look fer any subversive materials."

The major's gaze went to the small table. He stepped over and picked up the paper. Bringing it back to where Gaines now stood, Monteith shook it at him. "It's a copy of the damn *Royal Gazette.*" His voice rose. "Which my wife gave her." He shook his head. "Can either of you men read?"

Gaines squeaked out, "I . . . can, sir."

An exchange on the other side of the room diverted all their attention.

"No. I don't think so," Molly protested.

"Hey, you a damn shake and my coin is as good as any," Reeves smirked. His hand went to Molly's breast and he squeezed.

Jamie slapped Reeves's hand away and stepped in front of Molly. "The lady said no."

Reeves, much taller, stared down at Jamie. "She ain't no *lady.*" Then back to Molly, "What's the matter? Is it these two?" He caressed the scars etched down the sides of his face, one after the other. "I got them scars from two feisty females." He grabbed his crotch. "They loved it and so will you."

Undaunted, Jamie stared up at the ugly soldier. "You *will* leave her alone."

"And what ya goin' do about it, *kid*?" Reeves reached for the bayonet at the end of the rifle.

"Reeves!" Monteith's voice thundered across the small room. "Private, what are you doing here?"

Reeves grinned widely, showing rows of brown teeth, and Abigail had a flash of ugly memory in the barn back on Long Island. He said, "Sir, ya told me to stick close to ya. I was jus' doin' as ordered."

Monteith's gaze swung to the soldier who'd entered with Reeves. "Davis, *escort* Reeves outside." He jerked his head to Harrison and Gaines. "You two join them. I'll deal with all of you later."

All four men made their way toward the door, but not before Reeves leered at Molly and blew her a kiss. "I'll be back." Abigail watched them leave, trembling, the scene in the barn flashing back.

"Once again, I apologize for my men," the major said, addressing Abigail.

She said, "Uh, thank you, Major."

Then he glanced at the others. "That goes to all of you." He reached into a pocket and threw a coin onto the bar. Nodding at Levi, who'd slunk into a corner during the whole encounter, Monteith said, "That's for your troubles."

He took a few steps toward the door and turned. "And, Miss Trench, I trust you will be all right." He stopped as if searching for the right words. "I mean, Elizabeth and Henry would be quite unhappy if I let any harm come to their teacher. We will see you tomorrow?"

"Yes, I'll be there," Abigail rasped. Watching the major stride out the door, her gut clenched. She feared she hadn't seen the last of Private Reeves.

55

The next morning Abigail got herself to the mansion on Water Street, but it took all her resolve. The encounter with the soldiers at the Gooseneck Inn rattled her, not to mention Reeves's confrontation with Molly and Jamie. Standing in front of the house, staring at the tall columns and the beautiful wooden door, she wondered, what if Gaines had explored her schoolbag further and found the *American Crisis* pamphlet? Would she even be here? Or would she be rotting in some jail somewhere? Or worse, like her poor brother?

She still trembled when she recalled it all, but then a kind of fury replaced the fear. All because of something they were *reading*. Was this new British government going to try to control everything they read now?

Glancing down the rows of impressive houses—one tall mansion after another, clusters of colorful flowers in front of the homes flowing like the East River itself—she had trouble reconciling such magnificence with the realities of life elsewhere in the city. She no longer recognized anything about New York as what she knew as British. Where was the traditional respect for law? The tolerance for individual liberty?

Once the soldiers left and she and Molly calmed down, Abigail decided they were too unsettled for any more reading instruction. She agreed to return to pick up where they were and left Molly with a big hug.

Later, she learned their experience was hardly unique.

Yesterday, all through the city, teams of Redcoats had stormed door to door, combing the houses and shops for "rebel sympathizers." The results were disastrous and not surprising.

When Abigail got home, she fixed supper for Father, who came in with a grim look on his face. Seeing his expression, she pushed, and he explained. On his trip home from the wharf, he'd spied a pall of smoke a few streets over. Concerned, he drew closer and saw a building on fire, the structure fully engulfed in flames. Adults and children stood there, holding each other and staring at the inferno, trembling and crying out loud. He asked around but no one would talk at first, the onlookers' eyes darting from the fire, then left and right. Finally, an older man in soiled breeches and shirt told him soldiers had found some "suspect" material inside and decided the place housed rebel collaborators. Three Redcoats simply burnt it to the ground, laughing at the spectacle.

Abigail did what she could to comfort Father, then decided it best not to burden him with her own close encounter with His Majesty's soldiers. After supper, the two spent a quiet night together reading.

And today, she was back at the house of a British officer.

She put on a brave face, raised her hand, and knocked on the massive door. Opening it immediately, Louisa greeted Abigail with a warm hug, the woman's nearly white dress engulfing her, and Abigail took in the scent of the white flower in Louisa's hair. After ushering her inside, Louisa repeated her husband's apologies from yesterday. She grasped Abigail's hand in hers and squeezed. "Are you all right? Parker told me about what happened, uh . . . with the soldiers. They can be such brutes." Louisa's blue-gray eyes held pools of sympathy.

Taking a slow breath, Abigail inhaled the sweet scent of the white gardenias floating in a bowl near the entrance and offered a weak smile. She glanced down at the black-and-white checkered pattern of the floor and then brought her gaze up. "I'm all right . . . and Elizabeth and Henry always make things better." And she meant it.

"That they do . . . when they're not driving me crazy. Like I've said before, we're lucky to have you. The children *and* the major and I." She squeezed Abigail's hand again and released her. Louisa called up to the children and then turned back to Abigail. "Parker mentioned some officers will be over later today. So if they get loud, close the door and do your best to shut them out."

The children hurried down the stairs and Abigail herded them into the library. Within a few minutes, both Elizabeth and Henry were concentrating on their respective lessons, legs tucked underneath the tables, pencils grasped in small hands. Abigail had decided to switch things up, Elizabeth working to read a science article Abigail had found and Henry starting on basic addition facts. She handed Henry some small pebbles she picked up along the way to use as counters as he worked on his sums. Next, she listened as Elizabeth tried to decipher the words on the page, much as Molly had done yesterday.

Abigail struggled to keep her attention on the children's lessons, though, as her mind kept returning to the close call yesterday . . . and to Reeves. She resented how the trauma haunted her and she needed to do something to deal with it. She had no idea what. Thankfully, her students wouldn't let her dwell as they kept demanding her help, bringing her back to the present, over and over again.

Midday, loud voices echoed in the foyer, announcing the arrival of the officers. She heard that arrogant prick Hollister and one other voice as the major welcomed the visitors. The men seemed to be arguing strategy as they made their way in the front door and through the foyer.

"I applaud General Howe's efforts to sweep up the rebel collaborators. The locals have no illusion about who is in charge now," Hollister pronounced in a haughty voice. "But I tell you, Andre, he's not going to send men north to help Burgoyne."

"But Burgoyne needs the help," the other voice said.

Hollister chuckled. "Of course he does, but Howe is never going to divert troops from New York. The city is too big a prize and he's scared of what move old George might make."

Abigail glanced at Henry and Elizabeth who seemed unperturbed, intent only on their schoolwork. She decided to get up and close the door anyway. When she reached for the handle, she glanced across the hallway.

The two newcomers stood in the doorway to the office, their backs to her. She recognized Hollister, short and rotund, and took in the second—Andre, she deduced—a younger fellow, maybe late twenties, tall and thin with a full head of black hair. Hollister let the younger man go ahead of him, and turned as the maid entered the foyer, balancing a tray with a wine bottle and glasses. His face lit up and he greeted her, "So good to see you, Ruth." With a flip of his hand, he invited her to precede him as well and then glanced at Abigail across the space. He faced her in his pressed red uniform, one blue feather dangling from a button. With a curt wave, he smiled, nodding at her. Hollister turned and continued on, his voice still clear as he disappeared inside the office. "Howe won't take that chance, I'm telling you."

As she pulled the library door shut, catching the last of the exchange, realization struck her.

PARKER

56

Major Parker Monteith was nervous, unusual for him.

From his first day in His Majesty's service, deferral to authority had been inculcated into him. From that day years ago when his father purchased his commission as an officer in the British army, he had understood the responsibility to follow orders and not question the authority of those in charge. It was the essence of military protocol . . . and he concurred. On the battlefield, chaos would reign if soldiers could decide which orders they chose to follow and which to ignore. He had seen men whipped for violating this rule.

Yet, he was here anyway, ready to question orders, if not to ignore them. This week had altered his resolve. When the orders came down to search and root out rebel collaborators and sympathizers, he had led his company of men to their assigned quarter of the city. After hours of searching, rousting locals, and tossing businesses and homes, his hundred men had little to show for their efforts. Worse, all they seemed to accomplish was to anger residents who were already on the verge of revolt and push them into the arms of the rebels. He spent half his time trying to calm tavern owners, furriers, and smithies furious with the intrusion into their businesses, and using his own money to pay off locals to soothe their anger and compensate for the turmoil his men had caused.

After being summoned by his men, Parker found the blacksmith, a squat man with broad shoulders, massive arms, and a face surrounded by a mass of black hair and beard, pacing back and forth and threatening his two soldiers with a glowing iron. The man's brown eyes huge and his teeth gritted, he waved the hot chisel in front of his leather apron, poking toward the terrified soldiers. "I think it good when you Redcoats take the city, but now I realize I wrong. People are so scared, my business drop. Then you put ugly soldier in my work and home. He not only eat everything, he scare my customers. Now today, you search for supposed rebel papers." He spat on the ground at Parker's boots. "Is too much."

Parker agreed, it was too much.

All his company had recovered after hours of rousting residents and repeated confrontations between his soldiers and locals were a few worn and tattered copies of their "Declaration of Independence." Some rebel propaganda. Via the grapevine at the camp, he had heard other companies had "uncovered" some supposed rebel collaborators, but when he heard what counted as evidence—a few copies of pamphlets and rebel literature—he doubted any of it constituted treason against the crown. And for this, the soldiers had torched three more houses.

He found Cain and Hollister on the soft sofa and love seat, both smoking cigars. In a chair next to the pair, Parker recognized the young man who had visited his home last week, Major John Andre. His red uniform spotless and white wig atop his black hair, Andre sat bolt upright, as if he had a stiff board up his back. By way of greeting, the man nodded and smiled. Parker returned the nod but not the smile.

Cain's uniform appeared still pressed, and when he crossed his legs, his breeches looked clean and fresh. Parker guessed the lieutenant colonel had not been up all night at Martha's Place. Hollister, on the other hand, looked disheveled, his red greatcoat unbuttoned, the silly blue feather dangling. Watching him approach, the two officers blew white smoke rings, the odor of sour cigar smoke heavy in the room. He stopped a few feet in front of the group.

Cain was the first to speak. "Ah, Major Monteith. We're glad to welcome you back to your old lodgings." He glanced at Hollister and chuckled. "I'm afraid our offerings here pale by comparison to your wine cellar." He picked up a glass half-filled with a dark red liquid from the side table. "All we have to offer is this port." He took a long swallow.

These officers were drinking at this time in the morning. Though he noticed Major Andre had neither cigar nor drink. If Cain and Hollister were drunk, it would make this discussion that much more difficult.

"I am fine, sir," Parker said and cleared his throat but did not say more.

Hollister's eyes narrowed. He tossed back a drink and set the glass down on the wooden table with a bang. "Well, out with it. What brought you up here and out of your fancy Water Street mansion?"

Realizing there was no easy way to start, Parker jumped in. "Sir, I have come to register a major concern." He paused and then went on. "A formal complaint."

Cain and Hollister exchanged glances, and both started laughing. The two older officers hooted so hard, they both began coughing, their eyes tearing up. Parker watched the two and waited. When the half-laugh, half-cough began to settle down, Hollister looked up again. Pointing the lighted cigar, Hollister got out, "He wants to register a formal complaint," and then he launched into another fit of laughter. Within seconds, Cain joined him. The third member of the group, Major Andre, remained stoic.

Parker stood erect and at full attention. Fighting the inclination to ball his fists, he managed to keep his fingers flat on the side of his greatcoat. He shot a quick glance at Andre, who raised his eyebrows and shrugged. It took all his patience, but Parker waited, deciding both men were indeed drunk. He held his tongue, watching the two colonels giggling like schoolgirls, ignoring their cigars, which dropped hot ashes onto the blue fabric.

It took a few minutes before Cain said, "Well, don't just stand there like some statue. Why don't you share your concern with your superior officers? We're all ears."

This last comment set Hollister laughing. He glanced at Parker's stoic face. "Sorry," he said and then chortled again. He caught himself and brought a fat finger up to his lips.

Parker's gaze went from Hollister to Cain, whose features got serious. Cain scowled at him. "Well, out with it, man."

"Sirs," Parker started, noticing his throat had gone dry. "It . . . my concern is about our assignment last week." Both officers stared back with blank faces. "Our orders to roust the locals, looking for rebel sympathizers."

"What about it?" Hollister snapped, his bloodshot eyes fierce.

"Sirs, as you probably know, my men carried out our orders in our sector . . ." Parker stopped, suddenly unsure how to proceed.

Cain ordered, "Get on with it. We don't have all day. What about your orders?"

This was proving even harder than he had thought. Parker began to doubt his intention. He tried again. "Sirs, not only were last week's efforts to find rebel sympathizers and saboteurs unproductive and wasteful, all we succeeded in accomplishing was to alienate and anger more and more residents, many of whom are loyal to the crown. Or at least, used to be."

Hollister sat up and glared at Parker. "What do you mean *used to be*?"

Parker began recounting his experiences, starting with the blacksmith and then adding the comments of several other merchants. "I used my own money to soothe over their injuries, but I am not sure it did much good." When neither responded, he added, "To win this war, we need the locals on our side. I believe all we did last week was push the residents into the arms of the rebels. Many did not say that in so many words, but from my conversations with them, I could tell our actions strained their loyalty even further."

Setting his cigar down, Cain pointed at Parker. "Further than what?"

Parker stared from Cain to Hollister and finally to Andre. "You cannot be serious. Have you not traveled through those parts of the city? Have you not seen the state of those locals since . . . since the fire?"

Hollister blurted out, "The fire Washington's army started as they abandoned the city."

A fury now seized Parker and he leaned toward Hollister. "Come, Colonel Hollister, we are not before the ignorant soldiers. Remember, I was there. I saw you light that fire."

Hollister's eyes went wide. "You forget yourself, *Major.* I can have you court-martialed for your insolence."

Parker was in this deep, so he pressed on. "It matters little. General Howe promised to restore the city. And here we are almost a year later and how much have we done?" He faced Cain. "People remember such promises."

Hollister blustered, "General Howe believes the rebels were responsible for the fire and should be held accountable for it."

Parker turned his glare back to Hollister. "But we know that is not true."

Hollister started to rise, his fat legs struggling to lift his bulk from the couch, but Cain reached a hand out to restrain him. Hollister sat back down with a "Humpph."

Cain asked, "What does all this have to do with your current concern?"

Parker released a sigh, glancing first at the ceiling, then at Cain. "These people, the local residents and merchants, have been pushed to their breaking point. Since the fire, many have no decent place to live and nowhere to earn a living. And those who are working, the merchants and shop owners, make little money because so many people have nothing to spend." He now looked at both his superiors. "All the soldiers' actions did last week was inflame the locals further and drive them into the arms of the rebels."

It looked like his words were having little effect. Parker braced himself for a scolding *to remember his station.*

ABIGAIL

57

"I'm settled now, but I was pretty rattled then, I can tell you," Abigail said to Robert when he showed up the next day at her place. He'd asked to accompany her on a walk and, after checking on Father, she let him escort her.

She hadn't heard from Robert in a few weeks and assumed, with all the Redcoat activity in the city, he was trying to keep a low profile. As they strolled away from her flat, the evening warm and humid with the threat of rain hanging in the air, she told him about the events at the Gooseneck Inn and the close encounter. When she related Reeves's actions, she felt Robert go tense next to her.

"At least, I can talk about it now." Abigail released a sigh. "Between fearing what would happen if they found the pamphlet and worrying Reeves would whip that bayonet off—" She stopped and shook her head. "I'm just glad it's over."

Robert said, "I'm relieved you're all right. You're one tough woman."

Saying no more, he took her hand and they strolled. She figured Robert had a destination in mind and she was content to go along. A folded cloth over one arm, he led and she followed, turning at street corners and down a few roads. As they passed some of the devastated parts of the city, Robert hurried her past the remnants of charred, decaying wood.

Robert muttered, "The British can't even bother to clean up and rebuild this area. And it's been almost a year."

They passed a two-story building—or at least what used to be a two-story structure—still smoldering. She realized they were looking at one of the recent torchings by Redcoats on supposed rebel collaborators. As they walked past, they saw a family nearby, a mother and three small children, all in tattered clothes and with filthy faces. The woman's wide eyes pleaded and the children wept, but no one said a word. Releasing Abigail's hand, Robert reached into his pocket, pulled out a few coins, and placed them in the woman's palm.

She cried and managed, "Bless ya, sir."

Together, she and Robert made their way down Cherry Street to the dock area, where a few structures had been cleared and rebuilt, though many collapsed buildings still sat in the disarray from last year's inferno. At the wharf, Abigail saw three ships anchored in the harbor, their hulls slowly rising and falling in the current of the river. Pointing to the second ship with the word *Friendship* painted across the bow, she said, "That's where Father's been laboring."

As they crossed the wharf area, Abigail noticed a man standing alone in the shadows. She couldn't see much of him but noticed he was dressed in soiled dockworkers' clothes and had a full head of black hair with a matching, bushy beard. There was something about his presence, though he didn't seem threatening. As they passed, the man gave a curt nod.

Robert urged her a little farther along the shoreline past the piers and around a bend to where a tall oak tree, full in leaf, shadowed a gently sloping hill. Opening up the cloth he carried—which turned out to be a beautifully crafted quilt in brilliant colors of gold and red—he spread it out beneath the tree and invited Abigail to recline. She did and he joined her. Away from the hubbub of the dock, the noise died away. They lay side by side staring at the sky slowly changing from blue to indigo.

Casting a glance back toward the harbor, Robert asked, "How is your father?"

Abigail turned to look at him. "You know Father. Stubborn and insists on going down to work at the dock every day. He says he's fine, but I can see the toll it's taking on him."

Robert said, "He is one tough man."

When he didn't respond further, she turned her gaze back to the clouds gathering in the sky. They lay there in silence, water tumbling over rocks at their feet the only sound. After a minute, Robert asked, "How goes your tutoring?"

"Well, the Monteiths haven't set me packing." She chuckled. "Both Elizabeth and Henry are doing fine. Oh, and you won't believe how much progress Molly is making. By the way, thanks for the Paine pamphlet."

"What did you think of his writing?" Robert asked, glancing around.

"Seditious words," she whispered, "according to the *Royal Gazette*."

"You know of the *Royal Gazette*?"

"I am a teacher, remember." Then she explained the Monteiths received editions and she had used an old one to teach Molly.

Robert smiled, reminding her how much she enjoyed that smile. Then he looked around as if searching for possible eavesdroppers. He lowered his voice to a whisper so quiet Abigail had to turn toward him and lean closer to hear.

"First of all, I apologize I've stayed away," he said, contrition etched in his features. "I didn't want to but thought it a necessary precaution."

"I didn't know what to think."

"I probably shouldn't have told you about that." He shook his head. "It's just . . . I don't know. After your brother's death, you seemed so desperate. I wanted to give you some hope and couldn't think of anything else." He extended his hand to her.

Abigail grabbed it. "I'm glad you trusted me with your secret. I've told no one and never will."

"I know. I was never concerned about that. But it's been hard to stay away. I want you to know I care about you, Abigail. That hasn't changed. Still, I thought it best to keep my distance until I could be sure it was safe." His gaze swept the area again. "I believe it is now."

He continued, "Besides, it has taken me a while to set up my network. I have a network of people I can trust to keep me informed of . . . um, important matters."

Abigail released the hand and sat up. "Like the man at the wharf?"

He joined her, surprise igniting his features. "How did you know?"

"I didn't. I guessed. A man who could keep an eye on the comings and goings on the wharf would be a valuable source of information. And he seemed quite, um, comfortable with you."

"I'll have to remember never to try to outsmart a teacher." He smiled.

"Are you satisfied? I mean with your contacts around New York?"

"I'm still building my network, slowly." He shook his head. "I fear this will be a long war and I'll have to stay vigilant if I want to be of help. And stay alive doing it."

Robert grabbed a stone from the ground next to the quilt and tossed it into the water. Together they watched as the pebble skidded across the waves three times and disappeared below the surface.

Abigail took a deep breath. She figured she might as well go for it. "Could you use one more? Informant?"

58

"Do you know someone?" Robert asked, his eyes narrowing.

Abigail said nothing and merely stared at Robert, raising her eyebrows.

"You can't be serious." He shook his head again. "Abigail, this is dangerous work." He took both her hands in his and stared back at her. "Deadly work. You saw what happened to Nathan."

"Just listen—" she started.

"I could never forgive myself if something ever happened to you." He shook his head hard.

"I don't want anything to happen to me either." She stared across.

"I can't take that chance." He dropped her hands and one finger traced the sewn pattern.

Abigail shrugged, glancing at the water. "Fine. Then I guess I won't bother sharing what I overheard about the plans for Burgoyne's campaign." When he didn't respond, she added, her voice lilting, "Information Washington might find quite helpful in deploying his army."

Robert got up and paced around the tree while Abigail sat, staring out at the harbor. She studied the British man-o'-war bobbing in the waters, sailors scurrying about the deck. Farther downriver, she barely made out the outline of the prison ship where her brother died.

Robert stopped, hands behind his back, looking down at Abigail. "Even if you do have some valuable information, I can't simply give it to Washington. It doesn't work like that. The general doesn't even know who I am. I'm just one part of a ring which eventually ends up with Washington."

"The Culper Ring?"

"Yes . . . and I shouldn't have even shared the name," he said, shaking his head.

Neither spoke for a few moments. Taking a deep breath, Abigail said, "Why don't I tell you what I've learned, and you can decide how valuable it might be?"

Robert sat down again, facing her. "That doesn't mean I agree with you becoming an informant, but of course I want to know any information you might have."

Abigail relayed what she'd overheard about General Burgoyne's plans to attack upstate New York and Howe's reluctance to send reinforcements. He listened intently, stopping her twice to ask her to clarify a point or repeat what she heard.

When she finished, he started nodding. "This *could* be very valuable information to General Washington."

Encouraged, Abigail explained how the British officers frequent the Monteith house. "I think they come mostly for the Monteiths' wine selection, which they drink quite a bit of. Anyway, while they're there, they often talk about army plans and even discuss war strategy."

"Parker Monteith openly talks about such things?" Robert shook his head. "He seems quite the buttoned-up soldier from the few times I've met him."

"No, the major simply hosts these gatherings. I've never heard *him* saying much. Usually, it's one of the higher-ranking officers, like that cruel Hollister . . . the one who ordered the couple burned."

"And they just talk about army plans? With the door open and everything?"

"What else do they have to discuss?" Abigail asked. "Talk of Martha's Place can only take so long." She shrugged. "They ignore me. After all, I'm just a lowly teacher tutoring children. What interest would I ever have in important affairs of the army? They treat me like a servant, or the furniture."

"Abigail Trench, you continue to surprise me." He leaned in and kissed her, his lips lingering.

Abigail stared at the man across from her, seeing him in a different light. From their first encounter, he had seemed quiet, confident, and even guarded. A simple and unassuming businessman. His generosity and courage became evident only in a crisis, like the fire. It was not part of the public man. She took all this to be his nature but realized now it might also be for his own protection in his new role.

"Can you get the information to Washington? I mean, how does it work—" she started and then broke it off. He said he didn't want to share the details. Still, she was dying to know . . . something. She kept her voice quiet. "I know you can't tell me much, but how do you get your information?" She glanced at him and her eyes brightened. "I bet you hear a good deal from the soldiers who come to your store. Do the soldiers talk as much as Hollister?"

He shrugged again. "You'd be surprised. Sometimes they're bragging, sometimes they're drunk, and sometimes they just let something slip. I pretend not to listen."

"That's all it takes?"

"Oh, I have a few informants who feed me information from time to time, like the man on the wharf."

She paused and then asked, "You think you can make any difference?"

"I believe I *can* make a difference." He took both her hands in his. "Think of what it would've meant if, last December, Washington had learned of the British plans to surround Fort Washington. The Continental Army would have been able to slip away and not get captured."

"And my brother might still be alive."

He reached across and hugged her. "I wish I could've done something to save your brother," Robert said. "That battle convinced me I needed to do something."

The horrible images she'd witnessed flashed by—Reeves's ugly face while he raped her, the anguished eyes of the couple as the fire climbed up their bodies, the grimace on Nathan's face as he was hanged, the icy feel of her dead brother's skin.

When Robert released her, she eased back and faced him. "I want to become one of your regular informants."

Robert was shaking his head before she finished. "Absolutely not. Like I said, it would be too dangerous for you."

She stiffened. "Oh, it's not too dangerous for you but it *is* too dangerous for me? Because I'm a woman?"

"No, I didn't mean that. It's just that, just that . . ." He stopped. "Like I said, I don't want anything to happen to you."

She stared back at him. "You can teach me. Teach me how to be careful, what to watch for, what to listen for."

Robert still shook his head, but his motion held less conviction. "I don't know. It's very risky."

"Yes, but think about it. I wouldn't have to sneak around. All I have to do is my job. Like I told you, Major Monteith meets with other officers at his house once or twice a week." She began talking quickly, though her voice stayed low. "And they talk about all kinds of stuff. Where I tutor is just across the foyer from where the officers gather and drink. I hear them all the time. I can't help it."

He asked, "Have you thought this through? Could you still go about your tutoring all the while you're eavesdropping? Could you do *this* to the Monteiths?"

The Monteiths had been quite kind to her. Could she betray them? Louisa had confided to her the Monteiths were planning to stay in America after the "conflict," as she'd called it. The children would need to be educated to make their way in this new land and, if the rebel cause did prevail, Abigail might be able to ease the Monteiths' transition to becoming "American," as people were starting to say. Not only would she not have to compromise her tutoring, but Abigail's position in their house could actually help the Monteith family if the colonists prevailed. And if the British won, it wouldn't matter anyway.

Provided she was not found out and hanged for treason.

Then she thought about snippets of conversations she'd overheard at the mansion, arguments about orders, and even remembering hearing Nathan's name spoken. If she could hear of some plans that might save other Olivers in other battles *and* advance the rebel cause, she'd be happy to do it. She would no longer feel helpless.

"I realize it's dangerous. I'm no fool. I will need to be as cautious as you, though hopefully others would never think of a woman doing anything as devious as spying." It might be *devious*, but it was wholly necessary. She stared into Robert's eyes. "I will just need someone to teach me what I need to know."

He released a breath. "I may be able to help with that." He reached his hand to her chin and kissed her.

V

SPRING–SUMMER, 1778

59

Abigail was distraught.

Last fall she had convinced Robert she could contribute to the cause, that with her position in the Monteith household, *she* could make a difference. For weeks after, Robert trained her, though the lessons were always conducted under the guise of his courting her. She realized the courting was not all a charade, for either of them, and both prospects excited her.

He called on her on a regular basis, and they were often seen together, talking, holding hands, and smiling. She doubted anyone, even Father, had any inkling there was more than romance afoot.

To others, their relationship appeared to be one of flirtation and romance. And she was glad to have that as well. She melted a little every time he leaned down that beautiful head of reddish-brown hair and kissed her. On more than one occasion, he professed his devotion to her as well. But, at the same time, it all made for the perfect cover.

The sessions, as Robert called them, were never hurried and were conducted in several different locales. Sometimes, they sat on the bright red and gold quilt on the riverbank at Cherry Street, pretending to stare at the water, all the while she was learning how to be a spy. Other times, he would escort her to a dark corner of the Phoenix, the tavern he had first taken her to after Oliver's death, and they would conspire together like secret lovers. Sometimes, he would give a lesson as they walked on the street, two friends and lovers, as long as no one was within earshot.

With a quiet and patient manner, Robert taught her what to listen for in the officers' conversations and how to understand British military jargon. He instructed her on how to see through the sheer bragging and boasting for information that might be valuable. Then, he schooled her in memory tricks to help her remember critical details and retain them in her head without having to write as much down.

"Information recorded on paper can mean the rope," he warned her. She pictured Nathan swinging from the hangman's noose and shuddered.

Robert also advised her to remain impassive and unperturbed, even if what she overheard was life-threatening. "Your most important asset is your brain. Regardless of what you overhear, you must conduct yourself as if nothing is out of the ordinary. You must continue to be the *lowly tutor* they believe you to be."

She nodded. "I have to remain simply part of the furniture."

"Exactly." He leaned across and kissed her again. "A beautiful piece of furniture."

As it turned out, Robert was himself quite a good teacher. But when he showed her how to use invisible ink to convey secret messages, her heart thumped with delight. That evening they sat close together—intimate like the lovers they were becoming—in the corner of the dirty tavern, the place deserted. Mesmerized, she watched as Robert scratched the words "You are beautiful" with the special ink onto the page and then slid the piece over to her. By the time it arrived in front of her, the letters simply disappeared. She gasped. He grinned at her surprise, the sides of his mouth arching broadly. Then, he applied another liquid from a small bottle. The words reappeared! She squealed with excitement and he had to shush her, even though they were the only two in the tavern besides the sleeping barkeep. Robert even gave her a small vial of what he called "sympathetic ink" to use for special occasions. It still sat in a dark corner of their flat.

He explained the spy ring had developed a type of code to communicate and minimize possible exposure, using numbers to represent common words like garrison or power or even places like New York or Long Island. It had taken a while, but she had committed a number of the code words and numbers to memory.

She learned members of the Ring had been assigned a specific number to use in essential correspondence. They were only to know the next person in the chain, and individuals were referred to as their number.

Those weeks of training and learning had been heady, and Abigail started off full of hope and anticipation. But her training had ended almost six months ago. Since then, she had discovered very little. Some spy. Once again, she felt a failure, feared all of it was for nothing. The best she'd been able to do was pass on some plans for troop movements and what she'd heard about a large shipment of arms heading to Boston, but she'd not found out if any of the information proved to be of use.

Oh, she learned the British northern army under Burgoyne was defeated in September, thanks in part to her information, Robert told her. She had been thrilled and excited that her information had helped win that battle. It raised her hopes for her role as a spy. But after that, each month seemed to bring only news of more failures and setbacks for the Continental Army, their faltering condition matching her despair. And she had learned nothing that could help the cause.

Of course, she'd learned about the confrontation at Brandywine . . . after it was over and the Continental Army trounced. A few days after the battle, she'd overheard the haughty bass voice of Hollister bragging.

"Well, our boys gave old George another thrashing. Can you believe we took more than eleven hundred prisoners at Brandywine? I don't know how much longer George can hold his ragtag army together."

He laughed so loud that day it even disturbed Henry and Elizabeth. Abigail remained stoic, though her insides churned.

As if that defeat weren't enough, Howe and the Redcoats then took Philadelphia, routing the colonials and chasing the Continental Congress to someplace called Lancaster. And she learned all of this from the boasting officers *after the fact*, when the knowledge was too late to do anyone on the rebel side any good.

Her dreams of making a difference were being chipped away, month by month, her hopes waning with each passing week. That insidious paranoia started creeping in on her, and she wondered if somehow the officers, Hollister and the others, knew she was eavesdropping and had deliberately been careful what they said at the Monteiths'. In her worst moments, she feared it would all come crashing down. Struggling to keep a brave smile as she greeted Louisa and the major each day, she kept waiting for them to announce she was being arrested for treason.

Abigail realized this scenario didn't make sense. Robert continued to call each week, and, in their quiet moments, he explained the network was operating without interruption. The soldiers and officers continued to frequent his store, and he saw no signs of British suspicion. If no one suspected him, then it was unlikely anyone would suspect *her*. She knew all this, but some days her emotion overrode her head.

In recent weeks, she had begun to contemplate what life would be like under permanent British rule in America—which looked more and more likely. From snatches of conversation of the visiting officers last week, she had learned Washington and his army had suffered badly through the winter, a great many soldiers succumbing to cold and disease. If she could believe the Redcoats. Hollister bragged the surrender of the Continental Army was only weeks away. That prospect frightened her. For months, she battled her encroaching despair and feared she was losing the battle, and the Continental Army the war.

Until the first week of March.

On that frigid day, she stomped her feet to get rid of the snow she had gathered on her cold trek across the filthy streets of the city. By the time Abigail trudged through the front door, the officers were already crowded into the small study, arguing. It took her only a few moments to recognize their optimistic mood of last week had vanished. Before she got her coat hung up on the rack, she heard words that made her heart sing.

"Damn the French!" Hollister hollered loud enough to be heard throughout the whole house. "Why the hell would they want to side with the upstart colonies?"

"Because they want to stick it to England!" another voice called.

"Damn. Washington isn't going to quit now."

As she herded the children into the library, Abigail felt her smile widen. Maybe, all was not lost. She would stay the course, keep her ears open.

60

Like Robert had taught her, Abigail tried to be patient, though it wasn't easy. He explained over and over spies mostly waited and, most times, nothing happened. Every day she reported to the Monteith mansion for her lessons with the children, all the while keeping her ears open.

She had to admit Henry and Elizabeth provided her with a real sense of accomplishment, each time their eyes sparkled when they read a new passage or mastered a new set of numbers. Abigail tried to tell herself it was enough. In former days, it would have been enough. Now, she wanted more.

Though, she was not unhappy. In recent weeks, as Robert continued to call, their relationship deepened. They exchanged intimacies and shared more of their history. In time, they moved to more than mere kissing. Often breathless, she found herself wanting him more and more, wanting to be part of his world, his secret world. When his strong hands caressed her body and teased her breasts through the layers of fabric, she wanted to find some way to reward him for the thrills running through her.

Abigail felt he wanted more as well. His heavy breathing matched hers after they came up from an especially prolonged kiss. Her fingers explored him as well, his hard chest and strong arms through the wool of his shirt. When she felt compelled to let her hands drift lower, where she felt an incredible stiffness bump her, she held back. Society's morals restrained her . . . but that didn't mean she was satisfied.

"What is this word?" Elizabeth asked, dragging her teacher from her musing.

Abigail stared at the page of the *New England Primer* the girl pointed at and focused her eyes. She glanced at Elizabeth's face, then used her own finger to underline the word. "We've read this word before. Break it apart. Ex-hort."

The girl repeated, "Ex-hort," then put the two syllables together. She scrunched her features. "Exhort. But what does it mean? Exhort one another?"

"It means encourage. In this line, it means encourage people to be good." She pointed to the text again. "To avoid the deceitfulness of sin."

Elizabeth read the words aloud and then continued on, a bit haltingly but with little further trouble. Abigail heard the girl pronouncing the words but only half-listened. A few minutes ago, she'd heard the front door open and close and Hollister's brass voice. From the cacophony across the foyer, she recognized three voices besides the major—Hollister, one she had come to recognize as Colonel Cain, and a third who sounded younger. Though she couldn't catch most of the words, Abigail could tell by their tones they were excited about something. Something that might be of interest to her.

Her hand on Elizabeth's shoulder, Abigail gave a smile of encouragement as she rose from the chair. She walked over to where Henry sat, a few feet closer to the door. Pencil tip in his mouth, the boy worked his way through a list of minus problems. He looked up, a question in his eyes. Abigail scanned the paper he was working on and pointed to the fourth problem in the row.

"You might want to take another look at that one."

Henry pursed his lips. "Is it wrong?"

"Just check your work."

She stood there watching as he pointed his pencil at each digit in the problem. Then his eyes sparkled as he announced, "I see it. I'll fix it." His fingers got busy scratching through the wrong numbers and replacing them with the correct ones. Abigail nodded and Henry beamed.

She ambled toward the doorway, grateful the children seemed engrossed in their lessons today. They'd come a long way.

"The French fleet is due soon," announced Hollister in a haughty tone, his words slurring a bit. Abigail figured he must've drunk a good bit already. "Washington thinks his ship has come in, or rather ships," Hollister continued and then laughed, the chortle ending in a fit of coughing. "This, this'll fix him . . . good."

"Are you certain the French will take this route?" asked the third voice, the one she didn't recognize. Abigail figured the officers were looking at some map. She leaned but, in the open doorway to the office, could only see the back of one officer, red coat and white wig.

Hollister laughed again, the laugh half mirth, half scorn. "Yes, we're certain. We have sources inside Washington's circle."

Cain asked, "So, if we stage our troops and artillery here, we can attack the French fleet before they're even able to come ashore?"

Abigail desperately wanted to know where "here" was and was saved by Hollister's bluster.

"Hah. General Clinton has quite the surprise waiting for the French at Newport." He chuckled again. "In the form of ten thousand regulars! He may cut the legs off the frogs right there and end the war."

Newport, Rhode Island. She needed to get this information to Robert.

61

After what she'd overheard, Abigail struggled to contain her excitement and continue teaching. She did her best to hurry both Elizabeth and Henry through the rest of their lessons. Then an idea hit her.

"You both have been working so hard lately, I thought I'd let you finish early today," she offered. "What do you think?"

Elizabeth and Henry glanced at each other and answered in unison, heads shaking, "Thanks."

"Let's finish up what we're working on here and we'll call it quits for today."

Five minutes later, both children had turned their work in. Abigail packed up, slung the worn bag on her shoulder, and stepped into the foyer. Thinking she better cover for herself, she leaned into the office. The odor of alcohol wafted across the small space. A wineglass sat in front of each man. All four turned to face her and their conversations ceased.

She'd been right. The third visitor was a young officer, about her age she guessed, and he flashed her a wide smile. With his pressed uniform of red and black dotted with shiny brass buttons, he looked striking. He was the first to speak. "Good afternoon, miss." He nodded his head, the powdered wig firmly in place.

His name popped into her memory. She did a small curtsy. "Major Andre." When she came up, she said, "Major Monteith, I apologize for intruding on your important business."

Hollister slurred, "An interrup-shu-un by someone of your beauty is never an intrusion."

She wanted to say, "Keep your drunken comments to yourself." Instead, she smiled demurely and said, "Why, thank you, sir." She turned to Monteith. "Sir, I simply wanted you to know your children did quite well today. So well, in fact, I let them out early." She grinned. "I've learned a little reward goes a long way."

The major stood at his desk. "Well, thank you, Miss Trench. Louisa tells me the children continue to make excellent progress under your guidance."

Abigail said, "It is mostly them, sir. I'm just showing them the way. They're the ones doing the work and making the progress."

Monteith shook his head. "I doubt that, Miss Trench. Remember, I knew my children before you came along." He laughed at his own joke and the others joined him. "I . . . We . . . are grateful."

Abigail nodded. "Thank you again, sir. I'll take my leave, then. I'll see the children tomorrow." She backed out of the doorway as the men mumbled their goodbyes.

Once outside, she released the breath she'd been holding. Sometimes, it helps to be a mere woman and a lowly teacher.

She wanted to get this secret to Robert as soon as she could, though they had decided not to meet at his store. As she hurried into the city, her steps crunching on the pebbles, she decided her best bet was to leave a note for him at the Phoenix. The barkeep there served as a post office of sorts for him. Her feet moved quickly, the bag slapping her side as she strode. One man she passed looked at her askance and she decided she needed to check herself so she didn't look suspicious or draw attention. She slowed her pace a bit.

It was a cool spring afternoon, the air smelling crisp and fresh. As she passed warehouses and two-story buildings, the city even looked brighter, the water of the East River sparkling under the high afternoon sun. Abigail realized this was mostly the lens she viewed the city through, at least this afternoon, but she savored it just the same.

When she turned the corner onto Williams Street, she breathed a sigh when she saw the small wooden sign with some crudely drawn bird above some tongues of fire. The Phoenix. When she first saw the name, she had to search her memory to recall the phoenix was a mythical bird that was supposed to rise from its own ashes. On an earlier visit, she asked Robert if the name of the inn held any special significance. He'd chuckled and said, "I think the owner liked the sound of it. I don't know if he even knows the story about the phoenix."

As she passed under the carved sign, swaying back and forth in the breeze, Abigail was not so sure. Perhaps the Continental Army was supposed to rise from the ashes . . . with the help of the French, whom she might be able to save. She stepped out of the bright sunlight into the dark interior of the tavern. It took her eyes a few moments to adjust and she sighed when she didn't see Robert hunched over one of the scarred tables. Not that she expected to find him here. She was merely excited to see him, for reasons both romantic and secret.

In fact, she didn't see anyone at the tables. The only occupant was Harry, the barkeep Robert trusted. Leaning on the bar, he glanced up at her as the door closed behind her. He grinned, displaying a mouth of missing teeth. "You a sight fer sore eyes, Miss Trench."

She smiled. "Has Mr. Townsend stopped in today?"

Harry shook his head. "I expects him sometime, though."

She pointed to a small table in the back, near one of the oilcloth windows. "I'm going to write a note for him. Would you bring me a drink?"

"Comin' right up."

By the time she stripped off her cloak and set her bag on the other stool, Harry set the mug in front of her. Seated, Abigail shot a glance at the door. She had no choice. She'd realized she had to use the code to record the information. Shooting another glance around, she reached into her bag and withdrew the algebra book by Euler. From inside the back cover of the text, she pulled out the folded papers with small lettering and flattened them on the surface of the table.

The Culper Ring had devised a complicated set of numbers to correspond with words. Robert had instructed her on how to piece together a set of numbers that would look like, well, a list of numbers to anyone else, but those with the code would know how to translate the numbers into words that made up a message. Even though the numbers had been assigned mostly alphabetically—words starting with *a* and *b* had lower numbers, while those starting with *w* and *y* had much higher numbers—Abigail quickly learned there were far too many to memorize. So she kept the code hidden where she was confident no one would look, in the pages of Euler's *Elements of Algebra.*

She needed to think this through. Which words would she need to locate code numbers for? She started scribbling on another paper—which she'd have to burn when she was finished. *French* or *France. Fleet. British. Ambush. Newport.* That would suffice. She turned to the code. She remembered the places were at the end and found *France* quickly enough, 755. She wrote the number above *France.*

Then she moved up the alphabet, looking for *fleet* but couldn't find it. That was one of the problems with the code, Robert had explained. They couldn't have a number for everything. So she tried to think of another word that would work and might be on the list. As she sat there leaning over her note, she realized she had the tip of the pencil from the Monteiths in her mouth, much as she'd seen Henry do earlier today. She pulled it out as the word came to her—*ships.* She searched and found it, though it was *ship*, singular. It would have to do. She wrote 592 above *ship.*

"What you doing there?"

Abigail jumped and knocked the mug onto the floor. Terrified, she turned and saw the smiling face of Robert, his brown and gold eyes shining. She slapped his arm.

"You scared me, you cheek!" She felt her racing heart slow a bit.

He stifled her protest with a kiss. When they broke, he pulled up a stool next to her. "Harry, looks like the lady needs another drink and I'm mighty parched as well." He kissed her again.

When they came out of it, Harry stood at the table, two tankards in hand. He set them down and used a dirty towel to wipe up the spilled rum. As soon as he left, Abigail leaned close and whispered, "I have news. Important news, I think."

He pointed to the paper with the words, his brow scrunching as he read. "Looks like you were putting together a message."

She placed her hand over her writing and continued in a quiet voice, "It's about the French fleet."

Robert said, "They're due to land in the next few weeks, I hear."

Then she shared what she'd overheard and pieced together at the Monteiths'. As she talked, Robert listened intently but didn't say a word. When she finished, she asked, "Well, what do you think?"

He eased back on his stool. "I believe, Miss Abigail, you have proved you are anything but useless. Your information may just alter the course of the war."

VI

WINTER–SPRING, 1779

62

The information she'd overheard did in fact save the French fleet from a British ambush, though it didn't end the war. Still, she savored the fact she'd made a difference. She no longer felt useless.

But that had been months ago.

The week after the British plans to bottle up the French fleet failed, she heard the officers arguing and complaining, recriminations flying. She didn't need to eavesdrop. She couldn't help but hear. Hollister led the finger-pointing, his whining voice echoing across the foyer. Was the British information on French plans incorrect? Had the French received some kind of warning? With officers arguing, they blamed in turn the Royal Navy, incompetent government in London, and rebel spies.

When she overheard the last accusation, she froze, mid-sentence in Henry's lesson on long vowels. Would their suspicions point to her? Her gut clenched. Still, she waited and listened, straining to overhear.

"How do you say this word again?" Henry asked, his little finger pointing to the word she had scratched on her hornbook.

She dragged her attention back to her student, while still keeping an ear cocked toward the conversations going on across the foyer. Mustering up a teacher smile, she said, "The word is *sail*, like your mom, Elizabeth, and you sailed across the ocean."

Henry pronounced "sail" and scrawled the four letters on the surface of the hornbook. He went back to his lesson copying the other words on the list and Abigail returned to her fear, but nothing came of it. It seemed she was safe. For now.

For weeks after, the officers hadn't even showed up at the Monteith home. Day after day, the major's office had remained quiet with him working on correspondence alone or absent. The silence across the hall made the waiting harder and only fueled her paranoia. Were the officers avoiding the Monteiths' because they feared discussing plans anywhere but at the officers' quarters? Perhaps new orders went out, and they were ordered to be tight-lipped outside of headquarters.

In those weeks, she seldom saw the major and never spoke with him. So Abigail tried to engage Louisa to see if she could sense any change in their attitudes. Louisa expressed her gratitude for Abigail teaching, and she couldn't detect any shift in the mother's manner. Still, Abigail fretted. When she shared her concerns with Robert, he told her the staff officers were probably off conducting battles on Long Island or New Jersey.

His assurance helped, but still she fought her paranoia. She tried to focus on her lessons with the children . . . and wait. All the while, the rumors swirled around town. Some said the rebel cause was lost, and Washington was getting ready to surrender. Others said the Continental Army was proving to be stubborn. British soldiers were getting restless for home and would soon give up the fight. She had no idea what to believe.

That fall she cringed when she learned of more British atrocities in the Little Egg Massacre. Some cowardly loyalists surprised fifty Continental soldiers, but instead of taking them prisoner, they bayoneted everyone in their sleep. Each month seemed to bring some new fresh brutalities by the British. How much worse could their tactics get?

All this steeled her resolve.

Another Christmas came and went, and she was grateful to be able to cook a goose for Father and her, and Robert. His humor and funny stories about shoppers of his store, especially drunk Redcoats, helped to make the holiday bearable. Both Monteith children gave her a present—Elizabeth, a short story about faeries, and Henry, a drawing of a turkey. Their gifts nearly brought her to tears. And Molly gave her a beautiful beaded pocketbook—no doubt lifted by Jamie—but Abigail cherished it still. The small celebrations gave her a bit of respite from the anxieties of war, at least for a few days.

A few weeks after the holiday, the officers returned to the major's office, always Hollister and Cain and sometimes a third or fourth man would come, all eager to sample more of the Monteiths' wine cellar. Through it all, Abigail kept up her work, day after day, to teach Henry and Elizabeth, and to listen. Though she eavesdropped from the library door, nothing she overheard proved helpful.

Weeks melted into months. Then one afternoon, as a late March snow thawed and a cold sun made its appearance, something changed. By then, Elizabeth was making tremendous progress in her reading and Abigail had guided her through several sections of the *New England Primer.* Today, she was working her way through the text description of the Ten Commandments.

Elizabeth read aloud, "Q. 72. What is forbidden in the seventh commandment? The seventh commandment forbiddeth all unchaste thoughts, words and actions." She stopped her halting reading and glanced at her teacher, her blue eyes narrowing. "What is un-chaste?" She broke the word apart like Abigail had taught her.

Abigail stuttered, "Well, um, unchaste, um . . ."

How could she explain chaste to an eleven-year-old? In her head, Abigail tried a few definitions or synonyms but they all led to details not appropriate for such a young girl, even a very inquisitive one. Pondering possible explanations of the word, unchaste thoughts of Robert flooded her head and she felt her body get hot.

Something must have shown on her face because Elizabeth asked, "Are you all right, Miss Trench?" Worry etched on her young face.

"Um, I'm, um, fine," Abigail stammered. "Let's leave the seventh commandment for another day. Let's move on to the eighth."

Still looking a little puzzled, Elizabeth went back to reading the *Primer.* Thankfully, the eighth dealt with stealing, a much safer topic. As her student progressed down the page, Abigail was able to return her attention to eavesdropping.

Today, three visitors crowded the major's office, their voices boisterous at times. A good deal of discussing and arguing came from across the foyer, so loud, Abigail thought, they would distract the children. Both continued their work without even glancing across to the office. Obviously, Henry and Elizabeth had become so accustomed to the visitors, they tuned out the voices. Abigail did the opposite.

The officers sounded animated and, from their tones, not with recriminations or allegations. Rather they seemed excited about something. They sounded so energized, they talked over each other. All this made it difficult for Abigail to make out anything. Checking once more on Henry, she rose and stood just inside the doorway, head cocked toward the library. In the babble, she caught the words "colonial economy," "currency," and "bankrupt."

The officers left midday while she was still tutoring, the office suddenly going quiet. When she reviewed what she'd heard, she still had no idea if it meant anything. The officers had been agitated, so that must spell trouble for the rebels. When the time came, she released her students, complimenting them. "You two did a fine job, keeping your concentration on your lessons, especially with all the commotion coming from across the hall."

Both students beamed at the praise and Henry said, "I was working so hard on those long words, I didn't even notice them."

He surprised Abigail with a quick hug and both children disappeared out the door. Abigail listened to the clatter of their feet on the stairs. She gathered up her hornbook and the New England Primer, stuffing them into her worn schoolbag. When she hoisted the bag on her shoulder, she noticed two new holes in the worn fabric. She'd have to sew them shut later.

Abigail stepped into the foyer, still trying to puzzle out if the words she'd eavesdropped meant anything. Though she heard the children's pounding upstairs, the downstairs was quiet. Even Louisa must be out shopping.

She stepped across the hall and leaned into the office, studying the interior. No one. She was confident the major had left hours earlier with the other officers, but if she'd found him silently working behind his desk, she would've simply apologized and given him an impromptu update on his children's progress. She chuckled. She might've warned him his daughter might ask a question or two about unchaste. But the desk sat empty and the office silent.

She turned to head for the front door when she saw them. Two pieces of brown paper lay on the floor behind the one chair. She bent down and picked them up. They were colonial bills of credit. She studied them.

The Monteiths always paid her in British currency. It was worth far more and not subject to fluctuation. Louisa had said they never allowed Continental bills in the house. Abigail felt sure these officers would only carry British coin and paper. Why would they have Continental money? Even as she pondered this, she noticed something about the bills. She rubbed the brown paper between her fingers. Something about the paper felt different, felt *off*. Then she put it together. The snippets of conversation she'd overheard now made sense.

She needed to get this information to Robert.

63

She hurried along the city streets, her cloak open and flapping as she stepped. The more she thought about it, the heavier her secret felt. If she were right about what she'd put together from the words she'd overheard, the colonies were in trouble. Major trouble. Continental currency was iffy at best. Some merchants refused to even accept it. They already insisted on hard coin or British paper.

She turned the corner onto Dock Street and stepped up onto the wooden walkway. While she'd taught the children, the day had turned warmer and most of last night's snow had already melted, leaving small patches of gray slush clinging to the posts. Although still chilly, the air carried with it the promise of spring. She filled her lungs with the crisp afternoon air and, energized, hurried on.

As her feet clattered on the boards, she thought the whole thing through. If the British started printing fake currency and circulating it, the Continental bills of credit would be worth . . . nothing. Such a move would infuriate *all* the businessmen. Even loyalist merchants would suffer, because they depended on customers, both rebel and Tory. The entire economy of the colonies would collapse.

She stopped and glanced around her at the businesses up and down the street. The furrier, the blacksmith, the dry goods store, inns and taverns—they would all suffer. They wouldn't be able to feed their families. In the harbor, three merchant ships bobbed in the waves. Who would have money to pay for goods transported across the ocean?

Sweeping her gaze across the workers scurrying in and out of warehouses, on and off the ships, another thought came to her. Without Continental currency, there would be no way to fund the war. The only currency anyone anywhere would accept would be British pounds.

Oh God! Abigail wanted to head straight over to Robert's store on Broadway, but he had warned her against overreacting.

"No matter how big a secret you discover, you'll give yourself away if you appear overanxious or too excited," he had told her. "As much as possible, stick to your normal routine and find a way to get a coded note to me when you can. A zealous appearance is your enemy."

But this was so big, and the consequence so damaging, could she afford to wait? The urgent desire to get word to Robert and the need to maintain a calm appearance warred within her. In the end, she decided to heed Robert's advice and stick to her schedule. She had promised Molly she'd come by today for another lesson, though Molly was progressing so well Abigail was not sure how much she needed her teacher. Abigail smiled at the thought. Perhaps soon, Molly would be able to consider another way to earn a living. Her math skills had improved to such an extent, she thought Molly could get work in a shop or for some merchant. She knew how to deal with people—she had certainly managed enough unruly *clients* to prove that—and she had a quick head for figures. Maybe she could ask Robert if he'd consider hiring Molly. Abigail grinned at the prospect.

Another thought occurred to her. It was good she was headed to the Gooseneck Inn. She had to be careful what she told Molly or Jamie—she didn't want to put them in any danger—but maybe, if she asked the right questions, she could find out if Jamie had gotten wind of any counterfeit bills. He'd developed quite a network around the city, and he seemed to pick up on things faster than most.

Abigail was so caught up in her thoughts, she almost missed the turn onto Crown to get to Williams. The wind, which so often blew off the East River, seemed to die down today, making the city streets still. Hopping from one walkway to the next, she made good progress and, when she turned the corner onto Williams past the two-story boardinghouse, she moved the bookbag to her other shoulder and strode down the street, each step with purpose.

She'd taken a few quick steps down the walkway when she heard a voice from the alley ahead, a voice she recognized. Too well. She froze.

"My money's as good as anyone else, ya little whore!" It was Reeves. Here.

Molly called, "I don't hafta. Get your hands off me." Then, "Lemme go. That hurts."

Abigail took a deep breath and tried to stop her shaking. Molly needed her. She hurried to the end of the walkway. There, at the foot of the alley, she saw Molly squirming in the arms of a much larger man in uniform. The soldier stood with his back to her, but Abigail didn't need him to turn around. The ugly orange scarf around his neck gave him away. She pounded down the dirt alley and called ahead, "Just let her go, Reeves. Go find yourself another jack."

Reeves turned at the words, releasing one arm. When he saw Abigail striding toward him, he grinned, a lecherous smirk revealing the ugly broken teeth she remembered from Long Island. "Abigail, er, I should say, the fine Miss Trench."

Molly wiggled, but Reeves's one hand held her fast. "Lemme go, ya blackguard!"

Reeves's gaze went from Molly, still in his grasp, to Abigail, closing in on him. His grin broadened. "This is even better. I'm gonna have this here jack and good old Abigail can watch." He grabbed his crotch.

Rage burned in her gut. She had no idea what she was going to do, but she wasn't about to let Reeves rape Molly. She kept bearing down on him and slid her bag off her shoulder.

Reeves's eyes got wide, and he laughed, a lewd, horrid chortle. "Naw. I got a better idea. First, I'll do this here young poll and then I'll have a rut at Miss Trench."

Abigail ran full out and, three feet from him, swung her schoolbag at his head. It collided with his skull with a thud. He dropped the arm holding Molly, who scurried away.

Dazed, he shook his head, then glared at Abigail. His lips curled in a snarl. "Ya bitch!" He rubbed the side of his head. "You'll pay for that. You just assaulted one of His Majesty's soldiers. I can arrest ya jus' fer that."

Molly ran over to Abigail, the two women huddling together. Abigail said, "You are one sorry example of a soldier. When I report this to the major, he'll have your hide."

"Like hell ya will," Reeves said, his eyes glaring now. "Ya got me in enough trouble b'fore. On the Green. I ain't about to let that happen again." His hand reached to the side and he tugged. In seconds, the hand came away with a large silver bayonet. He waved it back and forth at the women.

Abigail saw the blade and froze. The memory of that spring afternoon flooded back, her on the floor of the barn, Reeves over her, the same bayonet at her throat. She shot a glance at Molly and saw her own fear reflected in the young girl's features. Molly's gaze jerked out to the front of the alley and Abigail guessed the girl was trying to figure if she could get help in time. Abigail calculated they were only about six feet away from Reeves, out of his reach even with the bayonet, but not far enough.

Reeves smirked, ugly teeth showing, and Abigail saw saliva drip out the side of his mouth. He advanced on them and both women started backing up, though they didn't take their eyes off him. A few steps back down the alley, a door opened in the siding and Jamie came out.

"What the hell?" He stared at Molly and Abigail, no doubt seeing the abject fear in their faces, and then turned toward Reeves, both hands up. He tried his smooth manner. "Good sir, we don't want any trouble here." He extended one hand and waved toward the inn. "How about ya come on inside and I'll get ya a few drinks, the good stuff? On the house, a'course."

While Jamie was talking, Molly and Abigail kept backing up, still keeping their faces toward Reeves. They had widened the distance, now more than ten feet. Jamie took a step toward Reeves, putting himself between the soldier and the two women.

Reeves's gaze jerked from Jamie to the retreating women, having to look around the small figure of Jamie. Then the smirk returned. "Naw, I don't think so." In one swift move, he shoved the blade toward Jamie.

Abigail saw the bayonet strike flesh, and then Jamie froze mid-step. Beside her, Molly screamed, "No!" and took off in a run toward Jamie and Reeves. Abigail had to follow.

Jamie dropped to his knees and Reeves bent over him. The soldier tugged again and again at his bayonet, making Jamie's thin body jerk with each pull. But the bayonet did not move. Seeing the women running at him, Reeves let go and sprinted around them out of the alley.

Jamie buckled, falling sideways, the handle protruding from the fabric. His shirt, which had been a dull white, now bloomed crimson, the blood turning the gray pebbles around his body a deep red. Ignoring the fleeing Reeves, Molly ran to her partner. Right behind her, Abigail's legs felt like they were going to give way, so she knelt beside her friend before she collapsed. Molly leaned over Jamie, her tears running so fierce they were dripping and mixing with the blood. She cradled his head in her hands and Jamie opened his eyes.

"No, no, no!" she cried, each syllable getting louder. "Don't ya leave me. Don't!"

Jamie tried to smile but managed only a half grimace. "Well, looks like I got it good this time, babe." Then he coughed and blood bubbled out of his mouth. "Sorry."

Molly pulled harder on his head. "No. Don't ya dare leave me."

Abigail stared at her first two friends in this city and her heart ripped out. She studied Jamie and could see color draining from his pretty face. Abigail's gaze traveled down his body, and she saw the knife just beyond his outstretched hands. Then she watched as the pool of blood widened, a mass of red framing his whole torso. So much blood and the sickening smell so strong. She'd never seen so much blood and realized there was no hope. As she watched, Jamie's brown eyes fluttered as he fought to keep them open.

He gasped, "I love ya." Then his eyes closed and his body stilled.

Molly's fist hit Jamie's chest so hard, the limp body flopped with the impact. "No, it can't be!" she screamed so loud Abigail thought the Monteiths could've heard.

64

Dear God, how much more could this war rip from her?

She remembered Molly needed *her* right now. In a tender voice, she said, "He's gone now," her tears flowing as freely as Molly's. She pulled the young girl in closer and tightened her embrace, even as her own tears dripped down the girl's back. Molly crumpled in her arms and looked every bit the young girl she was.

The next several minutes were a blur, but Abigail heard other people come down the alley, heard their gasps at the sight of Jamie. Levi shooed the others back in a gruff voice and, a minute later, returned with a large sheet, which he wrapped around the still body.

"I got him," the barkeep whispered as he lifted the corpse on his shoulder as if it weighed next to nothing. With his other hand, he opened the hidden door in the side, turned, and carried the body inside. Molly followed in a trance, and Abigail shadowed her, one step behind. They all watched as Levi gently eased the body off his shoulder, laying him out on the bar, the cloth covering him flopping open. The sheet, which had originally been some tan or brown color, now had long swaths of red, the scarlet darkening whole sections.

Once done with the body, Levi ducked behind the bar and came out with two mugs of ale. Abigail drank hers down right away, noticing it was stronger than normal. Good, she needed it. Molly didn't touch hers. She simply sat on the stool, staring at Jamie's lifeless body. Her only motion was to use her arms to wipe the tears from her eyes from time to time. The green in her pupils had turned almost opaque and red circled the irises.

"Here, take a drink," Abigail urged and held the mug to Molly's lips. The young girl turned her head and looked at Abigail, her curls drooping. The blond hair was streaked with red. Molly took a sip and then coughed, hard. She wiped her mouth with the back of her hand. After that, she took the tankard in both hands and drank the entire contents, her throat gulping as the liquor slid down her throat.

Abigail tried to figure out what she could do, what to do next. She noticed several patrons creeping closer, so they could hear the story. With an angry wave of her arm, Abigail shooed them back and Levi took care of the rest. In a few minutes, the tavern emptied out and they were alone, she and Molly and Levi . . . and Jamie's body. The inn quiet now, Abigail placed her hand on the girl's arm and kept it there. She didn't speak and waited.

Molly started and stopped her crying three different times, weeping, sniffling, coughing, and even hiccupping. Still, Abigail waited, her hand resting on the girl's arm. When Molly leaned toward her, Abigail wrapped the girl in her arms and let her weep into her own dress. When the sobbing slowed and Abigail felt the young girl settle down a bit, she eased Molly back up and looked into her eyes, which seemed empty of life. Both women sat there, silent, breathing together.

After a few moments, Abigail whispered, "Can you tell me what happened? Before?"

Molly nodded slowly and started in. "I was done with Phillip, my usual Wednesday, and when I slid me dress back down and turned, *he* was there." Her eyes went dark and she took in a long breath before she continued.

"That Reeves jus' showed up. He musta seen Phillip leave and snuck down the alley. He wore that ugly smirk we'd seen when he was in the tavern and said, 'My turn.' When I heard his voice, I turned and saw 'im, them ugly scars on each side of his face and all them black teeth. I 'membered the man. I said no."

She stopped and stared at Abigail, both eyes red and wet. "Oh my God. I got Jamie killed. I got me love killed!"

Abigail held her as the girl cried. She tried, "No, it's not your fault. You can't blame yourself. Reeves is an *evil* man. He's to blame."

As she pronounced the words, they sounded hollow, even to her ears. Blame. Abigail realized, if anyone was to blame, it was her. *She* was the one who brought that evil soldier into Jamie and Molly's lives. He might never have even known them or come to the Gooseneck Inn if it weren't for her.

As she held her, their faces only inches apart, Molly stared up and asked, "Jamie was me world. What am I goin' t'do now?"

"I'm here for you. We'll figure it out." Abigail patted the girl's arm, knowing there was little she could do to ease the young woman's pain. She'd been there.

But Abigail knew what *she* was going to do. What she had to do.

Later, when Molly's crying so exhausted her, Levi helped her up to her room and settled her on their bed, collapsed and sleeping. When he returned, he asked, his voice timid, "What do you want me to do?" His gaze went to Jamie's corpse on the bar.

Abigail fought to steady her voice. "Clean him up. I'll see if I can get some help with the . . . um, arrangements." She stared at the lifeless body, one whole side drenched in red. She reached down and grasped the handle of the bayonet sticking out of Jamie's side. It was slimy with his blood. She used the hem of her dress to wipe off the handle, the dark red smearing the bright yellow fabric. She glanced down at her outfit. Her gown wore blood stains all over the front—handprints, smears, and drops. Now an elongated smear across the bottom.

She tried to pull the handle free, but it wouldn't budge. Wrapping both hands around it, she yanked. Still, it refused to give way. She eased closer to the body, leaned over the top, and pulled with all her strength. The blade still stuck. No wonder Reeves fled without his precious bayonet.

Levi returned, a dirty rag in his hand. "Miss Abigail, ya don't need to do that. I'll hep ya."

When he stepped next to her, Abigail shoved him back. She needed to do this. He stared at her and then put up both hands in surrender. The lanky bartender took a step back and watched.

Abigail turned back to Jamie's body and examined the wound, the blade buried deep. She lowered her head closer so she could get a better look. The metallic smell of blood was so strong she closed her eyes and held her breath. Then she opened them and peered again. The bayonet went in so deep the guard was caught on something. Abigail realized she had to turn the blade to get it out. She rotated the heavy bayonet, hearing it scrape bone. Abigail cringed. Another slow breath. She grabbed it again with both hands and, using all her strength, pulled. It came free, and Abigail stumbled to the floor. Both hands still held the handle, and her fingers were now covered in Jamie's blood. Holding her breath so she wouldn't vomit, Abigail used her dress again to wipe off her hands. Levi threw her a towel, and she wiped off most of the gore.

Glancing around, she located her schoolbag and, using two fingers, carried the bayonet over and dropped it in, the metal blade still covered in red and white. She closed the bag and hoisted it on her shoulder. She had to travel across half the city, and it would not do for soldiers to see her carrying a bloody bayonet.

65

Abigail didn't knock. She simply opened Monteith's huge front door and barged inside, the heavy door slamming behind her. In three steps, she strode across the foyer and through the doorway. The major sat at his desk, quill in hand. Briefly, his eyes flashed surprise.

"Miss Abigail—"

Before he could say more, Abigail reached inside her bag, pulled out the bayonet, and threw it on top of the papers on the desk. The bayonet bounced once and flipped, dripping its white and red contents onto the letters.

The major jumped back in his chair. He scrambled to his feet, his gaze jerking from the bloodied blade to Abigail. His look turned from surprise to anger, his green eyes going dark. "Miss Abigail, what is the meaning of this?"

"This," she sputtered, "this . . . I'm just returning some property to *His Majesty's army*!" She laced the last three words with as much venom as she could muster. "I thought the owner might want it back so he could go on killing."

Seeing the major's face bloom in rage, she realized she might well be sacrificing her tutoring job—and with it, any chance to continue spying for Robert—but her own anger burned so hot she didn't care.

"Where . . . where did you get this?" Monteith studied the bayonet but still did not touch it.

"Oh." Abigail felt her voice crack. "Oh, I just pulled it from between the ribs of the lifeless body of a friend of mine."

The major's eyes went from the bloody bayonet to Abigail. "But how did it get there?" His voice got louder, his impatience showing.

"One of the fine soldiers in His Majesty's army stuck it there."

"Who? Why?"

Abigail spat out, "Your man Reeves. And because he's an evil, cruel bastard."

"Reeves?" Monteith's manner shifted, his arrogance cracking. "What happened?"

Abigail choked and yelled, "Reeves tried to force himself on a woman. She refused him and her man came to her defense. Reeves just pulled out his bayonet and stabbed him."

Just then, Louisa came into the room. She glanced at her husband and then at Abigail, her eyes going wide. "Abigail, are you hurt?"

Abigail looked down at her outfit, the plain dress splattered with red stains down the front. Her hands were filthy, covered with dried blood. She recalled the strange looks as she traversed the city blocks back to the Monteith mansion. Now she understood. She must look a fright.

Abigail glanced at Louisa. "Not mine."

Monteith asked, "You are sure it was Reeves? Are you certain this happened as you described?"

"I saw it all with my own eyes," Abigail said, recalling Reeves thrusting the bayonet into poor Jamie. "And yes, I'm sure. These are friends of mine." She choked back a sob. "Well, he was a friend of mine."

Louisa gazed at her, the pain showing in her blue-gray eyes. "Robert?"

Abigail stifled a cry. "No, Jamie."

"I'm so sorry." Louisa looked at her husband. "I met him at the funeral for Abigail's brother, Oliver. A nice, polite young man."

Monteith nodded to his wife and seemed to gather himself up to his full height. "This is a very serious allegation. You are sure?"

Abigail started, "Because . . . because I know Reeves. Reeves almost stabbed me with the same bayonet." Her angry finger pointed to the weapon, now dripping more blood onto the papers.

"You mean when Reeves challenged you and your friend on the Green—" Monteith offered.

Abigail shook her head hard, interrupting him. "That's not it." She glanced from the major to his wife and swallowed hard. "On Long Island, Reeves invaded our homestead and stole our livestock. When I tried to stop him, reason with him, he laughed at me. Then he raped me all the while holding *that* bayonet to my throat."

She had no intention of sharing that. She didn't know where the admission came from. It just erupted from her mouth before she realized it.

The major's response was predictable. "Wha-a-at?"

But Louisa's response surprised her. The woman came over and wrapped her arms around her. She gave her a tighter hug than Abigail would've thought possible. "Oh, I'm so sorry. And you've been carrying this around all this time."

Abigail could smell the fresh scent of the white gardenia bloom in Louisa's shining yellow hair as Louisa clung to her. Right now, Abigail really needed the mothering. Without letting go, Louisa turned her head and asked, "This Reeves, he's one of yours?"

Monteith exhaled. "Sadly, yes. And one of the worst."

She let go of Abigail and looked across at her husband, the two exchanging glances. She said, "You're not surprised?"

"He has pulled other things before and had to be disciplined. But not murder."

Louisa kept one hand on Abigail's arm. "Well, then don't give this woman the third degree. Ask her for the details so she can get back to her friends." She caught herself. "Friend."

Louisa sat Abigail down in one of the office chairs and sat next to her. Abigail spent the next half hour recounting everything she could about the attack. At the end, she was spent and only wanted to get back to Molly . . . and Robert.

When she got up to leave, Louisa rose with her. She turned toward her husband and said, "You know what you need to do about this. You need to make this right."

Abigail muttered, "It'll never be right."

Louisa said, "Of course, you're right." She patted Abigail's arm with a light touch. "You let us know if we can do anything . . . for the funeral or you."

66

The day of Jamie's funeral could not have been more different than when they had buried Oliver.

That was Abigail's first thought as she rode to the graveyard in the wagon with the blond wooden coffin in the back. The day had dawned a beautiful spring day, the sky a perfect azure stretching from horizon to horizon, with not a cloud anywhere. But Abigail felt just as cold as she had the day they lowered Oliver into the hole in the earth.

When they buried Oliver, the day was so bleak and her grief so great, she hadn't taken note of the graveyard surroundings. Today, with a clear sky and a warm spring breeze, she glanced around and saw what a beautiful area Robert had found for a final resting place. For Oliver and Jamie. The hillsides surrounding them burst with color, splotches of gold and blue and orange dotting the countryside as if some benevolent painter had added just the right touches of color to the flowing green grasses. Off in the distance, she could make out the glistening waters of the East River as it snaked through the hills below.

Again, Robert had stepped forward, securing a plot in the cemetery next to Oliver, after asking if that was all right. He did it all in two days. Her only comment was, "Oliver would've liked Jamie."

There was one major difference, though. They were hardly alone today. She, Father, and Robert were accompanied by Molly and Louisa Monteith, who had once again insisted on coming in her fancy carriage with her footman. Levi had closed the Gooseneck Inn and came as well, his lanky frame bent over in grief.

But word of Jamie's death had spread. Dozens of other knucklers and friends in his network heard about it and showed up to pay their respects. A few of the young men were dressed in fancy waistcoats and breeches and even a bowler, but most of the buzzers, as Jamie called them, looked the part, in shabby clothes and shoes with holes at the toes. Many of the guys were accompanied by a woman or girl, likely the pair making their way on the street, like Jamie and Molly had. Although two had horses, most had come on foot, a journey of more than an hour from the city.

When the service was complete and the preacher had done his best, each of the mourners filed past the recently dug hole with the wooden casket at the bottom, tossing a handful of dirt into the grave. Then, one by one, they came over to Molly to pay their respects. Abigail, Father, and Robert stood at a discreet distance, silent and watching. Some of the knucklers wrapped Molly in a hug and the women kissed her on the cheek as they hugged her. Abigail saw some of the men slide some coins into the pocket of Molly's dress. Then, in pairs or small groups, the knucklers and their partners headed back the way they came, starting the long trek back to the city on foot or horseback.

Abigail's heart broke for this poor young girl. Not even eighteen and the only man she'd loved stripped from her. Seeing the girl weeping, her blond hair bobbing to each passing mourner, tore at Abigail's heart. It tore open her grief for Oliver, raw again.

Abigail let her gaze drift over the hillside, and she noticed rows of small white crosses dotting the landscape. She heaved. How many other girls or women had stood up here on this hill and wept at the loss of someone they loved? How many more boys and men would sacrifice their lives for this war?

Molly appeared beside her. "I think I's ready to go back now." Her face still bore streams of tears, but the girl's weeping had slowed.

"You can come stay with us." Abigail pointed to Father, who smiled through his salt-and-pepper beard. "We'd be happy to have you, at least for a while. Till you figure out what's next."

Molly looked up to her, her green eyes glistening. "I'd like to git back to our place." Her gaze slid over to the grave and back. "I wanna be with our things . . . to 'member Jamie." She sniffed. "We'll see about tomorrow."

Louisa insisted on taking Molly back in her carriage. "It's the least I can do for that poor girl." She even invited Levi to join them. Surprised, the tall man nodded at Abigail and climbed in next to Molly.

Before her footman helped her back inside the carriage, Louisa turned to Abigail and whispered, "The major *is* working on doing the right thing." She, too, glanced back toward the recently dug hole. "I'll be so glad when this war comes to an end, one way or the other." To Abigail, she said, "If you need some days, feel free to take them. I'll tell the children a friend of yours has perished and you need time to grieve. They don't need to know the grisly details, but we cannot keep the horrors of war away from them completely." With that, Louisa Monteith turned and headed to the waiting footman.

Together, Father, Robert, and she headed to the open wagon with heavy steps. The two horses, both with shiny brown coats, stood in front of the wagon and pawed the ground. As they came alongside the horses, Abigail stopped and petted the closer one, her hand running down the tan mane. Father stopped beside her and placed a hand on her cheek. "Wish there was something I could do for you, child. Some way to ease your pain."

Abigail tried to muster a small smile for Father. "You know us, Father. We're survivors."

He patted her cheek, his touch gentle. "That we are."

She looked up at him. "If it's all right with you, I'd like to spend some time with Robert."

Father dropped his hand and nodded. “Of course it is.” He turned to Robert, who stood a step behind. “Take care of her. She thinks she’s tough but she’s really fragile.”

Robert stepped up beside Abigail and took her hand from the mane and held it. “I’ll do my best. I’m here for her.”

67

The clatter of the wagon wheels made conversation nearly impossible, so none of the three spoke on the return trip. Abigail's thoughts tortured her, reeling from Reeves's ugly smirks to Oliver's cold blue skin to the bloodstained bayonet sticking out of Jamie's ribs. After *returning* the bayonet, Abigail did her best to clean her precious books, but the *New England Primer* still bore lurid red stains on its cover and the edge of its pages. The blade had chipped a corner of her hornbook. Ugly reminders of the horrors of war. When the children saw the primer and hornbook in their next lesson, they'd no doubt notice.

When Robert dropped off Father at their flat, he turned to Abigail. "I think we'll head to my store. I closed it for the day, so we'll not likely be disturbed. I figured the last thing you want is a hundred people around."

She nodded and choked back a sob. "Thanks."

Once in the city, Robert navigated the wagon through the crowded streets, dodging workers who ran in and out of warehouses, their naked shoulders bowed under heavy crates and their dark skin glistening with sweat. Twice, he had to stop as a herd of animals—first chickens, then pigs—crossed in front of the horses. The entire city seemed to go about its business as if nothing had happened. Abigail wanted to scream. Another young man's life had been snatched away.

Not ten minutes after leaving their flat, Robert tugged on the reins, stopping the two horses. Jumping to the ground, he extended a hand to help her down. Abigail grabbed her schoolbag from the back and took it. When she took in her surroundings, she realized she'd been here before. At least, she'd passed by here. Nathan had accompanied her down this street on her first visit to the Green. Had that been nearly three years ago? She blinked, fighting another flood of tears, and swept her gaze from left to right.

To the left, on the far west end of the street, rose the skeleton of Trinity Church, its steeple now only blackened boards clinging to charred supports. Beyond the burnt-out church, rows of one- and two-story structures lined both sides of the street, some rebuilt with new wood, others still partially charred. Warehouses, a smithy, tavern after tavern, a ropemaker, a mason, a barn with animals being herded in—all stood on both sides of the street, though some looked as if they could collapse at any moment. The businesses then gave way to shacks and painted structures, which looked even more dilapidated and housed the brothels and tippling shops.

"Aye, sir. There ya be," called a tall man who burst out of a door and down the wooden steps into the street. His bald head bobbed as he smiled, showing rows of missing teeth. He nodded to Abigail. "Miss." Grabbing the reins, the man climbed into the seat. "I'll take care of the horses." He flicked the reins once.

As the noise from the horses' hooves and the clatter of the wheels died away, Robert said, "That's my man, James." He extended a hand. "Allow me to show you my humble domain."

He led her up onto the walkway and to the door the man had just exited. Over the door hung a wooden sign with the word STORE burned into it. As he held the door open, Abigail stepped inside. The interior was dark, and it took a moment for her eyes to adjust. While she blinked, trying to focus, Robert scurried around the room and lit two oil lamps. The flames inside the fixtures flickered and burned, dispelling the shadows.

Abigail could now see it all, and she stood and gaped, trying to take it in. The store was much larger than it looked from the outside and held all manner of things. As the room brightened, she could make out barrels of coffee beans and trays with stacks of cheeses, their earthy and smoky scents hanging in the air. Next to them were shelves with rows and rows of candles, the tapers ranging from white to deep green. Another section held all kinds of guns and knives, laid out in formation on two long tables, their silver blades reflecting the flickering lamplight.

Fascinated, Abigail roamed the room, her worn bag bumping against her hip when she turned corners and headed down another aisle. She hadn't seen so many goods since . . . since the stores in London. Another area held clothing, everything from flowing European dresses in pink, green, and yellow, with the accompanying petticoats, to men's waistcoats in the muted colors of brown, green, and tan. The next display held new breeches and white shirts, some with fancy ruffles and collars. Alongside these clothes lay red, tan, and black furs, no doubt procured from natives or frontiersmen. This section even held various men's and women's shoes, a few with silver buckles that blinked in the flickering light.

She moved farther into the space and saw an area with foodstuffs. Baskets of eggs sat next to plates of dried meats. Even some early-season scallions were displayed, ready for purchase. Abigail turned her astonished gaze from the goods to Robert, who had come alongside her.

Laying his hand gently on her arm, he asked, "What do you think?"

"Is all this yours?" Her eyes scanned the room again.

Grinning, he shrugged. "This . . . and what's in the storeroom."

"By all that's holy, that's a lot." Her eyes met his, and for a moment, she felt her crushing grief lift a bit.

"Come on, and I'll show you the rest. The part few others get to see." He took her hand and led her to the rear of the room. He opened a small door in the back wall. "After you." He made a sweeping gesture with his hand.

The space she stepped into held a darkness similar to the store. Robert edged around her and lit another oil lamp on the back wall. The long, narrow space was shrouded with sheets strung on ropes, one after another. Abigail could make out little in the dim light. He led her past the first rope. Beyond it stretched another line with breeches, shirts, and bed dresses dangling from it. A third rope held a dirty sheet stretching almost to the floor.

Pulling it back, he pronounced, "Voila!"

Staring, she stood rooted to the spot. Beyond sat a large metal contraption, black and hulking in the dim light. Abigail squinted, peering at it.

"It's a press," Robert whispered, as if anyone might be listening. "A printing press. Pretty rudimentary, but it gets the job done."

Abigail stared. She knew British soldiers searched for any rebels with printers and destroyed all they found. "But you said Redcoats are in and out of here every day. Surely, one of them wanted to search back here." Abigail pointed to the press. "How did you hide this from them?"

Robert's grin broadened. "Easy. The Redcoats believe I'm their friend, a loyal Tory who gives them discounts. When they demand to see what's in the back room, I show them this." He pulled back the other curtain, the one they'd stepped around.

The newly revealed space held a small bed with a straw mattress, a wooden chair, and a stone washbasin. Next to the bed sat a round table with a candle, burnt halfway down.

Robert said, "I tell them sometimes I work late and sleep here. If they are persistent enough to search more, I let them see my laundry." He beamed and then peered at her face. "Are you all right? Do you need to sit down?"

Abigail felt flushed and lightheaded. She felt suddenly as if she might collapse, her legs buckling under her. She let him guide her to the bed, where she sat down hard, the schoolbag hitting the floor with a thud. He hovered over her, then knelt in front of her, his features betraying his anxiety.

She tried a few long, slow breaths, in and out, in and out. Sitting there, exhausted, she felt the tears welling up again. She didn't hold them back this time. She stared at the floor, watching the drops fall onto the fabric of her green dress.

"What can I do?" Robert asked, his voice anguished.

She glanced over at him through moist eyes. "Just hold me. Please."

68

He wrapped his arms around her and pressed his forehead to hers. His hug felt so good, but somehow, even that comfort made her sorrow more acute. Withering there on the cot, Abigail shuddered, her sobbing growing louder in the confined space.

"Shh," he whispered, his mouth inches from her ear.

Another spasm of grief shook her. She couldn't help herself. She reached her arms around his middle, trying to calm her quivering nerves. "Poor Jamie," she uttered, the words dissolving into more sobs.

"I know. I know. Try to breathe deep."

She gave a slight nod, their two foreheads moving together, and took in a lungful of air. She did it again and finally a slow, third time. The weeping ebbed, and she looked up at Robert's face through teary eyes.

He said, "I'm here. We're here. It'll be all right again."

She inched her face up a bit more, staring at those deep brown eyes, the single gold stripe shimmering with wetness. She leaned in close and then kissed his pale pink lips. His eyes widened before he returned the kiss. His was urgent, and she felt his arms pull her closer. Then he released her and leaned back, both hands on her shoulders.

"Abigail, are you sure? You just lost Jamie. You're lost in your grief. You—"

She silenced his protests with another kiss, this one more earnest and passionate. He didn't fight it but still did not move to hug her again. When they broke the kiss, he leveled his gaze at her and said, "I know you're hurting. I care for you deeply. But I do not want to take advantage of you."

Abigail freed one arm and used it to wipe her eyes. Then she raised both hands to his chin, her fingers feeling the stubble. She sniffed back more tears. "What I know is death has stolen another piece of my world. Right now, I need to feel alive."

Holding his face in her hands, she kissed him—slow, long, and hard. Robert slowly raised his arms and encircled her shoulders again. When they broke the kiss, she tugged on his chin, and he rose from his knees. She patted the cot, and he sat on the bed beside her. Abigail's hands went to his dark brown waistcoat, and her fingers began undoing the brass buttons. He stilled her hands with his own, making her glance again into his face.

He whispered, "Are you *sure* this is what you want?"

Abigail nodded, feeling another tear slide down her cheek. "I think I love you, Robert Townsend." She took his hand in hers and brought it to her breast. "And more than anything else, this is what I *need*."

He leaned closer and kissed her while his hand cupped her breast and squeezed. She shut her eyes, reveling in the sensation rippling through her body. This is what she craved. Although the ugly memory of her trauma still lingered, she realized at her core this was so different. With Robert, she felt safe and loved.

Her hands returned to their task, and when she finished with the row of buttons, she tugged at his white shirt. When his hand went to her other breast, she caught her breath again. She pushed his hands away and rose. Robert stood up quickly, surprise registering on his features.

Abigail reached behind her and turned around. Over her shoulder, she said, "I need you to help me out of this dress."

Later, when they finished, their bodies spent and wet with perspiration, they lay there, still wrapped together in a desperate embrace, feeling the warmth flowing between them. For a few minutes, neither spoke, and Abigail drank it in, this warming sensation flooding her mind and body until there was no room for sorrow or grief or despair. Robert had allowed her to take the lead in their lovemaking, realizing she needed to be in control. Through it all, he had been gentle, the touch of his hands on her body tender, the sound of his voice in her ear a loving whisper. Perhaps because she had told him about Reeves and the assault, he had been gentle, slow, and passionate and made her feel cherished, not used.

Relief and ecstasy flooded through her, and she felt tears running down her face again, their saltiness on her lips. Robert, seeing them, kissed the tears and said, "I'm sorry if I hurt you."

"Sh-h-h. You were wonderful." She sniffed and managed a small smile. "These are tears of joy."

He kissed her again, his muscular arms wrapped around her, making her feel safe, at least for now. Abigail snuggled against this strong, sensitive man and drifted off to the most peaceful sleep she'd had in a long time.

69

Abigail opened her eyes to see the first tendrils of dawn creep in through the small window. Robert must have gotten up in the night, stoked the woodstove, and opened the door to keep the space from freezing. And then climbed back next to her under the blankets, their two naked bodies still touching in a hundred places in the morning. Hearing his quiet snore, she glanced up at his handsome face and felt his warm breath on her hair. Memories of last night flowed back, and she felt her body tingle at their recall. Emotions cascaded through her mind, one after the other—sorrow, desperation, relief, and finally, joy. She snuggled a little closer. Perhaps there *was* a chance for something other than sadness and helplessness.

Robert stirred, shifting his arm around her back. Slowly, his eyes opened and met hers, the brown orbs still heavy with sleep. He smiled at her, and she watched his eyes light up. "Good morning, beautiful," he whispered, his voice hoarse.

She placed a hand on the few auburn hairs on his chest. "You look pretty good yourself."

He said, "I could get used to this." His hand slid down her back to her buttocks, and his smile widened.

She adjusted her position on the cot and was pleased to feel his hand move with her. She jutted her chin to indicate the world outside. "I wish we could stay like this and not have to go back out there."

"I feel the same." He took a slow breath. "But your father is out there, and he needs you." He waited a bit and then added, "And Washington is counting on me. On us." He pressed his forehead to hers.

"Washington! Oh, crikey, I completely forgot." In a sudden move, she pushed him aside and sat bolt upright, sending the cover to the floor. Climbing out of the small bed, she scurried about the back room. "I knew I had it with me. Where did I drop my schoolbag?" She turned and saw Robert staring at her. In an unconscious gesture, she covered her nakedness, then thought it silly, considering what they'd just done. She lifted her arms in the air and pointed at him. "Stop staring, please."

"I can't help it. You're an incredibly beautiful woman." He grinned.

She felt her face flush again and the blood rush to other parts of her body. "Come on, don't just sit there. Please get up and help me find it. It's important."

"Don't worry. It's around here somewhere. It's just an old bag. I'll gladly get you a new one."

She stopped at the edge of the sheet hiding the printing press and turned. "Mother got it for me . . . before she died."

"I didn't know. I'm sorry." He stood up quickly, his eyes scanning the small room. "I'm sure we'll find it. Maybe you set it down on one of the tables out in the storeroom."

"Besides, it's not the bag. It's what's in it." She looked past his handsome, naked body standing in front of the bed and saw the bag lodged under the cot.

She stepped over and reached under the bed. Pulling out the brown schoolbag, she set it on the mattress and sat down next to it. She started fumbling through the bag. Robert perched on the other side and peered inside. From the bottom, she pulled out the *New England Primer* and opened it to the back. She withdrew two papers. "Here's the ticket." She handed him the two slightly wrinkled currency notes.

He took them and rubbed the paper between his fingers, his eyes widening. He held the bills up to the light streaming in through the window. "These are fake Continental currency." Meeting her gaze, he asked, "Where'd you get these?"

"In Major Monteith's office."

"Major Monteith?"

She shook her head. "No, the other officers brought a pile of these and must've dropped these two and not noticed." Robert nodded, so she continued. "From what I overheard from Hollister, the British have some kind of scheme to use fake currency to paralyze the economy."

"You're not only the most beautiful woman I've ever seen. You are also one of the smartest. This might be an even bigger coup than your learning of the British plan to trap the French fleet. What you overheard and these"—he held up the fake bills—"will convince Washington to do something. And soon."

"I'm sorry. I've been carrying those around with me for three days. I was heading to meet you when Jamie—" She stopped mid-sentence, picturing the horrible scene again. She stifled a sigh. "I should've gotten these to you sooner."

He took her hand and squeezed it gently. "Abigail, after what you've been through in the last few days, it's amazing you remembered at all."

"But shouldn't we get these to Washington? Right away? I mean, wouldn't this cripple the war effort?"

Robert stood, took the bills, and disappeared behind the curtain, talking as he went. "We have time. These bills aren't printed on the right paper. It means the British are still working out the plan. Besides, I have to work through the network. I can't afford to compromise secrecy."

"What should we do, then?" Abigail was excited to be part of this. For now, her grief didn't completely consume her.

"I'll lock the papers you found in a safe place. Tonight, I'll get them to the next link in the chain, along with a coded message."

"Tonight? Shouldn't you get on it now?"

"I have a regular rendezvous set for eight o'clock tonight. If I try to contact them before, it might raise suspicion. I'll pass them on then."

He glanced at the first beams of sunlight streaming through the two windows of the storeroom. It shed enough light for them to see their way around, though the back room remained in shadow. “I’m not scheduled to open the store for another few hours. I think perhaps we should return to bed for a little more sleep. We didn’t get much last night.” He grinned at her. “And maybe we’ll think of something else while we’re there.”

PARKER

70

Parker stared at the livid face of his wife.

"They decided to take *no* action? No action at all? Reeves gets off scot-free?" Louisa's voice rose with each question.

"No *official* action. They decided to take no official action."

She shot both hands to her hips. "What does that mean?"

"I am still not sure." He shook his head. "I think it means they did not find him innocent of the charge."

"But he gets no punishment." Louisa's eyebrows rose. "It amounts to the same thing. What's the difference?"

"Cain emphasized the *official* part." He sighed. "After the formal hearing, after they dismissed me, Cain followed me outside to talk. I was so upset at that point, I was ready to ignore him. Just get on my horse and ride back here."

His wife leveled a look at him. "But you didn't."

"No, I stayed and listened. For what it was worth."

"And what did the good lieutenant colonel have to say?"

"He said he agreed with me that Reeves deserved to be punished."

"But." Louisa's impatience showed in the single word.

"He claimed the decision on Reeves's case was decided at a higher level. They're worried Reeves's hanging could damage morale. And with some of the losses the army has suffered lately, he said General Clinton is getting nervous about the progress of the conflict."

Louisa's mouth formed an O. "They think they could lose? We could lose?"

Parker shook his head. "Oh, Cain would never admit such a thing. He said the general's staff is worried that hanging Reeves might send the wrong message, said there is much grumbling among the troops wanting to quit and go home."

"So we're back to where we started. Reeves gets off scot-free."

"Not exactly. Cain intimated he would not mind if something happened to Reeves . . . as long as it does not track back to command."

"Those cowardly fools. So it all falls on you. They expect *you* to find a way to exact some kind of punishment for Reeves, without involving any formal British army channels. They simply want to make sure the command doesn't get its hands dirty."

"Oh, it is not that simple. Nothing can come back to me either, as I am part of the command."

"Oh, that's rich. How are you supposed to accomplish this feat?"

"I have not yet figured that out."

Louisa huffed. "Sometimes I wonder what we're fighting for." She stared at him with a serious look he seldom saw. "Parker, sometimes I wonder if we are fighting for the right side."

"Louisa?" he said sharply, but before he could get out any more, she cut him off.

"Maybe it's time you consider resigning your commission."

He never expected to hear that. He thought Louisa reveled in being a major's wife. When he met her gaze, he saw she was deadly serious. Before he had a chance to say more, she asked, "What are you going to tell Abigail?"

"That worries me almost as much. I promised her I would make this right, and I have clearly failed."

Louisa said, "You did your best, but the blasted army let you down. Again." She let out a loud sigh. "I hope this doesn't cost us Miss Abigail. You'd better decide what you're going to tell her. She left word she planned to return today to resume her lessons with both Elizabeth and Henry. I expect her later this morning."

"Please send her to me when she arrives."

Parker retired to his office and tried to concentrate on his correspondence but found himself staring at the same paper for minutes on end, its script blurring before his eyes. He replayed his wife's words. *Sometimes I wonder if we're fighting for the right side.* Those words might well be deemed treasonous, but in the quiet of the night, had he not considered the same thing?

And this latest demonstration of cowardice by Cain, Hollister, and others up the ranks only fed his doubts. Was a mutiny really possible, or was it all simply the normal complaining among the troops? *He* had heard very little such talk in his company, except for the few who always grumbled.

Were the generals really afraid of the men's possible reactions if Reeves were hanged, or was that merely an excuse?

When he received this posting of major with command of a full company, he had had high expectations. But very little about this posting had turned out as he had hoped. Except for being here in America with his family.

The Continental militia should have been no match for the powerful British army and navy. Their ill-equipped and untrained troops should have been easily beaten and captured. Every senior officer had claimed the conflict—they never deigned to call it a war—would be over quickly and victorious Redcoats would be home before their hearths by Christmas. Christmas, two years ago. Somehow, the bands of Continental soldiers and rebel fighters had been able to strike and escape, again and again, always out of the reach of a British brigade or battalion. In fact, here they were, three years into "the conflict," and from all Parker could tell, the British army was no closer to victory than when they had taken the city. Rather, victory seemed farther from their grasp.

He replayed Colonel Cain's words. "The fight was not going as anticipated. The soldiers, privates like Reeves, are getting restless. There was talk among the troops of simply quitting, even deserting and going home."

Mulling the comments over, Parker allowed himself to think the unthinkable. What if the rebels won the conflict? Most other soldiers, certainly all the officers, would be on the first ship back to England. Once a treaty was signed. But the Parker Monteith family had decided to stay in the New World. Louisa and he had discussed it several times and had agreed. It would be exciting for them to start a whole new life here, away from relatives and home obligations. Envisioning the possible future for his family here, a cold shiver ran through Parker. When he received this posting, he pictured a life as a ruling officer in a peaceful British colony after the conflict. But what would happen to a British major in a rebel America? And to his family?

He heard his wife's urgent words again. *Maybe it's time you consider resigning your commission.*

71

"Major, Louisa said you wanted to speak with me." Miss Abigail appeared at his door, derailing his bleak train of thought.

"Please come in, Miss Abigail." He indicated the chair near his. Sitting across from her, he took her in. She was a pretty young woman who always presented herself well, but today she looked different somehow. She had done up her hair, with a brown bun atop her head. Those deep-set blue-green eyes still held remnants of her grief, but a small smile tugged at her lips. Her features remained serious and expectant, but she exuded a lighter air, as if her steps were not quite so heavy.

His information was probably going to devastate whatever good spirits she clung to. "I wanted to inform you of the disposition of the case involving Private Reeves." The young woman looked at him, her eyes intent. "I took the full case to my superiors and gave them everything you told me and Miss Brighton confirmed."

He gulped, his throat suddenly dry. He reached for the silver pitcher, poured some water into a mug, and drank it all in one long swallow. Then he remembered his manners and offered Abigail a drink as well. She declined and continued staring at him, waiting. He could put this off no longer.

"I am sorry to say the panel decided to take no official action against Reeves. I have failed to put this right." He paused. "I failed you."

Miss Abigail's mouth hung open. "So Reeves is going to get off? Just like he got away with what he did to me!" As soon as she said this, her face darkened. She hissed, "Another fine example of the British justice system." She gave a frantic wave around the room. "This is *nothing* like the England I left."

It looked less and less like the England he remembered.

She looked desperate, close to tears, and he wanted to give her something, but all he came up with was, "I understand how you feel." He longed to say he agreed with her, to share his own disappointment and disgust with his superiors. But he held his tongue.

"Do you?" she asked, her tone sharp. "Who has this war stolen from you . . . sir?"

"You are correct, Miss Abigail. I should not have said I understand your pain. I plainly do not." He tried to clear his throat but could not. Grabbing the pitcher, he poured more water and took another long swallow. Before he could find his voice, Abigail spoke.

"But sir, *you* know what kind of man Reeves is . . . after all I confided to you." Her voice broke toward the end.

Parker looked at her anguished face, and his heart ached. After promising he would get justice for her friend, he had failed. But he had the kernel of an idea. Meeting her gaze, he said, "I certainly agree. I do know what kind of man Reeves is. In addition to what you shared with me, I have had to discipline him on multiple occasions."

Abigail's eyes hardened, her eyebrows scrunching together. "I don't think any *discipline* would be sufficient for Reeves."

Parker said, "I can only think of one."

Abigail shook her head slowly, pursing her lips. "You said you reported everything Molly and I shared with you? After all that, they didn't believe Reeves killed Jamie?"

Parker struggled with how much he could say—he did not want to cause even greater offense. This woman had suffered so much. Abigail waited, saying nothing, though her anxious eyes begged for a response. He decided he had best tell her the truth, at least most of it.

"Reeves claimed he killed Jamie in self-defense." She started to say something, but he hurried on. "He claimed the same thing when I talked to him. I had already spoken with you and Molly. I knew he was lying."

"And you shared all that with your superiors?"

"Of course. Yes."

"Then why did they take Reeves's word over ours? Molly's and mine?"

He had trouble forming a decent answer, and a few seconds of silence elapsed.

Her eyes opened wide. "Let me guess." Her voice dripped with bitterness. "It's because Reeves is a British soldier and Molly is some gutter prostitute."

He let that go because he did not want to reveal their perspective about a teacher being an unreliable witness. "Still, the panel did not find Reeves not guilty," he tried, but even he heard how feeble the words sounded.

"But Reeves still gets off scot-free!"

He noticed Abigail and his wife had used the same expression. This woman deserved to know. "The truth is, they know, or at least suspect, that Reeves is guilty. That he did murder Jamie. But they are worried that hanging a British soldier will have a detrimental effect on morale."

"Morale? A murder, and they're worried about morale!"

Abigail's voice rose so much that Parker worried the children might overhear. He stood and closed his office door, something he seldom did. Back in his chair, he reached over and laid a hand atop her two, clenched together so tightly the knuckles were white.

"Miss Abigail, I think all is not lost."

She was weeping now, tears flowing freely. She sniffed once. "I don't understand."

Parker scanned the empty room, searching for the right words. "All right, I will simply come right out and say it. One of my superiors shared that they know Reeves is a danger and they would not mind if something *happened* to him." He searched her face to see if she understood his message.

"Well, I'd like to be the *something* that happens to him."

"Not what I meant. Reeves is a dangerous man." He looked away, then shifted his glance back to her. "Louisa shared the funeral for the young man, Jamie, was quite well attended. She said there were men and women like . . . well, like Jamie and Molly, from all over the city there at the cemetery."

Abigail released her grip and wiped her eyes with one hand. "I was surprised. There must've been fifty or more." She peered at him through wet eyes. "What are you getting at?"

Parker gulped again and charged ahead. "Let me ask you a question. I would guess many of Jamie's friends have little use for British soldiers, especially soldiers like Reeves." When she nodded, he continued, "Would some of them be willing to exact a little revenge for Jamie? On Reeves, I mean?"

ABIGAIL

72

After meeting with Major Monteith, Abigail had been so shaken by the news that she had to beg off teaching Henry and Elizabeth. Louisa met her when she opened the door and said she would explain to the children that Miss Abigail wasn't feeling well. That was certainly true. Instead, she'd gone straight to Molly, first to tell her about the panel's cowardly decision.

Molly blurted her reaction through angry tears. "Well, I's espect nothin' less from the stinkin' British."

After Molly's crying eased a bit, Abigail explained the major's idea. A wicked smile lit up the younger woman's face. "I'd be glad to be one of them that brings justice for that bastard Reeves." She sniffed. "Jamie woulda liked that."

After that, they had put the word out, and knucklers from every neighborhood stopped by the Pelican night after night. Hulking men and small, wiry boys came by and gave a listen. To each, they laid out the plan and explained that they had to be patient and wait. Every single one wanted in.

It took a while for the stars to align, so long that Abigail wondered if the major had had second thoughts. Then, more than three weeks after Parker had shared the panel's decision, he again called for Abigail. This time he didn't even wait. As soon as she entered, he closed the door behind her and sat down.

"Tonight I am giving Reeves the evening off, and he has bragged he is going to celebrate with some shake named Marybeth, somewhere over on Williams Street, my men tell me." His eyes did a quick scan of the empty room as he talked. "I have made sure he will be out alone. All of his fellows have been given duties tonight. They will not accompany him." His gaze returned to her. "But even alone, Reeves will be dangerous. He keeps that bayonet with him at all times now."

Abigail assured him they'd be careful and thanked him. On her way up Water Street, she passed a pickpocket named Stu, a wiry, short man with a half-toothed grin, an acne-scarred face, and a head of unruly jet-black hair, sitting along the walkway begging. Weeks ago, Stu had been one of the first to stop by the Pelican to express his condolences to Molly and offer to help. Every day since then, he'd crouched at his spot on Water Street. To passersby, he appeared to be begging—"Can ya spare a halfpenny?"—but he was merely waiting for her signal. Today, when she bent to put a penny in the dirty black cap, she also dropped the small paper she'd scribbled on as she gathered up her school things. After that, Abigail left everything to the knuckler network.

Evening fell slowly, the late spring sun surrendering at last to an encroaching dusk. She went home, fixed Father some supper, and cleaned up. After that, she paced the floor like an angry cat, glancing out the second-story window. When Father asked after her, she put him off. She'd tell him tomorrow . . . if all went well. A few hours later, she heard a soft knock at the door. When Father rose to get it, she beat him to it. Stu stood at the door, his shabby hat in his hands, his breath ragged.

"We got 'im," was all he said.

He turned and headed back the way he came, and Abigail grabbed a cloak and hurried after him, ignoring Father's questions. She and the short pickpocket made their way through the city blocks, the darkness closing in around them. The air felt cool on her face. Halfway down Williams Street, she heard yelling coming from an alley off to the left.

"Blast! Git your filthy hands off me."

Abigail turned into the alley and saw the huddle of figures around a man on the ground.

"Zounds! I'm a British soldier. I'll get you all for this," he screamed.

Two shabbily dressed sentinels stood at the entrance to the alleyway. They nodded to Abigail as she entered. Farther down the alley, Private Reeves lay on the hard dirt, his arms and legs pinned by four of the bigger knucklers. Molly stood over him, hands on hips. A small crowd of others stood around in the semi-darkness, mumbling. When Abigail approached him, Reeves's eyes flashed and his face flushed, the twin scars reddening. Abigail realized Reeves probably didn't recognize Molly—he had accosted so many women, one didn't matter—but his gaze locked on hers, and recognition flashed across his features.

Abigail stood at Molly's side, and the two women peered at Reeves. He squirmed and spat at them but missed. "Lemme go now, an' I won't kill ya," he hollered, thrashing to try to break free. He flicked his gaze from the two women standing over him to his four captors. "The army's goin' to hang ev'ry las' one a ya." The heavy stink of alcohol flowed off him.

One of the young men hobbled out of the huddled group, and Abigail recognized Benjamin, the Continental soldier Jamie had helped escape and she had patched up. He limped forward and lowered his good leg to Reeves's chest. He slammed Reeves's body to the ground and, one hand fumbling through the soldier's uniform, came away with the bayonet.

Reeves shrieked, "That's mine."

Benjamin ignored him and handed it to Molly. "Ya said ya wanted t' be first."

Molly took the blade, grasping the hilt in both hands. She turned to Benjamin. "Can ya move your foot down a little? I need t' aim right there." Her head tilted toward the side of Reeves's chest, where he'd knifed Jamie.

Reeves's eyes got huge, and he screamed, "You can't. I'm a king's soldier. Help!"

Another boy stepped forward, yanked the ugly orange scarf from around Reeves's neck, and stuffed it in his mouth. "Ump-uh-um," was all that came out.

Molly gritted her teeth. "This is fer me Jamie." She hefted the bayonet over her head. Reeves's red eyes grew impossibly large. She thrust the blade straight down, making a sound like knifing a watermelon.

"Ow-w-w!" came the muffled cry. Then Reeves peed and soiled himself, the stench thick in the enclosed alley. The knucklers laughed.

Molly pulled the blade out, nodded at her work, and turned to Abigail. She handed her the bayonet. Abigail stared down at the man who had tormented her and saw recognition in his eyes. She said, "I think I'll aim a little lower." She thrust the blade right into his groin, and Reeves tried to scream, though the rag muffled it.

After that, it went quickly. One by one, knuckler after knuckler stepped up, grabbed the bayonet, pulled it out, and thrust the blade back down again, until the body and uniform were covered with gashes and the oozing pool of blood darkened the dirt so much it looked black.

From the back of the alley, two more men dragged out a cart. The men still surrounding Reeves grabbed the four limbs and together threw the now-limp body into the back. A woman came forward and spread a dirty cloth over it.

Stu had been the last in line. He walked over to Molly and laid the bayonet in her hands. "This is yours now. Jamie would be proud of ya. I'll take this bastard and drop 'im in the East River. I know jus' the place. We'll let the fishes feed on 'im."

Molly stared down at the heavy iron weapon, the blade covered in blood and gore. She looked back at Stu. "Take this damn thing and drown it in the river too. I don't ever want to lay eyes on it again."

When Stu took back the bayonet, Molly walked over to Abigail and hugged her, her body shivering. Abigail held the frail young woman in her arms and squeezed, whispering in her ear, "It's over now. We've sent Reeves to hell, where he belongs."

VII

SUMMER, 1779

73

It had been an eventful three months. And things were changing in the Monteith household as well.

After Reeves was killed—or rather, brought to justice, Abigail thought—she was surprised she felt little guilt. She, Molly, and the knucklers had simply done what the British high officers were too cowardly to do. She knew of no one who deserved that fate more than that scar-faced gutter rat. The world was better without him in it. Reeves represented everything ugly about the British army and the worst of the British lot. There were still those who were honorable, like the Monteiths, but there didn't appear to be many, and they weren't in charge.

As promised, Major Monteith had kept his word and, when Reeves didn't return that evening in late May, a brief manhunt was conducted, but in the end, the major had simply recorded him as deserted. No other official action was taken. Still, the tale of Reeves's capture and execution circulated among the street community, and Abigail had little doubt rumors made their way to the troops. Perhaps that was one reason British soldiers grew more anxious. According to Stu, who'd overheard conversations of some Redcoats, soldiers believed locals had executed Reeves and wondered if they could be next.

Abigail got confirmation of this. One afternoon, while helping Henry write his first letter—this one to thank his father for a gift—Abigail overheard the officers grumbling about dwindling troop numbers.

"Our soldiers are out-and-out complaining and want to go home," Hollister's whiny voice called from across the foyer. "Our numbers are so low, Clinton wants us to start enlisting the loyalist merchants to join our ranks. Can you imagine these locals with their axes and shit shovels jumping into a battle?"

From Robert, she had learned her information and evidence of the fake currency had made it to Washington, and he had informed the Continental Congress. The political leaders had decided something had to be done to thwart the British counterfeiting plot and were debating what drastic steps to take. Since then, she'd not overheard any more about the planned forgery in the conversations coming across the hall. Still, the success of the secret steeled her resolve. And Jamie's murder by Reeves gave her even more motivation.

As she strained to listen each day, the mood of the officers who gathered in Monteith's office and drank wine seemed to change from day to day, week to week. When they received word of the British victory in the south, Abigail heard Hollister announce, "To the Battle of Stono Ferry!" and the men cheer. The next week, the group grew quiet, nursing another round of wine as they complained about losing some fort in New Jersey, something about Stony Point. When Spain also allied with the "disgusting rebels," she could almost sense the officers' trepidation.

And it wasn't only the visiting officers. In the passing weeks, the atmosphere around the Monteith household had altered as well. Her students appeared the same, boisterous and complaining one moment and then pensive and industrious the next. They were . . . well, children. But Abigail sensed subtle changes in both Louisa and the major.

Abigail had become quite adept at eavesdropping while still attending to the children. She had learned to listen not only for secrets or details of troop deployments but had also become attuned to the nuances of the men's voices, at least the regulars like Cain and Hollister and, of course, Major Monteith. To her ears, the major's replies seemed less enthusiastic lately, and he let the others do most of the talking. From what little he spoke, Abigail sensed a growing discontent.

Then, one day two weeks ago, Louisa came into the library when Abigail was packing up and commented that the family was growing tired of living in smelly, dirty New York City. She said they were considering moving somewhere, perhaps to a quiet countryside. When Abigail pressed, Louisa said she and the major were just talking for now. "Considering our options."

The following week, Louisa added more details. "The major and I are quite pleased with your work with the children. I hope you know that."

Abigail stuffed the primer into the worn schoolbag that had somehow sprouted another hole. She poked her pinkie through it and looked at Louisa. "Thank you, ma'am. I'm very grateful for your support."

Louisa sighed. "And Henry and Elizabeth think you hung the moon."

Abigail felt her face redden. "I've grown quite fond of them as well. You have two bright children."

"Thank you, Abigail. I love both Henry and Elizabeth but thought they were dolts before you came along."

Abigail grinned. "Nonsense. They've both made excellent progress over the last three years."

Louisa shook her head. "Three years. They certainly have. That's why I wanted you to know . . ." She stopped as if searching for the right words. "If our lives change and we are no longer able to have you continue as their tutor, it won't be because of anything on your part."

Abigail stopped her packing and stared at Louisa. She appeared composed, her yellow dress rustled under two petticoats, and her hair done up on top of her head, a golden flower through her curls. But there was something about her, her composure a little strained. "Ma'am?"

"Parker and I have discussed some possible changes in our lives, and these may necessitate our leaving New York City."

Abigail asked, "Are you returning to England? Has Major Monteith been recalled?"

Louisa chuckled. "Nothing like that. Whatever happens, we hope to stay in this new country, but perhaps not here in New York City."

Abigail wasn't sure how to respond. "I'll be happy to serve as your children's tutor as long as I can. I appreciate the opportunity to work with them."

Louisa patted her on the arm. "Well, try not to worry. There won't be any immediate changes. Perhaps in a few months."

Hiding behind the schoolbag atop the desk, Abigail caressed her abdomen. *The Monteith family's changes might just coincide with changes in her own life.*

74

"Wow, you've learned your times tables quite well. Almost as well as me," Abigail announced to a beaming Molly, both of them sitting behind the counter at Robert's store.

One good thing—perhaps the only good thing—to come out of Jamie's death was that Abigail had talked Molly into getting off the street. A few nights after Reeves's execution, as Abigail lay in Robert's arms, she pleaded for his help. "Would you consider bringing Molly on . . . at the shop?" When he didn't respond right away, she added, "I want to get her off the street. It's too dangerous without someone to protect her. And I think you'll find she can be quite a help. She's good with people—she's had to deal with enough rough types—and she's come a long way in her reading and numbers."

Robert had agreed, on a trial basis. He loaned Molly a modest, tan dress, saying she'd have to work to pay it off. It turned out the young woman performed remarkably well with both the women and the men. Robert found a pretty face with golden curls helped increase sales. And the Redcoat soldiers lingered around her, flirting, talking, and bragging, which turned out to be good for business . . . and good for the spy business. Molly had been working at his store for more than two months, so Abigail conducted her tutoring lessons here.

"Pretty soon, Robert will be asking you to do the books," Abigail continued. Robert came up behind her, leaned down, and kissed her cheek. She turned toward him. "What do you think, Robert?"

"Molly has been a real asset," he said, smiling at the young woman.

"Thank ya, sir. I 'ppreciate the chance to prove meself." Molly nodded, her smile widening.

"On that note, I best get going," Abigail said. "I need to go tutor my students while I still can." She had shared with Robert Louisa's comments about the family's possible future. But she hadn't yet gotten the courage to talk to him about her own.

As the store sat a few blocks farther from Water Street, it took Abigail a little longer to reach the Monteiths, though she made it on time. When Louisa opened the front door for her, Abigail heard the commotion of several voices coming from the office. Her gaze strayed there, and Louisa said in a quiet voice, "The major has several visitors today. I hope they don't disturb you too much." She raised her voice and called upstairs, "Children, Miss Abigail is here." When the sound of steps echoed from the second floor, she gave Abigail a pat on the arm. "I'll leave you to it."

While the children pounded down the stairs, Abigail glanced toward the office. The voices of Cain and Hollister came across clearly, brassy and whiny in turn, but she heard two other voices, besides an occasional word from the major. In a chair facing away from her, she caught sight of a man sitting, stiff-backed in a pressed Redcoat uniform with a white wig atop his head. Ushering the students to their seats, she racked her brain for the name of the man, a man she'd met before.

Knowing her time in this house was limited—and with it, likely her role in the Ring—Abigail came every day, watching and eavesdropping, hoping she could uncover at least one more thing. For the past three months, she'd heard curses and cheers from the office, but nothing of any real value to the cause.

She turned to her two students. "Henry, I think you are ready to try some more passages in the primer." Pulling the slightly battered *New England Primer* out of her bag, she saw again the smear of dark red along the edge of the book. She steeled herself. *He* was dead now.

"Elizabeth, I've prepared a page of more challenging subtraction problems for you." When she saw the girl scrunch her features together, she added, "I think you're ready for them, but if you have trouble with a problem, skip it, and I'll help you with it when I get to you. I'm going to start with Henry. Let's get you started, then."

As both children settled in, getting book, paper, and pencil ready, Abigail shot another look across the foyer. This time she saw a different man, dressed not in a British uniform but in street clothes. In her glance, she couldn't make out much—a head of dark hair and, when the visitor moved across the space to take a glass of wine, a limp.

"What is this word again? I know we read it yesterday, but I don't remember."

Henry's question drew Abigail's attention back. For the next hour, she alternated between helping Henry decipher words and reminding Elizabeth how to borrow. All she could pick up from the men in the office were some mumbled voices and laughing.

The children finished their first session, and Abigail switched their subjects, reading for Elizabeth and sums for Henry. When they were settled again and working quietly, Abigail stood behind each in turn, peering over their shoulder and offering quiet encouragement. Then she strolled around the library, her fingers running over the spines of the volumes stacked neatly on the shelves. She would miss this library. As always, she ended up by the doorway, listening.

"Colonel, you need to give us something. A few details at least," said a voice Abigail had heard before. She racked her brain to recall the name, and then it came to her. A handsome officer, about her age, dressed in a perfectly pressed uniform and wearing a white wig. Major Andre. Her eyes lingered on both students, while her ears stayed attuned to the voices in the office.

Someone over there cleared his throat and spoke in a raspy voice. "I have every reason to believe George will soon give me command of the fort. The fool." The visitor? It was not a voice she'd heard before. "Then I will be able to hand it over to you."

"It can't be that simple." Abigail recognized Hollister's whiny voice. "Why would you do that?"

The new voice gave a loud, throaty chuckle. "Well, sir, because I tire of the incompetence and jealousy of the Continental buffoons. And because Major Andre has assured me you will meet my financial requests. Which is more than I can say the rebels have done."

"We have considerably more funds than Washington. But the amount you've requested is quite large." It was the cocksure voice of Cain this time.

"It will be worth every penny, I assure you," the gruff voice said.

Abigail struggled to process what she'd heard. This man, this colonel, was dressed not in a British uniform but in civilian clothes? A colonel in the Continental Army? The man claimed to be friends with Washington and that he was going to be given command of some fort? A fort he was ready to hand over to the British for money?

"Officers, think about it," the raspy voice continued. "From there, you can control the entire Hudson Valley."

Worried her presence by the door might be noticed, Abigail moved to an alcove and sat in the window seat, trying to grasp what she'd heard. She had to get some of this down. Now. She pulled a piece of paper and a pencil from her bag. For the hundredth time, she felt grateful to be in a British house with ready access to school necessities like pencil and paper. Then, while keeping it below the rim of the bag, she peeled open the back cover of the Euler algebra text, where she'd hidden the code list. She extracted the sheet with tiny letters and numbers. She scanned the list, trying to decide what words and numbers she should use. She recorded the numbers: *traitor*—642, *fort*—192.

Her glance jerked from the paper to the doorway. She checked on the children. They continued working, unaware. She took another breath and shot another glance at the doorway. No one there.

She returned her attention to the code sheet. She couldn't find a code for *colonel* or *officer*. She decided on *jealous*—556 and *battery*—298. Her eyes ran down the rows again and again but came up with nothing else. She'd have to spell out the other information in the complicated alphabetic code, and that would take time . . . and privacy. Besides, she'd have to use the invisible ink for the words.

"I'm finished," proclaimed Henry.

"Me too," added Elizabeth.

Abigail secreted the code sheet inside the back cover of the algebra book and made sure the seal on the cover looked tight. She tucked the Euler text beneath the other books. Jumping up from the alcove, Abigail said, forcing calm into her voice, "All right, I think that will be enough for today. You did well, and I'm proud of you."

Needing no more encouragement, the two children scampered out of the library and up the stairs, the sound of their loud footfalls echoing behind them. Her insides churning, Abigail gathered up the students' work and stuffed papers and primer on top of the other books in her bag.

Slinging the worn bag over her shoulder, she headed out of the library, only to find the foyer congested with the military gathering. She stopped, hoping to let them head out first. Hollister recognized her, and his mouth broke into a leer. Abigail nodded back, forcing herself to remain polite even as her insides squirmed. The stranger stared at her. She froze. His eyes narrowed and went from her to Major Andre. She watched as the two men exchanged some unspoken agreement.

The man dressed in civilian clothes rasped, "I didn't realize anyone else would be here."

Major Monteith said, "Gentlemen, this is Miss Trench, my children's tutor."

The stranger leaned over and whispered something to Major Andre, whose eyes grew huge. Major Andre stared at Abigail but spoke to Monteith. "Sir, I realize this is your house, but the colonel and I would feel much better if we could search the woman's bag." He nodded the white wig toward Abigail.

75

Abigail's heart beat so hard she swore the others could hear it. She struggled to control her breathing. In and out. In and out. Her stomach roiled. She pasted her teacher smile on her face.

The major stepped over and laid a hand on her shoulder. "Sirs, I can assure you that is hardly necessary. Miss Abigail has been with us for years. I warrant she is a woman of fine character, and I have found her to be quite trustworthy."

Abigail kept the smile on her face. Her mind whirled. She had to think of something. "So good to see you again, Major Andre," Abigail said in her most unassuming teacher voice.

Andre's eyes widened. "Have we met, ma'am?"

"Louisa introduced us when you were visiting a few months ago, and we happened to be leaving at the same time." Abigail dropped her gaze, going for demure. She kept her hands over her stomach, glad for the broad green fabric and the wide, white bow that camouflaged the bulge. "I'm not surprised you don't remember—it was merely a chance meeting—but I remember you. A young woman would have to be blind not to remember such a handsome, young British officer."

Hollister chuckled. "See, Colonel? Miss Abigail is merely a simple woman. More than that, a simple teacher." He waved her away with a swish of his hand.

Abigail kept her gaze slightly downcast. Her heart pounded against her rib cage.

Monteith tried to intervene. "Miss Abigail, I trust my children were not too much trouble today." She met the major's glance. "Sir, they were well behaved as usual." She offered another reassuring teacher smile. This might just work. How ironic that the officers' disparagement of her profession might well save her. "They worked hard today. Did you know Elizabeth is getting good at complicated subtraction—"

"I still want to see what's in that bag," the stranger blurted out. He stabbed a finger toward Abigail's shoulder.

"Oh, for George's sake, Arnold," Major Monteith said, releasing a sigh. He rolled his eyes. "Abigail, let the man inspect your schoolbag." He indicated the nearer desk in the library.

Abigail was stuck. Seeing no other option, she turned, went to the desk, and set her bag on top. "Please be careful. The books are expensive and hard to come by." She tried to make her tone calm, but even she could hear the edge in her voice.

The stranger limped over to the desk and pushed her aside. He stuck his hand inside and started pulling out books and papers. Abigail watched as he removed the *New England Primer* and dropped it on the wood surface with a plop. Next came a piece of expensive paper, neatly folded in thirds.

"What's this?" The man opened the folds, and his gaze went from the script to her and back to the paper. He read, "This woman, Miss Abigail Trench, is in my employ and under my protection." His gaze went farther down the page. "Major Monteith." He pointed to Abigail. "Why would *she* have such a letter?"

Abigail felt a trickle of sweat roll down the side of her face. She tried to speak but found her throat so dry she couldn't get anything out.

Monteith again rescued her, snatching the letter from the stranger's grasp. "I wrote her the letter to grant her safe passage, especially during the early days of our occupation. So overzealous soldiers wouldn't victimize her." The major's tone conveyed his rising exasperation.

The stranger's attention went back to the bag. As the man held it up, he took notice of the holes patched with brown and black fabric. "Maybe it's time you got a new sack for your school things."

Abigail felt the heat rise in her face but bit back her reply. The man's hands came out with the papers Abigail had stuffed hurriedly into it. His gaze took in Henry's page of sums with his scrawled answers and Elizabeth's sheet of two- and three-digit subtraction problems with her neat, feminine numbers. Then he pulled out the paper she had been working on to record the particulars she'd overheard.

"What are these numbers? 642, 192, 556, 298?" he asked, flapping the paper at Abigail.

"Those," she started and had to clear her throat. Her heart thumped harder. *Breathe*, she ordered her brain. She inhaled. Exhaled. "I was just working ahead. I was preparing another page for Elizabeth for tomorrow and started with those numbers." She picked up the page of problems Elizabeth had completed and held it next to the paper in his hand. "See?" She tried the demure teacher smile again. "I was just working ahead so I wouldn't have quite so much work to do tonight."

The man's eyes went from her to the paper to the major.

Monteith asked, "Satisfied, sir?"

The man Monteith had called Arnold didn't answer. He dropped her code paper and pulled out the single remaining item from the schoolbag. Abigail started to exhale and then caught her breath again. The man opened the Euler algebra text, held it upside down, and fanned the book, no doubt to drop any papers stuck between the pages. She prayed he wouldn't find the hidden compartment. Once again, Abigail held her breath. She was done. Her whole body tensed. What would she do if—? What could she do?

The stranger closed the book and held it in one hand, his long fingers grasping the cover. Twisting it in his palm, he eyed the book. "Why would the Monteith children need to know algebra? Just like a *teacher*, having children study useless subjects." He turned to the other men and laughed. "Why would anyone need to know algebra? All anyone needs to know are the basic operations, so he can get paid, keep track of troops, and make sure we're not cheated. Right, Major Andre?"

Andre looked uncomfortable with the colonel's sport. He turned to Abigail. "We apologize if we offended you, Miss Abigail. Let me help you." He shot his plain-clothed colleague a scornful look and reached to place the books and papers back in the bag. Abigail grabbed the algebra text and placed it inside herself.

Monteith parted the officers and opened the front door. "Miss Abigail, thank you for indulging our colleague." He shot a glance at the stranger. "The children will see you tomorrow, then?"

She hoisted the bag on her shoulder. "Of course, sir. With your permission, I'll take my leave." Abigail stepped through the doorway.

As she navigated the stone steps, she cast a glance back at the opening and saw the four men together, watching her descend. She waved to them and kept her teacher smile fixed on her face.

76

Once the front door shut, it took all Abigail's willpower not to run. Instead, she forced herself to walk. When she turned from Water Street to Smith, she took a few steps down the first alley she found and leaned against the side of a building, her breath coming in short bursts now and her stomach protesting. She tried to breathe slowly, in and out, in and out, but her lungs wouldn't cooperate. Her body shook, tremors racking her frame so badly she had to lean against the wood until she could get herself under control. Her gaze swept the alley and the street. She worried someone was watching her, but as she looked all around, no one seemed to take notice.

Hollister and the others had not appeared yet, but she knew it would not be long. They would likely come this way as well. She needed to get moving. Lowering her head, she strode down Smith Street, trying to look purposeful but not hurried. She felt her pulse jump every time she passed a Redcoat, certain he would stop and arrest her. When any of the soldiers cast a glance at her, she flashed a veneer of a smile. And kept moving. She suspected it took her the usual time to cross the city blocks to Broadway, though it felt like forever. When she stepped through the door to Robert's store, she was relieved to find it empty, except for him, counting candles near the rear.

As she entered, he looked up. "Abigail," he said, but his look of joy turned to panic. "What's wrong?"

Abigail scanned the interior of the store, making sure no shoppers lingered in the corners. Her heart still pounded. She shook her head. "Not here. In the back room." Without another word, she threaded her way around the tables, heading for the back door.

Robert said, "I'll run to the storeroom to get James. He can watch the store for me." Robert bolted out the door and disappeared. In a few seconds, he returned, the elderly assistant a few steps behind him.

"Ma'am," James said and nodded his bald head toward her. The assistant passed, heading for the front of the store where a well-dressed woman had just entered. "Anythin' I can hep ya with?" he offered.

Abigail turned and stepped through the doorway, where Robert stood waiting. As soon as she was through, he closed the door, grabbing her and pulling her into his arms. "Oh, Robert," she cried and buried her face in the smooth fabric of his waistcoat. Then she erupted in sobs, her body shaking with each one. At first, Robert simply held her, resting his chin atop her head. Her body still quivered, but wrapped in his strong embrace, she felt her heart rate slow a bit. She sniffled, trying to get herself back under control. He waited.

When her weeping eased to a trickle, he asked, "Think you can talk about it now?"

Abigail nodded, her right hand wiping at her eyes. "I'm sorry. I'm so emotional lately. I don't know what's come over—" She stopped. She did know but needed to tell him the other first. She took a deep breath and said quickly, "I was almost caught today."

Robert hugged her a little tighter. "Well, you're here now. You're safe." He eased her onto the cot and sat next to her, one arm still wrapped around her shoulders. "Tell me what happened."

She did feel safe here, with him. Looking into his deep brown eyes, she took a slow breath and began. She told him first about the Monteith visitors, including the man dressed in civilian clothes and her guess that he was an officer in the Continental Army. "The others addressed him as Colonel." She paused and then added, "I heard Monteith call him 'Arnold.' Does that mean anything to you?"

Robert's eyes widened. "I think it might. What else did you hear?"

Then she explained what she overheard about some fort and her hurried effort to get some details down. "This man, this Arnold, said something about the Hudson Valley."

Robert's features darkened, but he didn't interrupt her. Abigail gulped and then told him about the stranger accosting her, searching her schoolbag, and finding her scribbled code numbers. Robert remained still and let her talk. Finally, she shared the colonel's interest in the algebra text and his handling of it.

"After that, Major Monteith intervened, and I made a hasty exit." She stared into his eyes, tears welling up in hers again. "Robert, I was so scared." She handed him the Euler text and then peeled back the hidden compartment with the code sheet.

Robert's eyes went wide again. "But he didn't find the codes."

"No." She sniffed back more tears.

Robert reached into her schoolbag and pulled out the paper she'd written the codes on, studying it. When he looked at her, he smiled. "Pretty quick thinking. That part about putting together another page of problems for your student."

She shrugged. "It was the only thing I could come up with." Staring at the paper in his hand, she asked, "If this Arnold *is* an officer with the Continentals, could he know about the codes?"

Robert shook his head. "I doubt it. I'm only one link in the chain, but besides the others in the Ring, only Washington knows about the code. At least, that's what I've been told." He looked at her. "Tell me about this stranger. What did he look like? What was he like?"

"Well, he was middle-aged, about Major Monteith's age, I think. Mid-thirties or forties. Handsome enough fellow with a youngish-looking face. And he had a pronounced limp. It was quite obvious when he crossed the foyer to the library." Abigail looked Robert up and down. "Not as tall as you, and he had a very prominent nose and dark hair." She brought her finger to her lips. "Brown, I think. Oh, and he had a very arrogant attitude."

"How so?"

"When he was rifling through my bag, Major Monteith tried to intervene and advocate for me, but this stranger acted like he was above the major. Like he didn't need to even pay attention to what the major said."

Robert jotted notes while she talked. "And I'm no expert on military protocol, but I doubt a colonel would be given command of a fort. You didn't hear which fort?"

Abigail said, "I never heard a name, just that part about having control of the Hudson Valley, I think?"

"All right. This is really good. You know that, right? You might've been scared."

"Try terrified."

"But you kept your wits about you and remembered the important details. I'll get the sympathetic ink, and we'll put everything down. Then I can include the note with a bill of lading I have going to my contact tonight. It should get to Washington in a day or two."

Abigail took another deep breath. "We can't get the information to General Washington any sooner? I got the impression whatever was going to happen would happen soon."

"You're right, it sounds really important. But we need to follow protocol. If we deviate, we put ourselves at risk. It would put *you* at risk. I won't do that." He shook his head, bringing his fingers to his chin. "If this man is successful and the British get a hold of this fort, that might tilt the war toward them." He stared at her, his eyes brightening. "This information is new. Something the network hadn't heard anything about. I'm incredibly proud of you."

"Not bad for a simple schoolmarm, eh?" She chuckled and felt her abdomen stir again.

Neither spoke for a while, and she leaned against his strong shoulder. After a few minutes, Robert broke the silence. "Maybe this is telling us it's time for you to hang up your spy boots." When she started to object, he continued, "I told you from the start this was dangerous.

Now you've witnessed just how dangerous. I couldn't bear to see anything happen to you. I couldn't stand to see this beautiful neck stretched."

He ran his fingers across her neck, and she felt the tingle again. His hand cupped her chin, and he kissed her. She turned to meet him and brought her arms around his neck. The next kiss became longer, more passionate. She wanted to do more than kiss.

Abigail gazed into his face and saw caring and tenderness there. She could've been captured and killed today. Maybe it was time to tell him. After they kissed again, his one hand on her breast, Abigail leaned next to his ear and whispered, "Robert, I'm pregnant."

77

Robert slowly edged back and pulled his hand from her breast. "You're what?"

"Pregnant. With child."

"You're certain?"

Why did men always ask that? "Yes, Robert."

"How . . . how far along?" he asked.

"About two months. And, in case you were wondering, you're the only man I've been with."

"I wasn't." He breathed in and out. "Pregnant, huh. That alters things a bit."

Abigail bit her lip.

"I mean, with your spy work, my spy work." Then he shrugged, and a wide grin broke across his face. "I'm thrilled. We're going to have a boy . . . or a girl."

"You're thrilled!" she repeated and practically bounced on the cot like a schoolgirl.

Robert tilted his head sideways a bit. "Maybe I shouldn't have said 'thrilled.' It will certainly create complications. But I love the idea of having a baby with you." He shook his head. "What about your tutoring? You know, when will you start to show?"

Abigail put a finger on her lips. "I'm not sure, maybe another two, three months." Her hand went to her belly. "But I can already feel him move every once in a while."

"Him?" Robert placed a gentle hand on her abdomen, his features lighting up.

"Or her." The sight of his hand there and the joy on his face erased the fear that had gripped her earlier. She loved this man.

"Well, that settles it. I can't have the mother of my child risking her life and the life of my son—"

"Or daughter."

"—or daughter in dangerous spying activities."

She placed both hands over his on her belly. "Whoa, there. I'm pregnant, not incompetent."

"But the Monteiths will see you, and—"

She interrupted him. "I think the Almighty might be helping out a bit there." Robert's eyes came up to meet hers. "Remember I told you the Monteiths were thinking about packing up and leaving New York? Louisa told me they plan to be gone by the end of summer, regardless of what happens with the war. I don't think I'll be showing by then, so it should all be fine."

Surprise showed on his face. "Major Monteith is going to give up his commission?"

"Louisa confided they were all tired of New York and the bureaucracy of the British army. They want to move to the countryside. She said the major was working out the details."

"Has the major informed the other officers?"

"From what little Louisa said, I don't think anyone else knows yet. She only told me because she wanted me to be able to make other plans. She knows I'll need the money."

Robert grinned and glanced down at her belly. "Well, you've certainly taken her at her word about other plans."

"Robert, I didn't plan for this to happen. I'm sorry—"

He cut her off. "Don't. Don't ever say you're sorry about having my baby, ever. Our baby."

"All right, but I don't think I should quit the Monteiths, at least not yet." Seeing the question in his eyes, she went on, "Not after today.

If I quit after that colonel's suspicions, and we can stop this Arnold's betrayal, it might raise some uncomfortable questions." She shook her head. "No, I need to go back tomorrow like everything's the same."

"That makes sense." Then he thought of something else. "Do you think the officers will still frequent the Monteith house? I mean, if the major wants to distance himself from the army?"

Abigail grinned. "I suspect he will not say much . . . until he has to. From what I've overheard and seen, Major Monteith has little affection for those other officers."

"But they will still come?"

"In the words of that haughty Hollister, 'To the greatest wine cellar in New York,'" she whined, then changed back to her normal voice. "No, they'll keep coming as long as they can get free wine."

"You need to be extra careful, then." He patted her stomach. "For both of you."

"I will."

Neither spoke for a while, the only sounds the quiet babble of voices from the store, indistinct but there. Abigail's gaze went from his hand still on her belly to his face with its wide grin.

"I've had more time with my condition." She patted her stomach. "At first, I was terrified, then I realized . . . maybe it's a sign."

Robert pulled his hand away and looked at her. "A sign?"

"Yes. After all the death and tragedy around us the last few years, I think this baby is . . . oh, I don't know, a sign of hope. You know, hope for the future. A better future. I hope, a better country." Her voice broke toward the end.

His hand returned to her stomach, and he held it there. "I like that. Well, I'm not sure what the future holds, but when you need to quit the Monteiths for whatever reason, you'll not have to worry about money or anything else. I'll take care of you and our baby. And I promise to do everything in my power to make it the best possible future for you and my son."

"Or daughter," she said, her eyebrows raising.

Robert wrapped his arms around her, and she felt the warmth of his strong body. He kissed her, and she kissed him back, savoring the moment. There was still much to talk about—marriage, where they would live, Father—but for now, Abigail basked in his love and commitment.

PARKER

78

"Will there be any complications, I mean from Cain or Hollister . . . or General Clinton, about you resigning?" Louisa asked her husband.

It had been two weeks since she and Parker had made the final decision to leave New York City. They were seated in his office, the door closed. They spoke in quiet voices, as they did not wish Elizabeth and Henry to overhear. The children knew nothing of their plans.

Parker said, "I am certain there will be repercussions. But in the end, there is little they can do."

"Really?" His wife's pretty eyebrows went up.

He liked it when they did that. "I signed on for ten years and, between my time in Ireland, the West Indies, and here, I have more than completed my commitment. I am not an enlisted man, and they have no way to bind me."

"With how the war is going, they can't be happy to lose 'one of our best majors,'" Louisa said, doing a perfect parody of Hollister's tinny voice.

He chuckled at her impersonation of the nasty little man. "From what they said, General Clinton is the most distressed. Cain and Hollister are a little closer to the fighting men. They know which way the wind is blowing."

"You think they believe the tide is turning?"

Parker said, "Oh, they won't admit it, but I've heard them talk about our losses at St. Vincent and Grenada. The French joining with the rebels is making all the difference." He shrugged. "And with Arnold's failure to deliver West Point, control of the Hudson Valley is in great doubt. Our losses at Stony Point and Paulus Hook proved that. And the capture and execution of Major Andre really shook their confidence."

"Do you think the end will come soon?"

Parker shook his head. "Not likely. We British are nothing if not persistent."

"Still, since we've decided, I'll be in a state until it is done." She glanced at her husband, a pained look on her face. "Will we still have to put up with the officers swilling our wine?"

"Oh, I am certain Cain and Hollister, and a few others, will miss the chance to raid 'our excellent wine cellar' more than anything else." He realized his impersonation of Hollister paled in comparison to Louisa's, and he gave a short laugh. "But in the end, I gave them no real option."

"You what?" The eyebrows went up again.

"They are under the impression that you and the children are ill, and we are sailing back to England for convalescing."

"But we're fine." The blond eyebrows arched sharply. "And we're not going to sail back to England, are we?"

He leaned close and patted her hand, caressing the slender fingers. "No, we are not going back to England. We are starting over with a new life in this new country, just as we planned. But they do not know that. When we pack up to leave, they will assume we are heading for a ship. We will even time our departure to coincide with the sailing schedule. For appearances, I think I will even purchase tickets for us."

"Is all that . . . subterfuge necessary?"

He patted her hand again and let go. "Probably not. But I will feel better if I cover all the bases."

"And when we don't show up?"

"By the time the last of the passengers have boarded and they realize we are not among them, we will be well north and will have disappeared. We will leave them a little mystery."

"North?"

"I know we had talked about Virginia, but I have learned it is staunchly pro-slavery, and I know how you feel about holding any other person in bondage. Slavery is far less tolerated where we are headed."

"Good." She nodded her head twice.

"Oh, and I have made arrangements to free Ruth and the others once we leave. I met with a solicitor and have drawn up all the legal papers. And I have provided a little something to get their new lives started as well."

Louisa grabbed her husband's hand and squeezed. "You don't know how happy that makes me. I'll miss Ruth and Israel and the others, but I'm so glad for them . . . and for us." Then she asked, "Where are *we* going, then?"

He smiled. "We're headed to this beautiful valley up north, in the Hudson River. They tell me the views are breathtaking. I purchased a nice parcel of land there. I think you and the children are going to love it."

"Far?"

"Far enough but not too far. It will take us a few weeks to travel there."

Another question showed on Louisa's face. "Since you'll no longer be a major, what will we do there? How will we live?"

He grinned. "With my family's money, we will be fine. Perhaps I will become a gentleman farmer. We will need to see. There will be much to do, for you, me, and the children, to build a new life there."

Louisa got up from her chair, leaned down, and kissed him. Staring into his eyes, she said, "As long as we're together, I'll be happy with you."

79

TWO MONTHS LATER

"Henry. Elizabeth. Time to climb aboard," Parker Monteith called across the yard where his two children were playing. Both children ran one more loop in their game before staggering toward the street, both laughing hard.

Louisa stood at his side, staring up at the impressive structure they had called home for the past three years. He followed her gaze to the majestic columns, oversized wooden door, and eight tall windows flanked by polished black shutters.

One arm around her, he squeezed her shoulders. "Where we are going, we will not have anything nearly as nice as this."

She looked up at him, those beautiful blue-gray eyes a little moist. "It has been really nice here. But like I told you when we started, Parker Harrison Monteith, I could live in a hovel if I get to be with you." She chuckled. "Maybe not a hovel." She gestured to the mansion. "But we don't need anything as grand as this to be happy."

The squealing of his children interrupted their reverie. His first reaction, anxiety, turned to relief when he saw the cause of their distress.

"Miss Abigail, you came," Henry squealed. "You came!"

Elizabeth said, "I was afraid I was never going to see you again."

Miss Abigail Trench caught up with the two children, her ever-present schoolbag swinging on her shoulder. "I couldn't let you go without one more hug." She reached into the worn brown bag. "And I brought something for each of you."

Henry jumped up and down. "Me first, me first."

Parker and Louisa strolled over, and Parker said, "Henry, wait your turn."

His son hung his head. "Yes, Father. Sorry, Miss Abigail."

Miss Abigail grinned. "No worries, young man." Her hand came out with a book wrapped in paper, and she handed it to him. Henry tore off the paper, and his eyes grew huge. She said, "That's a book with pictures and stories of all kinds of animals. My friend Robert was able to get it for me."

Henry opened the book and started turning the pages, his gaze jumping from page to page, picture to picture. Miss Abigail turned toward Elizabeth, who was trying to wait patiently, but Parker could see her heels bounce up and down.

"And for you, Miss Elizabeth." The teacher handed her another wrapped book.

Elizabeth did not wait either. She tore off the paper and read the title. "*Evelina?*"

Miss Abigail smiled. "It's new. You're reading so well I thought you might enjoy the story of a young woman entering society in London. You're twelve now, and it won't be that long before it will be your turn."

Elizabeth said, "Thank you so much, Miss Abigail."

Henry jumped in. "Yes, super thanks. My book looks great."

Both ran to her and hugged her, almost knocking her down.

Elizabeth stared up at their teacher. "We'll miss you."

Henry added, "A lot."

Miss Abigail patted both children on their heads. "I'll miss you both," she said, her voice catching.

Parker called, "All right, children. Time to get going, or we will never make it to our new home." He watched as Henry and Elizabeth untangled themselves from their teacher, tears in their eyes and books clutched in their hands. They ambled over to the carriage.

Parker's gaze returned to their former tutor. "Miss Abigail, I hope you know how much Louisa and I appreciate your hard work with our children."

"It was my pleasure, Major," Abigail said with a sigh.

"Not 'Major' any longer," Parker said. "Only Mr. Monteith."

"Move aside, Parker," Louisa said, and he did. His wife went up to Miss Abigail and held her at arm's length. "You look . . . radiant, you know that." A huge smile broke across Louisa's face, and she wrapped the teacher in a big hug. "I can't thank you enough. You brought out the best in our children." She glanced over at the waiting carriage as one of the huge horses pawed the ground. She turned back. Without letting go, she said, "I wish only the best . . . for both of you."

Parker watched as Miss Abigail's eyes widened, and he heard Louisa say, "A mother knows." Louisa gave her one more squeeze and then let go, but not before slipping an envelope into the schoolbag. She walked back beside him and slid her arm through his. "All right, Mr. Monteith, let's be off."

Arm in arm, they walked over to the carriage, the driver hurrying down from his perch to open the door for them. Parker spoke in a quiet voice only Louisa could hear. "I saw you slip that envelope into Miss Abigail's bag. A little something to tide her over to her next job?"

Louisa stopped them and whispered in his ear. "I did because they are going to need it, both of them."

Parker pulled away slightly. "Both of them?"

Louisa leaned closer. "I'm almost certain Miss Abigail is several months' pregnant."

Parker shot a glance back at the woman who stood by the road, schoolbag in front, waiting for the carriage to pass. *Life goes on*, he thought. He and Louisa alighted. The footman closed the door, shook the reins, and they were off in a clatter of wheels and a pounding of hooves. As they passed, Miss Abigail waved frantically, tears streaming down her face.

ABIGAIL

EPILOGUE

FOUR YEARS LATER

"Robbie, come on in and wash up," Abigail called from the porch.

The little boy turned and glanced at his mother. "Just a little more. Jimmy and me was havin' fun."

"Jimmy and *I* were having fun," his mother corrected. It seemed Abigail was always trying to correct her son's words. No matter how hard she tried, he kept imitating the language of the other kids. She knew it was only natural, but still. Even though he was only three, the boy loved to play with the older students, five- and six-year-olds, from her school. He was almost as tall as some of them anyway. "Still, you need to come. Your father left word. He's on his way . . . and he says he has important news."

The boy looked up, his brown eyes going wide. "Father!" He turned to his playmates. "Gotta go." He ran across the yard as fast as his little wiry legs would carry him, the late autumn wind tossing his auburn hair. "When?" His gaze went past his mother and searched the road leading up to their house.

"Soon, I think, from his note." She tilted her head to the front door. "You best get in and make yourself presentable."

The boy disappeared through the door, leaving it partway open. Every time she looked into that cherubic face, she couldn't keep from smiling. He'd managed to steal some of the best features from both his parents, those deep brown eyes from his father—though without the gold stripe in one—and a petite nose and chin from his mother. Robert Townsend Jr. they had named him, but Abigail had trouble calling a little boy that grown-up name, so it was Robbie for now.

She glanced in the distance, the road snaking down the valley toward the East River and out of her view. No sign of Robert yet. Well, it would take him a while to make the trip from New York to out here on Oyster Bay. She wondered what news he brought—something good about the war, she hoped. Ever since Cornwallis surrendered to General Washington two years ago, rumors had been rampant everywhere.

She looked at the house they'd built and the schoolhouse not far down the road. It was hard to believe they'd been here a year already. After the Monteiths had left, and her job with them, she and Robert had discussed their future. They had decided she would move in with him on Broadway. She was able to help him out in the store, and she loved working with Molly.

With her loss of the position at the Monteiths', her ability to provide inside information for the cause ended as well. She knew it had to, and with the close call with that traitor Arnold, she had to admit she was relieved to be out. Still, her news about Arnold's planned betrayal of the fort had helped, some. Arnold wasn't caught, though Major Andre was. But they were able to get the news through the Ring to Washington in time to spoil Arnold's plan to hand over West Point to the British. When she thought about how some of what she learned helped the cause, she was thrilled to be a small part of the final rebel victory. At least, she hoped that was the news Robert was bringing.

One time, when they were alone in bed, she asked, "Culper Ring, huh? Where did that name come from?"

He shrugged. "I don't know. I've been told Washington came up with it. And he gave me the designation of Culper Jr., even though he doesn't know who I am. That's how I sign my messages."

"Culper Jr. What name was I given?"

He leaned up on his hand, his elbow on the cot. "None. No name. Only a number—355." When she started to ask, he finished. "No one but me knows who you are. Only the number, 355. I didn't take any chances. A name, even a code name, could've made it more dangerous for you. I wasn't about to let anything happen to you."

She leaned in close and kissed him, and he returned the kiss, pulling her atop him.

For a while, Abigail made regular trips between Robert's house and the apartment she shared with Father. But as she got further along in her pregnancy and the trips became more strenuous, Robert offered, and she begged, and eventually Father had joined them at Robert's place as well. There was plenty of room. Eventually, Robert convinced Father to give up work on the docks and hired him for warehouse work.

And when her time came, he made sure she had the best midwife help available, and the birth went off without any trouble. Mother, Robert, and Father—now Grandfather—beamed at the beautiful, healthy boy. Robert was ready to bust when she said she wanted to name the new arrival Robert, after his father, so the Junior was added. When Robbie was born, she wasn't sure who was prouder, father or grandfather. Both doted on the boy. That had been more than three years ago.

For the first two years, life on Broadway went well. She helped with the store, and when Robbie was born, she had help with the baby. Father and Molly often fought over who would take care of the little one. When he was old enough, Robbie loved to crawl along the aisles and investigate, though they had to be careful he didn't stray into trouble. Robert even said having a young son helped with business, both kinds. Customers oohed and aahed over the boy, especially the soldiers, who missed their homes and families. Robert said the domestic scene made him appear even more trustworthy.

Abigail had brought up the subject of getting married a few times, but Robert had brushed her off. "We're in love, and we have a beautiful little one. Who needs a paper to make it official?" She thought his reluctance might have something to do with spying. If he were caught, heaven forbid, he worried things would go worse for her if they were husband and wife. Would that change after the war?

Then, last year, he told her he wanted to get her and Robbie out of the city. The war was coming to an end, and he feared the final battles would be fought in and around New York. So he had this nice place built in Oyster Bay, near his folks and close to the town schoolhouse. Then, last summer, after the schoolmarm left, he had prevailed upon the town fathers to hire her as the new teacher even though she had a child, his child—often against the rules for teachers. So she was back teaching, and not that far from where she, Oliver, and Father had started their life in this new country. Robert made regular trips from his store in the city to their new place on Oyster Bay.

She sighed. She would've preferred to be married, but overall her life had turned out quite well. Robert's love and her work as a spy helped her move past her trauma, and now she found the role of teacher comforting and reassuring. There was a new generation of *Americans* to educate, and she felt blessed to assume that responsibility. And she had Robert Townsend Jr. to raise.

"He's coming!" Robbie bounded through the door and pointed down the road. A rooster tail of dust nearly cloaked a horse and rider, but Abigail recognized the figure sitting high in the saddle. Within a few minutes, the horse galloped up to the front of the house and stopped. Robert climbed off and patted its nose.

Robbie, unable to wait another second, burst from the porch and assaulted his father, clasping his legs tightly. "You home. You home!"

Robert reached down and grabbed the boy, wrapping him in his strong arms. "I am, and for a while. And I have news."

"What? Is it good news? Mother said you had good news."

"The best." Robert's glance went from the boy to Abigail, and he grinned. "You are one beautiful sight."

She walked over, and he wrapped his arms around both of them. He leaned down to his son. "Go inside, get me a cup, and then pump me some water from the well. My throat is parched, and I have much to tell you both."

Without a word, Robbie took off like a shot and hurried through the door into the house. In ten seconds, he was out and headed around back to the well.

Abigail asked, "Is it over now? For good?"

He nodded. "We received word they signed the Treaty of Paris last month, England and us. I can finally hang up my spy boots. And have more time for you and young Robert." He leaned in and kissed her. "I believe this calls for a major celebration."

Abigail recognized the passion in those adorable eyes. "Well, get on inside and tell us all about it. Later, we'll see what we can do to do some proper *celebrating.*"

ACKNOWLEDGMENTS

Contrary to popular belief, an author's journey is never solo. Behind a man with a computer are many people encouraging, assisting, supporting, critiquing, and cheerleading the concept, the story, and eventually the manuscript—at least, so it is for me. This, my seventh published novel over a little more than a decade, and I've had a good deal of help along the way. For this and every novel, my beta readers were the first to read my writing as it emerged and provided me with feedback that only helped to improve the narrative. This novel would not have been nearly as good without the suggestions, criticisms, and recommendations of my talented colleagues in the Dayton Tuesday Evening Writers Group. My editors and friends, Beth Terrell and Cindy Stanley, made sure my ideas and words were clear, correct, and pretty much error-free. And I especially want to thank Ellen Scordato and the team at Stonesong Press LLC for helping find a great home for the novel at Diversion Books. Most important of all, I'm grateful to my wife, Cathy, and my extended family for their unflinching belief in me as a storyteller and a writer.

It turns out it takes a village to make an author as well, and I feel blessed to have mine.